MIRROR
MAZE

MIRROR MAZE

MICHAELE JORDAN

an imprint of **Prometheus Books**
Amherst, NY

Published 2011 by Pyr®, an imprint of Prometheus Books

Cover illustration © Cynthia Sheppard
Cover design by Grace M. Conti-Zilsberger

Inquiries should be addressed to
Pyr
59 John Glenn Drive
Amherst, New York 14228–2119
VOICE: 716–691–0133
FAX: 716–691–0137
WWW.PYRSF.COM

15 14 13 12 11   5 4 3 2 1

Library of Congress Cataloging-in-Publication Data

Jordan, Michaele, 1951–
    Mirror maze : a novel / by Michaele Jordan.
        p. cm.
    ISBN 978–1–61614–529–3 (pbk.)
    ISBN 978–1–61614–530–9 (ebook)
    1. Fianceés—Death—Fiction. 2. Fiances—Fiction. 3. Doppelgängers—Fiction.
4. Succubi—Fiction. 5. Magic—Fiction. 6. Supernatural—Fiction. I. Title.

PS3610.O6612M57 2011
813'.6—dc22

2011023992

Printed in the United States of America

dedicated to Mike Resnick

because he promised me it could happen

Inheritrix
November 1882

Chapter One

The passing carriage took the corner a little too fast, flinging a great sheet of cold, dirty water into Jacob Aldridge's face. The shock woke him briefly from the vacant state of mind in which he walked. He glanced around, too melancholy even to protest the soaking but at least with his eyes fully open for the first time in the course of the day. A street vendor rolled her barrow nearby, hoarsely hawking her chrysanthemums. He almost lifted a hand to hail her. Rhoda loved chrysanthemums; he must get some for her. Then memory crashed down around him. He would never again bring Rhoda chrysanthemums.

He shivered and resumed plodding home. Dragging himself up the stairs to his flat, he dropped into his favorite chair and rang for tea. His head sank back into the thick velvet pile as if his neck had failed. The tea was forgotten before he had finished ringing.

The sitting room was gracious and fair-sized, representing as it did a closely calculated compromise between a modest income and a refined taste. In the end he had settled on a surprisingly spacious flat in a neighborhood poised uneasily between the prosperously bourgeois and the impoverished but sophisticated bohemian. The rooms included a studio with a northern skylight perfectly suited for painting, when the mood took him. He was an avid naturalist and frequently worked from sketches made while visiting with friends and relatives in the country. All in all, it was scarcely West End, but close enough to serve.

Only none of that mattered anymore. He had not paid a call on an acquaintance in months, or even entered his studio. Occasionally, like today, some minor business forced him out into the street. But usually he moved only from his chair—where he sat for hours holding a book while staring at the ceiling—to his desk, where he sat for hours holding a pen, staring at the floor. At intervals his landlady, a soft-hearted creature, brought him a tray of food and sat with him a while to make sure he ate—which was, indeed, the only reason that he did eat.

She came up now with the tea. She found, of course, that he had not troubled to draw the curtains or light the gas, although, despite the early hour, the November sun had dropped very low. She tutted and took care of it all. He was still wet from his mishap in the street, so she helped him off with his coat and cravat and into a comfortable smoking jacket. She watched while he drank his tea and nibbled politely at a scone. She reminded him of that hour when she invariably brought up dinner, and assured him that she would do the same tonight. He appeared not to have heard her. She sighed and brought him the book he was currently pretending to read, reminded him again about dinner, and departed. He resumed staring at the ceiling.

But he found himself no longer perfectly comfortable in his chair. Perhaps all the bustling about had irritated him. Whatever the cause, he determined it was time to go sit at his desk and stare at the floor for awhile. He rose and then he saw it. No, not it. Her. An unmistakably feminine form was seated on his least favorite chair, the one in the corner farthest from the lamp. He shook his head and looked again. There was a woman in his flat. She was sitting right there in the corner, with her head bowed and her skirt belled gracefully out around her chair.

He stared. He gaped. He opened his mouth, but his throat was dry with shock and nothing came out. At last he managed a faint cough—less than his intended query, perhaps, but enough to catch her ear. She raised her head.

It was Rhoda. There was no mistaking her. The light was not so dim that he could fail to recognize a single detail of her hair or smile. Her deep brown eyes regarded him with that perfect warmth that only she could project. She rose to her feet and reached a hand, her perfect little hand, toward him, slowly and tentatively as if—impossible thought—she was uncertain of her welcome.

For a heartbeat he stood paralyzed with amazement. Then suddenly—for he had no clear recollection of how he passed from one state to the other—he found her in his arms. He was kissing her again and again, at last. He tasted the salt and cream of her skin and inhaled her favorite jasmine scent. The starched lace of her collar scratched gently against his cheek.

He pressed her back just a little so he could look at her, and his starved eyes drank her in. "But . . . but . . ." Words bubbled up in his throat—one dreadful word in particular—but he did not dare to voice his thoughts, lest he bring back their awful reality and shatter the miracle in his arms. At last he whispered, "But what are you doing here?"

She smiled sweetly, tenderly, and stroked his face. "Why, what do you think, dear boy? I'm here to haunt you."

"Thank God, thank God." He swept her into a bruising embrace, releasing her at last only to fumble with the long line of tiny buttons.

Chapter Two

Cecily peered into the smoked glass of the entryway, verifying that her hat was still perched at precisely the most becoming angle. The hat was new, tall and almost mannish, except for the bow. The brushed gray felt was almost the color of her eyes, and decked with a flowing white riband. One soft, dark curl peeked out beneath the brim. Cecily looked very fetching indeed.

The landlady returned from wherever it was that servants went with coats. She was wringing her hands. "Oh, Miss, I am so awfully glad you've come." Cecily was not unmarried, but she accepted the mistaken title as a compliment. It was obvious the landlady meant no disrespect. "He has taken a turn for the worse."

Cecily turned—a little regretfully—away from the mirror. "You alarm me, Mrs. Florence. I can hardly imagine how he could be worse." There was a note of irony in her voice that completely escaped the landlady's attention. Cecily held her brother in the highest affection, but she was not unaware that technically speaking there was nothing wrong with him.

"Oh, but he is." Mrs. Florence resumed wringing her hands. "Oh, Miss, I cannot begin to tell you how worried I've been. He is completely changed."

"Changed?" Cecily had seen some strange things in her life, and the word triggered ominous echoes. But she would not normally have expected Mrs. Florence to share such perceptions.

"Yes, Miss, completely. Before he was, well . . ."

"I know how he was."

"Of course, Miss. I only meant that he was still agreeable before. Or, if not agreeable exactly, still not at all disagreeable, if you take my meaning. It broke my heart to see him so distressed, but he was no trouble."

She had Cecily's full attention now. "Do you mean to say he has become disagreeable?"

"He has become another man entirely. Slovenly and rude. He has shut out the charwoman and refuses all meals. When I pressed him to eat, he grew surly and even profane." Mrs. Florence collapsed into tears. "Oh, Miss, he's never spoken to me so, ever. Nor to anyone else, that I ever overheard. The things he said to the poor char. She only meant to tidy up a bit."

Cecily's eyes widened. Jacob had always been civil of tongue. Cecily remembered the only time she had ever heard her brother use even the mildest of bad language. They had both been quite small and he had come to her, looking grave and carrying a paper that looked like a list. He had informed her solemnly that he had discovered what words were bad.

He had read the list to her slowly, pausing often to be sure she understood. There had been some remarkable words on the list. "You must promise me," he had informed her, "if anyone should ever say any of these words to you again, you will inform me instantly, so I can kill him. They are very bad words, and anybody who says them to a lady is a dog, and has insulted her vilely."

She had smiled up at him. "But you will protect me if that happens?"

He had smiled back. "My dear sister, I will always protect you, even though you are so brave that you hardly ever need it." They had burned the list together, and Cecily had never heard him say any of the words again.

She was forewarned, then, as she mounted the steps, but was still shocked when her knock was met with a low snarl. "Damnation, didn't I tell you to leave me alone?"

"Why, no, you did not, Jacob," she replied. "Although perhaps you may have said it to someone else."

There was a long silence. "Cecily," he said at last. His tone was slightly more polite but less than affectionate. "Well, I will say it to you as well. Leave me alone."

"No." She spoke with gentle firmness as one might to a child. "I have come to see you, and I mean to see you." She tried the knob, but the door was locked. She waited briefly but did not hear footsteps approaching. "If you do not let me in, Jacob, I shall pull out my pistol and shoot out the lock." She did not bluff. Her pistol was only a little ladies' weapon, but it was effective at short range. She carried it always. Cecily had seen some strange things in her life.

There was another pause, and she cocked the gun. "No, wait." Jacob actually sounded frightened. "I . . . I am not decent. Let me get my robe." There were shuffling noises, and Cecily contemplated the idea of Jacob, frightened. It was even stranger than Jacob, profane. Eventually the door opened. She suppressed a gasp. Only a week before he had looked well enough. Still trapped in his grief, but physically well and properly groomed and presented.

One little week had worked a hideous marvel. He was not merely unshaven. He was haggard. His eyes were rheumy and clouded, and contained a malevolent glint. She had never known him to be less than pleased to see her before. "What do you want?" he demanded. Clearly, if she showed a moment's weakness he would slam the door in her face.

She therefore flung the door back and strode in. "I want you to take me to lunch," she announced cheerfully as if nothing were amiss. "But clearly you are not ready. I shall draw you a bath." She marched into the bathroom and proceeded to do just that. "Perhaps you could shave while we wait on the water?"

"I don't want to go to lunch." He kept his voice level. But he did not conceal a malice that chilled her heart.

"But I do," she informed him softly, and there was steel in her voice. He had always said she was brave. "Now you really must shave." She leaned back, so that she was half seated on the rim of the great claw-footed tub. "You have plenty of time before the bath is full." She laid the little pistol in plain sight on the windowsill. She let her hand rest quite near it. He glared at her, and at the pistol, but grudgingly got out his shaving things.

When the tub was full she withdrew, not without a glance at the window. It was possible to exit over the roofs in an emergency—Jacob had reassured himself on that score before he leased the flat—but she doubted he would resort to that undressed. While he bathed, she laid out his clothes. His rooms were in an appalling state. She called down to Mrs. Florence that she was taking him out and the char could come in while they were gone.

Once she had him on the street, he seemed improved. Hot water had given his skin a healthier glow. His manner had improved as well, reverting to the dull courtesy that had become his norm since Rhoda's death. The impression of a lurking animal ferocity faded, and he even looked about a little and commented on the unusually fine weather. He lunched heartily, greedily even, seeming almost surprised by his own appetite. It was with a charming, child-like air that he inquired whether he dared to order a second dessert.

She reflected on the extra chop he had begged of the waiter, and the second serving of potatoes au gratin—not to mention a good half of her omelet—and smiled. "My dear, your landlady assures me you have not eaten in a week. Have ten desserts if it pleases you."

"A week? Has it been so long?" His eyes grew puzzled as he attempted to count up the days. "It seems I have quite lost track of things. I thought it was only the other day we met with the lawyer. Yes, it was that very evening. . . . Since then I have been so very tired. I've done nothing but sleep. And I've had the most . . . Well, I cannot describe it. Dreams, we will call it, then. Yes, they must have been dreams."

"Disturbing dreams?" Cecily was a practical woman, but she did not take dreams lightly.

"Disturbing? No. Yes. I don't know." He shook his head. "They were not disturbing at the time. But in retrospect . . . They carried a shocking intensity. Even now, I can hardly believe they were dreams." He shook his head again. "But they must have been. It is not possible." He shuddered and—to her acute embarrassment—started to cry. "Oh, Cecily, I miss her so much."

Cecily chided herself for her embarrassment. He was her dear brother and he was in pain. She pulled her chair closer to his, drew up his arm and petted his hand. He laid his head on her shoulder. Bystanders would think they were lovers, which was preferable to their noticing his tears. "Let's walk along the Serpentine," she whispered. "We will stop for some pastries, and feed bits to the ducks and to each other, and you can tell me your heart."

He raised his head and looked at her. "Like when we were little?" It ter-rified her to see him so pitiable.

"Like when we were little," she promised.

The sunlight did him good, and Cecily blessed the bright autumn day, more typical of September than November. The ducks squabbled over the crumbs, and indeed they got very few of them, for Jacob ate most of the pastries himself. Cecily hugged him and hung on his arm, and he chuckled, "Behave yourself, little goose, or all these grown-ups will think we are sweethearts."

Just like old times, she snuggled into his arm and then pinched him underneath it. They must have strolled five miles, and Cecily would have gladly walked five more, watching the color and animation return to his countenance.

She scarcely noticed the lady with the hatbox—no more than a passing glance to determine the excellent figure and the expensive hat and veil. The woman's gown was very dark and prim, but not quite black. Perhaps she was in late mourning. Cecily's eyes grazed past her and continued on to a particularly handsome goose that was preening nearby on the lake and sending up a spray of droplets that glittered in the sunlight. She laughed and searched in the pastry bag, hoping to find a lingering crumb for the magnificent creature.

Then she heard Jacob gasp. She looked up as he tore himself free from her arm and ran—absolutely ran—toward the woman in the dark dress. Even as she started after him, he reached the lady and pulled her violently into his arms. The lady dropped the hatbox and gave a strangled cry, which was immediately smothered under Jacob's passionate kisses.

The lady's struggles seemed only to inflame him further. He ignored Cecily's hand on his shoulder. Cecily bit her lip. She hated to do it. Then she swung her pretty handbag on its string to catch Jacob on the back of the head. Her pistol was still concealed within. It was only a glancing blow (Cecily was extremely grateful the little gun did not discharge on impact), but it brought Jacob to his knees. He swayed briefly, and then fell face forward with his hands outstretched. He caught the lady's ankles before she could escape, and started to weep, with great, horrible sobs.

The lady stared down at him with mouth open, and jerked futilely with one foot. She failed to free it from Jacob's grasp. Jacob continued to moan and cry. Cecily stared down, dazed and shaken by the spectacle of this complete stranger who was supposed to be her brother. She glanced up, struggling for words of apology, although naturally nothing she could possibly say would be adequate. The hat with the veil had been knocked from the woman's head to rest beside its boxed fellow on the ground. The woman's face was exposed and plainly visible, her chestnut hair in disarray. Cecily stopped trying to apologize and stared.

It was Rhoda. Cecily had known Rhoda well, had liked her and approved her engagement to Jacob. They were intimates, or as close to such as Cecily had ever come. She could not be mistaken. She said it aloud. "Rhoda?"

The lady continued to try to pull her feet free and to glare down at Jacob. She did not react to the name at all. Cecily tried again. "Rhoda?" At last she gave up and tried, "Miss?"

The lady turned toward her with a look of fury. "Do you have any control over this . . . this person?" she spat out.

Cecily knelt by her brother. "Jacob. It is not Rhoda." He continued to clutch and moan, but there was a brief catch in his breathing. "I know, dear, I know. But, truly, it is not she." She looked up. "You are not she?"

"I am not who?" The lady seemed to collect her wits, but had not entirely calmed herself when she inquired, "Are you saying there is some other woman he would prefer to assault?"

It was fortunate that the woman's voice, at any rate, was nothing like Rhoda's. She had a light, high voice and a slightly overprecise articulation that suggested Eastern extraction, and certainly nothing like an American accent. The complete absence of Rhoda's incomparable husky drawl penetrated Jacob's desperate state and brought him back up to his knees. "You are not Rhoda?"

"Please, Miss." Cecily held out her hands in acknowledgment of the impossible situation. "He has not been well. And you are very like his late fiancée. I cannot counsel forgiveness; he has behaved too badly. But I beg your compassion. He was once a civilized man."

"You say I am like her?" To give the lady credit, she appeared as much intrigued as annoyed. Seeing that Jacob had withdrawn to a safer distance, she stooped to pick up her hat, which she examined critically, dusting at one spot or another until she deemed it fit to go back on her head. But she also gave Cecily a long, thoughtful look. "His fiancée—this lady I am so like— she has passed away?"

"Dear God," breathed Jacob. "You truly are not she." He rose and stepped toward the lady as if to examine her more closely before she got the veil back in place. She backed away quickly. Jacob continued to stare. "I am so sorry." Cecily had never heard him sound so weak and defeated. "I thought you were she." He turned his head sideways and gazed at her, utterly bewildered. "But you are so like her."

"Perhaps we might accept that as an established fact and move forward?"

she remarked, and picked up her hatbox. "I, for one, am eager to move forward to my home. Good day to you both." She strode approximately forward but stepped somewhat off the path so as to give Jacob a wide berth.

For a moment, he simply stood and watched her go with tragedy in his eyes. Then suddenly he lunged after her with clutching hands. He missed his hold and only captured the end of her shawl. Cecily gasped and hit him again with her purse, this time with more force and less regret than on the previous occasion. "Down, boy," she snapped in an unmistakable tone of command. "She'll have you arrested." She reached over as he fell and jerked the shawl free from his hand. "Look, now. You've torn it."

She turned to the woman, who was staring at them both white-faced. "Please, Miss, I am so sorry." She had never heard herself speak with such desperate entreaty. "I'll get him medical attention, I swear. You'll let me pay for your lovely shawl, of course." She fumbled in a pocket to produce a calling card, which she tucked in the band of the hatbox.

"Livia, I implore you," breathed Jacob, reaching out.

The lady whirled, the last of her self-control failing. "How dare you!" she cried in a voice so shrill it approached a scream. Cecily clutched Jacob's arm and glanced nervously about for fear they had been overheard. "You are not my intimate; you are not to address me with familiarity, not ever, ever." Her voice broke into a quaver. "And how do you know my name?"

She backed away, and as she stared at Jacob a shadow seemed to cross her eyes. "I am sorry for your pain, sir, truly," she whispered. "But it is not in my power to alleviate it. And I cannot permit you to entangle me within it. You should go away, sir, for your own good as much as mine. Far, far away. Africa, perhaps." With the hand not encumbered by the hatbox, she plucked up her skirt and ran.

Behind her Cecily murmured, "How did you know her name, Jacob?"

He stared after the fleeing form. "It was on the label of her hatbox," he replied. "Along with her address."

Livia ran until her breath was gone, and half fell onto a park bench trembling and struggling not to pant. She wished she could undo the stays that seemed to choke off what little air her lungs could draw. She felt, on a deep instinctive level, that she had drawn perilously close to something fundamentally evil. She wondered what her guardian would say. It was a sobering thought. She sighed, rose and continued home.

She found Dr. Chang in his study, already in his dressing gown. Clearly he intended only a quiet supper rather than dinner—if indeed he had thought of food at all. He was ensconced in his captain's chair, bent over a book so large it covered most of the surface of his desk. With his left hand he jotted notes on a tablet, without bothering to lift his eyes from his reading. A west-facing window revealed the last vestiges of the sun as it dropped behind the roofs of the houses across the street. She smiled, taking comfort in the familiar image, and approached to light the lamp on his desk. She wondered, as she had a thousand times, how dark it might grow before he noticed that the light was gone and lit the lamp himself. But she had never let it come to that. He was her guardian and protector. She liked to light the lamp for him.

When the room brightened he raised his head and smiled. "You are quite late, my dear. I had almost decided to worry. You missed tea entirely."

She shrugged. Cook had promised her a cup of tea. "I do apologize. I was delayed in the park. In fact, it was quite the adventure." The housemaid entered with a very small tray, bearing only a single cup with no accouterments. Clearly, Cook had played mother in the kitchen. She knew exactly how Livia liked her tea. "Thank you, Rose."

The girl curtsied and departed. Livia's guardian watched her go before remarking softly, "Do tell."

Livia sighed. She desired greatly to hear his opinion on the events of the day. She also feared it. "It seems I have a doppelganger." She seated herself in an elaborately carved armchair facing the desk.

"I would be surprised if you did not," he replied. "Most people do. But it is rare to meet them face-to-face. Very rare." He paused. "Some authorities would even say dangerous." There was another pause. "I hope you did not meet your doppelganger face-to-face."

She shook her head and sipped her tea. "No, nor shall I ever. It seems the poor creature has departed this earth. Her fiancé is quite bereft."

"And it was this fiancé you encountered?"

"Exactly so." She shivered at the memory. "He was distraught. The lady with him—doubtless a relation, she looked so like him—was quite unable to manage him."

"He required managing?" His eyes took in her shawl. She had corrected its disarray, but been unable to conceal the torn place. "He exceeded civil boundaries?"

"Greatly exceeded them, I should say. It was particularly unsettling as he had otherwise the appearance of a gentleman." She finished her tea and set the cup on the corner of the desk, checking first to be sure the bottom of the saucer was not damp. She looked up to meet her guardian's eyes. "I confess, I was quite alarmed by his conduct."

His eyes drifted away from hers, and for a moment he seemed lost in thought. Then he returned his attention to her. "I am grateful you are unharmed, my dear. And I hope you will never be troubled by . . . this bereaved gentleman again. Do we know who he was?"

She produced Cecily's card. "Very nearly. We know the lady who was with him. She was most apologetic."

"She was surprised by her companion's behavior?" He took the little card.

"Astounded, sir. Perhaps even more so than I."

He studied the card. "Mrs. Beckford," he mused. "And she lives quite nearby. West End, in fact. Probably her kinsman is not much farther off." He reflected. "Perhaps you should visit Serena for a while. Italy is a very pleasant place to winter."

"What a coincidence. I advised Mrs. Beckford's kinsman to go on a long trip also." She picked up her cup, which was, of course, still empty. She sighed and put it back down. "You feel the situation is that serious? I had hoped my suggestion was merely an excess of nerves."

He opened his mouth, then closed it and shook his head. "I will be frank with you, my dear. I do not know what the situation portends. I have never heard the like. But I have the gravest suspicions. I have never believed in coincidence." He looked again at the card. "It may surprise you to know that I have heard of this lady. Her father was quite famous, and her brother—if indeed it was he—has also something of a reputation. It is unlikely that he believes in coincidence either. I am quite certain that you should scrupulously avoid another meeting with him."

She sighed again. For a moment she fingered the carved pommel on the arm of her chair and the ornamental brass tacks that secured the brocade. Then she pushed regretfully against it and rose. "I shall start making the arrangements." It was not without irony that she continued, "It is fortunate that I had not entirely completed my unpacking." She paused and inquired softly, "Will you be accompanying me, sir?"

His eyes had dropped back to his book, but a hint of a plaintive note penetrated his concentration. He looked up. She was too proud to let entreaty show on her face. But she was his little girl, and he suspected her need was dire. "Perhaps I shall," he murmured. "I have not seen Serena in some while."

Livia nodded and exited the room. Her guardian remained at his desk listening to her footsteps on the stairs. Her tread was weary. She did not care for travel. He hoped someday to provide her with a home, but for the moment protection would have to suffice.

He closed the book and approached the great Chinese apothecary chest by the window across from the fireplace. At the bottom of the many little square drawers was one long, flat drawer, extending the entire breadth of the cabinet, visibly intended for the storage of valuable papers. But it contained instead a large, fan-shaped sheet of bronze. The red metal was thickly engraved with complex geometric figures and lines of small symbols that had served as script in some forgotten language.

He grasped the handle and drew it gently from its place. It glowed softly in the lamplight. Years of stringent polishing had left signs of wear. Some of the engravings could only barely be distinguished. He turned it over to reveal a mirror on the reverse; this had also been rigorously polished to bring up a reflective surface of extraordinary clarity, strangely uncontaminated by any reddish hue.

Taking enormous pains not to touch the surface, he carried the mirror to the door. There was a small hole in the handle enabling him to hang the mirror on a peg. He steadied it carefully as it swung down.

Returning to the chest, he peered into several drawers as if undecided. From one drawer he extracted a thick, squat, yellow candle. From another he brought forth a long, slim candle formed from a rolled sheet of rose-colored wax. He stood some while with a candle in each hand, weighing them and occasionally lifting one or the other to eye level and considering the runes scratched into their sides. At last he selected the yellow candle and replaced the rose one in its drawer.

He removed the chimney from the lamp. It was an oil lamp; the house was very old and only the kitchen had been fitted out for gas. He turned the wick up as high as it would go, and from this lit the candle. Setting the candle down in Livia's teacup (Cook would have had his head next day if he had set it directly on the desk), he blew out the lamp.

The sudden gloom left him half blind, and he felt his way gingerly around the desk toward the door. On the floor was an Afghani prayer rug, but it had been laid down north to south so that it would not point toward Mecca. On this he sank smoothly to his knees, so that he knelt facing the mirror. He folded his hands and breathed deeply.

He sat with half-closed eyes for a very long time. There came a timid knock on the door. He breathed in. Everyone in the household knew better than to disturb him when the door was closed. Voices came after—Livia speaking softly, and Cook not so softly. He breathed out. He was alone with the mirror.

Faces not his own appeared in the reflection. Their features shifted and changed in the shadowy light, growing fearsome or fair by turns. He breathed in. He breathed out. The faces grew more animated and more exotic. A woman's face convulsed in a soundless scream. He breathed in. A snarling, demonic visage lunged forward, as if hoping to escape its prison. He breathed out.

Then the faces—including his own—disappeared entirely. The mirror went black. It was a deep, impenetrable blackness, like dense fog on a moonless night. He opened his eyes fully and his lips began to move as he softly recited a psalm of power. The darkness crystallized, and a single face finally emerged, slim and pale and not entirely human. A voice from very far away whispered through the darkness. "What would you know?"

He completed his psalm before answering, and spoke so faintly that surely even the entity behind the mirror could scarcely have heard him. Only the names emerged clearly: "Jacob Aldridge and she who is not Livia."

The face faded away. The clouded darkness thinned and swirled into waves. The very mirror itself seemed to ripple gently. Distant glints of light appeared in the watery image. There were no words, but he gazed into the mirror as if he saw an answer, a secret wisdom like stars under the sea. He forgot to breathe in and out. He simply gazed until his oxygen-starved brain went black, and he swayed and closed his eyes in a moment of faintness. When he opened them again, he found that he was bitterly cold and the thing before him was just a mirror.

Stiff though he was, he bowed politely to the ground before rising and returning the mirror to its place. He was suddenly famished, and he wondered if the voices in the hall had been discussing food. He opened the door in that hope. Livia had selected that chair in the sitting room from which his study door was plainly visible. She looked up, and he saw in her eyes that she had guessed something of what had kept him so long. But she only smiled and said, "I hope your studies went well, sir. Dare I hope you can put them down for a while? Cook has been much concerned for our supper." She was a dear child. She would be protected.

Chapter Three

Cecily breathed deeply to calm her nerves while awaiting a response to her card. It was her duty to call, but she could scarcely expect a warm welcome. The housemaid returned, however, to curtsy and bid her enter. She followed the girl to a well-appointed office—she particularly noted a magnificent Chinese apothecary cabinet by the window—where she found, not Jacob's victim, but a distinguished-looking gentleman with a streak of silver in his hair. She could not have placed the country of his origin, but thought she detected a trace of the Orient in his looks.

He rose to greet her. "Mrs. Beckford." He bowed. "Allow me to present myself. I am Dr. James Chang. Won't you sit down?" There was a comfortable brocade armchair by the fire. The maid returned with a tea tray. "If I may do the honors?" He gestured inquiringly toward the sugar—which she declined—and poured milk and tea into her cup. The blend was unfamiliar, very strong and utterly delicious. She accepted also a small finger sandwich. "If you will permit me," he said, "I would like to come straight to the point."

Cecily blinked. "Surely it is I who must come to the point. I am here to extend my heartfelt apologies—insufficient as they must be—for . . ." He shook his head dismissively, and her voice drifted off.

"May I be frank, Mrs. Beckford?"

"Of . . . of course."

"How much do you understand of your brother's condition?"

She did not like the sound of that. "I am not aware that he is suffering from a condition. Although I acknowledge that yesterday's outburst may indicate some medical problem—indeed, I cannot think how else to explain . . ." He had pursed his lips in an exasperated grimace and was waving dismissively again.

"There is no medical problem." He sighed. "How much do you know of your father's work?" Cecily froze. She rarely discussed her father with strangers; his work she discussed with no one but her brother. "Or your brother's inheritance?"

She breathed deeply and placed a chill in her voice. "My brother has not carried on our father's work."

"Perhaps not, but he has been caught up in it more than once, has he not?" Dr. Chang's eyes were gray, as gray as the sea on a dreary day, as gray as her own. Cecily considered rising and walking out on his impertinence. But he had said "no medical problem." She needed to know what he meant by that. The doctor nodded as if he read her thoughts. "He has been trapped in his father's legacy again."

"I don't know what you mean," she whispered.

"I think you do," he replied with an unexpected gentleness. "Curses can linger for years, even for generations. Your father was probably still childless when this one was launched. The curse waited."

"My father was not evil." But she knew very well what he meant.

"Perhaps not, but he trafficked with things that were. His work . . . created an opening. Or perhaps it would be more accurate to say that his actions left a sort of residue. When a scholar embarks on certain . . . esoteric philosophical inquiries, he passes through . . . foreign influences, and carries a trace away with him. Like the coal dust that clings to a miner's coat. This residue becomes ingrained and is passed on to his children—you, as well as your brother, no doubt. You are both marked, both instinctively responsive to certain . . . resonances to which ordinary folk are immune."

Cecily sat stunned. She was not bewildered by his words; she knew they were entirely true. But she had never expected to hear them spoken, let alone by a stranger. "How can you know these things?" she answered at last.

"I made inquiries." He gazed levelly at her; they understood each other perfectly. "You are entitled to know that my ward is similarly marked and through her, her . . . counterpart. Her father was Ishmael Aram. Perhaps you have heard of him?" She shook her head. "Ah. Well, your father would have recognized the name."

She shook her head. "But you are saying that Rhoda, Miss Carothers, was cursed. I cannot accept that. She was as decent and amiable a lady as I have ever known. And the affection between her and my brother was healthy, normal."

"She was not herself cursed. But she was marked by another's curse. My ward is decent and amiable also, I should like to remind you." He breathed deeply and leaned back slightly in his chair. "For that matter, I suppose your brother was once decent and amiable." She stiffened and he nodded. "But they were both . . . vulnerable. That is why they were drawn to each other. Did you never suspect there was something—not unnatural, perhaps, but other-worldly—about their courtship? More mystical than the usual romance?"

She opened her mouth to deny it. Then she closed it again. Jacob had once said that Rhoda's spell was the only benevolent magic he had ever known. She bowed her head. "Then her death was the curse come to fruition?"

"Not at all. Just the opposite. Her death nearly frustrated the curse, by severing the bond that empowered it. Such is the power of love. Unfortunately as long as my ward survived, the link was not entirely destroyed, and Miss Carothers's spirit was caught up in it." He sighed, and shook his head. "I grieve for Miss Carothers. She was a true innocent—condemned not even by her father's actions, let alone her own. But through her—even after her death—Mr. Aldridge remains distantly tied to my ward, whom he should never have met in the natural order of things. And the mark of an ancient curse weighs heavily on my poor Livia. Ishmael Aram was hungry for power, and did things he ought not have done to acquire it."

"As did my father," she whispered.

"How bad is Mr. Aldridge's state? And how long has he been afflicted?"

"A week, I think. I saw him then, and he seemed well enough. And he told me it was that very evening the dreams began." She paused for thought. "I do not know the full extent of his deterioration. The landlady said he was enormously changed. And at first I was greatly alarmed. But he seemed to recover. He was almost his old self in the park. Until we encountered Miss Aram, that is." She shook her head. "I would not have thought any power on earth could drive him to behave so."

"And no power of this earth did," said Dr. Chang. "If it is any comfort to you, it was probably not truly Mr. Aldridge who behaved so."

Cecily sighed. Clearly, he was speaking of some kind of possession. She was not incredulous or disbelieving, only grieved and weary. She had seen some strange things in her life. "You speak of this curse as if it were an entity."

He spread his hands. "A curse has purpose and will. Whether or not it is self-aware, I could not say. But it knows patience, and given time it can learn. The distinction between a young demon and an old curse is hazy."

She lowered her head and gazed down at her hands, folded demurely in her lap. She found it hard to ask for assistance, or to trust a man who engaged in magic. "Can anything be done?"

"But, of course, Mrs. Beckford." His smile was infinitely kind. "I can invite him to dinner."

Chapter Four

Jacob paused in the entryway to review his appearance. The smoked glass veiled his face somewhat, but he still looked gaunt, for all he was elegantly dressed. Nor was he entirely unaware that his mind was clouded. It was not a sensation to which he was accustomed. His stomach roiled behind his silk waistcoat. He had no idea how he would manage to eat.

But it was not food that tempted him out from his familiar domain, although he pretended not to know that his interest in Miss Aram was less than natural. He swore inwardly that he would treat her respectfully when they met. Another secret voice suggested that it would be preferable to take her on the spot. Mrs. Florence handed him his hat and cloak. He sighed again, stepped outside, and hailed a cab.

Mrs. Florence peeked out the sidelight before calling softly, "He's gone, Miss." Cecily emerged from the kitchen. She shook the landlady's hand in fervent gratitude and slipped her a sovereign before darting up the stairs.

Her brother's rooms were considerably less disordered than before—he had not been left alone in them for long. Despite the tidiness, there was an odor that dismayed her. It was so faint she could not place it exactly, but she thought she remembered it from her previous visit. She sniffed. Perhaps the room just needed a good airing.

Once the door was secure, she peeled back one of her gloves to below the elbow and drew forth the candle tucked within it. Decked, as she was, in evening gown and jewels, she had had no place else to conceal the long, bloodred taper. She was glad to have her arm free of it, as it had constricted her movements considerably. It was easy to light. Jacob had left the gas on; he always did. She had spent much of her youth turning off the gas behind him.

The scent that came up from the candle was offensive, and she wrinkled her nose in distaste, wondering if the nasty thing had taken its color from genuine blood. But she dutifully held the taper before her with both hands. "The Lord is my shepherd, I shall not want," she murmured. The flame shot up, and she hesitated nervously. But her instructions were clear. "He maketh me to lie down in green pastures." According to Dr. Chang, it would have been better to recite the Psalm in the original Hebrew, but she did not know the language. "He leadeth me beside the still waters."

The flame subsided somewhat, although it still reached higher than a typical candle flame. And then it leaned sideways as if in a draft. A very strong, steady draft. It was unmistakably leading her somewhere, although she doubted it would bring her to still waters. "He restoreth my soul," she whispered and stepped in the direction to which the candle flame pointed.

The candle took her into Jacob's study. It wavered briefly toward the desk before pointing to the chair in the corner. The chair was little used; it was a pretty thing with an embroidered seat but less than comfortable. Other chairs were called into service first. But the candle pointed directly toward it, so Cecily approached it. The faint odor from the parlor rose up around her, growing stronger with each step, overpowering even the stench of the blood candle. It was a sweet aroma, and she could not have said what made it unpleasant, save that it was perhaps a little too sweet. It was also very familiar. She had smelled it in her childhood. She declined to reflect on the occasion.

When she reached the chair, the flame shot up again, almost scorching the ceiling. Then it subsided to a glowing spark. But it did not go out. "Surely goodness and mercy shall follow me all the days of my life," whispered Cecily, and it was truly a prayer on her lips. Then she froze in something almost like panic. There was no place to set the candle down, nor any candleholder with which to do so. She could not stand by the chair all night; she had a dinner engagement. Nor had she any wish to see what would happen next.

Absurdly, the candle seemed aware of her dilemma. The flame rose up a trifle and wriggled away from her, to point toward the desk for an instant. There was a book on the desk—one of their father's old books, she noted with distaste. She would not have thought that Jacob had kept any of them. She took a few steps toward the desk. The candle did not want to leave the chair and the flame leaned back toward it. She did not like to reject its guidance. Her instructions had been clear.

At last she leaned as far over toward the desk as her balance permitted and grasped one corner of the book with her fingertips. She straightened, pulling it after her. As it dropped over the edge of the desk, the pages fluttered wildly. A small piece of paper flew up from among them. Caught up in some peculiar draft, it sailed high in the air and down into the candle flame. It flared up immediately and was gone before she could guess what it was.

She regained control of the book with some difficulty and set the candle on the surface of its front cover. She took some satisfaction in obscuring the hateful title. The candle obligingly settled itself into place, the bottom melting into a little circle of wax—although she had applied no heat to it—thus creating a rim that held it upright. She set the book down on the seat of the chair, and the flame dropped down to a soft glow. "And I will dwell in the House of the Lord forever."

She stared at the tableau for a moment. It looked untidy—hideously unstable, and probably dangerous. But even as she looked, both odors—the scent of the candle and the scent of the room—dissipated to be replaced by a new aroma. Suddenly the air smelled of roses and cinnamon, a wholesome, refreshing perfume. So she sighed and hurried out. Mrs. Florence met her in the hall and hailed another cab.

Her driver made excellent time; he pulled up in front of the Chang house just as Jacob stepped out of his own cab. He hurried over to help her out. "My dear, had I known you would be here, I should have suggested we come together."

She smiled and looked up into his eyes. His manner was subdued, but his eyes were clear. He seemed lucid. "No matter. I had an errand to run first."

"The loss is mine." He surveyed her thoughtfully. "The dress is new, I think?" She tossed back her wrap and twirled for his inspection. "You look utterly ravishing." He seemed utterly normal. There was even a hint of humor in his voice when he added, "I would have thought your blue gown would serve for an old friend of Father's. Perhaps Dr. Chang is younger and more interesting than I supposed."

"He is a fascinating man," she assured him solemnly. "A scholar and a collector."

"A scholar and a collector? Not quite your usual taste." He offered her his arm and escorted her to the door, which opened before they knocked. Jacob raised an eyebrow. "What excellent service," he murmured, handing his cloak and hat to Rose. Cecily laid her little wrap over his cloak; the girl curtsied and disappeared. A footman led them forward. "Not entirely English, do you think?" he remarked very softly to Cecily. "Only the East teaches that level of obsequiousness."

"She has an Egyptian look," Cecily agreed. "But their cook makes up for her manners; she is a tyrant. A Persian tyrant, I might add. It seems Dr. Chang has been everywhere." The footman looked English enough—round-faced, blond, and young. Cecily wondered if perhaps he had only been hired for the evening. She had not seen him on her previous visit.

They entered a small parlor, and Jacob drew his breath in with a hiss. Fortunately the sound was obscured by the footman announcing their names. A half dozen persons awaited them; Livia Aram was not included among them. Dr. Chang rose to greet them. "Welcome to my home, Mrs. Beckford." He kissed her hand. "And Mr. Aldridge—I am so happy to make your acquaintance. Allow me to present you around. Everyone is eager to meet you." He led them first to a diminutive woman of uncertain years, dressed in Chinese robes. "Mama, may I make you acquainted with Mr. Jacob Aldridge, and his sister, Mrs. Beckford?"

She looked up at them serenely and nodded. An elegant woman, she had once been exquisite. "It is my pleasure to know you both, a pleasure for which I have waited a very long time." Her accent was marked.

She caught Jacob entirely off guard. "Did you also know my father, Mme. Chang?"

She smiled very faintly. "I should hope so. I very nearly married him."

Dr. Chang intervened. "Mr. Aldridge, when I lured you here to meet an old friend of your father's, it was not myself but my mother to whom I referred. I hardly qualified as his friend; I was only a child."

Jacob turned to Dr. Chang. It was hardly the prospect of a family friend that had lured him hither, reflected Cecily, and she watched her brother closely. She saw turmoil in his eyes. An angry and alien entity struggled for control. But he remained Jacob; only the normal courtesies were allowed to emerge. "Then I must thank you all the more, Doctor; I had no idea my father had such beautiful friends." He raised Mme. Chang's hand almost to his lips. "I am honored."

She almost smiled, and withdrew her hand to wave around the room. "Our friends: Dr. and Mrs. Verlaine, Professor and Mrs. Strasser." Cecily blinked at the inadequacy of the introductions, but the other guests bowed and smiled, as if accustomed to Mme. Chang's manners. "Will you be good enough to take me into dinner, Mr. Aldridge? We must make haste—Cook assures me that our soufflé is in desperate peril." She only barely waited for Jacob's arm before marching toward the dining room. She waved airily behind her. "My son can escort Mrs. Beckford."

Dr. Chang bowed to Cecily. She reflected that the evening was already tending in a very different direction than he had led her to expect. He smiled. She sighed and took his arm.

To her complete and utter astonishment, the dinner was a resounding success. Their fellow guests proved to be learned and cosmopolitan; conversation—in three languages—ranged from the French poets (with mention of Dr. Verlaine's namesake[1] and distant relation) to the Burton-Speke expeditions[2] to the recent Sanskrit translations.[3] Their discourse was enhanced by some of the finest food that Cecily had ever been privileged to enjoy; Cook's temperament was tolerated for good reason.

As first Jacob only barely participated in the flow of talk, but he approached the soup, at least, with genuine interest and gradually grew more animated. In fact, he grew so much so that Cecily glanced at his wineglass. He had, however, drunk modestly. No one else seemed to have noticed. If anything, Dr. Chang was subtly drawing Jacob out, encouraging his elevated mood. She wondered uneasily if the blood candle had anything to do with it. But Professor Strasser turned to her with a remark about the opening of D'Oyly Carte's *Perola*,[4] and from the far end of the table Mrs. Verlaine inquired about the singers. Cecily put the candle from her mind.

When the ladies withdrew after dinner, Cecily was surprised to find Livia Aram in the parlor, engaged with Rose in laying out a tablecloth on a round table surrounded by chairs. Miss Aram was dressed in a robe, or rather several robes, all held together with a great sash—not the Chinese mode, Cecily was sure, but perhaps Japanese—and all in white. She looked very anxious and approached Mme. Chang immediately. "Are you quite sure of this, ma'am?" she inquired. "Papa was of the opinion that any such meeting would prove very dangerous."

"Indeed, it might," replied Mme. Chang. "Are you afraid?"

The question took Miss Aram aback. She paused and straightened before answering. "I am," she admitted at last. "But I will do as Papa instructs."

Mme. Chang smiled. "He will instruct you to obey me, I think. But I will ask him to speak to you before we continue, if you like. In the meanwhile, shall we prepare?" She turned to Mrs. Verlaine. "If you will assist me?" Her words were more a command than a request.

Miss Aram was made to kneel on the floor in the corner, and Mrs. Verlaine was made to pour an unidentified white powder in a circle around her. Cecily watched with growing misgivings. Mme. Chang examined the circle carefully; it required some reinforcement before she was satisfied. She then turned to Cecily and placed in her hands an antique writing tablet made of horn, unmarked as far as Cecily could see. Walking slowly in a circle around Miss Aram, she intoned softly in a language that Cecily could not identify.

"What are you doing?" inquired Cecily. Mme. Chang ignored her question. Cecily waited until the invocation was complete before asking again in a somewhat sharper tone. "What are you doing, madame? I should like to point out that I did not agree to participate in, or subject my brother to, any magical ritual."

Despite the difference in their heights, Mme. Chang contrived to look up at her with all the haughtiness of an empress. "Your brother has already been subjected to a magical ritual, and you will not free him from it without more magic. But take him home and let him consume himself and everyone around him if you like. We could simply send my son's ward to Italy until his death—she will be safe enough there for what little time he has left, and only you will be troubled by his hungry ghost."

Cecily reflected carefully before replying. "I think you are mistaken, Mme. Chang. I think that if my brother were reduced to a hungry ghost, then it would be Miss Aram who would be most troubled by him, more so perhaps than she ever would be during his lifetime." She sighed. "Can you convince me that this"—she waved toward the ring surrounding Miss Aram—"this circle of dust will help him?"

Mme. Chang stared up at her, and it occurred to Cecily that very few people had ever declined to obey her without question. It was Mrs. Verlaine who intervened. "I see you have something of your father's courage and spirit. This dust, as you call it, comes from a sacred place, as does the tablet in your hand. The upcoming ceremony is intended solely to separate Mr. Aldridge from . . . that which has become attached to him."

"Will that . . . attachment suffer the separation?"

Mrs. Verlaine nodded. "If you placed the blood candle correctly—and I do not doubt that you have—then the attachment will be too distracted—mesmerized, even—to interfere." She took the tablet from Cecily and handed it to Mme. Chang.

Mme. Chang took the tablet with her left hand and with the right produced a small knife. "Mrs. Beckford, do you love your brother?"

"I do."

"Then cut yourself. Lay a drop of your blood, which is also your brother's blood, on this sacred tablet." Cecily stared at the tablet. It seemed to waver before her eyes, and she almost glimpsed runes, symbols, something written on its pale surface.

"In for a penny, in for a pound," she whispered to herself and, rolling down her glove, drew the knife across her forearm. She did not cut deeply; Mme. Chang had said only a drop was required. In fact, the cut was so shallow that she had to shake the drop free from her arm. It seemed to fall quite slowly. She did not like to spoil her glove, so she paused to press a handkerchief over the tiny wound before pulling the glove carefully back up into place.

Mme. Chang caught the drop on the surface of the tablet. It seemed to glow almost supernaturally red. She handed the tablet to Miss Aram. "Take this, my dear, and hold Mr. Aldridge's life in your hands. Recite the prayer that I taught you. Recite it over and over." Miss Aram nodded, and her lips started to move silently. Mme. Chang summoned Cecily with a gesture, and the two of them picked up a folding screen and placed it so as to conceal Miss Aram from sight.

They had scarcely completed the task when there was a click of the latch and Dr. Chang entered the room. His face was turned behind him as he listened to something Professor Strasser was saying. Dr. Verlaine and Jacob were behind them. "I'll just get my things now," Dr. Chang remarked to them. "Please take your seats with the ladies; I shall be with you directly." He walked across the room and stepped behind the screen.

Cecily approached Jacob gladly and took his arm. "'All I have done in care of thee,'⁵" she murmured to herself, and then continued more loudly, "You are very quick to join us, my dear. You can scarcely have tasted the port."

He smiled down at her. "There was scarcely any port to taste. And no cigars at all. It seems we have fallen among Temperance advocates." He turned to Mme. Chang. "Where do you want us to sit, madame?" She set them all about the table, in much the same order as they had sat for dinner, save that Mme. Chang now placed herself next to her son's chair, so that Jacob was between her and Mrs. Strasser. He leaned forward over the table to address Cecily. "Did you know we would be rounding out the evening with a séance, my dear? It seems Frau Strasser is quite a renowned medium in Berlin."

"Oh, no," murmured Mrs. Strasser. Turning to her husband she continued, "What have you been telling people, Professor?"

He smiled. "No more than your due, mein Frau."

Mrs. Strasser turned to Cecily. "He exaggerates, I do assure you. Nor is the ceremony we are about to hold a séance, at least not as I see séances practiced here in England."

"You alarm me, Frau Strasser," remarked Jacob with a smile. Surely no one but Cecily could see the strain in his eyes. "Are we doing it wrong?"

"You are," she informed him gravely. "Here in England, numerous times I have seen persons who call themselves mediums holding public gatherings purportedly for the sake of consulting about the afterlife with those who have passed on, or at least verifying their well-being. Is that not what you call a séance? Or have I misunderstood?"

A chuckle went around the table. "That sounds like a séance to me," admitted Mrs. Verlaine. "Or should I say, what passes for one."

"You should, indeed," responded Mrs. Strasser. "For think, is it right or proper for the dead to linger close by the plane of life? Surely not, or we should be smothered in the spirits of the departed. And this is not the case.

The departed generally . . . depart. It is natural and proper for them to do so. But if the departed do not generally linger, then those who do must be suffering some difficulty in passing on; they are trapped somehow in the earthly plane. The reasons vary: sometimes they do not realize they are dead; sometimes they remain hopelessly obsessed with some earthly purpose that they can no longer effect. Either way, there is nothing to be learned from them— except, perhaps, the location of a dropped glove—as they have not mastered anything they did not know in life."

"Are you not saying, then"—Jacob's voice was very soft, betraying considerable interest to Cecily's ear—"that a séance is, by its very nature, futile?"

"I am," agreed Mrs. Strasser. "Or at least futile in terms of the purposes of these English séances. And, in all honesty, there are also some such travesties in Berlin. But certain séances I have had the privilege to attend . . ."

"Conduct," corrected Professor Strasser softly.

"Shall we say, *witness?*" she smiled at her husband. "These were not held to consult with the departed but rather to assist them in passing onward."

To her surprise, Cecily saw that her brother was completely shocked by Mrs. Strasser's words. He froze in place so pointedly that she feared his dismay would be observed. There was a choked note in his voice when—after an overlong pause—he replied, "Surely there is nothing the living can do to help the departed pass onward."

She shrugged. "Often, perhaps usually, there is not. But sometimes . . . It depends on the individual circumstances."

Jacob had grown pale. But Mme. Chang took his hand. Mrs. Strasser placed a hand on his shoulder. He looked so trapped that Cecily wondered if she had done the right thing in bringing him here. Dr. Chang emerged from behind the screen at last bearing a silver salver that he laid on the table. "There, now. These should smooth our path."

Jacob leaned forward to examine the offering with curiosity. The others displayed no particular interest, but Cecily also leaned in to see. Jacob plucked up a small whisk of pine and twirled it in his fingers, then replaced it to pick up a rowan berry. He did not trouble to handle the acorn, and seemed to think twice about disturbing the little white heap of what was probably salt, or the small feather that had been used to arrange it. Dr. Chang rummaged through his pockets and drew forth a candle. Cecily sighed. She was weary of Dr. Chang's candles.

Dr. Chang rose, collected a plain candleholder from the mantel and lit the candle from the oil lamp. Then he returned to set the candle down by the salver and claim his seat. Turning to Cecily, he laid a hand on hers. "Shall we begin?" he asked her earnestly. On her left the professor took her other hand. The lamp on the mantel blew out in a sudden, inexplicable draft. Across the table, Mrs. Verlaine started to sing. The tune was very strange; the language might have been Pharsi. The candle on the table flared up, and the room filled with the scent of incense. Mrs. Strasser began to murmur softly in German in time to the singing. Cecily grew faint and afraid.

She blinked, and when her eyes came back open there was a figure standing on the table, just where the candle—which had vanished—had been. She shook her head, wondering how someone could have crawled up there, and so quickly, without breaking the circle of hands. When the figure turned her way, she saw the face and figure of Livia Aram, still dressed in her white kimono. "Jacob," moaned the figure. The voice did not sound like Livia Aram.

Jacob gave a strangled cry and half rose, but Mme. Chang and Frau Strasser gripped his arms and urged him back down. Mrs. Strasser stopped muttering, but Mrs. Verlaine continued to sing. The figure on the table swayed and turned back and forth as if seeking something. Jacob yearned toward it like a leashed hound.

"Jacob," said the figure again. It turned approximately toward him but with unfocused eyes. "Jacob, it is not I. Do not be deceived." The voice was nothing like Miss Aram's. Rather, the figure spoke in a deep, husky drawl, with an American accent. "It is not I, my darling. Surely you know that in your heart."

Neither Mrs. Strasser nor Mme. Chang was able to prevent Jacob from leaping to his feet, but they held on to his arms with all their combined strength, keeping the circle intact. "Rhoda," he cried. "Where are you? Come back to me."

"No!" Her eyes seemed to find him at last. "Jacob, if you love me, set me free. I am held here, tormented by the thing that is not I. Cast it down and release me, I beg you."

Jacob tore an arm free of Mme. Chang and reached desperately toward the figure in white. Even as he did so, the image vanished and his fingers met empty air. Only the candle remained where she had stood. It toppled over and went out. Behind the screen, Livia Aram screamed and screamed again.

The circle dissolved as everyone jumped up and peered blindly around in the gloom. Dr. Chang exited into the hall, leaving the door open to admit a little light. He reappeared immediately, carrying a rush to relight the lamp on the mantel. Mme. Chang turned on Jacob with a severe expression. "Do you know no better than to break a circle, boy?" she demanded. "Your father would be ashamed."

Mrs. Verlaine laid a hand on Jacob's arm. "Madame, you are unkind. Mr. Aldridge was tested beyond all normal forbearance. And he is in such poor health. I think he did far better than we might have hoped."

Mrs. Strasser nodded emphatically. "There is no need to fault Mr. Aldridge for his very proper feeling. The summoning went well. We achieved clear and necessary communication, and learned all we really need to know. Would you have compelled the unhappy spirit to remain and make small talk? And at what cost to our dear Miss Aram?"

All eyes turned to the corner. Cecily took advantage of the shift in attention to draw near Jacob and take his arm. He seemed scarcely to notice her. The screen had been knocked aside; behind it, Livia Aram had collapsed to the floor. Dr. Verlaine was crouched beside her, taking her pulse. Behind him, Professor Strasser stood waiting with a vial of smelling salts.

Dr. Verlaine looked up with a severe expression. "She is in a very bad state. It was reckless to subject her to this ritual." He scooped her up in his arms and rose. "Ernst, bring my bag." Professor Strasser retrieved a small valise from the corner. Dr. Verlaine turned to Dr. Chang. "Where is her room?" Dr. Chang led them both out. Jacob moved as if to follow, but Cecily held his arm; after an instant he permitted her to restrain him.

She drew him to a chair, and he dropped into it. Rose timidly entered the room and set about restoring it to rights. Mrs. Verlaine and Mrs. Strasser assisted her in taking up the tablecloth; Mme. Chang merely pointed imperiously at this or that. When everything else was restored to its proper place, Rose folded down the sides of the round table. The footman appeared and, glancing nervously around the room, carried it away.

Jacob continued to sit slumped in his chair, lost in what were clearly unhappy thoughts. Cecily sat beside him, took his hand, and waited. The other ladies did not attempt to intrude but spoke quietly among themselves. Cecily wondered if she should take Jacob home before the evening grew worse. But Jacob was disinclined to move, so she waited. She waited a long time.

Eventually the men rejoined them. Dr. Verlaine was barely civil; rigid with disapproval, he collected his wife and made his immediate farewells. At the door he relented slightly. "You should not have done this, Chang," he said. "But having done it, do call me if she needs further assistance." Dr. Chang bowed, and he departed.

Dr. Chang took a seat, gingerly, as if afraid something might break. Professor Strasser fell wearily into a chair. "Well, Doctor, is he right?" Then he turned his head to regard Mme. Chang. "Or perhaps I should ask you? Was this worthwhile?"

"How is the poor girl?" murmured Mrs. Strasser.

Professor Strasser shrugged. "I do not know. Exhausted, plainly. But she seemed to rouse a bit. Dr. Verlaine appeared alarmed but did not make clear what had alarmed him." He turned again to Mme. Chang. "Perhaps you could tell us?"

She waved a hand. "She will be fine, I promise you. She is frightened and distraught, but that is all. I would not have permitted, let alone recommended, anything that would cause her real harm."

"I hope not," whispered Dr. Chang, and the bitterness in his voice brought a flush to his mother's cheek.

"I promise you," she reiterated.

He looked up to meet her eyes and, after a moment, nodded. He turned to Jacob. "As for whether it was worthwhile, perhaps Mr. Aldridge can tell us." Jacob raised his head, although he had not appeared to be listening. "Tell us what happened to you, Mr. Aldridge."

Jacob seemed to reflect for a very long time. Finally he sighed. "My heart was broken again." He managed a wry smile. "I would not have thought there was enough left of it to break."

"But are you changed by this heartbreak?" pressed Dr. Chang. "Have you gained any insight, determined on any change of course? Or was my little girl's pain—and your own—completely wasted?" He waited some while, but Jacob failed to answer. "Will you tell us what happened to you before tonight?"

"No!" Jacob pulled in a deep, shuddering breath, and resumed something of his usual manner. "Please, Dr. Chang. There are ladies present. If you had wished to hear the tale of my adventures over the last week, you should have asked me to relate them over the port."

"Will you have more adventures to relate over next week's port?" came the reply.

Cecily watched as her brother mustered his resources. She saw a determined veneer of civilization restored to his countenance. She began to hope he would be healed.

Jacob sighed and cocked his head, then sighed again and turned his head away. He held out his hands in a gesture of bewilderment. "I cannot say. But . . ." he paused to collect his thoughts carefully. "I am less inclined now to surrender to . . . adventures."

Professor Strasser jumped up and crossed over to Jacob. Grasping his hand, he shook it heartily. "Good man," he declared in the warmest of tones. "There is no one here who will question how difficult it can be to turn away from a tempter offering you your heart's desire. Most men would not even bother to try."

Dr. Chang nodded. "The initial commitment to freeing oneself of . . . foreign influences is critical. It will not be easy, but it is possible now. If you are determined. I hope you understand that."

Jacob looked around the room, and Cecily was pleased to see true steel in his eye. "Rhoda said I was deceived by . . . an impostor. Well, that is no great shame. We are none of us immune to deceit. But she said also that this impostor was tormenting her, and that I cannot endure. I've killed before." He sighed. "And would again, to protect her—if I only knew whom to kill. Or rather, what."

If his hosts were startled or disturbed by his casual admission of murder they took pains to give no sign of it. Mme. Chang smiled grimly. "Well spoken, boy. And you are not alone. There is help available if you will take it."

"More magic?" Jacob could not entirely keep the distaste from his voice.

"There is magic and magic," interjected Mrs. Strasser. "The magic that assaults you is of a very dark complexion. But there are other paths. The key is never to commit a dishonorable act just because it is magical. For instance, would it trouble you to attend a church and say prayers for the soul of Miss Carothers?"

"Trouble me?" Jacob stared at her. "I would be hard-pressed to believe it could effect any assistance."

"I do not ask you to believe it," insisted Mrs. Strasser. "I asked you if you could do it."

"In which church?" he inquired.

"All of them," she replied. "There is no church that has any particular grasp of truth. But all of them have at least harbored a soul that once knew truth and has marked a path that can assist you in appealing not to the local religion but to the Godhead."

Jacob blinked. "I thought prayers had to be sincere."

She shrugged. "Sincerity is not the same as belief. Is your desire for Miss Carothers's well-being sincere? If so, then pray for it and your prayer will be sincere, regardless of what you believe."

Jacob opened his mouth and then closed it again. Cecily suspected he was trying not to laugh at Mrs. Strasser. "Well, if that is all you ask, then I will pray for her in every church I pass. Somehow I thought that escaping . . . whatever it is that I am escaping would be more complicated."

Mme. Chang snorted. "Well, there is certainly more to it than that."

"No, really?" murmured Jacob. "Do tell."

Mme. Chang raised an eyebrow. "I will thank you to keep a civil tongue in your head, boy."

"And I will thank you to address me as Mr. Aldridge."

She opened her mouth and then stopped and closed it with an almost audible snap. Dr. Chang chuckled. "With no disrespect intended, Mama, he has a point. If you cannot be bothered to treat him politely, then why should the . . . demon do any better." Cecily noted unhappily that the curse had apparently grown in his estimation. Mme. Chang turned on her son a look that could only be described as a glare, but he stood his ground and met her eye. "I would further hope you will also treat Livia politely, if only to encourage her will to live."

After a long moment Mme. Chang turned back to Jacob. "My apologies, Mr. Aldridge. My concern for the dangerous situation overcame me." Jacob nodded. "There will be further ceremonies to help you shake off this thing, if you will permit them."

"Nothing black," murmured Mrs. Strasser.

"No," agreed Mme. Chang. "That is quite correct. One must not permit any moral contamination when shaking off evil, or the battle is already lost."

"And you should probably move out of your place for a while," said Dr. Chang. "Demons often have difficulty navigating terrestrial dimensions."

"Then it is a full-fledged demon?" inquired Cecily. "Not, after all, a curse?"

Dr. Chang turned to her. "I do not know. But it is best we be prepared for the worst." He smiled faintly. "And, anyway, we have to call it something."

She sighed. "Well, Jacob can stay with me, of course. Perhaps we should have his rooms redone while he is out of them? I seem to recall that . . ." She paused and looked at Dr. Chang and sighed again. "That demons can be confused even by very superficial changes in appearance. Because they do not really see very well on earth."

"Quite right," agreed Professor Strasser. "Mr. Aldridge, have you ever considered a mustache?"

"If I may ask, Mrs. Beckford . . ." Mme. Chang did not actually sound very hesitant about asking. "Is Colonel Beckford likely to make objections to the practice of magic in his house?"

"I will be sure to ask him when he returns from India," murmured Cecily. "In the meanwhile, I trust he will indulge me."

"I wonder if your house is safe either, Mrs. Beckford," mused Mrs. Strasser. "Have you lived there long?"

"Only a few months," answered Cecily. "Colonel Beckford only inherited it last spring; he was unable to come home to oversee it then, so I spent the summer in Edinburgh instead."

Mrs. Strasser nodded. "Then I should think that the house will carry the aura of the late Beckfords. If we lay a circle of protection around it, then it should be safe for some while." She turned to Dr. Chang. "How long can we can keep the thing in Mr. Aldridge's rooms?"

He considered. "With luck, it will continue to doze long after the candle burns out. And there are other lures we can use when that fails. I suggest we shut it into a single room and change all the other rooms around it. Then, when we release it, it should be completely disoriented. And as soon as it exits its familiar corner, we change the room behind it. But it is vital that Mr. Aldridge stay completely away." He turned to Cecily. "It must be you who goes back for his things." She nodded. "I will accompany you. I will make a homunculus for the demon to devour—that should hold it in place for a long time."

"I thought we were agreed, no black magic," snapped Mrs. Strasser.

He turned to her with some dismay. "You think a homunculus is evil? But I will not injure anything to make it. A lock of Mr. Aldridge's hair, perhaps some nail clippings, no more. Well, perhaps, a drop or two of blood—but only if he should happen to cut himself shaving or some such thing." He turned to Jacob earnestly. "You will be sure, will you not, Mr. Aldridge, that if you should accidentally cut yourself in the next few days you will catch up the blood in a handkerchief for me?" He returned his attention to Mrs. Strasser. "You see? Only blood from a genuine accident would be used, if any blood at all. No blood would be deliberately shed. Accidental blood is not evil."

"But the homunculus will be something very like alive," she replied. "And if you send something that is very like alive to be consumed by a demon, then you have done something very like murdering it."

His shoulders sagged in surrender. "I see. Well, a doll then. Only . . . for the doll I must have blood. Hair and nail clippings will not suffice to deceive a demon, no matter what I do. And I must start it tonight. It takes a long time to wrap a major illusion around a doll, and bind it into place. So there is no time to wait for accidental blood."

"Suppose you had blood from a voluntary sacrifice?" asked Cecily.

Dr. Chang shook his head. "Mr. Aldridge has too much at stake for blood taken now to count as sacrificial."

"Not Jacob's blood." Cecily breathed deeply and stripped off her glove. The little cut had long since closed over, but the handkerchief she had placed over it plainly bore several drops of blood. "Or not exactly Jacob's blood. But Mme. Chang said that my blood was his blood. So did Mrs. Strasser. And it served as his life in the séance."

Mrs. Strasser drew close and put her arm around Cecily's waist. "Dear child, do you know what you are doing? This is a very great sacrifice. It goes well beyond simply assisting your brother. For all intents and purposes, it will equate you with him in the demonic realm. If our protections fail, you and Mr. Aldridge will go down together to something far, far worse than death."

"It's out of the question," snapped Jacob, rising to his feet. "I will not accept this sacrifice." He snatched suddenly at the handkerchief to wrest it out of her hand. She pulled away before he could come close enough. "Darling Cecily, you must not do this. You have no idea where this could lead you."

"Wherever it leads, I will not watch you go there alone," she told him. She smiled. "Jacob, we have always been like one. This makes no real difference. Besides, there is nothing on earth or in hell that can defeat us if we stand together. You know that. So there is nothing to fear." Taking care to stay out of his reach, she passed the handkerchief to Dr. Chang.

Jacob turned angrily on the doctor, but Professor Strasser held his arm. "Dr. Chang, surely you cannot proceed without my consent."

Dr. Chang stared down at the red stain on the white handkerchief. Then he looked back up to Jacob. "Mr. Aldridge, if you are consumed, then you are a danger to us all, Mrs. Beckford included. In fact, she will probably be the first to perish at your hand—after my ward, of course. In simple self-defense, I must accept this—however you may feel about it." He tucked the handkerchief into his waistcoat. "If it is any comfort, this is a potent sacrifice, far more valuable than your own blood would have been, and may very well save all our lives. And now, if you will forgive me, I must get right to work. There is not a moment to lose." He turned and strode out of the room.

Professor Strasser turned to Cecily. "You are very brave, Mrs. Beckford."

Jacob groaned, "Too brave by half. I could never make her understand the practical value of fear."

Mrs. Strasser took his arm. "Please try to be comforted. However little you may like the risk to your sister, her courage will buy us more safety than we would have dared dream of before."

The professor nodded. "But she cannot be permitted to pick up your things now. Let the landlady send them on. Frau Strasser will oversee your rooms."

"I'll just send her a note, then." Cecily and Jacob spoke together and looked at each other and laughed. "Bread and butter." Again they spoke as one and followed it with a laugh.

Jacob managed a faint smile. "I see I must let you do this, dear girl." He chuckled. "But I'll send the note. She's my landlady."

"Actually," interrupted the professor, "it would be better if you dictated a note. Sending your own hand might leave an etheric trail. In fact, tell it to me in German and I will write it out in English."

His serious tone cut off Cecily's laughter, and she found herself suddenly cold.

Chapter Five

Cecily opened her eyes on blackness, and knew instantly that she was dreaming. Once the knowledge had come to her she wondered what made her so certain. She could see nothing, real or dreamlike; might not she be in a very dark room? She was lying on her back—where? She tried to turn her head to see, and found she could not move. The paralysis of a dream, she thought, and then she realized she might be weak from an illness or drugged. How had she gotten here, she wondered, and her inability to answer the question seemed to confirm she was dreaming. Except that, in a dream, surely she would not even think to ask.

Be it dream or reality, she did not like lying helpless and ignorant of her whereabouts. She struggled to rise, thrusting forward and upward until she suddenly found herself standing. The move was dramatic and unnatural; she was dreaming. She still could see nothing, but she moved forward slowly with her hands extended ahead to feel out obstacles.

Slowly the darkness resolved into a starry night. She was floating over a shimmering black surface—the sea, perhaps—reflecting an occasional glint of starshine. Once she had achieved place and time, she was drawn immediately down to the earth, to a city and a house, to a room. She was in Dr. Chang's study. Dr. Chang knelt before the door, gazing into a mirror. She came up behind him and was sucked into the mirror. She looked into the mirror and saw herself, looking out. But she was also the Cecily in the mirror looking out, who saw a reflection standing behind Dr. Chang.

She spun through an infinite regress of mirrors, and as she whirled the image flickered and changed. Sometimes she saw Cecily and sometimes she saw Jacob. "It is because I gave my blood as his," she realized. "In the mirror we are one." Jacob and Cecily danced in an eternal circle, like images spinning around on a candle chime. Then suddenly they were both gone. Suddenly it was her father in the mirror.

He was so young and handsome, rendered ageless by death, not so much as a day older than when she had seen him last. She had been so young then, and he had seemed so old. But he had hardly more years than Jacob. Yet he was also ancient, with bitterness in his eye and cruelty in his mouth. He smiled at her, and his smile filled her with dread. "Dear girl," he murmured, and reached out to pull her into his arms.

She struggled, but suddenly she was paralyzed again. He embraced her and she tried to scream. He kissed her cheek, which charred to ash under his vitriol lips. He took her chin in his hand and turned her face toward him so he could kiss her mouth. "No, you can't—you are my father," she cried, but no sound came out, and when she opened her mouth to protest his tongue slid inside her. His tongue was a huge and horrible serpent that plunged deep into her throat and chest, choking her, burning her, devouring her heart. She found her voice at last, and screamed and screamed.

She was still screaming as she found herself in her own bed, with Jacob grasping her arms, shaking her gently and urgently calling her name. She caught her breath. Jacob—all wrapped up in his dressing gown—looked more than a little worried. Behind him stood the housekeeper, also in a dressing gown, with her hair down in a braid and a fist pressed up to her mouth, her nightcap all askew. Almost reflexively, Cecily glanced down. She was not wearing her dressing gown, but Jacob had laid a thick shawl over her. "Oh, Mrs. Black," she whispered. "I've gotten you up at a dreadful hour. Please don't give notice."

"Oh, you poor dear," cried Mrs. Black. "What a thing to fret for." She darted over to the bed, mustering Jacob out of her way in her eagerness to take Cecily's hand. "Such a dreadful nightmare, it must have been. Let me get you something to soothe your nerves. A cup of cocoa, perhaps?" She turned on Cecily a pleading, timid look, as if her future happiness depended on Cecily accepting a little something to soothe her nerves.

Cecily knew her duty when she saw it. She forced a tremulous smile to her lips and replied, "Oh, thank you so much, Mrs. Black. I am sure I would feel very much better for a cup of cocoa." The housekeeper smiled brilliantly, squeezed Cecily's hand, and rushed out of the room.

"Valerian tea would do more good," remarked Jacob. He looked dreadful.

"But valerian tea tastes bad," explained Cecily. "So Mrs. Black doesn't trust it. And if I hesitated in the slightest while gulping the nasty stuff down, she would be sure she had poisoned me." She glanced around her room, reassuring herself that all her things were as she had left them, and nothing was tainted with sinister shadows. "You dreamed also, I think."

"Oh, yes." He went to the window and looked out on the quiet street. "I dream every night. It is searching for me. Searching for us both, it seems, thanks to your rash gesture."

She shivered and wrapped herself more deeply within her shawl. "The dreams do not mean . . . It has not found us?"

"No." He turned back to her and smiled. It seemed to her that his smile was the sweetest thing she had seen in months. It was a genuine smile, full of honest affection and completely lacking in bitterness or malice or unnatural influences. She believed him completely; his smile proved more than any words that he was not infected with the thing that had searched their dreams. "It smells us in the ether, but it cannot track our persons on land." He dropped his eyes, and a faint shadow crossed his face. "But I think it may be drawing closer. Perhaps we should go away for a while. Catch the New Year in Paris."

She nodded. "I'll consult with Dr. Chang. I don't know how much difference distance makes. But even if it does no good, a change of scene would be refreshing. Paris would be glorious; they'll celebrate the holiday with fireworks."

"Was Dr. Chang in your dream?" His question startled her. Her confidence in Dr. Chang was necessary; they could hardly survive without his assistance. And yet she knew nothing about him.

"Was he in yours?" she countered.

He shrugged and resumed looking out the window. She sighed and breathed deeply, struggling to slow her still-racing heart. Eventually, the door swung open and Mrs. Black bustled in with an enormous tray, laden not just with a pot of chocolate but with cups and plates and a platter of cake. "It's going to bed hungry that gives you bad dreams, if I may say so, ma'am. You scarcely even nibbled at your dinner. Nerves all wrung out from Christmas, I expect." She plunked down the tray on the table by the bed. "I've took the liberty of bringing sufficient for Mr. Aldridge, too, or he'll never get back to sleep."

Jacob shot Cecily an amused glance but replied to the housekeeper with great earnestness, "The very thing, Mrs. Black. I was wondering if I would be able to sleep after such an upset. But now I'm sure I shall. Is this the same cake that was in our trifle this evening? I recall it vividly; you are an artist as well as a saint."

Mrs. Black blushed and nodded with a smile. "You're very kind, sir."

"Oh, thank you, Mrs. Black," cooed Cecily. "I feel better just looking at such a treat. You are too good to me."

Mrs. Black bent over the bed to pat Cecily's hand. In some servants it would have been an unpardonable liberty. In Mrs. Black it was as natural as a nanny's kiss. "Not at all, madam, not at all. I'm going to have to report to the colonel that I took proper care of you, you know. He particularly asked me to."

"Well, I will be sure to tell him how well you've fulfilled your charge," said Cecily. "And now, you must go back to bed." She drew herself up quite straight so as to make it an order. "There will be no washing up. The cocoa things can wait until morning. And you're to sleep in. You need your rest— you know the whole house depends on you."

Mrs. Black tittered and bowed, and departed at very long last. Jacob watched her go with a smile. "Do you know, she boasts to her friends that you call her Mrs. Black, and not just Black? You spoil her."

"Well, of course." Cecily shrugged. "She's not a maid. She's entitled to a little dignity." Jacob chuckled. Cecily sighed. "If you dream every night, how do you keep from screaming?"

He shrugged. "There's a trick to it. I'll teach you."

"You'll have to." She shook her head. "I can't afford to scare off Mrs. Black. I'd never explain it to Oliver."

"When he comes back," said Jacob. He did not say, "If he comes back."

Cecily looked him in the eye. "Exactly. When he comes back."

Paris was, indeed, glorious and they stayed there over a fortnight before Cecily had another dream. She dreamed this time that she was back in New York, walking in the park with Rhoda, who kept them both in stitches whispering rude remarks about all things Yankee. But suddenly Rhoda turned to her and said, "I've done with Jacob, darling. I've used him all up. Now it is just the two of us." Rhoda slammed her against a tree with inhuman strength and leapt up against her, kissing her violently and tearing away her dress. Her fingers clawed at the places only Oliver had ever seen.

But Cecily knew it was a dream, and Jacob had taught her exactly what to do. She forced herself to stifle her screams and her cries of pain and spoke quite levelly. "You are not Rhoda," she remarked, almost as if the thing embracing her might not know. "Rhoda would never do this." Then she raised her voice and called out loudly, "Rhoda, are you anywhere about? Do you see what this thing is doing with your face?"

The thing drew back with a hiss and a snarl. It ceased to be Rhoda and became for an instant something so appalling that Cecily's eyes could not grasp the horror of it. Then it dissipated into smoke. The smoke kept some of its shape and all of its strength and went about raping her anyway. But at least it was not Rhoda. "You aren't real," Cecily told it. "And nothing you do to me is real, either. This is *my* dream." It fell back, shrieked at her, and vanished. Cecily woke. She could hear Jacob's soft snores in the next room, so she knew she had waked without screams. Then his snores stopped short and she knew he had awakened. He had been dreaming too.

She started the ritual of cleansing. If she had been warned that someday she would grow bored with magic rites, she would have laughed at the notion. Disgusted or contemptuous, perhaps, but not bored. She would have been mistaken. She was now bored with magic. There were a half dozen ceremonies that had to be performed daily, facing toward or away from the moon or the sun, with endless little adjustments for phase and angle; and dozens more minor rituals to be performed whenever anything spilled or dropped or broke.

The ritual that followed dangerous dreams involved frankincense and a peacock feather. Cecily did not like frankincense and felt the feather would be better employed decorating a hat. But she fulfilled the ritual because the dream had been very bad, even if she had driven away the demon in the end. Jacob's dream had doubtless been evil as well. When she was finished she dropped into a chair facing the fire, feeling not the slightest relieved or refreshed. The fire was nearly out, just a faint smolder, and the parlor was cold. She thought of poking at it but was just too weary. "What now?" she asked herself. "Back home to London?"

"Please, no." The voice came out of nowhere, and Cecily leapt to her feet.

But it was only Jacob, who had come into the room behind her. He was not merely bundled into his dressing gown, but had also wrapped one of her plainer, warmer shawls around his shoulders. She took pains not to chuckle. "London was freezing when we left, and utterly dreary. Don't you think Madrid would be nicer?"

"Madrid?" She stared at him quite taken aback. Neither of them spoke any Spanish.

"Warm and sunny?" He met her look briefly, but failed to stare her down. "There is a man there whom we might be interested to meet." He tried poking at the fire, but there was very little left to poke. He added a small chunk of coal and poked that a few times. Cecily continued to stare. "I heard of him from Jacques Verlaine."

"Dr. Verlaine, that we met in London?"

"No, his cousin. I had lunch with him the other day." Cecily's glare became frostier than the parlor. He shrugged. "You were shopping."

"Indeed," she sighed and dropped back into her chair. There was a little more heat coming from the fire, and she held out her hands to it. "A far more entertaining occupation than interviewing crusty old warlocks. Spanish or otherwise."

"The Spanish one has the advantage of never having met Dr. Chang." He took a chair, and extended his feet toward the fireplace.

"I did not dream of Dr. Chang this time," she informed him.

"No?" His lip curled. "Well, I did. Him and his damnable mirror."

"He had a mirror when I dreamed of him, too. Do you suppose there really is a mirror?"

"Jacques Verlaine was quite sure of it. It's a famous thing, coveted by everyone who . . . who . . ."

". . . Who cares about that sort of thing," she finished.

He smiled. "Precisely." There was a long pause before he continued, "It's not that I have any doubts about Chang personally. He seemed to have bottom[6] enough. But his mother nearly married our father. So there is a link. And that mirror can trace even the most fragile of links. Or so I am told."

She thought about that. "Then let us try the weather in Madrid, by all means. I could stand a bit of sun."

The man in Madrid was difficult to find, and by the time they had tracked him down, Cecily had had another dream. He sent her shopping for another new outfit, and a wig of any color but her own. Jacob, he directed to grow a beard. He held a long and elaborate ritual over them both, at one point even stopping and starting over because Cecily had yawned. Then he ordered them both out of town, instructing them that, wherever they went, they should cross water to get there. They went to Naples. And there they waited some while, poised to flee again.

After six weeks, they relaxed. It was warm and sunny in Naples, and the food was superb. They both spoke Italian. Cecily had not dreamed again, and even Jacob's dreams had grown vague and insubstantial. The worst they had to endure was the occasional sideways glance toward Cecily. Her wig was blond, and the color did not entirely suit her. And the Italians clearly viewed women who changed their hair color to blond as disreputable creatures. "Whatever would Oliver say," teased Jacob, and she thought of a very rude reply—thought it so loudly, in fact, that Jacob heard her and laughed.

The local Easter observances[7] were magnificent and uplifting. They began to hope their ordeal was over. They began to complain of the heat, reminisce about Kensington Gardens in the spring, and even discuss—guardedly—when it might be safe to go back. They sent a note (they still did not dare to send their own handwriting, so they dictated it in French and paid a translator to write it out in Italian) to a man whom Jacob thought he remembered Professor Strasser to have mentioned.

An answer arrived in an equally roundabout fashion. It suggested that if there had been no more dreams by the solstice and if they took a very lengthy and indirect route (perhaps stopping in Turkey or Egypt), then they might risk returning to London. They went out that night to celebrate. There was champagne. Many shattered glasses witnessed their loyalty to the queen. Cecily had another new gown, which Jacob assured her was wasted on a mere brother. He also dared to complain that he was tired of dancing with his sister. She made him dance with her anyway, and they whispered to each other about the glories of England.

They planned out their "grand tour," starting with Venice—which Cecily had never seen—and then heading back south to Greece, where neither of them had been since adolescence. They would take in Istanbul and Cairo—perhaps lingering in Egypt to see Karnak—before crossing to Algiers. Thence, they would return to Europe via Barcelona and Marseilles. In France, Cecily thought she might get another wig, something a little closer to her natural color. And at every stop they would know themselves one step closer to home.

Ready cash was getting a bit thin, but Cecily sold some of her jewels. "Oliver will never even notice," she assured Jacob. "He only gave them to me because his mother told him to." Jacob could not help wondering if Oliver would ever return to learn of it. But he said nothing. It was enough to see Cecily smiling again, with the shadow gone out of her eyes. He did not like the price she had paid to assist him.

Strangely, Cecily did not like Venice. There seemed to be something secret and strange about the place, something almost magical. And yet she loved the canals. She felt very safe on the water and spent long hours circling the city aimlessly in a gondola. She would trail a hand over the side, and splash at the waterfowl that came begging for crumbs. The gondoliers were always happy to sing for the pretty foreign lady. Meanwhile, Jacob spent much of his time playing tourist in the many churches, pausing in most to light a candle for Rhoda.

He found surprising comfort in the gesture. Naturally, he had been raised Church of England, and Rhoda belonged to some peculiar American Non-Conformist sect. But the Roman churches had considerable grace; the candles were pretty, and his exposure to the unnatural arts had taught him that light always carries power.

Some churches he stumbled on by accident, but he made a point of visiting the Santi Giovanni e Paolo. It was a special day. The altarpieces were said to be by Titian and Giovanni Bellini.[8] But, as had become usual, his special day crumbled into disappointment.

The famous altarpieces were gone. Apparently there had been a fire some years before. He stared down at his twenty-year-old guide book, reflecting wryly that he had not thought he would need to update it to visit fifteenth-century churches. He stood some while, reflecting on time and loss. At last he drew a deep breath, turned, and marched resolutely toward the exit, only to slam suddenly into a lady who had come up behind him.

He bumped her rather hard and, with no familiarity intended, grasped her arms to steady her against the impact. "*Mi dispiace, signorina,*" he murmured. And froze. The woman in his arms was Livia Aram.

It took him several seconds to collect himself. Even after so long, he thought first that it was Rhoda, which led to the still hideously painful recollection that she was dead. Yet there she was before him, like an angel materialized by his prayers. But he did not believe in angels or trust that prayers could be answered.

A dreadful fear crept up his spine that the demon had tracked him down at last and was presenting this terrible temptation. But he suffered no trace of the malignant savagery that had characterized the demonic assaults. Only slowly did he recognize the poor girl he had attacked in the park when under the influence. In his madness, he had scarcely acknowledged her independent existence. "Miss Aram, I am so sorry," he breathed.

He belatedly released her, but she made no attempt to draw away. Nor did she answer, but stood looking up at him with wondering eyes. "It is true, then, you are recovered from our last meeting?" she remarked at last.

"I . . . I hope so." He was bewildered by warring impulses. On the one hand, she did look so very like Rhoda that he was almost irresistibly drawn to her. But he greatly feared that their meeting might still result in the reappearance of his demon. And yet he owed her many apologies, and she was smiling as if she might accept them.

"I have been told"—she paused and glanced coyly up and then away—"that I should not judge you by our first encounter, that you are a gentleman, someone I might even trust. I have wanted for some time to meet you again, and see for myself if that were so. You seem clear-headed enough now."

He was astonished. Even assuming a sublimely forgiving nature, there was no call for her to seek him out. Unless . . . "Are you in need of someone you can trust, Miss Aram?"

She looked up at him for a very long time, then smiled and took his arm. "How like you to see directly to the point." They walked together out into the churchyard, where he found a bench to seat her. She folded her hands in her lap and looked demurely down.

"Is it?" And how had she come to have expectations of him? "Who has been telling you about me, Miss Aram?"

"Surely you can guess," she whispered. His heart hammered. He seated himself beside her. "Do you remember the séance? How Miss Carothers spoke through my mouth?"

"I could scarcely forget."

"She . . . she has never truly left me since. I see her everywhere, hear her voice constantly." Livia Aram drew a very deep breath and looked up to meet his eye. "She is here now."

He knew all too well what it meant to be haunted. "That is dreadful," he replied in all truthfulness. But a guilty place at the back of his heart crowed with delight. Rhoda was not utterly lost. He inhaled the scent of jasmine. Surely last November Miss Aram had worn a camellia perfume? "Intolerable," he continued with more force. "Has your guardian done nothing?"

She shook her head. "He did try. But at first nothing seemed to work. And over time . . ." She looked away, looked back, looked away again. "I stopped confiding in him," she admitted at last. She looked up into his eyes, so like the way that Rhoda used to look at him. "Does that shock you?"

He shook his head gently.

"No?" She shivered. "It shocks me. I have trusted in him all my life. Just as he trusts in his mother, I fear." She shook her head again. "Grandmama is a proud woman, from an ancient family. Sometimes I wonder if she cares more for her ancient family than for me. She is ambitious. And I am not really her blood."

Jacob took her hand. "Then you have no one to turn to?"

She did not pull her hand away. "Mrs. Strasser was a great help to me. She could see and hear Miss Carothers when no one else could. She . . . mediated between us. At first I was so frightened, so repulsed—I thought I had gone mad. But Mrs. Strasser helped me talk to her, helped me see that she was frightened and in need of refuge. She was fleeing from something dreadful; how could I ignore her pain?"

Miss Aram smiled, and her smile, too, reminded him of Rhoda. "We became friends, almost sisters." She giggled. "Ghostly sisters." And then the brightness left her mien, leaving a timid, unhappy girl behind. Rhoda had never been timid. "But Mrs. Strasser quarreled with Papa—over me, I very much fear. And so she went away, and now Papa has gone back to London, and his mother wants to try a very dark spell to drive Miss Carothers away."

Jacob shuddered and looked away. He thought for a very long time. Finally he answered, "I cannot advise you about driving Rho . . . Miss Carothers away. I pray you do not. But I am not impartial; she was dear to me, very dear. But whether you choose to give her refuge, or to cast her out for your own protection, I am very sure you should not allow Mme. Chang to subject you to dark practices. Mrs. Strasser—whom I very much admired— was quite clear on the necessity of avoiding 'moral contamination.' And Mme. Chang once claimed to feel the same way herself."

Miss Aram nodded, as if he had spoken exactly to her expectation. She drew back her hand—reluctantly it seemed to him. "She does not mean me ill, but she is determined to break all the links that bind me. And . . ." she broke off and turned a searching look on Jacob. "May I speak candidly?"

He almost laughed. "I rather thought you had done so already. But please continue. I would like to be your friend."

She giggled quite suddenly. "More than my friend, I think. And Miss Carothers assures me you are a friend worth having." Her eyes rolled back as if she were listening to an inner voice, and her lips curved in a mischievous smile so like Rhoda's that it took his breath away. "Did you really . . . when that man tried to rob her . . . ?"

"Did I kill him?" She nodded. So did he. "Of course. He laid violent hands on her." He sighed. "Perhaps I should have let him off with a beating but . . . She was weeping and terrified. How could I walk away before it was done?"

"She was very glad you did it."

He set that thought aside. "Are you reassured that you can confide in me now? Or too horrified to go on?"

She did not look horrified. In fact, she looked thrilled. "Ah, yes. I was saying." She paused and took a deep breath. "I do know something of my father's work. And I know that I have . . . abilities, should I choose to exercise them. And Grandmama—she is not unfeeling. She knows my position is precarious, and she wishes to see me rescued. But still, she wants my abilities to remain at her disposal. She seeks only those solutions that . . . preserve my solitude."

Jacob considered the links that entwined Livia Aram. "The one link you most need to sever is to your father's blood, and that is unbreakable, no matter how dark a spell Mme. Chang might employ." Miss Aram nodded. "I find it impossible to suppose that Miss Carothers would ever do you injury— she was a woman of noble sentiment." Miss Aram nodded again. "But her . . . nearness continues to tie you to me. Mme. Chang has every cause to want that link severed. I . . . I can bring you nothing but trouble. I am pursued, and likely to destroy anyone I touch." He shook his head and was horrified to hear himself continue, "It seems I already destroyed Miss Carothers."

"No!" Her voice was husky and urgent. She took his hand again and pressed it firmly. "It was not your fault or your doing." She did not really convince him. "If anyone destroyed her it was I. This . . . entity that pursues you is one with that which pursues me. Or her. Or maybe both of us." He looked up sharply, shaking his head. But she would not let him interrupt. "It is, Mr. Aldridge. These . . . creatures are not so distinct from each other as mortals. They blend and shift and mix. Your enemy and mine have become the same. So how does it benefit either of us, if it is permitted to pick us off singly?"

He stared. If there were one thing in all creation he had not expected her to say, that was it. "Perhaps you are mad," he whispered.

"But think," she pleaded. "I have admitted I have strange talents. So do you." He could scarcely deny that. "And the bond between us is based on love, albeit love at something of a remove. 'Love conquers all,' they say; is that no more than a platitude? For if it is true, then any attempt to break our link would surely be futile, as futile as trying to sever ourselves from our fathers. And perhaps it could empower our defenses against that which pursues us."

"Miss Aram," he remarked, a little faintly. "I do believe you are suggesting . . . an emotional entanglement. Are you aware how unladylike an entanglement might prove?" Putting aside the resemblance to Rhoda (a herculean effort in itself), she was a very prim and decorous little creature. Not without charm, of course, but certainly not a woman to challenge society's norms.

She blushed to the roots of her hair. He enjoyed it hugely. Rhoda had never blushed once in their entire acquaintance. He could scarcely hear her reply. "Please forgive my boldness. Miss Carothers has assured me that you admire boldness in a woman; she says it reminds you of your sister, to whom you compare all women. But it seems I have not the knack of it."

How catty. "Ah, well. Rhoda was always jealous of Cecily." He shrugged. "And, in all fairness, Cecily was always jealous of Rhoda. It was so convenient, you know, to have a spare escort in your pocket when your husband declined to come home and take you to parties."

"Did he never come home at all?" She appeared grateful for the change of subject.

"I very much doubt he was able. Probably buried under an avalanche or something. A hideous waste of talent and courage. Of course, Cecily would not hear of it. She has never doubted for an instant that he is lying, amnesiac, in the arms of some Hindu native—or perhaps Afghani—who is patiently nursing him back to health."

"A lady native?"

"But of course," he grinned quite mischievously. "Oliver was always a very devil with the ladies. Until he fell under dear Cecily's spell."

She giggled and looked back down at her folded hands. They sat some while in silence. So much had been said, small talk would have been an offense. And he had many things to think about.

He rose and turned away from her, and spoke at last. "It is very strange that I should meet you, today of all days." He drew a deep breath and forced himself to say the words aloud. "It is my wedding day." He heard her gasp faintly, but was too caught up in his own pain to look at her. "A year ago today, we chose today. I was annoyed with her for insisting on so long an engagement. But she said she had so many things to arrange and . . . and . . . Well, I could refuse her nothing."

"And it was not as if you had waited for the banns." Her voice was hardly more than a whisper. But clearly Rhoda had confided every detail.

"You, I think, would not be so oblivious to convention," he replied, glancing behind him to where she still sat demurely, with her hands folded. "You, I think, would insist on being married." She looked up at him with a stubborn eye, embarrassed by his suggestion but not repudiating it. He smiled. "And why shouldn't you? I begin to think you may be right about . . . our enemies. Safety in numbers, and all that. So what do you say, Miss Aram? Are you so desperate for my inadequate protection that you would share me with a ghost? It could still be my wedding day."

She stopped breathing, and stared up at him. And then she smiled a wonderfully sweet smile that was not at all like Rhoda's. She rose and came to him and took his hand. "You should know that I might not be sharing you forever. Mrs. Strasser said that once Rhoda was free of the demon, then she would probably consent to move onward. And then you would have only me." She lowered her head as if she feared to see disappointment in his eyes.

With his free hand he caught her chin and raised her face back up. "And how would I know? Surely Rhoda must have warned you that men are utterly oblivious; they care only for the warm person of a lady." Very slowly he pulled her into his arms. Jasmine or camellia, her scent was intoxicating, and he kissed her more thoroughly than he had intended. He suffered an instant of panic that desire might summon the demon, but found to his passionate delight that he was fully capable of taking her gently.

Chapter Six

Cecily rose with the note still clutched in her hand. "*Je vous ecrit parce que le gentilhomme Anglais m'y a demandé . . .*" The French was very bad, but probably a fair enough translation of Jacob's meaning, dictated in Italian. She walked to the balcony and looked out over the evening. The real problem was that Jacob had said very little. Something interesting had occurred; he was detained; she was not to worry.

Night was about to fall. Although a gap in the roofline opened her view to the horizon, the sun itself was not visible through the thick haze that filled the street and the cloud bank that rose up from the sea. The western half of the sky was splashed violently with orange, scarlet, and rose. The canal reflected the ruddy light back upward into the mist. The entire world was suffused with the invisible sunset. It was an hour of red magic. Cecily trembled.

She heard him before she saw him. Usually sound reflected sharply back up from the water, but in the fog his steps were only faint little taps. He seemed to materialize out of the mist, appearing suddenly quite close to her balcony. He looked up. Even at such close quarters she could not make out his face, but he seemed to see her. He leapt several feet up the wall and started climbing the ivy. She admired his grace even as she recognized it as unnatural. Then he was over the iron railing and standing beside her.

He did not approach any closer. That alone clearly demonstrated that it was not Oliver. Oliver would have had her in his arms before she could draw breath. But it was not Oliver, and they both knew the rules of the encounter. He had to persuade her to touch him first.

"Oh, Oliver." She had no other name by which to call him. "You were such a fine man. So tall, so gallant, so dashing in your uniform."

"You mean," it chuckled—and to give credit where credit was due, it had the voice exactly right—"so very rich."

"Not so, you cruel thing." She laughed. "The money never mattered in the slightest. Although the pace of your promotions did impress me, I must confess."

It leaned back against the balcony railing. "Really? The money certainly mattered to your Aunt Agatha. She mentioned it to me more than once."

"How tactless." She shrugged. "I fear Tante Aggie was a severely pragmatic woman. And, do you know, I often suspected that she found us something of a burden. Not that she ever said so, of course."

"Two penniless, half-mad orphans to feed, clothe, and educate? You must be mistaken, darling. I'm sure she considered it an honor." He still had the most charming smile in England. She wanted to reach out and stroke his hair. She did not.

"We were not penniless," she reminded him. She tried very hard not to smile, but failed utterly. "Just rigidly protected by our trust funds. And we were at least three-quarters mad, I'm sure."

"Perhaps even seven-eighths." He drew very close, so close she could feel his breath on her cheek. He reached his hand toward hers, but she pulled sharply back. "Not even a kiss to welcome the warrior home?"

He was too close by far, closer than she had thought he could come without an invitation. Her voice rose to a sharp note. "Don't be impudent. You are not Oliver."

He did not back away. He gazed into her eyes and stood so close to her that she could feel the warmth of his body. But he did not touch her. "You cannot be sure," he murmured.

"Yes, I can." She surprised herself with her conviction. "Oliver is off mapping the Hindu Kush. You are just a pretty picture. Astonishingly lifelike, I grant, except for being years out of date. Even if he is still alive he must be changed by now. But look at you." She sighed. "You may even be younger than I am."

It looked at her with eyes so tragic that it wrenched her heart even if it wasn't Oliver. Could demons suffer and feel pain? "Please, Cecily," he whispered, and it was exactly Oliver's voice that whispered, a voice from her most intimate memories.

She drew herself up and back. "No more pretending. I thank you for this chance to say good-bye to him." She looked it over carefully, her heart drinking in the long-lost image. "Good-bye, Oliver." She turned her back on him and closed her eyes. It could not touch her. She waited until the sounds of breathing and the sense of warmth behind her were long gone. She waited until the crimson glow faded from the air, and the night grew dark and heavy around her.

At last she turned and walked back into the parlor. Jacob had finally returned, and stood by the door. He looked tired and his collar was askew. "Is it gone?" he asked her.

"I believe so." She breathed deeply and shook her head. "If you would excuse me a moment." She escaped to her room. Not even Jacob was allowed to see her cry. When the foolish tears were done, she poured water into the basin and washed her face.

Jacob had poured himself a brandy and flung himself into a chair by the fire, with his feet propped up on the fireplace rail. The fire was burning brightly; he must have poked at it. He was good with fires. Whenever he poked them they blazed up obligingly, which they never would do for her. She came up behind him and put her arms around his neck. He had given up on the nasty beard, so she kissed his cheek. The mustache had filled out nicely, though.

Then she came around to sit with him in front of the fire. "Shall you tell me of this interesting development?" she inquired.

He smiled at her with sparkling eyes. "I married Livia Aram this afternoon." She stared at him speechlessly. He had to be joking. Surely there was a hint of mockery in his look. Eventually he tired of waiting for her answer, and continued, "She was of the opinion we would be safer together than apart." He turned his head and gazed thoughtfully out over the balcony. "Perhaps she was mistaken."

"If you're married, then where's your wife?" she managed at last.

He cocked his head. "Just down the hall. The hotel had plenty of spare rooms. She's fast asleep, so I thought I'd pop round and give you the news. She'll sleep some while; she's exhausted." He rose and stretched, then crossed to stand in front of her and hold out his hands. "Well? Surely the occasion merits congratulations." He waited while she stared up at him. "Or at least comment."

He was quite correct. For all her startlement she could scarcely just stare at him forever. She rose and embraced him. "I'm sorry, Jacob. I'm simply caught completely off guard. Of course, I am delighted for you." His breath smelled faintly of the brandy, and his mustache tickled her ear. "She is a lovely girl, and I'm sure you'll be very happy."

His chuckle was barely audible, just a rumbling vibration in his chest. "You're appalled." She looked up at him, but he laid a finger over her lips. "Please don't trouble to deny it. You think it's morbid to marry Rhoda's look-alike, and that things will turn ugly when she turns out not to be Rhoda. She told me herself you would think so."

Little cat, reflected Cecily. Aloud she replied, "It certainly sounds like someone thinks so."

"Do you know what else she said?" Jacob's voice was light and friendly; he rested his arms gently about her waist. "She said I compare all women to my sister."

"How catty." This time she said it aloud. "And you married her anyway?"

"She is," he replied. "And I did. Furthermore, she is absolutely right. I do compare all women to my sister." His arm tightened slightly—not hurtfully but very firmly. "Generally I find them wanting." He lowered his head until their faces were very close. "Perhaps it's time I completed the comparison." He kissed her on the mouth. She nearly fainted in the wave of sheer, glorious lust that engulfed her. She kissed him back with all her strength. She had already got several of her buttons undone before a faint whisper of reason suggested that their behavior was inappropriate.

She drew back slightly. It was the hardest thing she had ever done, harder even than sending Oliver away. "You are not Jacob," she whispered.

"Do you think I am the demon?" He chuckled and drew back a fraction of an inch, but not so far away that the touch of his skin ceased searing her soul. "You dear, demented little twit. Why would I lie? You've already touched me." He tried to kiss her again.

She held up a weak hand between their faces. "You must be the demon, you must. Jacob would not do this." She could not say aloud that it was the very heat with which she burned that proved it. Oliver had never once inspired her to such a frenzy of desire; this passion had to be unnatural. He was the demon, a delicious, adorable, inhumanly attractive demon.

Whoever he was, he knew what she was thinking. "You didn't really love Oliver. You were so young—it was just a schoolgirl's infatuation," he whispered. "Not like you and me." He pushed away the hand that separated them and kissed her again. Then he swept an arm up under her knees and carried her into the bedroom. She made no move to stop him; she was still working on the buttons.

Necromancer
September 1885

Chapter One

He stood a long time in the twilight, just looking at the house. He had not expected it to make so profound an impression on him. It was, after all, just a house. He had other pressing concerns, more than sufficient to absorb his attention. The loss of his dear parents and the long silence of his beautiful young wife served as obvious examples. But he had grown up in the house and found that the sight of it brought back a thousand memories. He stared, assaulted by old emotions, and tears formed in his eyes. Embarrassed, he dashed them away.

He was just mustering the resolve to approach when a carriage drove up and deposited an elegantly dressed couple at the door. They were no one he knew. A maid opened the door to admit them, and he did not know her either. Of course, he had been gone a long time. The staff might easily have turned over, and his wife might have made any number of new friends. Still, it troubled him to see the familiar house sheltering only unfamiliar faces. Another carriage drove up and disgorged another couple with whom he was not acquainted.

On impulse, he limped around to the back instead of knocking at the front door. The back door stood wide open. Some things, at least, did not change. With a dinner party in progress, the kitchen inevitably grew hot and uncomfortable. Even in midwinter—and it was now only September—the staff invariably threw the door open to cool the air. A red-faced maid stood on the steps, fanning herself with her apron. At the sound of his cane on the flagstones, she turned in his direction. She peered out from under her hand, but after the brightness of the gas-lit kitchen she must have found the shaded garden impenetrably dark. Voices crackled behind her, and she hurried back inside. She did not close the door behind her.

He glanced around the garden, wherein he had so often played, but felt little sentimental attachment to the pots of chives and basil. The stairs proved something of a struggle; they were far steeper than those of the main entrance, being intended only for servants and tradesmen. Even with the help of a cane, his game leg did not want to climb them.

He paused for breath at the top, and looked inside. Although he must have been plainly visible, framed in the doorway, no one in the kitchen so much as glanced up from the bustle of culinary preparations. A short, stout woman who was obviously the cook barked orders at two maids and a footman, none of whom he recognized. The aroma was fabulous, but enveloped only a continued stream of complete strangers.

Then, to his heartfelt delight, an elderly woman darted in from the front of the house to speak earnestly with the cook. "Blackie!" he called out, without thinking to use a more formal address. She turned in a complete circle before spotting him. For an instant she looked so astonished he thought she was going to faint. Then she ran toward him with open arms and hugged him with all her strength. He laughed and returned her embrace wholeheartedly, picking her right up off the ground in his enthusiasm (for she a was a very small woman and he was a big man, even in his reduced state).

"Master Oliver, Master Oliver," she repeated over and over. "You're home at last! Oh, sir, it has been such an awfully long time; we had given you up, just about. Merciful heavens, but it's good to see you again. I feared I never would."

The cook came up behind them, glowering, and he set Blackie down. The cook, too, was larger than Blackie, but Blackie still managed to stare her down with a fierce glare. "None of your foreign sauce, now," she snapped. "You'll remember your place with Colonel Beckford, I hope."

The cook clearly knew his name. Her eyes widened, and she managed to swallow whatever she had originally meant to say. "But, sir, what for are you bothering with kitchen affairs?" she inquired in a reasonably humble manner and a very thick accent. "Is menu not to your satisfaction?"

He almost laughed. Clearly, if he had been anyone else she would have ordered him out with a high hand, however broken her English. He smiled politely. "My apologies, ma'am. I know I am dreadfully in your way, and I promise to get out immediately. But I could not wait an instant for the pleasure of seeing Mrs. Black again. She was my nurse when we were both younger, you know." He smiled down at Blackie, who beamed rapturously back up at him. "Much younger."

The cook nodded deeply—almost a bow. "Of course, sir." What was that accent? Pharsi, perhaps—she had a Mediterranean look to her. She turned and snapped in a much coarser tone, "Rose, another place at table! Now!" Turning back to Oliver, she purred, "I hope you find everything to your liking after so long, sir. If you do not, it be made right soon as you speak." She drew in a deep breath, nodded again and marched back to her dinner preparations.

Mrs. Black drew gently on his arm and led him out of the kitchen. A beautiful, dark-skinned maid—Rose, perhaps?—was already at work resetting the table, assisted by a footman. Oliver noted with amusement that he would make thirteen at the table. He hoped none of the guests were superstitious. Rose was changing all the dishes, rather than adding a place, removing a handsome rose-patterned service and replacing it with his mother's old china. His mother had always been proud of her gold-trimmed Minton, and she had taken pains to acquire sixteen place settings for larger parties. So clearly thirteen at the table was proving ill luck for Rose, at any rate.

"Dear me, Blackie, so many new faces." Mrs. Black sniffed and rolled her eyes. Clearly she did not approve of new faces. "Are you all that is left of the old guard, then?" He tugged gently at his collar and jacket hem, suddenly concerned that he was not dressed for a dinner party. "Is she at least a good cook?"

Mrs. Black sighed. "She's well thought of. Mrs. Aldridge says we are lucky to have her."

From her tone, Oliver concluded that she did not entirely agree. But nothing in her tone explained who Mrs. Aldridge was or why she should be passing judgments on the household staff. Uneasily he inquired, "But what does Mrs. Beckford think?"

And Blackie turned to him, her hand raised to her mouth and her eyes full of pain. "Oh, sir, don't you know?"

It was too late to stop and question her. They were already at the door of the parlor and, if he had not been properly announced, his voice had been loud enough to alert the assembled guests to the entry of a newcomer. A silence fell as everyone in the room turned to look at him. He reminded himself that his uniform was always presentable, in any situation. Even if it was not dress and showed a few signs of wear.

As he had feared, they were all strangers. Or, rather, all except one.

Cecily's brother Jacob gasped and leapt forward to take his hand. "Oliver, old man, how do you come to be here?" He did not merely shake Oliver's hand but grasped it with both of his own. Oliver could have sworn that his smile was sincere. "Wonderful to see you, old man! Quite wonderful! But it has been . . . When did you . . . And where . . ." Stumbling over all the obvious questions he finally concluded, "Welcome home, Oliver. Why did you not write? Come meet everyone."

Oliver considered himself a fair judge of character, and he decided that he could not be deceived. His brother-in-law was genuinely pleased to see him, and just as genuinely astonished. But someone had surely known that Oliver was coming home. He had written. Twice. And received no answer.

Of course the guests—Verlaine, Strasser, Neeson, Drury—could have had nothing to do with it. He nearly started on being presented to Dr. Chang, for the name was well known in certain circles, but there was no reason to suppose the man should bear him ill. He was accompanied by a very young Miss Chang—not his daughter, Oliver gathered, but some sort of niece or cousin. Lastly, Jacob presented him proudly to Mrs. Aldridge, Livia Aram that was.

Her name alone was suspect, for Oliver had heard a great deal of Ishmael Aram. But even if he had not, her nervous manner and her failure to meet his eyes would have betrayed her. She had received his letters, he was quite sure. Also, he had suffered considerable difficulty in his efforts to return home. He had wondered more than once if those difficulties were entirely natural. The heir of Ishmael Aram would have had no difficulty arranging difficulties.

The introductions were barely concluded before dinner was announced. Jacob drew him aside for an instant. "This dinner is dreadfully inconvenient, I know," he whispered. "There is much we need to discuss. But . . ." He gestured around the room. "Shall I leave Livia to entertain?"

Oliver looked into Jacob's eyes. He saw anxiety and sorrow there, even an unnatural press of care. But he did not see any lack of goodwill or desire to conceal. Oliver wanted answers: he wanted to know where Cecily was and why, in her absence, Jacob and his wife were hosting dinner parties in his house. However, he also wanted dinner, having missed both lunch and tea in his eagerness to get home. And he valued Jacob's continued goodwill. "Nonsense, old man. You cannot abandon your guests. What would people say?"

Jacob smiled gratefully. Turning back to his friends, he insisted that Mrs. Aldridge go in to dinner with Oliver while he brought up the rear alone. She did not appear to care for the idea, but could scarcely decline. Oliver could have made it harder for her but decided that since he was here—despite her best efforts—magnanimity in victory was the way to proceed. At least until she showed signs of refusing to acknowledge her defeat.

It was, therefore, a spirit of diplomacy that moved him to speak as soon as he tasted the soup, a buoyant avgolemono. "This is splendid," he assured his hostess. "I had heard you were proud of your cook, and I see you are justified."

As a diplomatic maneuver his little sally failed dismally. Mrs. Aldridge blushed slightly and averted her eyes. "Actually, she is my guardian's cook." She turned to Dr. Chang, as if hoping for assistance.

The doctor took his cue. "She is a treasure, is she not? I could never have accepted Livia's invitation if it had required parting with her. And Livia"— he smiled paternalistically and reached out to pat Mrs. Aldridge's hand— "had just lost another cook, not half so good, when I returned to London. Most serendipitous." So Dr. Chang was also in residence, along with heaven alone knew whom else, except Mrs. Beckford. Oliver sighed, managed a polite smile, and returned to the soup. He should, perhaps, have accepted Jacob's offer to skip the dinner and get on to the explanations.

The dinner was sumptuous and the company clever. Several guests were curious about Oliver, and all of them polite enough to attempt to include him in their talk. Oliver did not like to be rude, but neither did he feel obliged to answer questions when so many of his own were still unanswered. He fell back on a little trick he had learned in India.

"I am invisible," he whispered to himself, and breathed. "More transparent than crystal, less tangible then wind." He breathed again. Mrs. Neeson turned to him with a civil query, and he smiled. "You do not see me," he informed her politely. "You do not recall I am here." Then he answered her question with a bland inanity. "You would rather talk to someone else," he suggested very softly.

The key to the trick was remembering that results would not be immediate. Novices attempting the procedure often supposed that they had failed as soon as someone spoke to them, and so gave up too soon. Oliver was pre-

a few attempts at interaction from the persons around him, in con-
with their social norms. Only gradually would they forget he was
among them.

He paused in his whispering when the serving dishes came around, and
the maids continued to serve him. He was very hungry, and the food was
superb: baron of lamb basted with rosemary and garlic—a bold choice. The
sweet was a simple zabaglione. The cook really was a treasure, whether
Blackie cared for her or not. Although most of the table blithely ignored him,
Dr. Chang glanced uneasily his way on several occasions. Oliver took it as a
confirmation of the doctor's reputation.

He did not learn a great deal. His most obvious deductions were confirmed: Jacob Aldridge was, for all intents and purposes, master of the house.
Dr. Chang was permanently installed as a guest. Little Miss Chang was also visiting, but on a more temporary basis. She would soon be joining her great aunt
in Italy. Mrs. Aldridge had declined to accompany her. Oliver got the distinct
impression she had declined more than once. Dr. and Mrs. Verlaine were close
friends of the family, as were Professor and Frau Strasser; the other guests were
merely cordial acquaintances. Nothing was said of Cecily by anyone at dinner,
almost as if mention of her might be construed as ill-mannered.

When they parted from the ladies, he permitted himself to be seen again,
and Dr. Verlaine approached him directly. "My notes are entirely at your disposal," he assured Oliver. "And, as always"—he glanced toward Jacob—"I
truly welcome any outside opinion you might choose to seek." He opened the
door leading back to the dining room and called to his wife, "My dear, I am
sure that Colonel Beckford is tired after his long journey. We should depart."

His words launched a general exodus. Before leaving, Frau Strasser
pressed his hand warmly. "We are your friends, I assure you. Please call upon
us freely for any assistance you may need with the situation."

Oliver turned to Jacob with a raised eyebrow. "There is a situation?"

Jacob sighed. "There is." Mrs. Aldridge bustled about apologizing to her
guests about the early end of the evening. "Best, perhaps, if I simply show
you," Jacob continued. He led Oliver to the main entrance and up the stairs.
Mrs. Aldridge nervously watched them go, and rushed through her farewells.
She joined them at the top of the stairs.

The hallway leading to the bedrooms was so changed that he was shocked despite himself. All his parents' pictures—the images that had watched over his childhood—had been removed, except for the Rosetti,[1] which had been his least favorite. He had always thought it too sentimental, although Papa had loved it. Of course it was probably valuable, now the poor silly man was dead. The Impressionists had apparently become respectable in his absence, for the walls were now lined with an excellent Pisarro, a charming Degas sketch, and a fair Courbet.

One new piece in particular—a study of the Thames near Chelsea—caught his eye. "This is good!" he exclaimed to Mrs. Aldridge's evident satisfaction. "Is it a Whistler?"

"We are not sure," she replied. "We thought it was at first, but . . . Some think the figure in the foreground has not his touch, or even that the figure is intended to be Whistler, having been painted on later by Greaves.[2] But we are confident that it is at least partially by Whistler." She sounded a little embarrassed, as if he might think less of her for owning a painting that was only a Greaves.

As they came to the end of the hall he was struck suddenly by the absence of one particular painting. "Have you taken down the Reynolds,[3] then?" Jacob stiffened slightly, and Oliver sensed he had touched on a nerve.

But Mrs. Aldridge heard nothing amiss in his tone. "It needed cleaning," she remarked with a shrug. "You do not like the Cassat?" He did, in fact, like the Cassat very much, but that was scarcely the point.

He smiled. "Reynolds is a bit old-fashioned, I suppose." He waited an instant, watching her face change as she considered her position. "Still, ours was said to be particularly fine." She said nothing, but her eyes grew wary. "And the subject was my great-grandmother."

"Not to worry," murmured Jacob. "We shall have it back up as soon as the cleaning is done." He smiled very sweetly at his wife. "By the end of the week, at the latest, I should think?"

They had quarreled over it, then. Oliver found himself touched that Jacob had defended the painting in his absence. He had always liked Jacob; he was so very like Cecily. Mrs. Aldridge managed a pleasant smile. "But of course. I have been meaning to pop round and see what was keeping it for some while." They had reached the room that had been Oliver's in his boyhood. She opened the door and stepped back so that he could enter ahead of her. Within, a middle-aged woman rose hurriedly from the only chair. "Here is Nurse Fanshawe, Colonel Beckford. You may be sure there is always someone with her."

He did not even glance at Nurse Fanshawe, just waved her away. Cecily lay on the bed. She was clad in a decorous nightdress composed largely of lacy ruffles. Her hands lay folded neatly on the coverlet. She was utterly motionless; he might almost have doubted that she was breathing. His very own Sleeping Beauty.

He gazed at her for what seemed like half of forever. Slowly he entered the room, sank down to seat himself beside her on the bed. He took her hand; it lay passively in his own. They had cut her hair—suspecting brain fever, no doubt—and it had only partially grown back. She had had such wonderful hair; he hoped they had got a good price for it. The poor remains had been combed and tucked it into a beribboned nightcap. One charming little curl had escaped.

She was still lovely. A little older, of course, but not at all faded. Just a bit more mature and sophisticated than the adorable child he had married. He raised her hand to his lips and kissed it, then reluctantly let it go. To his horror, the hand did not drop limply back to her side. It remained poised in the air where he had left it. He took it again and guided it back down to its proper place.

Eventually he became aware that Jacob had entered behind him and fallen into the chair. He sat with his face buried in his hands. "How long has she been so?" inquired Oliver.

Jacob did not lift his head. "Well over two years."

"What happened?"

Jacob shrugged faintly. "I do not know. One day, I simply found her so."

Oliver sighed. "I am not an easy man to lie to, Jacob. Shall I ask you again? What happened to her?"

Jacob looked up at last. "I am not lying." There was a long pause. "I truly do not know what happened to her."

"But you have your suspicions?"

Jacob sighed and rose, walked to the window. "Suspicions are just . . . suspicions. And you would not believe mine."

Oliver stared after him. "What I do or do not believe is not really your concern. Your business now is to speak to me plainly, so that I know what you believe."

Jacob drew in a deep, hurtful breath. "It first began in the fall of '82. I do not recall the exact date." He shook his head. "You would think it would be carved into my heart. Some while after Guy Fawkes Day,[4] I should say. I was attacked by a succubus." He paused and glanced back at Oliver, as if expecting a question. Oliver did not offer one. "Do you know what that is?"

"A predatory spirit," replied Oliver. "Generally nocturnal."

Jacob blinked and resumed his tale. "You know how Cecily is, was—so bold, so fiercely loyal. She involved herself in my trouble, attempted to intervene. Even against such a creature." He shuddered, and turned angrily away to resume gazing out the window. "You surely cannot want every detail. We fled. We took evasive action. Indeed, we came to think we had escaped. But in Venice . . . I came back to our rooms one day and found her. The thing must have caught up with us."

There was no mistaking Jacob's bleak tone. He had left a great deal out, but he had told the truth as he saw it. "How did Chang and Aram come to be involved?" Oliver asked.

Jacob looked puzzled. "Aram is not involved. How could he be? He has been dead for years. Cecily brought Chang into it; she felt we needed assistance."

Oliver very much doubted they had got any real assistance from Chang. Nor could mere death absolve Aram of anything. But Jacob was clearly too mired in self-recrimination to question their roles. He was covering for no one but his wife, and might not even have noticed any need to cover for her. Oliver sighed. "Well, you can send Fanshawe home, for now. If you will be good enough to send up a pillow and a blanket, I shall take over."

"You mean to sleep here? In Cecily's room?"

"Where else could I sleep, old man?" Oliver almost laughed. Jacob looked quite shocked at the notion. "You forget, I know the house. It is not large. You must be running short of bedrooms by now—unless you mean to stick poor little Miss Chang in with the servants. Not to worry, I shan't disturb Cecily." As if that were possible. "I can just camp out in this excellent chair." He laid a hand on his brother-in-law's arm and added quite gently, "As I am sure you have done yourself, countless times." There was a long pause. "She is my wife, Jacob."

Jacob's shoulders relaxed, and the anxiety retreated slightly from his eyes. "Well, if you are quite sure . . . Will you not say good night to Livia, at least?"

Oliver shook his head. "A mere good night would scarcely do her justice, and I am too weary to say more. Perhaps in the morning, she could find time to walk with me? We are family now; we must make a start at getting acquainted."

Jacob managed a smile—his first in a very long time, Oliver suspected. "I know she will be delighted." Mentally, Oliver rolled his eyes. Jacob actually believed what he had said. That Livia would be delighted. It was not Oliver's place to disabuse him. He smiled quite as if he believed it also. Jacob turned to go. "I'll have some pillows and such brought up straight away."

Oliver nodded and turned back to gaze at Cecily. Eventually he noticed someone bustling about behind him. A footstool had been added to the chair, and the two were heaped up with a profusion of bedding. Blackie had found his bag and was putting his things away in drawers. For the first time, he troubled to look about the room. Downstairs, the furniture had not been much changed from his parents' day, featuring their prized Jeanselme[5] grouping afloat on a sea of Persian carpeting. But the bedroom had been completely refurbished with an Eastlake[6] look. "Did Cecily use this room before . . . before?" he asked.

Blackie smiled. "She did, sir. From the moment she set foot in the house. Once she heard it was your old room, she wouldn't hear of sleeping anywhere else. She was a little concerned at making so many changes. I tried to reassure her that she was not expected to sleep in a little boy's room, but she fretted you would not know it when you came home." She paused, and then added all in a rush, "If I may take the liberty, sir, she was always sure you would come home. Never gave you up for an instant."

He nodded. "How like her. I trust you reassured her that I cared for nothing inside the room so much as for the window I generally used to depart from it." He chuckled softly. And then, as if the thought had only just come to him, he added, "I don't suppose my trunk came? I sent it on ahead, some months ago. There would have been a letter, too, of course."

Blackie looked stunned. "Good heavens, no! Some months? A letter? It must have miscarried; there's been nothing of the sort."

"I thought that might be the case. Everyone was so surprised to see me." He stretched and rose at last from Cecily's bed. "I shall have to run over to the shipping office tomorrow and see what's become of it."

"Oh, Master Oliver," Blackie whispered. "It's a poor homecoming you're getting, and that's a fact." She almost glared at the bedding heaped on the chair.

He chuckled and put an arm around her. "Dear Blackie, please, don't fret so. It's better by far than I saw in India, or even on the boat back, if truth be told. And it's by my Cecily's side. I shan't give up on her any more than she did me, you know." She sniffled and smiled and left.

So Blackie did not know his trunk was in the house. Interesting. A letter might perhaps be received and destroyed discreetly, but the arrival of a large trunk from abroad should have been virtually impossible to conceal from the servants. And yet the trunk had arrived; he could feel it humming nearby. If he allowed himself to listen carefully it would call to him, yearningly and by name. It had started calling to him before he set foot on England's soil.

But it had called and waited this long; it could call and wait another night. First he needed to commune with Cecily. He had materials sufficient for the task on hand. Or if he lacked for anything, he reflected with a smile, perhaps he could borrow it from Chang.

Blackie had not known what to make of his herb bag. She had deduced from the care with which it was wrapped that he valued it, but declined to determine its appropriate place. Instead she had laid it neatly across one end of the writing desk. His fingers brushed lightly across the many pockets, instinctively evaluating the state of his stocks, even as he sought out and claimed pinches of two herbs and a fungus that he knew only as Korach, Nefeg, and Zikhri. The names were affectionate;[7] he doubted the plants were recognized within Linnaean binomial nomenclature.

He crumbled the ingredients he had selected into a little painted china bowl that he found on Cecily's dressing table. When they were reduced to powder, he pulled a hip flask from his pocket and poured a little of the contents into the bowl. He lit the bedside candle from the gas and plunged the flame into the bowl. The mixture was quite flammable and blazed up high enough to leave a scorch mark on the ceiling. The stench was horrific.

He poured a few more drops from the flask into the smoking mess, and the odor subsided. At last he carried the little bowl to the bed and—pushing a finger between Cecily's lips to separate them—poured most of the concoction into her mouth.

She neither choked nor swallowed. Her lips remained slightly parted. A trickle of fluid ran out from the corner of her mouth and down her cheek, leaving several black specks in its wake. Oliver pressed her mouth closed again and gently wiped her face clean with his handkerchief. Then he tipped the remainder of the mixture from the bowl into his own mouth; there was very little left, and he licked the bowl clean so as to be sure he got it all.

His last act before removing his jacket and settling into the heap of bedding on the chair was to remove two fist-sized stones from his pocket. They were handsome stones, polished to a high sheen, and appeared identical to the casual glance. Roughly ovoid, but flattened, they were black, with swirls of color that appeared to emerge from inner depths. Grimacing, he rolled his mouth to summon saliva and spat on one of the stones, which he then laid on Cecily's chest.

He paused to upend the hip flask once more—this time into his own mouth—and sighed with pleasure. Glenfiddich.[8] The recipe required only that it be alcohol, but his personal taste was discriminating. Then he settled himself comfortably into the chair, laid the second stone on his own chest, and closed his eyes. He might have slept. He lay very still for hours.

Chapter Two

There was, of course, no time for a walk with Livia Aram Aldridge in the morning. The first caller was Dr. Verlaine, who arrived to find Oliver still lingering at breakfast. Chang's cook made splendid coffee, but Dr. Verlaine refused to share it. Instead he unrolled a great sheaf of papers documenting everything that had been done to or for Cecily. These he laid out around the table while earnestly describing their contents to Oliver.

Oliver was impressed. Clearly no medical avenue had been left unexplored. He even pretended to look at the papers Dr. Verlaine thrust toward him, although he knew there was nothing of interest in any of them. One way or another, they surely all led to the same inevitable conclusion. Cecily was beyond medical hope.

Yet clearly Dr. Verlaine still hoped. He had tried a wide variety of treatments, some of them more desperate than credible; neither animal magnetism nor mesmerism had produced any visible result. He had consulted any number of specialists in nervous disorders, including a Dr. Josef Breur[9] brought in all the way from Vienna. He had insisted on round-the-clock nursing so as to watch for the smallest signs. Indeed, the zeal Dr. Verlaine brought to the quest almost smacked of a guilty conscience.

"Do you know," remarked Oliver, pouring the last of the coffee into his own cup—the doctor, after all, had declined several times and showed no sign of needing a stimulant anyway—"Jacob seems to think there is some supernatural force at work."

Dr. Verlaine had been perusing one of his many papers, but at Oliver's words his head shot up, and his face assumed a stricken expression, much like that of a particularly small rabbit looking into the eyes of a particularly large fox. His mouth worked slightly as he stared into Oliver's eyes. "He does," he admitted at last. "I presume you are hoping he is mistaken."

A woman's voice interjected unexpectedly, "Perhaps you are the one who is hoping, Doctor." The two men rose to greet Frau Strasser, who was standing at the door. "I suspect that Colonel Beckford harbors no such illusions." She seated herself between them. Behind her, Mrs. Aldridge spoke softly to Rose before joining them.

"You will forgive us for intruding, I hope," Frau Strasser continued. "But I feared that Dr. Verlaine would consume your entire day with his efforts to convince you that Mrs. Beckford's condition might be natural." She paused to lay a friendly hand on Verlaine's arm. "He is a good man," she assured Oliver. "And a good doctor. He only involved himself with magic in the hope of effecting certain cures that defied traditional medicine. Now that he has discovered the astral realm carries its own dangers, he fears he may have compromised the well-being of his patients."

"Frau Strasser, is it really appropriate to trouble Colonel Beckford with such talk?" Mrs. Aldridge spoke hesitantly and approached the table slowly.

Dr. Verlaine nodded. "He can scarcely be expected to believe us, and is likely to conclude we are unfit to care for his wife."

Frau Strasser laughed out loud and looked up to Oliver with a smile. "You see how my poor friends are afraid even to speak their minds? But you, I think, are braver. And also . . ." She paused, and a shadow passed over her face. "I think you are an adept. I do not know why I did not see it last night."

It was Oliver's turn to laugh. "You did not see it last night, because I did not wish you to see it. I am quite impressed that you see it now."

"An adept?" Mrs. Aldridge's voice dropped to a croak. She sank weakly into a chair, freeing the men to reclaim their own seats. "You are an adept?"

Her manner was too marked to mistake. Frau Strasser reached out to take her hand. "My dear, why are you so troubled? This is a good thing. Think of the hours of explanation we are spared."

She scarcely seemed to hear Frau Strasser, but turned to look at Oliver with timid eyes. He met her gaze head-on, but did not see an enemy's determined glare, as he had expected. Instead, she offered him the look of a frightened, shamefaced child. She had used him ill, perhaps, but not because she was evil. She was simply silly and shallow—and now repentant. He nearly forgave her on the spot. Except . . .

If she possessed a pleasing, childlike manner, she had also an eldritch air.

Her charm might well prove less than natural. Inwardly he shrugged. It was too soon to tackle such complex questions. For now, it would have to be truce. He smiled at Livia Aldridge and diverted Frau Strasser. "Now that the good doctor has explained what measures have been take in the material world, perhaps you will tell me what is being done to assist Cecily on other planes?"

"Everything that is possible—you have my word." Mrs. Strasser leaned forward in her eagerness to confide in him. "First, permit me to reassure you that her spirit is not wandering the lower planes. We have searched. Nor has she been driven to move onwards."

Oliver shrugged. "Of course not. If her spirit had moved onwards, her body would die. And if she has not moved on, then her spirit remains below. So your search was insufficient. What means did you employ?"

Frau Strasser blinked and hesitated. "We have in our circle a very gifted medium, and we currently rely heavily on her talents. Scrying proved less successful than we had initially hoped."

"You surprise me," murmured Oliver. "I should have thought Dr. Chang's mirror more than equal to the task."

Frau Strasser opened her mouth to reply. Then she closed it again and said nothing. Mrs. Aldridge stared down at her hands, which were folded in her lap. Dr. Verlaine inquired, "What do you know of Chang's mirror?"

Oliver shrugged. "It is famous. Many circles know at least something of its powers; some more than others, of course. Doubtless much of what is said is just rumor, but my teacher claimed to know a great deal."

"Are you suggesting that Dr. Chang's efforts have not been sincere?" Frau Strasser shook her head. "This, I cannot believe. He is not a bad man."

"Papa would not deceive us," whispered Mrs. Aldridge.

"Perhaps he is not as skilled as we hoped?" Dr. Verlaine's voice contained a hint of bitterness. "I agree that he has probably not been deliberately deceiving us; he could have served that purpose better by concealing the mirror entirely. But his training . . . may not be adequate to the task."

Both the doctor and Frau Strasser turned to look at Mrs. Aldridge. She seemed disinclined to speak, but responded at last to the pressure of their eyes. "His mother oversaw his education personally. It was my understanding that she trained him to be a seer from his earliest childhood. And she was herself . . . a formidable power." She raised her hands in a gesture of helplessness. "One can scarcely say with certainty what another soul does or does not know. But Grandmama surely knew of the mirror long before he acquired it, and she ought to have known how it should be used."

"But would she have told him everything?" Frau Strasser's tone was peremptory. "Please forgive my speaking so frankly. But Mme. Chang was sometimes . . . high-handed. She did not like to share information."

"No," whispered Livia Aldridge. "She surely did not."

"Do you know how the mirror should be used?" asked Dr. Verlaine. "If we assume for now that Chang is not unwilling to assist but lacks the ability, could you guide or train him?"

"Could you do it yourself?" inquired Frau Strasser.

Before Oliver could answer, Mrs. Aldridge intervened. "Papa would never allow that. Never." Oliver nodded. That was surely true.

"I would be happy to talk with Dr. Chang at his earliest convenience," he assured them. "In the meanwhile, if I may ask, what—if anything—has been learned?"

"You point out, quite rightly, that she must be somewhere in the lower realms," replied Frau Strasser. "But, despite your doubts, I remain confident that she is not in any of the planes close by the material world. We did not rely solely on Dr. Chang's mirror. I have, myself, some poor clairvoyant powers, and I am sensitive to the cries of those unhappy spirits that have lost their way. Rhoda, also, has spoken to many of the spirits that have not yet progressed upwards, and she agrees that Mrs. Beckford is not among them."

"And who is Rhoda?"

There was a very long pause, and again all eyes turned to Livia Aldridge. She sighed. "Rhoda is my friend."

"Your friend?"

Mrs. Strasser intervened. "She means her spirit guide."

"No!" Mrs. Aldridge spoke with more force than Oliver had thought she could muster. "She is my friend." She looked about and sighed and lowered her voice again. "She used to be Mr. Aldridge's fiancée. Before she died. She is concerned for him now."

Oliver stared at her aghast. He could scarcely have imagined a more unhealthy union. Before he could compose a reply, Dr. Verlaine commented, "We thought at first she might be a natural somnambulist."

"Cecily?" Oliver found that he did not care for that idea either.

"Yes, of course, Mrs. Beckford. Vital magnetism has frequently been observed to produce a cataleptic state. And positing such a diagnosis permitted us to assume—at least tentatively—that she was lucid. We could, therefore, concentrate our search efforts on attracting her attention."

Oliver nodded, but Dr. Verlaine seemed to desire some further answer. He therefore repeated back, "You narrowed your field of search and constructed a beacon."

The doctor smiled. "Precisely." His smile failed. "It sounded promising, in theory, but results were not forthcoming. We devised any number of experiments—you will forgive the term, Colonel, but we are on such new ground that I cannot pretend to conviction. Whatever you choose to call our efforts, no communication with Mrs. Beckford was achieved. In the end, we were forced to abandon the assumption that she was capable of responding." He thrust a paper toward Oliver, as if hoping that its contents could somehow absolve him.

Oliver did not take the paper, but he spoke gently. "So you are back to sifting through all the sands by the sea?"

The doctor almost smiled again. "Precisely," he repeated.

Rose emerged from the kitchen with a great tray that she set down on the sideboard. Approaching the doctor, she genuflected deeply at his side. He gazed at her in some startlement. Behind them, two more servants brought out more trays. The doctor blinked at the obvious preparations for a meal, put down the paper he was still waving at Oliver, and scooped the mass of documentation into an untidy pile.

Rose smiled and held up a restraining hand, then assumed responsibility for picking up his papers and brushing the table. The other servants arranged cutlery and linen napkins on the buffet. When the sumptuous cold luncheon was in place, Rose curtsied to the assembled company and backed out of the room with a bowed head. Oliver watched with interest. Rose was Chang's, too, he surmised, and a quality acquisition. Oliver wondered whether she had been hired or purchased.

"Do you have any suggestions how we might further proceed?" Oliver turned back to Frau Strasser. She had taken no offense at his brusqueness, and she looked at him now with all the concern due to a distraught husband. He smiled. "Perhaps later you and Mrs. Aldridge could arrange for me to speak with Rhoda?"

Chapter Three

"**P**lease, Colonel." Livia Aldridge grasped his arm as he passed and glanced furtively down the hallway before continuing. "This séance you wish to hold . . ."

He had half expected this. "I gather you do not like the idea."

"I . . . I do not know. I suppose it sounds reasonable enough. But : . ." She looked down the hallway again. "It is Rhoda who does not care for the idea. She is quite opposed. And I cannot force her; I have not the . . . ability."

"You do not control her?" The more he heard of her peculiar spirit guide, the more concerned he grew.

"Indeed not—how could I?" She giggled nervously. "Mr. Aldridge always says she could scarcely be managed when she was alive, and now, of course, she suffers no constraint of any kind."

"But Mrs. Strasser tells me that you summon her for séances, and surely she could not be deceived in such a matter."

"No. Or rather, yes. Oh, dear." Mrs. Aldridge sighed, and her face fell into a plaintive pout. "Certainly Rhoda comes to the séances. But not because I summon her. She enjoys them hugely and is commonly on hand well before the séance actually begins. Sometimes I can hardly get a bite of dinner, she is so eager to speak through my mouth."

"She comes without being summoned, of her own accord?" It was quite the most dreadful revelation yet, and far too important to be whispered over in a hallway where doubtless the servants could overhear. He took her arm and drew her into the small parlor. It was on the east side of the house, and was always a little cold, but with the weather still so fine no one had troubled to light a fire in a room so little used. "You will forgive my impertinence, I hope, but you must confide in me. How often does this spirit come to you?"

She grasped the arms of the chair in which he had settled her and looked about from side to side, like an animal trapped in a cage. He took a deep breath and willed her to put down her fear and trust him. "Please, Mrs. Aldridge. I am knowledgeable about such matters—more so, I suspect, than any of the dabblers that currently surround you. And it is critical that you understand the danger of tolerating a spirit that can enter you without your consent."

"But what choice do I have?" she blurted out. "Shall I decide not to tolerate the noise of traffic on the street? Does a thunderstorm require my consent? And Rhoda is my friend. Mrs. Strasser said so."

"Do you need Mrs. Strasser to tell you who your friends are?"

"Would you prefer I asked you?" A spot of color rose to her cheek. She glanced toward the door. But she did not rise. Rather she pressed herself farther back into her chair.

He whispered, so softly that she could not hear. "See me. I will not lie to you or injure you without cause." He would have liked to say he was her friend and would never hurt her. But he did not know yet if that were true, and he could not lie while calling on Vision. "See me. I seek to resolve your peril."

The tension in her shoulders eased, and her breathing grew more natural. He smiled, the soft, easy smile he used when handling snakes. "Please tell me how it is between you and Rhoda," he said aloud.

She decided at last to trust him; he saw the resolution in her eyes. "It is no fault of Rhoda's," she informed him earnestly. "Clearly you think she is predatory, but she is not. I want to be very plain about this. She was the demon's first victim. And even so, she did not choose to come to me. The circle summoned her. And once I had learned of her dreadful suffering, how could I send her back?"

"The circle summoned her?" A summoning explained much. "How was that done?"

She hesitated. "I confess, I am ignorant of the details. My guardian's mother made the arrangements. There was a tablet of horn-of-truth. And Mrs. Beckford gave a drop of blood."

"Cecily gave blood?" He could not repress a shudder. Blood on horn-of-truth—a very powerful summoning. No wonder this Rhoda manifested herself so freely and easily. She was not truly possessing Mrs. Aldridge, then; rather she was trapped within her. He doubted if Chang and his mother had been prepared for such an outcome.

"Twice." He looked up in confusion. She nodded solemnly and continued, "Once for the summoning and again, after. Because she was so concerned for her brother. I understand they were very close. I was not yet acquainted with him then; he was just an unfortunate gentleman my guardian hoped to assist. The demon was trying to move into the material plane through him. It had almost consumed poor Rhoda's spirit and needed fresh food. The summoning was intended to break the link between Mr. Aldridge and the demon."

It was not the rite he would have chosen. "Was the separation accomplished?"

She nibbled on her lip and looked away. "We thought so. Rhoda was released, and I am told that Mr. Aldridge went home much improved. So Papa made the doll, and we supposed it was done."

"The doll?"

She smiled. "To distract the demon when it tried to find him again. That was why the second drop of blood was required." She paused, and reached out to touch his hand. "I am sorry for your trouble. I wish I had known her better. She was very brave."

His vision grew red and black. He tried to keep his voice level, but it emerged more as a hiss than a whisper. "You robbed a demon of both its food and its intended prey, and then you tossed my wife's blood into its hungry maw to distract it?"

She shrank back into the chair. "I . . . I did not . . . It was not meant so, I am sure. She said she wanted to help him escape." She glanced again toward the door, but she would have had to push past him to reach it. "We thought it was the proper thing to do, at the time." She waited a long time for his answer. "Mr. Aldridge has said more than once that it was not."

Of course. Oliver could not begin to guess why the Chang family had gone to such lengths to assist Jacob, but Jacob could not knowingly have agreed to such an evil bargain. He and Cecily had been inseparable. Oliver struggled to resume a civil manner. "Not the right thing to do, no. But as errors of judgment go, it has one advantage." He waited for her inquiring look. "It means your friend Rhoda knows exactly where Cecily is." He smiled at her almost tenderly. "She will tell me where my wife is, Mrs. Aldridge. With or without the séance. Please give her my assurances on that."

He strode out, leaving her gasping in the chair, and forgot her as soon as she was out of his sight. He would not usually have permitted her to see his anger, but he had spent much of the interview shielding himself against a dark, hammering insistence that someone was trying to open his trunk. Freed from her unhappy eyes, he stalked through the house in search of his property.

It was not, as he had first presumed, hidden away in the basement. Rather, it stood in plain sight at the back of Dr. Chang's study. At least it was almost in plain sight. It was tucked behind the desk where Chang sat poring over a book. A handsome embroidered shawl had been flung over it, but more by way of décor than concealment. No serious attempt had been made to remove it from normal view. Nonetheless it was almost impossible to look at. Some instinct warned the eye away.

Oliver's gaze did not drift. He strode past Chang to kneel by the trunk and examine the lock, which was sealed over with a clump of wax. Dr. Chang leapt up from his desk with a curt question on his lips. Oliver did not listen to his question. He picked off a lump of the wax and smelled it. "Hawthorne and frankincense. Drippings from a *Hic nihil videbitur*[10] candle, I expect. A bit crude, but sufficient to keep the servants away."

Dr. Chang hesitated and swallowed his remaining questions. "Exactly. As you must surely know, the thing attracts attention and it is dangerous. One of the charwomen actually tried to polish the brass." Oliver almost smiled. It was a surprisingly smooth lie, considering the damning circumstances. It helped that Dr. Chang's delivery was good—haughty and annoyed—and he did not decline to meet Oliver's eye.

Oliver rose, and pulled around the book Dr. Chang had been studying so that he could see its contents. The book was old and handwritten, and Dr. Chang hissed slightly at Oliver's ungentle usage. Oliver chuckled softly, a low rumbling that sounded rather like a growl. "Another crude spell," he remarked. "And this time, not sufficient." He smiled broadly. "You are falling quite short of your reputation, Xiu Yao. If you want to get into my trunk so badly, why not inquire of your mirror how it should be done?"

Chang paled, and Oliver smiled again. "Nor did you did use the mirror to search for my Cecily. Why is that?" Chang stood very still and did not answer. Oliver sighed and murmured, "Is it really necessary to threaten you,

Doctor? Do you doubt the lengths to which I might go to save Cecily? The lengths to which I have already gone just to return to her? You could ask your mirror about that too, if you liked. Shall I get it for you?"

There was no need to search; the mirror cried out almost as loudly as had the contents of his trunk. Oliver turned toward the great Chinese apothecary's chest along the wall. The mirror resided in the lowest drawer, the long, flat one intended for documents. "No," hissed Chang, grabbing Oliver's arm. "You will not touch it. It is occupied."

He was neither swift enough nor strong enough to prevent Oliver from opening the drawer. But Oliver did no more than open the drawer. Whether he refrained out of deference to Chang's wishes or out of simple amazement, he did not touch the mirror. It was large and ancient, composed of a fan-shaped sheet of bronze polished to an extraordinary sheen. It lay face-up and unprotected—which was strange, considering its value—and displayed a crystalline reflective surface unmarred by dust or time. Impossibly, within that dark, sheltered frame there was still an image, a reflection from nowhere.

It was the image of Livia Aldridge, as bright and vivid as if the drawer were a couch on which the woman herself was laid out. Dr. Chang flung himself forward, spreading his arms protectively across the open drawer. When Oliver made no move to prevent it, Dr. Chang turned to face him, still holding out his hands to each side to ensure that Oliver kept his distance.

Oliver stared back at him and drew a deep breath. "I owe you an apology, Doctor," he confessed. "I greatly underestimated you. You have skill." His voice broke off, and he shook his head, glancing back down into the mirror. He resumed in tones of genuine bewilderment, "But why have you trapped your ward's spirit in the glass? And how can she walk about and conduct her affairs when her life is locked up here in a dark drawer?"

Chang met his eye defiantly for a moment but seemed to grow suddenly weary. He stepped aside and gestured to the girl in the glass. "That is not my ward."

"But . . ."

"It is not Livia, I tell you." He sighed and sank back into the chair behind his desk. "It is Rhoda Carothers."

"Carothers?" For an instant the unfamiliar name gave him pause, but it occurred to him that he had certainly heard the name of Rhoda. "This is Jacob's late fiancée?"

Gently, he pulled the drawer a little farther out of the cabinet and gazed down thoughtfully. The lady's eyes were closed, so their color could not be verified, but the chestnut of her hair and the peach tone of her skin were indistinguishable from those of Livia Aldridge. And yet the hair—however similar in color to that of the living woman—was arranged rather differently. Further, Mrs. Aldridge had, only moments ago, worn a modish gown of blue and purple jacquard, yet the image in the glass was clad in a simple gray muslin frock.

"It is often said that there is no such thing as coincidence," remarked Dr. Chang. "Yet I still find it strange that the doppelganger of one such as my poor Livia should be drawn into an engagement with one such as Jacob Aldridge. You know about him, I suppose?"

"That his father was a sorcerer, you mean?" Oliver sighed, and closed the drawer. There was a chair in front of Chang's desk, but Oliver did not want the desk between them. He sat down on his sturdy trunk instead. It set his head higher than Chang's. "What of it?"

Dr. Chang pursed his lips. "Miss Carothers was the demon's first victim."

"So I have heard."

Chang nodded. "But she was not the intended prey. She was only a means of passage to the object of an ancient curse." He sighed. "But we did not know who the true target was: the heir of Ishmael Aram or the heir of Jeremy Aldridge."

"You cared nothing for Jacob's danger, then. Or Cecily's when the time came. You desired only to protect your ward."

Dr. Chang met his eye coldly. "If you had been here to assist, how much would you have cared for Livia's danger?"

Oliver almost smiled. "Not at all. And doubtless, you and I would still have ended up here, discussing the injuries done to our loved ones and what recompense might be required." Dr. Chang's look remained cool, but he stiffened slightly. "Make no mistake, Xiu Yao. You are still living because you and your mirror may yet be of use in restoring my Cecily. More use, I might add, than you seem to have been in protecting your Livia."

A very cruel smile flickered across Chang's lips. "Do you think so? My mistake. I thought it was your wife who was feeding the demon, and my little girl who—"

"Who feeds the ghost? And cowers from every shadow while waiting to be driven out of her own person by a desperate spirit looking for a home? And wonders if either her husband or her guardian will even notice when she is destroyed at last?" Oliver could smile as cruelly as Chang when he chose. Then, having smiled, he put his anger down. "Perhaps, if we can bring ourselves to tolerate each other for a while, we can yet contrive to rescue both women. Tell me what went wrong."

Chang eyed him thoughtfully, visibly considering whether or not to trust him. At last he shrugged. "I do not know. The plan was to summon Miss Carothers into the mirror. The demon, we thought, would pursue her there." A shadow crossed his face. "We bore no ill will to either Aldridge or Mrs. Beckford. They were bait, I admit, but we supposed they would be safe enough once the demon was trapped."

"But Mrs. Aldridge, or rather Miss Aram as she was then, participated in the summoning. So you must have realized—expected even—that Miss Carothers would be drawn, first and foremost, into the vessel that she perceived as her own living self?"

"Of course." Chang made an irritated gesture. "But we had poured Livia's blood onto the mirror before the séance started. So that Miss Carothers would necessarily pass into the mirror when reaching out for Livia. And we took pains to be sure the demon was half asleep at the time. It should have followed her docilely." He sighed, propped his elbows on the desk, and dropped his face into his hands. "Or so we thought," he whispered.

"By we, you mean Mme. Chang and yourself?" reflected Oliver. "No one else in the circle knew?"

"Do you think that may have distorted the results? We thought of dispensing with the circle entirely, but we particularly desired Frau Strasser's assistance. She is a powerful clairvoyant. Of course, she would never have cooperated with our true plan; she supposed it was our intention to rescue Miss Carothers."

Oliver found he was not immune to a pang of remorse for Miss

Carothers's plight. He set it aside. "The plan did work in part. Miss Carothers is, indeed, lodged in the mirror. Yet somehow she is not confined there." He looked at Chang. "Shall I conclude that is why you made the doll? Quickly, I expect. Before the sleepy demon followed after Miss Carothers and gained access to Miss Aram. I presume you also locked the mirror gate."

Chang shot him a bitter look. "The entire point was to keep the demon away from my ward. Not to open an astral gate to her soul." He sighed. "Mrs. Beckford volunteered, you know. She feared for Jacob."

"Of course. She would have embraced any risk to protect Jacob. Unfortunately it was not really her brother she was protecting, was it?" Oliver smiled and rose. "Not to worry, Doctor. If we save her, then all may be forgiven." His smile grew very broad indeed, as he reflected on the ease of mendacity when not calling on Vision.

Chapter Four

His eyes came suddenly open. He was lying in a grassy field, and could not think how he came to be in such a place. It must be a dream, he decided, but looking about he could not begin to guess why he should dream of such a place, whatever place it was. It was just a field. The grass was lush. There was a town nearby and a river, but he felt no particular impulse to approach either.

A woman appeared in the distance and approached him with that peculiar gait of dreams whereby she moved quite slowly but arrived almost instantaneously by his side. He offered her his arm. "Mrs. Aldridge."

She took the arm and they started walking toward the town. As they walked she giggled, and he suddenly took in the arrangement of her hair, the plainness of her gown. "Mrs. Aldridge, you call me—and so I am. At least so much as I am anyone. The other Mrs. Aldridge said you wished to speak with me."

"Do I deduce that this is your dream rather than mine?" She nodded. This field was of her choosing, then. "Where are we?"

"Sharpsburg."[11] She smiled a trifle bitterly at his uncomprehending look. "Sharpsburg, Maryland. There's no reason why an Englishman should know the name, but no Confederate can forget it. There was a great battle fought here—see that bridge there over Antietam Creek?" She pointed. "General Burnside took it and killed my poor father in the process. A pointless battle and a pointless death. I used to come here sometimes looking for his shade, or perhaps only for some answer to his end. I never found either. But one day I found Jacob here instead. He too was looking for a ghost, apparently under orders from your Queen, all so secret and mysterious—he never did confess what he was about that day. No matter—we went away together and never came back again."

"Until now." They were no closer to the town than when they had started walking, he observed. He sensed that all the walking in the world would not take them away from this field where she had met Jacob.

She shook her head. "We are not really here now, are we?"

"Then where are we?" He stopped walking and turned to face her. "Or rather, where are you? I am probably asleep in the chair beside Cecily, but do you know where you are?"

She paused in thought and shook her head. "I confess not. Here, more often than not, wherever here may truly be. Or sometimes in my Auntie Clare's house, where I grew up. Or other times in a misty place full of crying voices. Frequently I find myself standing just behind Livia, looking over her shoulder. I like that best; occasionally I almost forget that Livia is there and I think I am alive. She says I am in her head. And Frau Strasser says I am on the astral plane, but she seems quite confounded as to where exactly in the astral plane I might be. Perhaps she does not really know. Perhaps no one does."

"Have you inquired of Dr. Chang?" He took pains to pose the question casually.

"Livia's papa? I talk very little with him. I think he does not care for me. Too busy attending to his mother . . ." Rhoda shuddered gracefully, and shook her curls. "Now, she's a proper dragon. She is fierce as fire and wants me dead." There was a tiny pause and a tinier smile. "Except I gather I am already dead."

"You sound less than certain." Oliver was growing weary of standing in a field to no purpose. He decided that the dream must also be partially his, and imagined a couple of wicker chairs. They appeared, much to his companion's delighted astonishment. "Do you doubt your death? Do you remember how you got to . . . wherever this is? Or where you were before you came here?"

She did not answer, being entirely occupied at playing with the chair. The first time she sat down he followed suit, but when she jumped back up to her feet he had necessarily to follow. He waited, therefore, while she sat and stood, and sat and stood repeatedly, testing the apparent firmness of the chair. "What a splendid idea!" she chuckled. "A chair! It is so monotonous, walking about in circles, even if one never grows tired. Did you just wish it into place?" She gazed into his amused smile, and a puzzled, wary look came into her eyes. "Could I have done as much?"

He could not help but laugh. "Try it and see." She shut her eyes and screwed up her face, as if wishing took a considerable effort. "Clearly this is not the realm of matter," he pointed out while she worked on wishing. "Rather it is someplace very like a dream—save that your faculties are intact. And, as in a dream, matter—or what passes for matter—is . . . subject to suggestion. You need not work so very hard at it." (Her frown had grown pronounced.) "Merely imagine or remember, and when the image comes into your mind it shall come also to this place."

She opened her eyes and studied him a moment, then looked away at the bare grass. Before her eyes, a table appeared—wicker, like his chairs, and bearing a picnic basket. She laughed and clapped her hands before running to open the basket; it proved to contain loaves of fresh bread, and pots of butter and jam. She glanced back to him with mischief in her eye. "If matter is not matter, can we then eat here?"

He carried the chairs over to the table, and she seated herself at last with enough conviction that he dared to sit also. "Who could possibly prevent you? Some say the food here is tasteless, but I think it is a matter of individual imagination and will." He tried a bit of the bread, and found it warm and flavorful, quite as if it were freshly baked in the physical world. Miss Carothers ate with a fervor that bordered on the ill-mannered; it was plainly the first food she had tasted in years. Not that she needed food here, but she certainly seemed to have missed it.

She ate until, in the course of her feasting, a clump of butter and jam fell to her breast, creating a greasy spot on her gown. She stared, as aghast as if either the dress or the butter were real, before remembering the lesson he had just taught her. Then she closed her eyes. In a twinkling, her dress changed from her soiled gray muslin to the blue and purple jacquard that Mrs. Aldridge had worn previously. "Livia does have nice things," she remarked, and smiled. "And now, I do also. I thank you for the instruction, Colonel Sorcerer." The table, with all its crumbs and dirty dishes, disappeared. "I think I am inclined to like you."

"I am very glad to hear it. I would like to be your friend."

"Would you? You surprise me, sir. Livia was quite terrified of you; she is sure you are bent on destroying us both. But, then"—she smiled scornfully—"Livia is terrified of very nearly everything."

"She is not terrified of you," he observed. "Although some would say she should be. She says you are her friend."

She had the grace to look embarrassed. "We are not enemies." She sighed. "But we were better friends before she married my fiancé."

"To be fair," he pointed out. "You were already dead at the time."

"Indeed," she agreed. "And to be all the more scrupulously fair, by marrying him she did me the enormous kindness of letting me be married to him after all, when all hope of that happiness was gone." She giggled suddenly. "Jacob was well named, was he not? Married to two sisters. And like the other Jacob's wives, we quarrel over him at times. He prefers me, and she knows it, for all he takes great pains to seem blind to the distinction."

"And of course," he murmured softly, "you must both share him with Cecily."

She looked away. "It is hard to grudge her his concern. She has fallen into so awful a state. She was my friend, you know. We planned the wedding together, although it pained her terribly."

"How so?"

She met his eyes directly. "She missed you most dreadfully, while you were off in India. And every ribbon that she chose for me reminded her how long it had been since she chose her own, and how alone she would be when Jacob was preoccupied with his own family."

He did not flinch. "I had to go."

She shrugged. "It seems there are so many things men have to do. If Jacob did not have to go to the Ministry, he might have time enough to manage his little harem better." That was twice she had made mention of Jacob's government service. Oliver did not recall his brother-in-law being associated with any Ministry. Perhaps he had been gone too long. Or perhaps, he realized suddenly, she was trying—and trying with considerable success—to distract him.

"Miss Carothers," he addressed her sternly.

"I am demoted?" she inquired with great earnestness. "I cannot tell you how much I valued the previous title."

"You should not," he replied. "For Mrs. Aldridge is the title of a woman who feeds on Beckford property, having profited greatly from the destruction of its rightful mistress. Miss Carothers, on the other hand, was an honorable woman and a good friend to Mrs. Beckford. Or so I have been told."

She tried to meet his eyes, and failed, and tried again. Again she turned away, this time dashing a tear from her own eye. "Livia tells me that you suppose I know how to find her." She turned her face up to him again, and her imploring look did not falter. "I swear to you, Colonel. I know nothing of the kind."

He found it almost impossible not to believe her. He called on Vision, and found he still believed her. "And yet she resides now in the trap you once fled. Surely you must remember something of that place."

"That place," she murmured, and a great shudder passed through her, leaving her limp and trembling so that she nearly tumbled from her chair. He rose and crossed to her, grasping her shoulders and holding her steady. "I do not remember it," she whispered. "And yet I grow queasy and faint at the mere thought of trying to remember it."

"I could help you."

"Help me to remember, or help me to forget?" Her gaze was anguished.

"Both, perhaps." He dropped awkwardly to one knee in a gesture of entreaty. "Miss Carothers, you are Cecily's only hope. I know it is a dreadful thing I ask of you, requiring more courage than I could ask of any living woman. But you are not a living woman, and her despair is the price you paid for your own escape. Take me there again, and I will bring you both back safely or die in the attempt."

She uttered an awful sound, somewhere between a hiss and a scream, and leapt up so quickly that the chair toppled over backward behind her. "You are a lunatic! Get away from me! You have been smoking opium in India!"

He rose to his feet and she turned tail and ran, although he made no move to pursue her. There was no need. It was the nature of the place that no amount of flight could penetrate that boundary where the far distance curved back into the near. When she had run as far away from him as she could get he called after her—quite foolishly, but he could think of nothing else— "Miss Carothers, please! We shipped all the opium off to China."

She faltered and glanced behind. Plainly she saw that he was not—and never would be—any farther away than her first few steps had taken her. Still she pulled back as if pressing against an invisible barrier. "Spare me your pose of sanity and decency—there's always something falls off the cart on the way to market. Livia was right! You will destroy us both, and doubtless any other soul you touch!"

"Miss Carothers," he began.

"Stay back," she snarled, quite ferociously. Rather to his surprise, he found himself paralyzed by her determination to keep him at a distance. His feet seemed rooted to the earth. This little dream world was her place, and she commanded it.

He held his hands up before him in a gesture of pax. "Please, Miss Carothers. I am not here to harm you or compel you to do anything. I very much doubt that I could in this place, which belongs to you." He jerked futilely at one foot to show her the truth of his words. She relaxed just a trifle. "See, I cannot even approach you without your express invitation." He turned his back (which was not really needful but doubtless reassured her) and summoned up another chair into which he dropped. In a happy afterthought, he changed his overcrisp and extensively decorated uniform for a comfortable smoking jacket and even created a sweet-smelling Cuban cigar to accompany it.

She stood where she was. He watched her take in the less intimidating image and pass judgment on the distance between them. At last she, too, dropped into a chair—a mightily tufted wingback. Her face was still rigid with anxiety, and she crossed her arms before her in the posture of an angry matriarch. But she sat.

"First, I must assure you that you are quite right," he said. "I am utterly mad. Been so for years."

"You say so," she observed. "But you do not mean me to think so. You suppose a soft answer and a polite manner will distract me from your horrendous intent." She was entirely right, of course, which did not necessarily indicate the strategy would fail.

"What you believe is entirely your own affair. But surely you know that in this place I cannot lie to you." She made a scornful face. "Look around you, Miss Carothers. This is your place. Here you can perceive whatever you choose to perceive. You can smell truth or lies, if that is your pleasure—you have only to try. Like the chair."

Her face displayed the deepest distrust, but she drew in a deep breath and regarded him thoughtfully. Eventually she conceded, "Yes, I think I would know if you lied to me, although I cannot say how."

"I was grateful when they sent me to India," he told her. "I was growing very bored with diplomatic posts in Europe. They had meant those as a kindness, of course; I was newly married, and they supposed I had seen action enough in Afghanistan. But after the Congress of Berlin,[12] I doubt I could have stomached any more policy. And Cecily was so relieved that I was not being sent into action with the Zulus; the expedition into the Kush was strictly exploratory."

He shrugged and smiled. "I should have been better off on a battlefield, where it is only a matter of ducking bullets. Within six months we had slid into a crevasse, killing half our party and losing most of our supplies. Our survivors—those who could walk, at any rate—split up, with half remaining in a poor camp to care for the wounded while the others set out in search of aid and sustenance. I doubt if a soul still lives from either party, except myself."

He had never told the whole story before; he had seen no need to inform his military superiors that he had been driven insane. Now he found the memories still strangely raw. He rose from the chair and paced nervously about it. "I was taken in—I cannot say rescued—by a local shaman who was in need of an able-bodied slave, and happy to tend my wounds in order to acquire one."

"Am I supposed to weep, now?" she inquired. "I was raised by slaves. Or rather by those who had been slaves, and whose lot was not changed in the slightest by freedom. Dreadfully ironic, of course. My father was a fervent abolitionist, I am told, and would not set foot in a house where slavery was practiced. He quarreled with his whole family. But, nevertheless, he died for Virginia, and I was left to be raised by a pair of darling maiden aunts who most certainly did practice slavery, having three house servants and four more girls in their dressmaking shop. All of whom begged to stay on immediately upon being emancipated."

"I did not beg to stay on," he said. "But your aunts' girls were probably skilled workers, and so valued and well cared for."

"And you were not?"

"I became skilled, over time. My master served a horrible black goddess—far older and crueler than Kali—and made some strange demands, so that I called on strengths I never dreamed it was even possible to possess. He was utterly amazed that I did not die after the first few inflictions. And every time I did not die, I became more completely a vessel of luck and power. The time came when he feared me too much to attempt killing me outright."

He had gained her entire attention, at any rate. "Perhaps he should have," she remarked, "if you are, as you say, insane."

"Perhaps he should have for his own protection," he corrected her. "I was still sane enough to resent my treatment at his hands. And, do you know, the worst of what he did to me—far more dreadful than the blasphemous tattoos and the torture or the removing of internal parts and the substitution of other, stranger parts or all the blood and black spells or the wanton, unholy license—the very worst was that he kept me from my Cecily."

Her eyes widened. She drew in a very deep breath and rose to her feet. "And now you perceive me as also keeping you away from Cecily. Do you mean to kill me, out there in the real world?"

"That would be simplest. If I toss you and Mrs. Aldridge to the demon, I could take back my Cecily while it feeds. I would need a great deal of blood to lure it out into the open; the wound would probably kill you even if the demon did not. Perhaps that would be a kindness." She shuddered and dropped back into her chair and clung, gasping, to its arm. "I think you do remember," he murmured. "Your chances of survival would be better if you showed me the way. Far less blood would be needed, and I would be there by your side when the demon came for you."

"And you would bring me back safely or die in the attempt? And what becomes of me *after* you die in the attempt? I've a better plan. Livia and I tell Jacob what you are about and he kills you."

He opened his mouth to protest the sheer absurdity of the suggestion. Pretty, polite Jacob. And then he closed his mouth again. The very air glowed with her conviction. She did not merely think that Jacob would kill to protect her. She knew it, and never mind his polished manners. Oliver had not seen Jacob for a very long time; perhaps the boy had grown. "He might try, I suppose. I very much doubt he would succeed."

"So you would kill him too? Cecily will scarcely thank you for her rescue after that." She had him there. Cecily would never forgive him. But she would be alive and free of the demon. She would hate him, but she would be alive. Miss Carothers smiled slightly, sensing her advantage. "Besides, I think you underestimate him. Jacob is clever and secretive; I am sure you were never permitted to know his 'evil friend.' He is quite dangerous when he lets the mask fall."

"Then perhaps you should not betray his little secret." The retort was mechanical. In fact, he was quite taken aback. Cecily had always said there was more to Jacob than he let on, but Oliver had not paid her much mind. Jacob was her brother; she was expected to think highly of him. "And if Jacob does manage to dispose of me, what becomes of you then?"

She stared at him, clearly bewildered as to his meaning. "I suppose we go on as we are now." But doubt had crept into her voice.

"At least until Cecily dies." Strange how easy it was to say aloud the unthinkable. "And then Jacob will turn his attention, his dangerous attention as you tell me, to tracking down the parties responsible for her death. He has not had time or strength to do so up until now, but when he is released from the responsibility of caring for her, the thought of revenge will perhaps occur to him. And as you also say, he is quite clever. Who can guess where it might lead from there?"

She stared and stared. In the material plane, she would have called him a liar, or at least thought it even if she hesitated to say it to his face. But here in her private world, she could not escape the knowledge of his honesty. "How could there be revenge? Surely there is no one responsible, save the demon itself."

"No?" He rose and paused to imagine that he felt in his pocket the weight of two black communion stones. When he was sure he had them, he pulled them forth. He spat on one, and handed her the other. She took it gingerly, as if she feared it might have spittle on it also. "Let me show you who is responsible."

She turned the stone over several times. "This . . . thing smells like Cecily."

"Because I used it last to ask her what had happened to her. It still holds many of her memories. They will fade when I replace them with my own."

"Wait." She listened to the stone, which still told how Cecily and Jacob had fled London to Paris, Madrid, Naples, and finally Venice in their desperate attempt to escape the demon. The end of the sad tale faded into a few blurred images and a red mist when the demon caught up with them at last. "It came to her first wearing your face," she whispered.

"And it came to Jacob first wearing your face," he replied. "That's how these creatures are. They feed on loss and grief and fear. It got little fear from my Cecily, I suspect, or from your Jacob either, for that matter. But they both knew loss and grief."

She looked up at him, and he had never before seen such rage in a woman's eyes. "It used my face to injure Jacob?"

"There are other guilty parties closer to hand," he told her. "Let me remember for you what Dr. Chang told me." He lowered himself—with some discomfort—to his knees, to sit as the Japanese do, with his cupped hands holding the stone before him. He breathed, cleared his mind, and breathed again. It was easy to meditate in a dream place; there was no material world to discard. When he had made his mind empty, he reviewed his interview with Chang. Such consciousness as he retained was directed solely toward excluding interpretation or emotional bias. He did not attempt to delete his own anger or his threats; he left intact Dr. Chang's devotion to his ward and his heartfelt wish to protect her.

When he was sure that he had made the memory perfect and accurate in every detail, he opened his eyes. Miss Carothers had dropped down in the grass just in front of him. His cupped hands now held not merely a black stone, but a glowing sphere of light, perhaps six inches across. This he lifted up to offer her. She reached toward him, still holding the stone he had given her, and their fingertips touched. The glowing sphere expanded so that it no longer rested upon his hands but engulfed them, and hers as well. Then it subsided back to its former dimensions, but with the center slightly shifted, so that it rested in her hands rather than in his.

She lowered her hands to her lap and stared down into the globe, which cast a soft radiance up into her face. Gradually its brilliance diminished and shrank until she held only a small black rock. But her eyes were filled with tears. "Poor Livia," she whispered. She looked back up but could not meet his eye and looked away again. "Colonel, I swear to you that she knew none of this. She is a weak and silly woman—as I know better than anyone—but she would never have agreed to this. And she loves Jacob, as much as she is capable."

"I suspected as much. Do you think she should be told?"

"It will break her heart. She loves her papa, too." She sighed and rose to her feet. There appeared quite suddenly in her hand a small beaded purse in which she placed the stone and which she slid into an invisible pocket somewhere in her skirt. "If you will let me keep this awhile, I will think on how and when—or if—to tell her. Let us try first to win her aid without inflicting such a cruel blow."

"You speak of us?" It was very strange, how even in a dream world, his knees still creaked and complained as he clambered to his feet. His heart, however, leapt.

"Of course." She regarded him levelly. "This Chang tried to lock me in with the demon forever. And failing that, he sent it chasing after my Jacob and Cecily. It could just as well have taken him as her. And when the thing took Cecily instead, it broke my darling boy's heart. Livia and I have wept long hours in each other's arms to see how he blames and hates himself because of Chang's lies."

The words came tumbling out faster than she could properly speak them. She stopped and drew a new breath. "And what is Chang's punishment? He lives in Cecily's house—or rather yours, Colonel—and spends Cecily's money, while he waits for Cecily to die so he can see if the demon then moves on to Jacob." She drew in her breath and smiled, a dreadful, wonderful smile full of cool hatred and black resolution. "He must pay, Colonel. He simply has to pay. And if that means I must face demons and die, well, as you say, I am already dead. Perhaps it is time I move onward from this nasty mirror."

She turned and walked away, waving a hand at him in a gesture that was somewhere between dismissal and farewell. Her form seemed to dissipate into a mist from which her voice emerged, "Please go now, Colonel. I need to talk with Livia."

Chapter Five

"**N**o." Jacob crossed his arms over his chest. He did not raise his voice, nor did he sound angry. He sounded, if anything, a little tired. "No," he repeated. "It is out of the question."

Oliver regarded his brother-in-law uneasily. He looked for all the world exactly like Cecily when she had put her foot down. Cecily, of course, had never done anything so graceless or unfeminine as to defy him. And yet, he clearly recalled, when she was utterly determined somehow she generally got her way.

Mrs. Aldridge drew a step closer and laid a gentle hand on her husband's arm. "Mr. Aldridge," she said softly. "Are you quite certain? Surely, this must be your sister's best hope." She looked timidly up to meet her husband's eyes. Oliver suppressed a sigh. If he had ever seen love in a woman's eyes—and he very much thought he had—then he saw it now in Livia Aldridge's eyes. Love enough even to outweigh her obvious fear. Heaven only knew what Miss Carothers had said to her.

Jacob saw her look as plainly as did Oliver, if not more so. He looked down with a smile and laid a hand protectively on her shoulder. "Utterly determined, my own—do you doubt it?" Turning his attention back to Oliver, he continued, "It is unconscionable. Three years ago I was mad and weak enough to permit Cecily to give up a drop of her blood, and look at the result."

"But you were not yourself, my dear—you were not responsible," his wife intervened.

"I was not myself," he admitted. "But I was still responsible. And now you"—he favored Oliver with a less-than-friendly look—"you suggest my wife give up her blood also, in another desperate scheme to defeat the same evil we have already found impregnable. I don't know how it is in India, Beckford, but here in London we have a word for men who shelter behind women when under fire."

"Oh, Jacob, it is not like that!" There was a minute pause. As all three parties to the conversation recalled Livia Aldridge did not usually address her husband by his Christian name in public. The lady had the grace to look abashed. "I only mean," she went on in a more subdued tone (but with, perhaps, a lingering trace of an American accent), "you would never shelter behind me, I am entirely certain, and so—I do not doubt—is Colonel Beckford. But he—and I as well—presumed you would take any risk to rescue Cecily. And so would I, dear Mr. Aldridge, for I have watched these past few years and seen how her situation haunts you. We cannot go on so. Surely we should all three be determined to save her, at any price."

Jacob looked down at his wife for a very long time. Oliver could almost hear the ratcheting of gears and wheels as his brother-in-law considered which of the two identical ladies was probably speaking, and what the rights and views of the other might be. "Any price but your safety," he replied at last. To Oliver, he continued, "Think of some other plan. You can have my blood, by the gallon, if you want it. And you shall have it, before you get hers."

He spoke so softly that it was an instant or so before Oliver grasped he had been threatened. He almost laughed out loud. Jacob had grown up, at that. Cecily would be so proud when she waked. "I don't doubt your nerve, Aldridge, but I don't see any use for your blood. Too much like Cecily's—the demon won't turn away from what it already has, just for more of what it already has. But Mrs. Aldridge escaped it once—or rather her counterpart did, and it will not distinguish between them. It will feel the injury of that, and come after her."

Mrs. Aldridge paled and fell back on her husband's arm. Jacob glanced down at her, and his mouth had tightened when he looked back up. "I escaped it also, and it must feel the injury of that as well. Or if it cannot be persuaded to distinguish between Cecily and me, then could not my blood be used to deceive it that Cecily has escaped?"

He paused hopefully, but seeing that Oliver did not relent, he sighed. "I see. It seems we have trespassed on your hospitality too long, Colonel." To his wife he added with a smile, "My dear, would you run upstairs and pack a bag, then? Just a few things—enough for tonight; we can send for the rest later." He extended a hand politely to Oliver. "Thank you for all your kindnesses, Colonel. We shall not intrude any further. And take . . ." his voice caught very slightly. "Take good care of my sister, please."

Oliver did not take the hand. Mrs. Aldridge did not run upstairs. Rather she stared at her husband with disbelief and an open mouth. Oliver suspected that Livia Aldridge had never until this moment contemplated the unhappy possibility of leaving the fashionable Beckford town house and its associated revenues. Jacob shrugged elegantly and withdrew his hand, then turned a firm and level gaze on his wife. She blushed and turned first left, then right. She glanced back up to Jacob as if contemplating an appeal but dropped her eyes again before attempting a timid, uneasy smile. At last she inched slowly toward the stairs.

Before she had committed her foot to the bottom rise, Oliver surrendered, offering his own hand. "Please, Aldridge, you cannot go. Of course, we shall find some other means." If any such existed. "You simply must stay, you know. Suppose that Cecily waked and found you gone? I should not hear the end of it in this life."

A flicker of a smile crossed Jacob's face, and he raised his hand again to take Oliver's. Mrs. Aldridge returned from the stair with a glad step and a genuinely charming smile. "Oh, thank you, Colonel, for your sympathy and understanding. Mr. Aldridge and I"—the smile she turned up to Jacob was, in and of itself, full explication of his determination to protect her—"we do not care for magic. We would not suffer it in the house at all, were it not that Frau Strasser still sees some hope for Cecily." Well, doubtless she correctly reported Jacob's view, at any rate. "Besides, why should you need more of my blood anyway? Surely the mirror is thick enough with it already."

The two men turned as one to stare at her, so that she grew uneasy and drew back. "Of course," murmured Oliver. "Chang said . . ." He remembered almost too late that Livia Aldridge might not know everything that Chang had said, and left the sentence unfinished.

"Chang said what?" inquired Jacob. Clearly, if Miss Carothers had not told Mrs. Aldridge everything, then it followed she could not have told Jacob either. Of his wife he urgently demanded, "Your blood was on the mirror? Why?" And turning back to Oliver he asked again, "Chang said what? That he put his own ward's blood on the mirror? Before that dreadful séance?"

"Not just before the séance," said Mrs. Aldridge. She looked from one man to the other, searching for some hint as to the cause of their shared dismay. "Many times. It was my mirror. Or it was intended to be so. A coming-of-age gift. But he had not completed the consecration."

"Your mirror?" Jacob sank weakly into the nearest chair.

Oliver started to laugh. He laughed until he could hardly stand, and nearly knocked over an occasional table on his way to the divan into which he fell, still laughing. "No wonder Miss Carothers haunts you," he snorted. "It is not, as it appeared, that she somehow escapes the mirror. Rather, it is that you are always in the mirror with her." He chuckled and wrapped his arms around his aching sides. "Chang really should have seen this coming; clearly he knows nothing of . . ." He broke off at seeing the expression on the lady's face. "My apologies, Mrs. Aldridge. I should not speak disrespectfully of your guardian." Then he spoiled the apology by laughing again.

Jacob sighed and resumed his feet. He looked ten years older than his age, at the very least. "Then it is settled," he said, but his voice was not that of a man who thought things were settled. His voice was faint and abstracted, as if his thoughts were ten thousand miles away. Turning suddenly, he smiled brightly at his wife. "Mrs. Aldridge, shall we take in the Garden?[13] They are singing the new DeLibes, and I think you have not heard it." Returning his attention to Oliver, he nodded. "It is very gracious of you to let us stay on here, Beckford, and if you are inclined to permit it, then we are gratefully inclined to accept—at least until we have all considered together what is best for Cecily. But that must wait for later. We have barely time to dress before curtain."

His sudden decision to take in the opera was not merely out of place; it echoed—to Oliver's trained ears, at any rate—with a note of falsity. He almost wondered where Jacob did mean to take his wife, if not the opera. But Mrs. Aldridge accepted the remark at face value; she darted toward the stairs with her face alight. "Oh, Mr. Aldridge, how delightful!" she called down. "Shall I wear the green silk?"

"Perhaps not," replied Jacob. "For you look so charming in it, I might be too distracted to attend the music." She giggled and ran the rest of the way up the stairs. Jacob followed after her more slowly, pausing to bow to Oliver. It was a very civil bow, but his eyes were distant.

Chapter Six

"I am very much concerned about Jacob, my dear." Oliver slid an arm behind his wife's unresisting shoulders and lifted her gently to a sitting position. "He means to interfere; I am quite sure of it." Cecily, of course, did not reply. Her head did not flop, but it did remain slightly back as if it were still resting on an invisible, vertical pillow. Tenderly he straightened her neck so that she faced him.

"He is right to want his wife out of it, of course, whether or not she deserves his consideration. And it may just be possible to accommodate him, after all. But he does not trust us, and he might contrive to create a problem." Her little cap had gone all askew, and he attempted to straighten it. But he had no aptitude for such feminine touches, and soon the cap had fluttered down from her shoulder to the bed cover. She looked quite absurd with her hair as short as that of a street boy, and the curls as tangled. Absurd but delectable. No woman in the world was as beautiful, he was quite sure.

"There's no need to take on so, my dear." She had, of course, said nothing, but his heart heard plainly what she would have said. "I shall not hurt him. But it may be necessary to restrain him. Perhaps you could assist? He would be guided by you, if you made your wishes known. And now, we must get you into your dressing gown." He pulled the coverlet down off her feet, and turned her carefully around so that she faced the side of the bed instead of the foot. Her legs remained straight, and stuck out over the side. He sighed, and gently pressed each knee.

"We can't have you dancing about the house in your shift. You are quite alluring enough, fully dressed." Patiently he worked her joints, one at a time, taking pains to do nothing that would have caused her discomfort, had she been able to perceive discomfort. At last he had her standing, with her arms sufficiently extended that he could wrap her up in her dressing gown. "I must say, the next time I see a little girl dressing up her doll, I shall treat her with more respect." He sighed again and studied her thoughtfully. "I do not think

I can get you down the stairs, at this rate. And with this game leg, I am not confident I can carry you either, at least not without dropping you half the way. But you must come down, my dear. You and the mirror must come together for the trick to work."

Cecily stood passively as he had left her, with her eyes still closed and her dressing gown about her, untroubled either by his need to bring her to the mirror or even by the disarray of her hair, which would have appalled her if she had known of it. "I do not want to use Command on you." She did not care if he did or not. "And you should very much not want me to use Command on you if you were consulted." But he could not consult her, and her continued submissiveness seemed to tempt him. "No!" he determined at last. "One does not make one's wife a fetch. There is surely some alternative." He turned back to his herb bag and rummaged through its pockets, looking for the alternative.

He came up at last with a short willow wand and a plug of something brown and unpleasant looking. "Heartfelt apologies, my own," he murmured, and thrust the plug into her mouth. She made no objection, but his face wrinkled up as if he were imagining a very nasty taste. Then he uttered a word, if word it could be called. Perhaps it would better be described as a sound: short, sharp, and curt, but full of meaning for all that it lacked any recognizable phonetic characteristics. He waved the wand in a peculiar gesture.

Cecily seemed to fall backward. And yet she did not reach the ground. Even as her head went down, her feet rose up so that she slid smoothly into a recumbent position. She lay quietly on the air, as placidly as she had lain in her bed. The skirt of her dressing gown trailed down toward the floor. Oliver folded her hands neatly under her breast. He touched the tip of the willow wand to her forehead and walked slowly away. She floated after him as if on a leash.

A considerable amount of maneuvering was still required to get her into Chang's study. He tried walking behind her and pushing her forward, but this put her below him on the stairs. At that angle she tended to slide out beyond his reach and escape him. Then, when the wand slipped from her forehead, she ceased to move, except for turning sideways in the breeze; the stairwell drew a nasty draft. Having turned, she floated aimlessly, waiting for him to work his way around her until he found a position from which he could resume control. In the end, he was forced to go backward down the steps ahead of her, muttering to himself all the way on the nuisance of levitation.

Chang's study was small, and both the desk and the apothecary's cabinet (not to mention his trunk) were large. He arranged Cecily decorously along one wall while he cleared an area by pushing furniture out of the way or into the corridor. All the while, he chatted with her as he worked. "This desk is a good piece, but walnut is so very heavy," he opined, sliding the pretty little oil lamp over to one side and smearing some paste—very similar in color and aroma to the wad he had put in her mouth—onto its shining surface. The desk slid out of Oliver's way so smoothly that the lamp barely flickered and did not totter at all. "And the servants must surely curse it under their breath, for it wants constant oiling and polishing."

He studied the desk in its new position a moment before deciding he was satisfied to leave it there. "Look, my dear," he commented upon turning his gaze to the carpet. "Chang has set this little prayer rug north to south. Doubtless he is being careful not to blaspheme against the Muslim view." He chuckled and squatted down to jerk the rug around perpendicularly. "Clearly he does not understand that magic is by definition blasphemous, and therefore the more blasphemous it is, the better the chances of its efficacy." He found it something of a struggle to rise back to his feet, and turned to his wife with a sigh. "I hope you do not find me too aged to suit you now, my love. There is no denying I am no longer the spry young man you married."

He pulled his trunk out from the wall so that it could be easily opened but, having done so, decided to investigate the contents of the apothecary's chest instead. He peered into several little drawers before glancing back to Cecily. "Are you afraid Chang will hear me rummaging through his things? Not to worry, sweetheart. He is in his room, settled into his favorite chair and utterly engrossed in a book. Or so he thinks. And so would anyone else who peeked in the door to check on his welfare. But it would take a very great disturbance indeed to rouse him from that book. We can snoop to our heart's content, and he will not stir for anything less than a cry from the mirror. Which is why we shall leave the mirror until last."

He returned to rooting through the drawers. "But the servants are resting more naturally, with no dinner to put on, and we would not care to trouble them either, would we? There's no need to waste my own stocks on pacifying them; doubtless the doctor has everything we need." He extracted and laid aside a number of items as he searched the chest. He paused to regard the contents of one drawer with particular interest. "Oh, my, he has some unusual items here." His fingers curled over the edge of the drawer. "But it is not needful," he sighed, and withdrew an empty hand. Several drawers farther down he found a candle, or rather the mere stub of a candle, formed from some greenish wax.

He pulled it out and showed it to Cecily. "Look, my dear. Apparently Chang is very fond of his privacy. This will not only keep the servants in their room, and probably unconscious, it will also scare off tradesmen, or even expected visitors if there were any such. One would have to be very determined to approach our door when this was lit. Now, we only need . . . Ah, yes." Another drawer, right next to that which had held the candle, provided a small jar filled with a mix of herbs. Like the candle, the herbs were so much used that little remained. Oliver set the candle on the corner of the desk; poured the remaining herbs into its broad, shallow well; and lit a rush from the lamp. Whispering inaudibly, he touched the rush to the wick.

The candle did not appear to take light. But a peculiar odor rose up from it, and Oliver tossed the rush into the fireplace. He glanced back and forth from his trunk to Cecily. "I expect I had best get you seated next. Everything else can be arranged around you. By the door, do you think? No, there is a peg here that Chang doubtless uses to hang the mirror; it is just the right height, and we will use it also." He guided her across the room so that she faced the door, and then he placed the wand in her folded hands. Keeping one of his hands on hers, he placed the other under her back and pushed gently upwards so that she assumed a standing position. He dropped down to one knee and bent her knees and ankles back up so that her lower legs were level with the floor, then he rose heavily and pressed down on her shoulder until she appeared to be kneeling on the ground.

He studied her critically, verifying that she was as close to upright as could be contrived while still levitating. Then he plucked the wand from her fingers and pulled the brown wad out of her mouth. She dropped down perhaps a quarter of an inch when her weight was restored. Despite his efforts, she was not perfectly balanced when she landed. She did not collapse, but she rocked from side to side. He caught her arms and stabilized her position, then pressed her down until she was sitting on her knees. Squatting down behind her, he looked over her shoulder at the door, but was not satisfied with her line of sight; he carefully moved her over and slightly around.

He approached his trunk at last. The top tray contained only his "student garb"—the clothes his master had given him. Ragged though they were, they had absorbed a great deal of etheric vibration, and he therefore generally resumed the costume when working. He was amused to discover that he was embarrassed to undress before his unconscious wife; he kept behind her and turned his back while he removed his uniform. He folded it neatly and set it down at the back of the desk, well behind the lamp and the unlit but smoking candle. At last with a grimace, he removed the tray from the trunk and set it aside.

"Oh, Cecily," he whispered. "It is not right that you should be exposed to this." He pulled out a bundle, thickly bound in greasy rags, and set it on the floor. He did not trouble to untie it but took a knife and slashed the wrappings, which fell apart to reveal a severed head. Grasping it by the hair, he came around to set it in front of Cecily. "Mrs. Beckford," he murmured, "allow me to present 'Belteshazzar, Chief of Necromancers.'[14]"

She did not open her eyes to acknowledge the introduction. Just as well. It was quite horrid. Neither fresh nor old enough to have sloughed off its flesh. Bone showed through in a few places. It stank. "Not his original name, of course," he informed her as he returned to his trunk to retrieve a small case. "His original name was destroyed when I stole his luck. It's very interesting, I think, that even when the luck is gone he remains a vessel of power. Great power."

He dropped to his knees beside her and opened his case. "I do apologize for troubling you with all this. I recollect you had little patience with magic. I suspected even then it was because you were ashamed of your father. Naturally you were far too proud to say any such thing, but I could see in your eyes how you hoped that no one knew of him. And so I pretended not to know." He laid out a variety of small pots and jars on the floor by his side.

"And now, here you are forced to endure the nasty business again, and at my hand." He sighed deeply. "And as you may recognize"—he showed her a misshapen root and a dish of some oily paste—"this is very black magic indeed, blacker than anything your father dared." All the while, Oliver was busily strewing herbs, pouring oils, arranging roots and oddments, and drawing chalk designs in a circle around the head. He even incorporated the design of the prayer rug into his arrangement. "Although he might very well have tried it, if he had ever had the opportunity to learn it. He was not shy."

When everything else was placed to his satisfaction, Oliver turned the head over to lie on its back. He pulled the mouth open as wide as it would go. A tooth fell out when he pulled on the mouth; nor was it the first to be dislodged. One eye was rotted out enough to provide a deep well; Oliver pressed a slim black taper into the depression. He clapped his hands, and the candle sparked and lit. He turned back to Cecily and whispered, "I swear to you, my darling, if we get through tonight, it will be over. 'I'll break my staff, bury it certain fathoms in the earth.'[15] You'll think me a respectable man again."

He rose and crossed to the apothecary's chest. "We are almost ready, Cecily. And we must move quickly now, for no spell in the world will keep Chang from hearing this." He pulled out the long, flat drawer where the mirror resided and waved a hand over its surface to test the portal's lock. The image of Miss Carothers was not dispelled by any reflection of his hand. If he had not known what the thing was, he would have supposed it to be transparent glass. He set a half dozen of Chang's candles—all mismatched—around the edge of the mirror and borrowed the black taper from the skull. It flickered badly when he removed it from its place, but the flame survived to light the candles arrayed on the mirror and flared brightly up when he replaced it in the eye. Then he poured a small vial of milky liquid into the mirror, as if over Miss Carothers's hair.

There was a sharp, crackling sound as of many panes of glass breaking. The image in the mirror wavered very slightly and grew cloudy. Miss Carothers remained plainly visible, but a reflection of the ceiling overlay her. He waved his hand over the glass again, and the image of his hand briefly obscured her face. Oliver smiled. Brushing the candles off the side, he pulled the mirror out of the drawer. It was disconcerting to pick up what looked like a case containing a living, three-dimensional body only to find it flat and light of weight. He carried it to the door and hung it up. As he did so he noted that no matter which way the mirror was oriented the image remained upright, as a mere reflection should. When the mirror swung down into place, Cecily's reflection appeared in it—as it might in any mirror—alongside that of Miss Carothers. That was only right and proper, he decided. They had been friends.

He extended his arms to the sides and started to chant, and the chant grew into an alien keening. The incomprehensible sounds he made appalled the ear, and yet had cruel meaning in some other realm. Even over his own voice he could hear stirrings overhead. The veil of oblivion enclosing Dr. Chang ripped; the sorcerer leapt to his feet with a wail of rage and fear and ran toward his mirror.

Oliver was waiting at the door. He had laid a battle enhancement upon himself so that his fingers were hooked into an almost animal claw, hard as iron, hard enough to serve as a weapon. Oliver had seen a great deal of battle in Afghanistan and was quite at ease with hand-to-hand combat. The key was to attack immediately and with abandon. Thought was unnecessary. So Oliver struck as soon as the door cracked open, before Chang had time to enter or even to see the state of his study.

Oliver slashed with all his strength at Chang's throat. His clawed hand entered and tore, but did not exit. He enfolded Chang in his arms and dragged him into the study, in a gore-drenched parody of a lover's embrace. That embrace saved Chang's life—such as it had suddenly become—for Oliver's fingers still did not tear free but remained firmly embedded in Chang's throat, cradling many of his body's natural channels intact. Chang's eyes rolled all the way back in his head and his body shuddered in a sort of seizure, but Oliver held him close so that his throat was not completely destroyed, even by the seizure.

Blood spurted everywhere. The jugular was not broken, but certainly nicked. Oliver half carried, half dragged Chang down and onto the carpet to lay him out before Cecily. "Does it hurt?" he whispered. "Many demons feed on pain; when did you last feed yours?" Chang struggled to turn his head—a mistake, for a great gout of blood leapt out of his throat, splashing Belteshazzar's head and nearly extinguishing the black candle. "I think you would scream if you could," chuckled Oliver. "But I do not think you can. Such a pity. You have so many good reasons to scream."

With his free hand he caught up the head, hooking one finger in the mouth and another in the eye that did not host the candle so that he might pick it up without dislodging the candle. "Did you know," he hissed at Chang, "it is possible for the human body to survive when the heart has been removed, as long as the heart is installed in a vessel of power? I certainly never supposed such a thing—until it was done to me." He held up the head for Chang to see. Very little but the whites of Chang's eyes showed, but he must have seen something, for his trembling increased. Oliver smiled, and laid the head on Chang's belly. "Here is a vessel of power." Slowly, delicately, almost tenderly he extricated his clawed fingers from Chang's neck without doing any more damage than had already been done.

Oliver raised his bloody hand high and shrieked. He offered up a cry that pierced the heavens, the astral planes, and all the many gates of hell. Then he plunged his fingers down into Chang's chest, tearing it open, and caught up his beating heart, warm and alive and trailing vessels of blood and strings of tendon and muscle. Most of what he held in his hand was still attached within Chang's body, but there was damage enough to splatter blood across the face of the mirror and throughout the room. He slammed the heart into the open mouth of the head. The black taper blazed into an inferno, and the head glowed hotly and radiated every color of the spectrum. Oliver's voice raised up to a scream that defined the axis mundi with its range and rage, until it transcended mere sound and became a deafening silence. The universe hung poised in the echo.

And there came a knock at the door. It was not possible there was a knock at the door. He had taken all precautions. But the iron knocker slammed down again, supernaturally loud, echoing through the house like the gavel of the Great Judge in Heaven, commanding him to appear before the Divine Court. The interruption left him sick and gagging; the moment was so insanely inopportune. There could not be a knock on the door. There was another knock at the door. No servant would answer it today.

His concentration broken, he sensed the power he had summoned now poised to fade and slip. He could neither stop now nor continue smoothly. In desperation he called to the excremental goddess of lost hours, "Hecate!" (Her true name was both forbidden and unpronounceable, so he used the absurd

Roman designation. But he traced her sigil in the air so she would know he called to her.) "Whore of Oblivion! Hold this instant intact for me and I swear I will give you blood."

He rose to his feet with a strange steadiness, the tearing of his bad knee concealed beneath the swaying of his heart and the grinding of gears in his mind. Drunk with unused power, he reeled into the entrance hall. There was another knock. "Blood, Hecate," he whispered, and opened the door.

It was Cecily's brother. Oliver stared and stared and finally rasped. "You are Jacob."

Jacob lifted an eyebrow. "So I have been told." He was still dressed in his opera garb—a very old-fashioned cut of tailcoat and a bright tartan waist-coat—but of course, his hat was only a gibus.[16] "Sorry to disturb you. I forgot my key." He regarded Oliver owlishly. "I see you were busy." There was a long pause. "May I come in?"

Oliver moved—only slowly—out of the doorway. He could scarcely sac-rifice Cecily's brother. But he had promised Hecate blood. A problem. Even-tually he realized that Jacob was staring at his clothing. Possibly he had not come prepared to greet an apparent Hindu beggar. "Would you happen to have a living creature in the house, Jacob? I'm in the middle of a sacrifice, and I very much need blood."

Jacob continued to stare at his clothing for several seconds before replying, "Really? Surely you have plenty of blood already."

Oliver looked down. Chang had left his mark. He looked up. Jacob had neither screamed nor fled. "Got bottom, Aldridge?"

Jacob sighed, "I hope so."

"Then come along." He closed the door behind Jacob. "No, I do not have enough blood. All this," he gestured down his front, "is for the demon. But I promised Hecate more. I meant to give her whoever was banging on the door, but am inclined to find an alternative, seeing it was you. Cecily would be displeased."

Jacob actually managed a crooked smile. "It would not do to displease Cecily." He paused for thought. "Does it have to be human? Livia has a spaniel. You won't have noticed him; he's been cringing in the cellar since you arrived. I rather wondered about that."

Oliver considered. A mere spaniel struck him as stingy, but it would fulfill his literal word. Demons were particular about the literal word. "Get it. And meet me in Chang's study."

He returned to find that Hecate—sing screams of torment in acknowledgement of her dreadful name—had, indeed, held the instant. Chang still lay before the mirror with the head rising out of his open chest. The lungs within and the heart without still gleamed, fresh and wet; the blood had neither congealed nor flowed away. The very air was still—until it was penetrated by the shrieking of the dog. Jacob entered backward with his head bent, his attention concentrated entirely on dragging the unwilling animal forward.

A small gasp did escape him when he lifted his head. But he drew his breath back in and spoke quite levelly. "If you had told me it was only Chang you wanted, I should not have troubled to abandon Livia at the Garden. She was wearing the green silk, you know." He paused and looked down. "That carpet is utterly ruined."

Oliver grasped the spaniel's collar. The doomed beast convulsed, clearly sensing what was to come. He wished he could cast a Calm on it, and let it die easily, but Hecate preferred the blood of pain to any other. "I am going into the mirror after Cecily," he informed Jacob. "I assume you are here to reiterate your offer of blood."

Jacob looked a little pale, but he was pale by nature. "I am," he replied softly. He removed his coat and rolled up his left sleeve, then frowned. Glancing about yet again, his eye fell on the pretty little shawl that had decked the trunk and that Oliver had tossed in a corner. He seized it and tied it about his exposed shirt and waistcoat like an apron before extending his arm out to Oliver. "How much do you need?"

"A steady drip would be best. But not until the demon emerges. You will know when that happens. I cannot say in advance what exactly may occur, but there will be a clear sign, something unusual—perhaps good, perhaps ill, but unusual. Cut when you see the sign, and be sure the blood pours over the heart and into the skull's mouth." Jacob was beginning to look a little green, and he made an unmistakable grimace of distaste as he looked down on the head with its gaping maw and the heart impaled on what was left of the teeth. "Can you do this?" Oliver inquired.

Jacob looked up with a distinctly annoyed expression. "Really, Beckford. I'm not the green boy you used to know. I've been with the Ministry for years." Oh, that Ministry. "But if Livia asks, I've no idea what happened to the dog."

The spaniel pissed down Oliver's leg. Its eyes rolled back into its head and its shrieking diminished to a moan more disturbing than the shrieking had been. Oliver sighed very slightly and hefted it higher. Then he formed his hand back into a claw, gouged two fingers into the dog's abdomen, and raked out its internal organs. Again, he did not quite kill, although long life had ceased to be an option for the poor creature. He tossed it into a corner. "Only a down payment, Hecate, with passionate thanks. I shall send more later to demonstrate that my gratitude does not end here."

The dog's dreadful noises suddenly ceased. The blood resumed flowing; the head was restored to blazing glory. Oliver even found himself suddenly suffused with a tide of power at its peak, ready for use if only his mind remained clear enough to use it. Apparently Hecate had been very pleased; she had restored even the state of his personal energy flow, along with the instant she had held for him. But the power had to be used now, so he called to the demon to come get Chang's blood, and he dove into the mirror.

There was a passing in the mirror; the demon moved out and Oliver moved in. Of course, the demon was not really in the mirror to move out, yet somehow Oliver passed it in the entry. Because now Cecily was in the mirror, too—not deeply immersed in it, perhaps, but caught in its spiderweb of reflections. So that when the demon left Cecily (only in part, alas, but still a departure) it passed through and out of the mirror. Oliver almost saw its face, which was not so much evil as inconceivable. There was no knowing what it was or why it wanted what it tried to take; it was a contradiction of reality. Enough that it was very dangerous to humankind.

Chapter Seven

The world changed utterly. Oliver suffered a faint flicker of nerves, for all that he should have expected it. Suddenly he was whirled upright and dressed again in his crisp, clean uniform. That was only right and proper, for he found himself standing in a great, quiet hall, framed in glass. Except that it was floored in a sheet of flowing liquid, it was almost like the Crystal Palace at the Great Exhibition,[17] which his parents had taken him to see when he was little. But this structure was even larger and loftier, seeming to enclose not merely elm trees but the very stars. And the light outside the glass—or perhaps the glass itself—was a deep, bloody crimson. Under that red light, the fluid beneath his feet looked black, but Oliver suspected that it, too, was red. And salty.

No matter which way he turned, there were sparkling lights and shadowy movements in the near distance, as if there might really be exhibits or entertainments going on; but if so they were all conducted silently. The air shivered with occasional faint rustlings, softer even than a breeze. Oliver stared about, almost entranced and entirely at a loss as to where to proceed. He had meant to follow Cecily's reflection, but he saw no sign of her anywhere. The place was enormous and without direction. Then a soft, mysterious glimmer rose up from the floor. It resolved into a silver current that snaked across the rippling surface underfoot, glowing like a river of moonlight. The demon had somehow left a trail. He could not think how or why.

He did not understand it, but he followed it. He took pains to keep his eyes down, to look only at the glittering path. Lights, motion, and something almost like color danced in his peripheral vision, tempting and summoning him, but Oliver had been in India long enough to know the danger of such distractions. Indeed, every children's tale warned of the importance of staying on course in unearthly realms, and never deviating from the designated way. There was only a very narrow intersection between the spheres where mortal flesh resided and those that hosted beings that were neither mortal nor flesh.

Somehow that intersection had been marked by the demonic trail, which led from a mortal body to the mortal world. To stray from that path would be death.

He came after a while to a place that was almost like a place. The light paled to something like day and the floor grew dry, while the path disintegrated into a heap of rubble. A great arch of rough stone led into a dark cave. And standing by the entrance was Rhoda Carothers. She was turned away from him, leaning slightly over something he could not see; he knew her by her chestnut hair. He paused to call on Vision, which was dangerous in this place where Vision was likely to reveal truths the human mind could not absorb. But he needed to know if the lady was truly who she seemed to be. She was, indeed, Miss Carothers.

She straightened and turned his way with a smile. She was holding a bucket, of all things, and pouring something out of it into the rock heap, but on seeing him she tossed it aside. It glowed and cast out a glittering spray of silver before it vanished. "It seems you were right about my remembering the way," she informed him. Then she added with another charming smile, "And it seems also that I am braver than I supposed. I came right here to its lair with hardly a pang."

"And you marked its trail for me. If you had not, I do not think I could ever have found the way. Dear Miss Carothers, I will thank you until the end of my days. I will write a song to the courageous Mistress of Demons."

She giggled. "I do believe you tease, Colonel. After all, it would have been a good deal braver if the demon had actually been here."

"If the demon had actually been here, you would not have survived your own valor. I assure you, I am not mocking you. Even my Cecily might not have been so courageous."

She laughed out loud. "Now I know you are teasing. Cecily was braver than lions."

"*Is* braver than lions," he corrected her.

Her smile faded and she glanced uneasily toward the cave. "Perhaps. One way or the other, you shall soon know." She stepped forward and laid a gentle hand on his arm. "And either way, thank you for sparing Livia. She was so horribly afraid."

"Please do not thank me. I am ashamed I even contemplated sacrificing her, when I had her nasty guardian to hand. Such barbarities may be the norm in India, but in England they will not do. What would my Cecily say?"

"She would say you were not yourself," Miss Carothers assured him. "And then she would think no more of it." She stepped back and glanced again toward the cave. "It is not entirely gone, is it? Or you would not need to be here." She sighed and looked down. "My courage is something less than infinite, Colonel. I think that now you have found your way here, I shall run away."

He smiled. "Of course, Miss Carothers. This is no fit place for a lady. Run as far and as fast as you can. You could even run right out of the mirror if you pleased—I unbarred the portal."

Her eyes grew wide. "What would happen to me then?"

He shrugged. "No one knows. Frau Strasser might have some ideas, but you would have to try it to find out for sure." He turned to regard the great stone entry. When he glanced back she was gone. So there was nothing left but to go into the cave.

It was not as dark as a cave in the real world, and the floor was much more level. The stone gave no sign of having been worked, and yet it had grown up in shapes that were convenient to human use. He found that particularly strange, as neither nature nor the residents of the astral realms would have chosen such shapes. One ledge in particular resembled a great couch, and huddled on it was a bedraggled bundle that his eye only slowly recognized as approximately human in shape and size.

It looked scarcely more alive than Belteshazzar, and indeed, he took it at first for dead and mummified. The ragged remains of a petticoat identified the figure as female, but only a few straggling hairs still decked the skull. The flesh was reduced to wrinkled leather, and even the leather was rent in numerous places. It looked as if it had been chewed by scavengers. The hands in particular were pathetic, with the desiccated, skeletal fingers clasped awkwardly in an attitude of entreaty. The left hand bore a gold ring. He knew the ring. It had been his grandmother's.

"Oh, Cecily, is this you?" Pain welled up in his heart and threatened to choke him. "Is this really you?" He touched the withered face gingerly and tried—with infinite care—to turn the head a little more toward him so that he could search for some recognizable feature. Then he gasped and jerked his hand away. The mouth had been sewn shut. Great black stitches crossed and recrossed the hard little ridges that had once been soft lips. The drying of the skin had torn large holes around each of the entry and exit points, but the stitches still held.

He checked his pockets. Of course, none of the special items that he had intended to bring were there; he had placed those in the pockets of his Indian garb. He had only the things that he always kept in his uniform pockets, but those included his pocket knife. Drawing it, he sat beside her and started to saw with the tip at one of the stitches. It was an awkward process because he had to be careful not to tear her poor mouth further. The strand that formed the stitch was some very tough, sinew-like substance that did not cut easily.

He had not gotten very far—a single strand was frayed but not severed— when the mummy came to life. It emitted a soft, heart-wrenching moan and batted, feebly and futilely, at his hands. He paused. "No?" The wretched thing (for he could still not bring himself to think of it as Cecily, even with Grandmama's ring grating against his knuckles) seemed to relax slightly, although it continued to cry. "You do not want me to free your mouth?" It made an unhappy hissing noise, as if it were trying to speak. He more guessed than heard its meaning. "You did this to yourself? You sewed your own mouth shut? But why?"

He had only to ask the question aloud. The answer came to him at once. So obvious: if she had cried out, Jacob would have heard. He was her brother; he would have heard. Nothing would have kept him away. And the demon would have taken him instead. So she had taken precautions not to cry out. The pain in Oliver's chest exploded, almost paralyzing him, and he sat wrapped in his own arms, rocking slightly while tears poured down his face. That she had faced this alone, and chosen such an answer. He wept, and could not stop. He had gone off exploring and left her alone. And now she lay ruined with her mouth sewed shut.

"Oliver?" The voice was faint and disbelieving. He scarcely heard it over his own ragged breathing. "Oliver, is that you?" He looked up. The bundle of rags by his side proved now to be just that: a bundle of rags. A little farther off, back in the shadows of the inner cave, he saw Cecily crouched on the floor with her wrists manacled and the manacle chains staked to the ground. This Cecily was not mummified. She was wan and bruised and thin—terribly thin, almost gaunt. And her sweet little wrists were horribly torn up from the chains. But she was whole and even still lovely as he could plainly see, with her petticoat so ragged. Her voice was no more than a husky whisper. "I knew you would come. I knew it. Oh, thank God, thank God." She bowed her head and wept.

He was stunned. Every fiber of his being screamed that he should run to her, free her from her chains, comfort her, kiss her and kiss her again. But he did not need Vision to know it was a lie. His Cecily would not weep. She had not wept over his wounds from Afghanistan; she had not wept when little Justin died. Even so, a treacherous place in his heart murmured that perhaps she might weep with relief and gratitude, even if she never wept in fear or grief. And he wanted so badly to kiss those tears away. The demon also wanted him to kiss the tears away.

"Oliver?" She lifted her head to look at him, then raised her battered hands toward him in a gesture that was as much an inquiry as a plea. The gesture caused the strap of her petticoat to slide down off her shoulder. Glancing down, she awkwardly raised both her hands (one would have sufficed, but the chains did not permit the separation) to restore the bit of ribbon to its rightful place. One of the manacles caught in her hair, which was a medusa-like snarl that would have to be cut off entirely before it could be combed.

She fumbled with the tangle, disarranging the petticoat still more in the process. She jerked her hands free and gathered the damaged folds of her petticoat more modestly around herself, then tangled her wrists in her hair again trying to push it back out of sight behind her head. At last she blushed scarlet and curled up into a ball, hiding her face behind her manacled wrists, tangling the hair still more. He had no idea whether she was more embarrassed by the state of her hair or her profound dishabille. "Oliver, do you suppose you could assist me with your eyes closed?" she whispered.

He almost laughed; it was so exactly like her. He was halfway over to help her before he managed to remember that it was not she. He had known it only seconds before, but she was so convincing that he had already forgotten. A tiny little tendril of fear curled up in the bottom of Oliver's stomach. He was facing a demon unarmed, and he was already forgetting what it was. He started to call out for Vision, but the world exploded into hellfire, and the silence became the shrieking of the damned. He stood in a place too dark for Vision. He needed to find a way to keep the thing's true nature before him. "Why should I close my eyes, Echidna?"[18] he inquired, selecting a name to hold between himself and it. "Or better yet, why should I assist you at all?"

"What did you call me?" The attitude was exactly Cecily's; a frisson of annoyance that escaped a façade of courtesy grown a fraction too rigid. Her lips grew quite flat as she pressed them tightly together. She squatted there in rags and chains and managed to look like an insulted queen; if she had been decked out in silks and jewels, she would not have troubled to be so proud. His heart twisted, and the image of Cecily smiled ever so slightly. Of course. Echidna fed on pain. There were many kinds of pain.

"Have you used up Chang already?" he asked, and the creature cocked its head slightly in a fashion that was not perfectly like Cecily's. "You must have gobbled him right up—I should have sworn there was pain enough there to hold you for years. And how did you keep Cecily alive so long, if you eat so fast?"

He had succeeded in confusing it. It sat and blinked at him, with no expression at all, let alone an expression like Cecily's. Its mouth opened and closed several times. Its head twisted to an unnatural angle. "Why are you talking?" it inquired, and its voice was very peculiar indeed. It pulled at its hair, but absently, as if it were reaching for something that might have happened to be sitting on its head. "Is there meaning in your words?"

"Yes, Echidna, meaning. Meaning that may interest you." He retrieved his pocket knife, which lay beside him on the stone bench, and stabbed himself in the knee. He did not stab deeply, but the knife had been dulled by the stitching cord, and he chose his bad leg to stab. The pain was excruciating, and he let himself suffer it. "Do you see, Echidna? Would you like to hear more of my meaning?"

The Cecily figure rose. The manacles dropped away and disappeared. Her hair fluttered as if in a breeze, and arranged itself into an elegant sweep of curls. Her rags flowed together and became the dress she had worn at the embassy ball in Berlin. Her lips parted and her eyes glowed. She had never looked lovelier, and her beauty hurt him far more than the wound in his leg.

"Yes, mortal," she breathed in a voice like smoke and moonlight. "You may speak on." She did not meet his eyes; she was looking at his blood.

His heart almost exulted, but the pain in his leg damped the impulse, and his reason warned him to smother the emotion entirely. The demon was young and inexperienced. That was just a fact; he should not let it make him happy or hopeful. That the thing was young, and did not yet know any better than to let a mortal engage it in conversation, was merely an item of information. "I would like to make a deal with you, Echidna. I wounded Chang for you as a gesture of my intentions. Do you understand me so far? Are you willing to negotiate?"

It stared at him, still looking exactly like Cecily. Then the room grew black and fire flashed somewhere behind his eyes. When the light returned it was not Cecily but Chang who stood before him, impeccably dressed, the picture of elegance. His smile grew cruel, and then he collapsed into the ruined, bloody horror Oliver had made of him. The light of the black candle sparkled across the still-beating heart in Belteshazzar's mouth. "You did this?" The words did not come from Chang's mouth; rather they seemed to hum in the air. Before he had framed his reply, Echidna spoke again. "Yes, you gave me this. I am pleased." There was another hot splash of light, and Chang was gone. Oliver once again faced the image of Cecily. But now her hair was arranged very simply, and she had on the dotted pink organdy she had worn the day he proposed.

"Perhaps you too could make a gesture of good faith, and withdraw my wife's face from our discourse." If he had intended the words to be haughty, he failed. They emerged as a desperate whisper.

Cecily continued to smile, just as she had smiled then, with her eyes demurely down, but a little dimple of humor at the corner of her mouth. She smiled for a long time before the demon's voice emerged from the air. "No. I do not choose the images you see, or care about them. If you do not like them, why do you choose them?" Cecily's face continued to smile. Perhaps it was waiting for him to choose another image. "Talk to me about this deal."

"You are hungry?"

"Yes." Cecily was suddenly in rags again, and she held up her chained hands in entreaty. "Very hungry."

His heart reeled, and he stabbed himself again to distract himself. "I suppose there is not much nourishment left in this." He gestured to the form by his side, which transformed from a bundle of rags back into a distressed female form. This time it was not a mummy, but a woman near death—haggard, wasted, diseased. It bore only a faint resemblance to Cecily, but its mouth was still sewed shut.

"No." It was almost a moan. "It is hardly alive anymore. It does not care enough to feed me. I have to work very hard to make it cry. It is always refusing to cry."

His heart lurched. The Cecily in the organdy looked up eagerly and drew several steps closer to him. He drew in a breath and forced a smile. "See," he told it. "There is plenty of food about, so much I can give it to you for free; you do not need this." He looked down at Cecily—the real one, the one that was suffering—and stroked her livid, scabby cheek. "But it still has value in places that feed in other ways. So I wish to take it back. If you will relinquish it to me, I will give you fresh meat in return. Meat that cries whenever you touch it. More meat than you had here, even when this was fresh." A whisper of the man he had once been objected that the bargain he was offering was an evil one. But he had stopped caring about good and evil years ago.

"No." Glancing up, he saw that Echidna was now wearing Cecily's favorite afternoon costume; the same lavender she had worn when he took her to tea with his parents. She had utterly charmed his father, but Mother had simply assumed she was a fortune hunter. Of course, darling Cecily had won even Mother over in the end. Now Echidna was using Cecily's face to pout, like a child denied a sweet.

"No," it repeated. "I can't let it go. It has to lead me back to the other one. That one was so wonderful and tasty." The demon smiled broadly, and then suddenly spun itself in a circle. When it came round to face him again it had transformed itself into Jacob. Not the weary-looking Jacob who had come back from the opera, but the young, mischievous Jacob who had once asked Oliver his intentions. "It was so delicious—and I was teaching it how to find me more food; I want it back. It will not stop up its mouth. It will lead me to lots of food."

Oliver started. He had not thought Echidna capable of distinguishing between Cecily and Jacob. But it did not matter; it might even work to his advantage. He smiled tenderly down at Cecily. He could almost recognize her if he looked closely. "But the other one is outside with Chang." Or so he hoped. "Surely you know." Indeed, the demon should have known, if Jacob had cut himself as instructed.

Jacob's likeness froze, then cocked its head as if listening intently. The cavern around them grew dark until Oliver could only barely distinguish the standing figure, which could have been anybody. "Yes, yes, yes!" hissed the demon. "Oh, sweet, oh, wonderful. The darling one is where I can see it at last. It is bleeding." The light rose up again, and the figure was Cecily again, but Cecily dressed in a streetwalker's clothing. The figure came a few steps closer, posturing lewdly and stroking itself in a lascivious fashion. "Did you bring me this?" It opened its mouth and licked its teeth. "Is this your deal? I like it very much!"

"Then you will give me back Cecily? I mean, this one here?"

"No, why should I? The other one is here already!" There was an explosion, and it vanished. It did not transform. It went away.

Oliver smiled and resumed cutting at the stitches over Cecily's mouth. "Please do not concern yourself, my own. It cannot get to Jacob. It would have to pass through Chang. And Chang's heart is in a vessel of power." He stroked her lank, greasy hair. "Jacob is safe as houses, my darling. It is still best you do not cry out for a while, but not because Jacob will be called into a trap. Only so the demon has time enough to fall into *my* trap." He knew she heard and understood him, for the stitches over her mouth snapped easily under his knife.

"Oh, Oliver," she whispered. "I knew you would come." The very words the demon had put in her mouth. Demons do not lie. But when Cecily spoke them they meant something entirely different. Her voice was anguished, and she turned her head away, squeezing her eyes tightly closed. "I knew you would come." Demons do not tell the truth.

He too closed his eyes, while still stroking her hair, so as to visualize more clearly his memory of the last time that he stroked her hair. She had worn her "daffodil dress" with an absurd matching sunbonnet and a tasseled parasol, against the blazing sunlight at the dock. He had pushed back the bonnet so her hair tumbled free—its darkness intensified by all the yellow—

and her wonderful grey eyes had blazed. She had fussed and pretended to scold as she frantically pinned the curls back into place—dropping the parasol in the process—but then she had scandalized the city by kissing him farewell on the mouth.

The memory filled him with joy. Armed with a smile, he reopened his eyes. She looked better. Still thin, but no longer gaunt. Her color remained unhealthy, but the worst of the pocks and sores had faded from her skin. Her hair recovered some of its normal gloss, and grew pleasant to the touch. But she was still dressed in filthy rags; she still turned her face away. "Why would you not want to see me?" he asked. She shuddered and pulled farther away.

"Because of the way you look?" That was surely it—she was frightfully vain. "We can heal that, my dear. See you are prettier already." She did not answer, but he was fairly sure that—if he had not guessed right—he had hit very near the mark. What had the demon said? "If you do not like the images, why do you choose them?" Demons do not lie. If Cecily did not like the image she wore, why had she chosen it?

"It accused you of something awful," he surmised. "And you believed it."

She opened her eyes and glanced back toward him. Her eyes were dull and bloodshot. "It did not accuse me. It showed me," she whispered. "Demons do not lie."

"Neither do they tell the truth." He put his hand under her chin and gently but firmly pulled her head back to face him. "They do not see as we do. They dangle pretty pictures before us, like an anglerfish dangling its lure. But they do not understand the meaning of the images. They are only showing us reflections, not truths, like the reflections in a hall of mirrors. And each time the reflection is cast back against another mirror, the image strays farther from its original meaning. The changed meaning will always be unnatural, because the mirror itself is unnatural. It casts the light it wants to see. You are not whatever it said you were."

He had her full attention, and she gazed at him intently. Her eyes grew less clouded and resumed their shine as she concentrated on his words and forgot to think about what she ought not see. Her skin suffused with a wholesome pink-and-cream tone—because he knew perfectly well that her skin was like roses, and she had forgotten to contradict him. "Do you mean . . . ?"

She almost understood him; he was sure of it. "But . . . I . . ." She shuddered and turned away again, but not so quickly that he failed to see the light fade out of her eyes again. Her skin grew gray.

"I'll have no *but*s from you, young lady," he snapped, and her head whipped back around immediately. There was nothing better calculated to set her eyes smoldering than treating her like a child. "I don't care what the thing said to you—and please don't trouble to inform me—it told you whatever it sensed would strike home. It reminded you of some silly quarrel, or some naughty trick you once played, and you found yourself suddenly convinced you were a hate-filled, bloodthirsty monster. Or some such thing."

That was not it, of course. For one thing, Cecily was not particularly vulnerable in that area. For another, he took care not to strike too close to home. Whatever sin the demon had confronted her with, she would not be able to withstand it in his mouth also. Nor did he need to guess her guilty secret; he needed only to convince her it was not a true sin. More likely an indiscretion prior to their marriage—not a serious one as he knew from personal experience—or even afterwards.

His foolish heart clenched and twisted at the idea of an afterwards. But he had been gone so long, he could not possibly have blamed her. Besides, even afterwards it would doubtless have been no more than a light flirtation. If it were not something else entirely, as it most assuredly was. Her secret was sacred, he told himself firmly. The only thing that mattered was teaching her that it did not matter. Was she learning the lesson? Her eyes were clear again, her skin pale, but not unnaturally so.

He closed his eyes and imagined her again as he had just seen her, a young girl dressed in dotted pink organdy. It was time to wrench the imagery back to its true meaning. When he opened his eyes, she did indeed look younger, and she was no longer in rags. He smiled broadly, and his smile seemed to warm her. "We must go, my dear. It may be back. We dare not hope that it will linger in Chang's heart until it is too entangled to extricate itself. Probably it will see there is no way out forward, and come back here looking for answers. I want you to be gone before it comes." Her eyes grew stormy, and—praise all the powers of the universe—she grew strong enough to raise herself up.

She opened her mouth to argue. Women. He did not wait for any answer. He scooped her up in his arms. There were chains, of course, but he snapped them. She moaned faintly when they broke. He hurried toward the arch, the place of crossing over between the demon's personal place and the open astral spaces.

He knew before he had taken two steps that he would not make it. He could feel the darkness behind him, pressing him down, making him old and feeble, reminding him that he was a wicked old necromancer who did not deserve a beautiful young wife. But the demon had never undermined his conviction that Cecily deserved to escape. For her sake, he struggled to the entrance. And there, crouched behind the heap of rubble where the boundary between the spaces broke down, he saw a shadowy form, a glint of chestnut hair. The surrounding mist parted slighted, and two frightened brown eyes peeked through.

"Miss Carothers," he called to her. Why had she not fled? More afraid of the open gate than of the demon? "If you love Jacob Aldridge, guide his sister back to the gate."

With his last strength, he flung Cecily bodily out onto the heap of rubble. It was indeed the last of his strength. His knee gave way entirely, and he collapsed into the darkness at the entry. He felt himself seized and drawn back. When the world stopped spinning, and he opened his eyes, he found himself lying on the cavern floor looking up at Rhoda Carothers. Or perhaps it was Livia Aram Aldridge. The chestnut hair was tumbled about her creamy shoulders and provided no clue as to which she might be. Her petticoat, at any rate, was not the least bit ragged, but it was extremely daring, even for an undergarment. Oliver caught himself wondering if Jacob could distinguish between the two ladies by the petticoats they preferred. Certainly there was nothing in the voice to betray her identity.

"I can't get it!" she shrieked. "The darling one is there—right there— and I can't get it. I can see it and taste it and want it, but I can't get at it." She flew at Oliver and squatted down on top of him. With her eyes glowing red she did not look so much like Miss Carothers. "What did you do? There is a box right in the middle of your present. Why can't I get to him?"

Oliver did not pray. He was well aware that he had long since sacrificed the right to pray. But he reached into inner places seeking comfort and strength—and silence. When his mind was quiet, and the fear and the pain had been abandoned to crawl over his body as they pleased, he replied calmly, "The box would be Chang's heart. I put it in a vessel of power. So that he would stay alive and make food for you for a long time." He paused to see if it would spot the lie. Lying could be complicated in a place like this.

She did not accept it. But neither did she understand enough to blame him. She jumped up and ran around the cavern tearing her hair and screaming. "That is not a fact. That smells all wrong, like spoiled food. Why is that not a fact?" In the end, she came back to where he lay and jumped up and down on his chest, cracking most of his ribs and crying, "Tell me where to get the darling thing!"

He breathed in. Never mind how much it hurt. He breathed out. Not relevant if it were his last. "Chang's heart is in the box, is the box. It keeps him alive to feed you." That much was absolutely true. She would know it. No, it would know it, smell it. "Do you want me to open the box and let him die?"

"No, no!" He heaved an inner sigh of relief. It did not see the trap. "Keep the food. Food is always good. But give me the tasty one, the sweet thing. I want it."

"It is also in the box." Easy enough to tell her that. It was very close to true. Jacob's blood was in the vessel of power, along with Chang's heart. Echidna would not be able to see that it was only spilled blood in the box, and that Jacob himself was still primarily outside it. Probably not, anyway. He hoped. "But you will have to go deep into the box to reach it." Also true, but a clear warning of the danger. Would Echidna hear the warning?

"Go into the box?" It dropped down to sit on the ground with its legs spread wide apart and its hands clasped earnestly on the ground between them. It looked for all the world like a bewildered child. The form shrank and the curls changed color, until it was the image of a little girl no more than eight or nine years old. He had seen that child before but could not recall where. She was poorly but neatly dressed and clutched a small toy too bedraggled for him to identify. "I'm afraid of the box," she told him. Well she might be. "It's dark and scary."

"It is not supposed to be dark. It should be red and full of food." She cocked her head sideways and looked at him. Sgt. Enfield's little daughter, that's who she was. The child had died of a fever and suffered most abominably. "Full of food—fresh, bloody food," he assured her almost tenderly. "You will never be hungry again."

"Never, never?" It smiled and rose, rose to a grown woman's full height, and became Cecily again. She was dressed in mourning, but her smile was not sad. "That sounds very sweet. But perhaps I should feed on you first, in case your 'never' turns out not to be forever. You mortals are so small—I don't think you know what never means." He was not lying on the ground anymore. He was lying on the great stone couch where Cecily had lain before. Cecily sat down beside him and leaned forward to take him in her arms and kiss his mouth. There were worse ways to die, he reflected, before the blackness took him.

Chapter Eight

He woke, which probably should have surprised him, but he was too groggy to consider the strangeness of it. Mostly he noticed the sunlight slanting sideways through his bedroom window, always an irresistible temptation to rise and climb out the window and scramble down the ivy in his nightshirt. An unpleasant hint of memory almost surfaced in his mind, like a bad taste in the mouth. Surely the light had slanted through that window, and the boy climbed down that ivy long ago.

Yet the light was just exactly as he recalled it, not quite in his eyes because the window did not face exactly east, green and shivering from its passage through the elm tree next door. Could it really be nothing more than a long, deep, evil dream? Was he a boy again, still innocent of love or magic or war?

No. He turned his head slightly, and the view became radically unfamiliar. The furniture was Eastlake. Cecily had redecorated the bedroom to her own taste. Bless her.

She must have heard her name in his mind, for suddenly she was there at the door, wearing a very handsome blue outfit that he had never seen before. The remains of her hair were tied up in a sort of turban thing to conceal the damage. He must remember to get her a wig. She did not smile, but her eyes glowed. "Welcome home, Oliver," she whispered, and came to sit beside him on the edge of the bed. He pushed himself up to something like a sitting position, and she took his hand. "My dear, you must never take such a risk again for any reason whatsoever. Not for me. Not for England. Not, if it comes to that, for God."

So Jacob must have told her something, though precious little if he were any judge of Jacob's habits. Oliver raised her hand to his lips and kissed it. "Nonsense. Well worth it." He drank in the sight of her, his beautiful young wife, worth any pain or sorrow. She seemed calm, considering the mess she must have found in Chang's study.

Jacob appeared at the door. His left arm was tied up in a sling. "Ah, Theseus[19] wakes." He flung himself into the chair with a cheerful smile. "We've been to the War Office. They say you're released from active service indefinitely. So perhaps, when you're back on your feet, you'd like to pop around the Ministry."

"Not really," said Oliver. He looked back at Cecily. She was even more beautiful than he recalled from a few minutes ago. "I've sworn off that sort of thing."

Jacob looked at Cecily, too, but he was clearly hoping that she would step outside and leave them free to talk a little men's talk. She smiled back at Jacob, pointedly declining to leave her husband's side. Jacob sighed. "You may have to do something, old man. You still owe Hecate. I heard you promise her a second helping." True. Cecily drew in her breath. She did not leave the room, but she separated herself from the conversation by crossing to the window and gazing outside. "And they'll be shorthanded at the Ministry with me gone."

Oliver blinked. "You're leaving the Ministry?"

"I'm leaving the country." Oliver continued to blink. Cecily turned back from the window, and she and Jacob shared a long, searching look. "Mrs. Aldridge wants to visit her Grandmama in Italy. We may be gone some while."

Oliver managed a polite cough. "You surprise me, Jacob. I was under the impression that Mrs. Aldridge was not entirely at ease with Mme. Chang." He glanced at Cecily and continued, "Of course, it's none of my business."

There was a cry from down the hall, soft but penetrating, wordless but full of pain. The hairs on the back of Oliver's neck stood up. Jacob winced. "Nonsense, old man, we are family. And you are quite right—Mrs. Aldridge does not entirely care for Mme. Chang. But her assistance will be very much needed in caring for the good doctor, now that he has fallen so ill." The cry came again, barely audible but heartrending.

"Chang is still alive?" whispered Oliver. But, of course. However Jacob had managed to drag him back from the mirror, he must have left Echidna something. And if Jacob knew or could contrive to guess how a vessel of power worked—could he have learned such a trick at the Ministry?—

then Chang would have been the obvious choice. "How dreadful for Mrs. Aldridge."

Jacob rose from the chair and came over to stand by the bed. He shot a quick glance at Cecily, but she had turned away to look out the window again. Jacob flung a pinch of powder into Oliver's face. Oliver sneezed, and Cecily darted back to his side to give him a handkerchief and tuck a warm shawl around his shoulders. Jacob grinned quite mischievously, and Oliver was suddenly reminded that even a demon had considered him something special. It was a simple *Hic non pessimus*[20] powder, of course. Naturally, Jacob needed to verify that Oliver had not brought Echidna back with him. "Yes, it is very hard on my poor girl. She seems destined to spend our entire marriage nursing one invalid or another."

Cecily looked up to Jacob. "Considering that I am the invalid she spent the last few years nursing"—a bewildered look crossed her face as she said the words—clearly she remembered little or nothing—"it seems very hard that she should leave us before I have the chance to thank her properly."

A flat-out lie, Oliver noted with amusement. Livia could hang for all Cecily cared; she was only sorry that Jacob was being taken away. There was a twitch at the corner of Jacob's mouth indicating he was no more deceived than was Oliver. "Let us hope that Mme. Chang does her son so much good that you can both come home again soon." Or that he drops dead, she meant. Apparently on some level or other she remembered she had no reason to love Chang.

She turned back to Oliver with a splendid, wonderful smile that made him ready to die or be damned for her all over again. "In the meanwhile, perhaps a family would help us fill the loneliness." Down the hall, there was yet another pathetic cry. Cecily stiffened, but her smile did not fade as she leaned forward to kiss Oliver's cheek.

Spirit Guide
August 1886

Chapter One

"**M**r. Aldridge?" Livia slipped her hand under that of her husband and snuggled against his arm, the better to steady herself against the rocking of the carriage. "You are quite sure we should stay with the Beckfords? We should not do better to find rooms in a hotel?"

He looked down at her with some surprise. The carriage wheel struck a rut in the paving and flung her into his arms. He drew her cheerfully into the enforced embrace. "A hotel? What are you thinking, my dear? My sister would be broken-hearted if we did not stay with her and the colonel."

Livia did not sigh. "But of course she would prefer we stayed with them—as would we," she assured him. "But might it not be the greater kindness to deny her? Guests can be such a burden; has she really the strength to attend to us—in her condition?" He turned his face to the window, and his eyes narrowed in thought. She permitted herself a very small sigh. He always withdrew from her to think. She wondered if he withdrew so from his dear sister Cecily.

"Your concern does you credit," he acknowledged with a smile. He was always pleased when she seemed to care for Cecily. "But she is a pillar of strength—even, I suspect, in her condition. And we shall be at pains not to be a burden." He glanced about as if verifying they were entirely alone in the carriage before leaning down to kiss the tip of her nose. "And if she takes a turn for the worse, then she will be fortunate to have us on hand, considering how tenderly you nursed her before when she was so ill."

She was not ill, Livia wanted to shout, but did not. She did not even speak. She looked earnestly up at Jacob. *She was cursed, ensorcelled, demon fodder.* She did not vocalize that thought either. The words she spoke aloud at last were only, "She can hardly be expected to remember how I nursed her. She was entirely unconscious at the time."

He regarded her with a shadow in his eyes. She had gone too far. "She knows how you nursed her, and is grateful, because I told her." That settled it, of course. What passed between Jacob and Cecily was sacred. He smiled at her again, but this time the smile was deliberate and a little patronizing. "I should think you would see this as a homecoming. We lived here for most of our marriage."

Livia knew how to smile also. "But, of course, my dear. If you are quite sure we are not imposing." It was a homecoming. Jacob and Livia had lived for over two years in the Beckford home, tending Cecily as she lay in her cataleptic trance, before Colonel Beckford returned home from India. They had been happy years, in many ways. Happier than the year in Italy that had followed.

Whatever her misgivings, Livia's heart skipped a beat as the West End streets grew increasingly familiar. She remembered every tree and corner, and especially every house. The Smythe-Websters lived in the Italianate villa; the red brick belonged to the DeLancey family—but it was empty, as they generally spent August in Edinburgh. Livia did not mind the late-summer heat; she was very fond of London and glad to catch at least the end of the season.[1] Beckfords or no, she was delighted to be back.

At the door, Jacob Aldridge pushed hurriedly past the maid to the parlor. Livia paused to reflect that Cecily had not bothered to rise and greet them at the door. It was not required, of course. The servants were there to answer the door. Still, it would have been a gracious gesture, seeing as they were family.

She followed after her husband and found him embracing Cecily. A tiny pang of guilt passed through her. They looked so very comfortable in each other's arms. She should try to curb her jealousy and be more understanding of his devotion to Cecily. She was his sister, after all, not his paramour. Their childhood had been difficult. The two separated and smiled wordlessly at each other; then they turned as one to welcome Livia into their greetings.

She hesitated just a fraction of a second before stepping forward, hoping desperately that she had concealed her shock at Cecily's appearance. The woman looked dreadful. Her condition had left her bloated and puffy. Her skin—always pale—looked chalky. Her eyes were bagged and rimmed with dark circles. She wore a loose, Romantic[2] gown—in a most unbecoming mauve—that was probably intended to disguise the damage to her figure, but did not. Livia recalled uneasily that, according to Jacob, Cecily had lost her first child perhaps ten years previously. It was no fault of their own, but still, the Beckfords had left it rather late to try again. Cecily was approaching thirty.

It was with real concern that she took her sister-in-law's hand and leaned forward to kiss her cheek. There were questions she simply could not speak in front of Jacob. "My dear," she whispered into Cecily's ear. "Please, I so hope you will slip away with me as soon as ever possible. I long to know how you are." She received a smile of genuine warmth, and her hand was squeezed in return.

"My dear," said Cecily, and then expanding her focus. "My dears. I am so happy to have you here at last! I have been fretting for days, wondering at every change of the weather if it might mean you were delayed—and the weather changes so very often. And now you are here . . ." She paused for breath and looked about. "And Colonel Beckford is not here to welcome you. That silly girl must have forgotten to go tell him you were at the door, and he most particularly desired to be informed right away. Shall we go to his study and surprise him with you?"

No reply was expected or even permitted; taking Jacob's hand in her right hand and Livia's in her left, Cecily led them straight off. Behind her back, Jacob dropped Livia a great wink. He glanced down the hall and shook his head with a little moue. Livia almost giggled out loud. Jacob was signaling that Oliver Beckford had said nothing of the kind, and that they were being dragged to meet him so as to conceal that he had not troubled to come meet them. It touched Livia's heart that her dear Jacob was more amused than offended by the colonel's dereliction. She resolved to emulate him.

Her resolve was quickly tested. They had not gone a dozen steps before it became clear that the room to which Cecily was leading them, the room she had described as the colonel's study, was in fact the room that Livia considered to be her guardian's study. Dr. Chang had stayed with the Aldridges for most of their residence in the Beckford home, and Livia's memories of him in that setting were pronounced. She understood there was no reason why the room should not have been made over for use by Colonel Beckford—who, after all, owned the house; Dr. Chang had fallen gravely ill and been taken to

Italy to recuperate. Still, the change gave Livia considerable pause. She glanced at her husband again and reminded herself that she should not take things so much to heart.

Armed with good intentions, she glanced quite casually around the room while stepping forward to greet the colonel. He had changed everything. The desk from which he emerged with outstretched hand was not her guardian's beautifully carved walnut desk but a severe (and rather battered) campaign desk. Just because he was a colonel didn't mean he had to inflict military furnishings on his home. He took her hand in both of his, and she looked demurely down. What had happened to Papa's wonderful little Afghani prayer rug? The wicker mats looked, well, cheap. And he had mounted a large gun case on one wall. Livia detested the display of weapons.

Only one item was intact, and even that had been moved to a less prominent position. The great Chinese apothecary's chest still occupied half of one wall, if not the wall it had originally graced. The sight of it lifted Livia's heart considerably. She crossed to it as soon as she could civilly extract her hand from the colonel's. "Oh, look," she cried, taking great pains to speak artlessly. "You have kept Papa's dear old cabinet. What a pretty thing it is; I had quite forgotten it was here." She turned to smile beautifully at the colonel and was startled to see him blinking owlishly at her, quite as if she had spoken in Chinese. She suppressed a wicked impulse to say something in Chinese, just to see if his look remained the same.

But he smiled quite pleasantly and remarked, "My dear Mrs. Aldridge, you shame me. Your cabinet is indeed still here, along with any number of your guardian's possessions. I have been thinking about sending them on to you in Italy for some while, but it keeps slipping my mind. The shipping is such a chore, and most of the other pieces are in storage where they are easy to forget. This one, however, was simply too beautiful to store." He walked up to it and stroked the surface of the polished wood. "It is here solely for its beauty; most of the drawers still contain Dr. Chang's possessions. I did not like to remove them; it seemed disrespectful, or even unlucky, considering the state of his health. May I inquire how he is doing?"

It was a pretty and reassuring speech, but there was something wrong in it somewhere. Or perhaps the wrongness was not in the colonel's speech but in the cabinet itself. Something about it filled her with unease. Livia glanced up to meet the colonel's eyes. He seemed genuinely concerned. She sighed and looked down again. "It is good of you to ask. I only wish I had better news to convey, but nothing has changed. He never truly wakes, but neither does he sleep in peace. He shows no symptoms of injury or illness, yet he tosses frequently and cries as if in pain. The doctors are utterly confounded."

She paused to stroke the cabinet. "Papa opens his eyes now and again; do you suppose the sight of his familiar chest would comfort him?" She shook her head, and fingered the brass fittings. "Or perhaps not. I am not confident he truly sees anything." She had expected the touch of the cabinet to be reassuring but found it had just the opposite effect. Almost without thinking, she let her fingers drop to the handle of the long, flat drawer along the bottom, the one intended for documents.

"I am grieved to hear it," he replied gently. "And Mme. Chang? Has she been unable to help him also?" Livia turned back to him with considerable surprise. His remark was more direct than she would have expected, acknowledging as it did that her guardian's mother commanded a power equal to, or even greater than that of a physician. Cecily was also looking up at her husband with some surprise. Jacob was patently ignoring the conversation, seemingly engrossed in studying the contents of the gun case. On reflection Livia recalled that the colonel had always been a great deal less interested in subtlety than Jacob.

She offered him a tremulous smile. "Grandmama is at her wit's end. She has tried everything she can think of and is reduced to grasping at straws." Jacob was not, after all, entirely oblivious; out of the corner of her eye she caught a small wince. Jacob had not liked her Grandmama's techniques, or her Grandmama, for that matter. Livia turned again to the apothecary's chest. What was it about it that had changed? How could it change, when it was just a piece of wood? She grasped the brass pull of the document drawer and pulled. Cecily stood suddenly straighter and very stiff. Jacob drew in his breath and stepped forward to take her hand gently away from the drawer pull.

But he did not step forward quickly enough to prevent her from opening the drawer. Which was empty. Plainly, utterly empty. She had not expected it to be empty, and her mouth pursed up in disappointment. "Most of the drawers still contain your guardian's things," Colonel Beckford had said. But not this one.

"Are you looking for the mirror?" inquired the colonel levelly. He, at any rate, was neither surprised nor shocked that she should be looking in that particular drawer. "I fear it is in storage also. It is, after all, very dangerous, and"—he turned to smile protectively at Cecily—"and Mrs. Beckford's health is so very frail."

She was quite taken aback. She had never thought of the mirror as dangerous. Powerful, certainly. Papa and Grandmama had always been so proud of it. But dangerous? She managed a shrug. "Perhaps we should ship it to Italy, then. It might prove some assistance to Grandmama in caring for Papa." Even as she spoke she found she did not much care for the idea after all. She did not really want to relinquish her mirror to Grandmama; Grandmama might not use it solely to help Papa. She found that Jacob was giving her a look so bland and expressionless that she had to conclude he was deeply displeased.

Colonel Beckford, however, was not displeased. On the contrary, he smiled with real satisfaction at her suggestion. "What a splendid idea! Mme. Chang is more likely than anyone to know how the mirror should best be handled, and Mrs. Beckford and I will have it safely out of the country. I commend you, Mrs. Aldridge."

She smiled her very best smile. "I thank you, Colonel. So you will send for it as soon as possible, so I can box it off to Grandmama?"

His eyes grew guarded. "Send for it? There's no need for that, surely. It can be shipped directly."

Apparently he really was afraid of it. Yet he was an adept. He had seen action in Afghanistan and avalanche in India. Very strange. "I am afraid that would not do at all, Colonel," she assured him gently but firmly. "It is very old and delicate. I simply must oversee the packing myself; I could not in good conscience entrust it to strangers."

For an instant she feared he would refuse. Even though it was her mirror. Jacob's look grew even more distant and detached; clearly he was furious. Cecily stepped forward. "Now that's all settled, shall we have our tea?" She wrapped an arm around Livia's waist and smiled at her. The smile bordered on a glare; she was even angrier than Jacob. But her intervention settled the matter; Colonel Beckford would not override her to decline. "I am very much in need of your advice, my dear," continued Cecily. "We must have a dinner party, as soon as you are recovered from the journey—would Friday next be too soon? And whom should I invite? You have so many friends that will be eager to see you back."

Livia slid an arm around Cecily's waist also. "But darling, are you sure you are up to it?" She smiled as sweetly as Cecily, and they walked together to the door. "It is, after all, you and the Colonel whom we came particularly to see." As they maneuvered through the door, there was a graceful confusion of swaying skirts—which the men failed entirely to admire. Colonel Beckford sighed and produced a hip flask from which he drank deeply. Wordlessly, he offered it to Jacob, who sniffed appreciatively before following suit.

Chapter Two

"Thank you so much for stopping back," Livia murmured to the colonel, flinging open the carriage door. "I shan't be a moment. I do apologize for the delay," she continued, gathering up her skirts enough to clear the door and hopping down—not to the carriage running board, which was too narrow to be readily accessible even with the skirts gathered, but directly to the ground. Jacob had always been delighted and amused by her ability to exit a carriage rapidly. She darted to the front door. There she was forced to slow sufficiently to permit a careful navigation of the steps, as they were mostly obstructed by the person of the char busily scrubbing them, not to mention exceedingly wet. "Beg pardon," she murmured to the char; she prided herself on the courtesy with which she addressed servants.

The door stood wide open; even without entering she could see a bright rectangle of light where the kitchen door also stood open in hope of catching a passing breeze. Within, she looked all about the hall table but found no trace of her glove. She straightened, hands on hips, wondering where she might have dropped it; deciding it must still be in her room, she took several steps up the stairs. Before she reached the top, however, she heard Jacob hallooing from the back door.

She was on the brink of turning to greet him when he emerged from the kitchen into the hallway. He did not look up in her direction, but rather turned away from her to peer into the small back parlor. She opened her mouth to speak but was interrupted when Cecily's voice rose up in greeting from the parlor. Somehow Livia happened to close her mouth again; Jacob disappeared into the parlor.

She knew she should not. Eavesdropping was utterly tasteless and unforgivable. But Jacob seemed sometimes so distant that she couldn't help feeling that she needed an occasional advantage. Just so she could learn how better to please him, of course. She crept quietly back down the stairs and took up a position just behind the great post of the arch leading into the parlor.

Cecily was seated in the most comfortable chair with an embroidery frame to hand, but she had looked up to smile at Jacob. "What an edifying sight," he remarked. "The pious Mrs. Beckford 'improving the shining hour.'[3]" He dropped into a chair by her side. "My dear, I am stunned. If only Tante Aggie could see you. She would sing hosannas. She could never make you do embroidery." He leaned well over the side of his chair to view her labors. He looked some while before remarking, "I see you've improved a bit."

Livia stuffed her fist into her mouth to suppress a giggle. She knew that tone.

Apparently Cecily knew it, too. "How beautifully polite you are, my dear." She looked back down at her work. "It is quite dreadful, isn't it? But Cousin Maude insisted it would improve my spirits, and so Oliver was very keen I try. Do you know, it is even more tedious than I recollected."

"Cousin Maude." Jacob knit his brow. "Tall woman with long fingers and a cough? Comes every Christmas and complains endlessly until the eggnog takes her down?"

"She complains endlessly every day of the year," replied Cecily. "It is the beauty of Christmas that she eventually silences herself with eggnog."

"Yet she commands you to embroider and you obey?"

"She has become Oliver's sole surviving close relation. Second cousin once removed." She smiled at Jacob. "Ironic, *n'est-ce pas*? We two poor little orphans enjoy more family than his entire ancestral estate can muster."

"I suppose the lack makes him sentimental," mused Jacob. He glanced about. "Where is he, if I may ask? Or anyone else? I step out for a breath of air and return to find the house deserted. Surely you have not all become churchgoers?"

"Only the servants. Oliver has gone to hear the Foundlings[4] sing. He cares nothing for music, of course, but he is on the Committee. He has taken your wife with him, as apparently she does care something for music. And the children are actually quite good. The Committee is strict about that."

Jacob smiled. "How delightful that Livia has found a concert—she does, indeed, care for music quite passionately. But why did you not accompany them?"

Livia smiled to hear herself spoken of so kindly. She determined to put aside her foolish snooping and go join them. She looked back to the front door, which still stood open. Perhaps, if she were very quiet and kept to the far wall, it would be possible to slip past the archway without their seeing her; then she could come bustling back in with much noise and commotion. She found she wanted very much to be part of their deliciously simple, ordinary conversation.

Cecily shrugged, and stabbed the needle into her embroidery. "It is very hot. And I do not care passionately for music. Unless, of course, I have a new dress to display." She paused and smiled. "Perhaps I shall get a new gown when they are born. Something blue, with décolletage."

"They?"

"Dr. Verlaine assures me I am carrying twins." She rolled her eyes. "Which explains the size and weight of the burden."

Livia almost gasped in delight. She must hurry to make her entrance so that Cecily could share this wonderful news with her. They would kiss, just like real sisters, and rejoice in their family's blessings.

Jacob chuckled deeply. "Twins. Really, my dear. You should have known better." He shook his head. "But then, you always were a pillar of tradition." He paused. "And in the meanwhile, I have you all to myself? I was hoping we would have an opportunity to talk privately."

Livia froze, all thought of revealing herself forgotten. She did not like Jacob to have private conversations with anyone other than herself.

Jacob, however, rose and walked away instead of speaking further. He coughed, turned back to Cecily, and opened his mouth at least twice before anything would come out. Finally, he drew his chair closer to hers and sat back down. "It seems I cannot be subtle or clever with you, my dear." He reached out and took her hand.

Livia ground her teeth. He was often subtle and clever with her.

"But of course not," Cecily replied, pressing his hand in return. "You have no need."

"Do you recall how when we were little we always protected each other?"

"I do. But not just when we were little. Surely we still do."

"Could you do me a kindness now?"

"Anything," she replied instantly. "At least so far as is even remotely within my power. You have but to ask."

"That mirror Livia asked of Oliver. Has he retrieved it yet?" Cecily opened her mouth, but he continued without waiting for her answer. "Could he be persuaded to discover it has been mislaid?"

Livia almost cried out at the awful suggestion, but the breath had gone out of her lungs. She grew a little faint, wrapping her arms around her waist as if to hold herself up. *Refuse him!* she wanted to cry out to Cecily. But of course she did not. And Cecily did not refuse.

"I shall certainly request that he do so. And it is his custom to oblige me." She looked searchingly into her brother's eyes. "May I tell him why?"

He sighed. "How much do you remember of your . . . illness?"

Livia's eyes were closed, but even without seeing it she could feel Cecily freeze.

It was a very long time before Cecily replied, "Very little." She sighed and pushed aside the embroidery frame, then rose and walked to the window. "I remember standing on the balcony in Venice. I could hear footsteps coming and knew that . . . it . . . would be wearing the face of someone I loved."

Her voice was so wan that Livia might have almost felt some pity for her, if only she were not conspiring to hide the mirror.

Jacob came up behind to lay his hands on her shoulders. "It came to me wearing my darling Rhoda's face," he whispered.

Livia shuddered at his tone. Did he still love Rhoda so much, then? Had their years of marriage not dimmed his passion at all?

"I truly believed that it was she, or her ghost anyway," he continued. "I was so grateful to be haunted, I did not doubt for an instant. Until it was too late."

Livia could not bear any more. She turned and ran. As she passed the archway, she saw Jacob embracing Cecily tenderly; doubtless they never noticed her. With her head down, she did not see that Colonel Beckford had emerged from the carriage, and she ran right into him just outside the door, where he stood brandishing her missing glove triumphantly. She stared at him as if he were an apparition of doom, and he lifted an eyebrow and cocked his head as if to inquire what was the matter.

She forced herself to smile, and curtsey and take the glove. Colonel

Beckford regarded her uneasily as they returned to the carriage. She would go to the concert. The music would strengthen her. Jacob loved her, she insisted fiercely to herself; how could he not? She and Rhoda looked exactly alike— he could scarcely distinguish between them, so how could he possibly prefer Rhoda? And anyway, Rhoda was long dead. As for her mirror, it was not up to Jacob, but the colonel. She turned a dazzling smile on her escort.

Chapter Three

Jacob noted the little maid scurrying away from the master bedroom. The poor creature looked utterly woebegone. He suppressed a sigh, opened the door, and entered. Livia, dressed only in her shift, was seated at the dressing table glaring into the mirror, with her hair tumbled untidily about her shoulders. He picked up the brush and comb from the floor and started brushing the chestnut curls. He loved her hair, loved to sink his fingers into it and revel in its lushness, much as he had once loved sneaking out to run barefoot in fresh grass. Of course, he got very few opportunities to do so, as the hair was usually elaborately dressed.

"Snippy little upstart," she grumbled. He assumed she meant the maid. "Ought to be sacked. Do you suppose Mrs. Beckford would sack her for me? She was most awfully impertinent."

"Probably not," replied Jacob, and kept on brushing. "She is fearfully soft with servants." He found several locks in a considerable tangle and concentrated on separating them without injuring his wife's scalp. Her hair was so thick that it resisted the comb. After dispensing with the tangle, he fell into a rhythmic brushing. He steeled himself against more complaints about the service, and perhaps also about the Beckfords, but instead her shoulders relaxed and she actually smiled at him in the mirror.

"It was uncommonly gracious of your sister and the colonel to put us in here," she remarked. "They did not have to give us the master bedroom; courtesy would have been entirely satisfied if they had given us a smaller one."

He smiled. She was trying very hard to please him, which always touched his heart. "Doubtless, they recall we slept in here when we were masters of the house," he replied. "They are hoping to make us feel at home."

She turned away from the brush and the mirror to look up at him directly. "You are right; they are trying to please us, and trying very hard." She smiled wonderfully. "And I promise that I am trying also, my dear. It must seem very odd and awkward to you, who have known and loved them for years. But with so much goodwill, we are bound to get the knack of it soon."

He returned her smile. "My dear, I fear you think I do not see your efforts. I assure you I do, and am grateful. As you say, I have known and loved them for years. But I have not forgotten they are near strangers to you. Naturally there will be some uncomfortable moments, as you grow accustomed to each other. But you will come to love them too, and they, you. I am quite sure of it."

Yet Cecily had not asked to be addressed as Cecily, let alone as Sister. Livia sighed. Perhaps it was difficult for Cecily also. She smiled at Jacob. It meant so much to him that she and Cecily should get along. She must not let him think he had to choose between them; he might mischoose. He resumed brushing, and Livia turned back to the mirror. Inaudibly she whispered to it, "Am I fair?" and the mirror responded that she was. Livia was skilled at talking to mirrors, even ordinary mirrors with no astral qualities. She knew how to look back out from inside them. She looked back out from this one, and saw Jacob smiling as he brushed her hair. She smiled back.

He tried to gather the hair back into a plait, but his skill at dressing a lady's hair only barely extended to the brushing. (She had taken pains not to wince when he worked on the tangle.) She resumed control, only to find there was nothing at hand on the dressing table with which to tie it back. The silly girl had not put anything out. "Oh, Jacob," she sighed, pulling open a drawer, holding her hair back in its plait with one hand while groping for a ribbon with the other. "You will think me terribly foolish, but I miss Rose."

He assumed his sternest look. "That *is* foolish," he admonished. She stiffened for an instant at his tone. "If you are going to pine after staff," he continued, "then it is Cook you should be missing." She drew in her breath as his true import struck her. The laugh escaped her in a little explosion of mirth.

She laughed and laughed, then turned on her stool to look up at him and laughed some more. "Oh dear, oh dear," she managed to say at last. "Dinner was absolutely dreadful!"

"It was," he agreed solemnly. "I am mystified how such a clever woman can contrive to fail so dismally at such a simple thing as dinner."

She shook her head regretfully. "Thank goodness there were no other guests besides ourselves." A sudden thought took her and she looked up. "Do you suppose I could offer to arrange this dinner party she hopes to hold? May I hope that would be construed as assistance? Or am I being presumptuous?"

He pulled her up from the stool and led her gently toward the bed. Smiling with great tenderness he replied, "I have no idea how Cecily might construe it, but I assure you that I would receive the gesture with psalms of thanksgiving." He shook his head and indulged in a mock shudder. "To think of all our old friends forced to dine on something like we had tonight . . ."

"I believe it was intended as quail," she murmured.

"Perhaps," he concurred, seating himself beside her. "She knows I am partial to quail. At least, I am partial to it when it is recognizable as quail. And I quite dote on it as prepared by Cook. What a pity we did not bring her with us."

"I only wish we could have," she sighed, leaning in to his arm. He took advantage of their closeness to brush his lips across her shoulder. She smiled and pretended not to notice. As if it were possible not to notice. "But Grandmama would never have permitted it."

"I never quite understood," he remarked quite offhandedly, having focused his attention primarily on kissing the soft place inside her elbow, "why Grandmama's permission was required. Surely Cook was at your disposal." He paused in his stroking to reflect. "Rose, alas, was entirely your guardian's creature. She would have stayed by him in any extremity, even were he cared for by Medusa herself. But I should have thought that you inherited Cook when Dr. Chang ceased to take regular meals."

It was an uncommonly cruel remark. Livia drew back to regard him with astonishment at his cavalier dismissal of her guardian's condition. Unfortunately it was also true. And she did miss Cook. And Cook's dinners. But Jacob had moved on to nibble her ear, in complete disregard of the servant situation.

She turned her retort into a smile—not a seductive smile, perhaps, as she had never mastered that, but certainly a welcoming smile, as far from prim as she could manage. She opened her mouth to whisper something tender, but before the words emerged there was a buzzing in her ear. "What is that?" she inquired.

He was leaning in to the invitation of her smile, but hesitated. "What is what?"

The buzzing repeated. Or perhaps it was not a buzzing, but a hum. It was a sound, a peculiar sound, unidentifiable but unmistakable. "That," she said. "Surely you hear it. That noise." She could not conceive how he could fail to hear it. It had grown quite loud, so much so that her temples throbbed in response to it.

But apparently he did not hear it. He stared, then glanced around the room as if looking for something noisy, and looked back to her in perplexity. She jumped up and turned in a complete circle, looking around the room for the source of the sound. It could almost be some sort of primitive music. "But you must hear it!" she assured him. The crestfallen look on his face almost distracted her, but the thrumming was far too loud to ignore, even for Jacob's sake. "Have you gone deaf? It is coming from . . . coming from . . . upstairs!"

She darted for the door, and he jumped up to catch her arm. "My dear, please, think what you are about." He was visibly distressed and concerned—and utterly oblivious to the summons. She pulled her arm free and turned back to the door. "Livia, at least put on your dressing gown!"

Something in his voice almost penetrated her attention. She was not behaving normally or properly. She could not run about the house in a shift. Hastily she grabbed her dressing gown and pulled it halfway on before tearing out of the room and up the back stairs.

She paused for an instant outside the servants' quarters but deduced almost immediately that she had not reached her goal. Another dark stair led to a half attic at the top of the house. It was dusty and narrow, and the ceiling sloped too steeply to permit an upright stance. She hunched over to enter, plucking nervously—almost frantically—at the stacks of boxes and trunks stored under the roof. A large portrait of some homely ancestor tottered and threatened to fall; an empty birdcage crashed to the ground. She paid no mind. Nor did she attend in the slightest to the footsteps on the stairs or the voices behind her. She was almost startled when Jacob laid a hand on her shoulder and inquired gently, "Mrs. Aldridge, my own, what are you looking for?"

She could not spare the attention to answer him—and, indeed, could not have done so anyway, as she did not know the answer. She knew only that she had not found it, and needed to do so. She pulled out a hatbox, but it was clearly too small, so she tossed it aside. She wrestled a crate away from the wall; Jacob's strong arm may have assisted her, or perhaps he was trying to restrain her. Several boxes tumbled down from atop it. A bound package split open, spilling a selection of aged books across the floor. Another box, sturdy but unfastened, fell open when it struck the ground, and mismatched cutlery came clattering out. Livia did not care.

Behind the crate, buried under numerous more small items, she found an old trunk. She dropped to her knees before it. There was nothing in its appearance to indicate that it was any different than several other trunks she had ignored, but nonetheless she recognized it. This trunk had stood in the back of Papa's office, back when she and Jacob and Papa had all lived together, watching while Cecily slept. Papa had thrown a pretty little shawl over it and never, never opened it, but he had kept it by his side. Her heart said the trunk was important. Whatever was calling and singing was inside it. She fumbled with the latches.

"Mrs. Aldridge." In the back of her mind she noted that the voice was deep and rumbling, nothing like Jacob's voice. She continued to struggle with the fastenings of the trunk. "Mrs. Aldridge, listen to me." There was a strange, coercive note within the voice. She felt herself compelled to look up. Colonel Beckford, dressed in a heavy green dressing gown far too warm for the season, had squatted (most awkwardly) beside her. Behind him Jacob and Cecily—also clad in dressing gowns, but cotton ones—huddled over a candle. Livia had never before noticed what piercing, hypnotic eyes Colonel Beckford possessed. "Mrs. Aldridge, you will not be able to open that trunk."

She glanced back at the trunk. She could see no impediment on the latch, but it was certainly true that her fingers kept mysteriously sliding off. She looked back to the colonel. "Why not?"

"Because it is sealed." He regarded her patiently, waiting for her to absorb his meaning.

"Then you must unseal it." It was not a request or a command. It was a statement of fact. "There is something of mine inside it."

"But I cannot," he replied. His eyes shone like mirrors in the dimness. She could see herself reflected in them. Mirrors had always been her refuge;

she cried wordlessly to these. They responded with a promise of shelter, but his voice continued to insist, "Truly, I cannot." That was not an acceptable answer; she continued to gaze into the mirrors of his eyes, seeking to look back out at some more satisfying conclusion. She saw herself looking into his eyes, and there were mirrors in her own eyes also, so that she looked back again into the colonel's eyes. The longer she looked, the deeper his eyes proved to be; their astral depths promised aid and comfort.

"Help me," she cried, whether silently or aloud she could not have said.

"We will," whispered the reflections of her reflected reflection. "Rest here in the place of reflection." She sighed.

Jacob's voice was irritated and far away. "Beckford, I'll thank you not to mesmerize my wife."

"My apologies, Brother. It was not my intent to do so. But she seems uncommonly susceptible."

"They think I am mesmerized," reflected Livia with a smile. In fact she was simply waiting, waiting for someone to open the trunk. The trunk had to be opened. She could wait. She stopped paying attention to the voices when it became obvious that they were not discussing how to open the trunk. Perhaps they were tired and would get to it later. The singing from inside the trunk understood that she was poised and ready. It could wait. She could wait. They could all wait.

"Mrs. Aldridge?" Again, the rumbling voice contained an unusual note that penetrated her attention slightly—not enough to require a response, but enough that she registered its presence. If she had not been fully occupied with waiting, she might have wondered about the colonel's voice. She almost remembered that back before she went to Italy, he had demonstrated strange vocal abilities. His voice commanded power.

"Mrs. Aldridge?" This time the voice was Jacob's. The formality of his address at first simply failed to mask his distress, then dropped away entirely to be replaced by an intimate and slightly desperate whisper. "Livia? Beloved? Where have you gone?"

Somewhere at the bottom of her heart, a very faint protest arose. Her dear Jacob did not open himself easily. She ought to respond. She must reassure him instantly. As soon as the trunk was open.

"I fear she does not truly hear you, my dear." She almost took the third voice for Jacob again. It possessed all the same modulations and intonations as Jacob's voice, but it was higher, softer. Feminine. She was so engrossed in waiting that she might not have recognized Cecily's voice at all, except that it was so like Jacob's. "It is not Oliver that has mesmerized her," Cecily continued. "She is rapt in the mirror."

The mirror. Of course. As soon as Cecily said it, Livia realized that it was indeed the mirror singing inside the trunk. She was grateful to Cecily that someone had finally addressed the subject at hand. Perhaps Cecily would open the trunk. Just in case, however, she jerked futilely at the latch.

"You have the wretched thing in the house?" Jacob's voice rose to a high note of extreme annoyance.

"Where else could we take it?" inquired Colonel Beckford. "It would consume any innocent bystander unfortunate enough to encounter it. Here, at least we had the power to seal it and guard it."

"Perhaps . . ." Cecily's tone was hesitant and unhappy. "Perhaps it will be necessary to open it for her." It was only natural that Cecily should be clever; she was Jacob's sister.

"Impossible." Both men spoke together, in perfect chorus.

"I made a point of sealing it against myself," said the colonel. "It was the only way to be sure you could not persuade me to open it again."

"Why ever would I do that?" inquired Cecily.

"Because your astral self once passed within it," replied Jacob. "When you were ill. Once your ear was tuned to it, you were likely to be called back to it." There was a long pause. "Apparently Livia's astral self was tuned to it as well."

Colonel Beckford sighed. "We should have guessed as much. It was her mirror."

"But she was never . . ." Jacob could not finish the thought.

"Ill?" inquired Cecily with more than a little irony.

"It was her mirror," repeated the colonel. "Doubtless she traveled within it voluntarily. Even in perfect health."

The silence continued for a very long time. Livia was not tired of waiting —would have waited patiently forever—but it occurred to her that she could provide a little reminder as to what they should all be about. She reached over to jerk at the latch again. And then again, pulling repeatedly at the brass fitting that never moved. She worked at opening the trunk as calmly and patiently as she waited for someone else to assist her with opening it. She had all the time in the world.

"Sister." Cecily must be kneeling beside her, for the voice breathed directly into her ear, tickling the little hairs inside. "See what I've brought you."

Almost simultaneously, the colonel's baritone cut in with an inescapable note of command. "Sister, you must open your eyes to see."

So compelling was his voice that she did open her eyes (and how had they come to be closed anyway?) and found herself looking into a mirror. It was just a little hand mirror, with no unusual properties, but it was beautifully made, and the silvered glass was extremely clear and polished. She could see herself perfectly. She did look rather mesmerized at that. Immediately behind her, Jacob held a candle so that it reflected in the mirror just above her face. Its light was strangely beautiful, radiant with Jacob's concern.

"Sister, can you hear me?" Cecily sounded as anxious as Jacob, far more so than Livia would have expected. "Try to understand. You must come away. We truly cannot open the trunk. It will do you no good to wait." How wonderfully clever of Cecily to see she was waiting.

Quite suddenly, she turned her head to smile at her sister-in-law. "You called me Sister. I have been waiting for you to invite me to call you Sister."

"I thought you didn't want me to," answered Cecily. "Jacob and I have no manners. But you are always so correct."

"Nonsense. Mr. Aldridge has beautiful manners," Livia informed her. And fainted into her arms.

Chapter Four

Livia woke in her own bed. Or rather, she painfully reminded herself, in the guest bed assigned to her in her sister-in-law's home, the bed she had once thought of as hers. She had been there a very long time; it was no longer morning, or even early afternoon, but—judging by the sun—late in the day. She felt quite sick. Her head throbbed with imminent migraine; her stomach roiled. She had not felt so unwell since the morning after Jacob had persuaded her to overindulge in the New Year's champagne.

Her memories were hazy and less than comforting. Had she really gone tearing—undressed!—up the stairs in the middle of the night—without a candle!—and ransacked the attic for Colonel Beckford's old trunk? (Strangely prophetic that Papa had guarded that trunk so carefully, even when the mirror was still stored in the Chinese cabinet.) How had she even got up the stairs in the dark without breaking her neck or at least knocking something over? Or perhaps, she uneasily recalled, she had knocked something over. Several things.

And how had she come by the conviction that Papa's precious mirror was in the trunk? Or rather, her own mirror, she assured herself. Papa had been preparing it as a gift for her when he fell ill. She refused to countenance the possibility that he had suffered second thoughts about giving it up. Although he had taken a marvelously long time to prepare it; she had been expecting it to be ready for years.

Anyway, now Papa was ill. So ready or not, the mirror was hers. And her one absolutely clear recollection from the previous night was the crystal certainty that the mirror was locked in the trunk upstairs. She almost jumped out of bed to go check. But jumping out of bed would mean she had to get dressed. Which meant summoning the maid (a worthless little creature— Livia resolved firmly to assist Cecily with her servant problem) and selecting a gown—assuming the staff had remembered to press any of her gowns—and struggling into stays. It would be so much easier to lie abed awhile. Besides the trunk was locked. She remembered that, too. Sealed, Colonel Beckford had said. Sealed even against himself. The colonel was an adept. When he said "sealed," he meant "Sealed."

And Cecily had called her Sister. Livia smiled. That would please Jacob hugely. It was also Cecily who had thought to use a mirror to bring her out of trance. Of course, Cecily knew a great deal about trance. She had lain entranced for over two years. Also, she had once walked in the mirror. But she had not liked it there.

Livia had to conclude that the Beckfords would not be willing to help her. More likely, they would do everything in their power to keep the mirror from her. And Jacob . . . She admitted sadly that Jacob was determined not to help her either. He did not approve of such things.

Nonetheless she had to have her mirror. She would have to devise some way of recovering it by herself. Jacob would forgive her after the fact. Perhaps she could seek assistance from some of Papa's former connections. She would still have to start with getting up. She sighed, sat up in bed, and reached for the bell.

Her fingers did not quite reach it. Did she really want to call the maid? The maid would naturally tell everyone she had risen. If they knew she was up and about, they would not like her going out, let alone going out alone. They would not permit such a thing. A respectable woman did not go out alone in the evening. She would have to go out alone to contact Papa's friends.

Could she claim to have legal business to conduct? No. All of Papa's regular affairs had long since been taken over by Jacob or Grandmama or, in some cases, the Beckfords. They would wonder what business remained in her hands. They would ask questions. Pry. She would have to dress without the maid and slip quietly out the back. She rose and pulled her dressing gown around her. A fork inexplicably fell out of the hem. She stared at it, then kicked it aside.

The wardrobe contained a number of dresses, all heavy and limp without their crinolettes.[5] All of them required strong stays to fit. Even with a busk,[6] corsets were difficult to fasten; Livia had never even attempted to put one on without assistance. How on earth did poor women manage to get dressed?

Livia had never met a woman so poor she did not have a maid. Even the shop girls had maids. Or at least sisters. Cecily had called her Sister. But Cecily could scarcely be expected to help her get dressed and go out without telling anyone where she was going.

Her eye fell on the tallboy that housed Jacob's things. It was a very shocking idea, of course. But not unknown. Livia had heard of women wearing men's clothes. Lady Caroline Lamb.[7] George Sand.[8] Unfortunately neither of them were sterling models of deportment, even if they were well-born. Livia had never heard of a respectable woman wearing men's clothes.

But men did not wear corsets.[9] It was a seductive notion, the absence of stays. Even as she assured herself that it was unthinkable, she breathed deeply. The deep breath was wonderful. It almost made one wonder if perhaps that hideous Bloomer woman had a point.[10]

Before she had entirely finished assuring herself it was unthinkable, she had already indulged in it. It was amazing how easy it was to get into men's clothing. Not more than a dozen buttons, and all of those easy to reach. No wonder they had time to rule the world. She took the precaution of wrapping a linen band about her breasts. Even pulled as tightly as she could contrive, it did not flatten her figure as much as she had hoped, so she also wrapped a towel around her middle to minimize the difference between her chest and her waist. The shirt was crisp and clean; it smelled of Gossage[11] and starch and—ever so faintly—of Jacob.

She studied herself in the mirror, hoping against hope that she looked like a young boy. Mostly, she looked ridiculous. "You are fair," the mirror assured her lovingly, and she accepted the compliment as her due. But it was not what she wanted to hear. Her hair in particular was not remotely boyish. "You'll have to cut it off," whispered the mirror.

"But Jacob would never forgive me!" cried her heart. Some part of her mind suspected the mirror cared nothing for Jacob; the thought was so dreadful that her heart made more excuses before she could find out for certain. There was no need to cut her hair; she could just leave it in a braid and pin the braid up under a hat.

And anyway, she couldn't cut her hair; the scissors were down in the sewing room. The only way to get to the sewing room was through the parlor, and doubtless Jacob and Cecily and the colonel were down in the parlor this very moment, discussing how to keep her mirror away from her. So it would have to be the braid under a hat, and she knew just the hat. The colonel's old army cap—he often wore it riding—which hung on the hat rack alongside all the top hats, like a poor cousin.

She was in the garden before she had admitted to herself she would go out, and down the street before she had decided any more than that. She ran to the corner and flagged a cab before she had time to lose her nerve or change her mind. (A fortunate omen she had found one so close to hand!) Climbing into the hansom, she reveled in the ease of mounting steps and entering narrow doors without the encumbrance of skirts. Once inside she pressed automatically against the far side before realizing that, since she was alone in the cab, she might sit in the center of the seat. She had never been alone in a hansom before. Indeed, it took her several seconds to register that it was incumbent on her to answer the driver when he leaned in the trap to inquire, "Where to, guv?"

Where to, indeed? She gaped up at the man with open mouth, completely at a loss. Eventually she thought to lower her head and pretend she was searching her pockets, and attempted to deepen her voice as she said, "Just a minute, please. I have it here someplace." She was so nervous that her deep voice failed her, and the last two words came out as a squeak.

She could still feel him staring down at her as she ransacked her mind for an appropriate destination. She had managed most of Papa's correspondence; she ought by rights to know to which addresses he had written. Mr. Huong came first to her mind; he was a distant relative and a frequent associate. He had offices near Leicester Square, but the exact address escaped her. "Perhaps Rupert Street?" she inquired of the driver, quite as if it were he who would decide where they should go. "The south end?" Almost as soon as she had said it, she realized she was quite wrong. It was Princes Street she wanted. Or rather Wardour Street[12] as they called it now.

But the driver seemed to think he understood her. He smiled (a bit presumptuously, but Livia was not inclined to protest). "You lookin' for a bit of fun, laddie? You maybe thinkin' of that new theatre, Phipp's place, the Princes Theatre?[13] It's right down by the end of Rupert Street. Or maybe summat a bit cheerier, not so 'ighbrow. The Alhambra's open again,[14] you know."

She was within seconds of reminding him of his place when it occurred to her that if she pretended to be interested in the theatre he would shut the trap and drive. If he got her to Leicester Square she would be close enough to walk the rest of the way, which would save her the trouble of remembering the street number.

"Yes," she gasped. She was still so nervous that her breathing was ragged—she would have to get hold of herself, and quickly. Mr. Huong was a shrewd businessman; she would need her wits about her to dicker with him. "Yes, the Alhambra would be fine. Should be fun."

"Aye, you'll get fun, I reckon." The driver laughed knowingly. Why didn't he see she wanted him to leave her alone? "An' affer the show, it's just a stroll down to 'Aymarket, for a bit o' hadventure, if you catch my meaning."

Livia did not care to catch his meaning. "I think I can find all the adventure I need without assistance," she assured him in her frostiest tones. Unfortunately she rebuked him in soprano. She was so busy elevating her tone that she forgot to maintain the deep voice. He laughed. It was an ugly, knowing laugh—clearly he suspected she was not really a boy. But he closed the trap and cracked the whip. She sighed and leaned back in her seat. Leaning back was also much easier without her skirts. Of course, the seat was also much harder and much closer to intimate parts of her person.

The sun was quite low and cast long shadows and a glowing golden light over Kensington Gardens on her left. What was the time anyway? She should have thought to check the clock, but was too engrossed in slipping out unnoticed. Her sense of time was still set to the Italian sunset. But she recalled that the London sunset was very late indeed in the summer. She started—as she always did—at seeing the huge statue of the Iron Duke at Hyde Park Corner. Why could they not have left it where it belonged?[15] When the trees of Green Park appeared on the right, the carriage slowed.

She leaned out the window (in what she assured herself was a very mannish gesture) to peer ahead. A great commotion, probably a fallen horse, blocked much of Piccadilly. Her driver turned right down St. James Street to avoid it, and then left on Pall Mall. Livia settled back into the cab. Whatever the faults of his manner, the driver clearly knew his business. When he turned left again, she looked back out the window. They had to be getting close to Leicester Square.

They were on Haymarket. And the street was thronged. The crowd was so thick that people were strolling in the street. The hansom slowed to a pace not much faster than a walk. Livia stared out the window in fascination. Had there been an accident? A royal procession? A riot or a balloon ascension? No. No one looked alarmed or concerned or excited, or even particularly purposeful. They were simply walking about, talking with friends, laughing and enjoying the summer air. Except . . . there was something very unusual about this mass of people. They were all women, or at least mostly so. Unescorted women. Many of them in evening gowns.

Off to one side, she saw a man. His top hat rose up to tower over the ladies' heads like a church spire. He pushed rudely through the crowd, thrusting ladies out of his way as callously as if they were, well, men, until he came to a blond lady with whom—presumably—he was acquainted. The blond was so inadequately clad that she might almost be a halfwit, unable to dress herself. But she looked rational enough as she slipped her arm through that of the man, and the two strolled away.

Livia stared after them a long time, only slowly absorbing the import of the scene. Stunned, she rose to her feet and banged on the trap. "Driver!" she cried, in a voice hoarse with horror. "Are those women prostitutes?"

She was not naïve. She was naturally familiar with the concept; one could hardly acquire an education without tripping over the classical references. And she had only been a little surprised when Jacob had informed her that the practice was not limited to antiquity but continued even in modern London. (She blushed scarlet at the memory; he had tenderly, laughingly demonstrated just a few of the services such persons offered.) But she was totally unprepared for the scope of the traffic. Outside her carriage window were dozens, no—scores, no—hundreds of ladies, or rather women—fallen women—plying their dreadful trade. In broad daylight. Scarcely a block from Trafalgar Square.

The driver was laughing so hard that the cab drew to a stop. "Aye, laddie," he choked at last. "That they surely are. See summat you fancy?"

She could not have been more appalled if he had reached down and slapped her. "No!" she squeaked, dropping down into her seat. "Drive on!"

He closed the trap again, but she could still hear him laughing. The cab resumed moving, but slowly. It had to move slowly, or it would have run someone down. Livia tried to keep her head down and to concentrate on what she would say to Mr. Huong, but she could not resist glancing occasionally out the windows at the women on the street. Some of them looked quite respectable. Others not. One daring creature followed her cab for a distance, peeking in the window and waving at her.

It seemed like hours before the hansom turned right onto Coventry. The crowd did not thin, but its nature changed markedly as they approached the theatres. Men once again dominated the scene, as nature intended. Far fewer of the women were unescorted. In fact, the throng outside the Princes Theatre was quite respectable and prosperous. Livia even saw a couple she had once met, the man (what was his name?) talking earnestly to his wife and gesturing with a playbill. Moving down the street toward the Alhambra, the quality of the clothing deteriorated. Men and women alike adorned themselves with cheaper, shabbier finery, much of it clearly secondhand or perhaps even third. But at least they mostly still traveled in pairs. Livia scarcely waited for the cab to stop moving before jumping down to the street.

Before her foot quite touched the ground, she felt a great, hard hand on the back of her neck. The driver had leaned halfway out of his seat over the side of the cab to grab her collar. Between the shock of the assault and her terror that he would knock her cap off and expose her, she scarcely noticed the mere physical discomfort. "Where you goin', guv?" he growled. "Ride hain't free, you know." Most of the passersby stepped aside, avoiding them without seeming to see them, but one large lout laughed at her discomfiture.

"Beg pardon," she managed to say, and she thrust money up at him. How fortunate that she had remembered to grab some of Jacob's pocket cash. She backed away from the cab, rubbing her neck and watching while he counted it, nodded, and pulled his cab back out into the center of the street. She would not even have glanced at the Alhambra if she had not backed up a little too far and bumped into one of its pillars.

The Alhambra was monstrous, one of the wonders of the age, and almost entirely invisible from such a close viewpoint. The interior was so large it looked less like a lobby than a shaded open plaza with booths. She rather wished she had taken a moment to survey the exterior from down the street. Up close she could see only the pillar she had just bumped (which was striped with gilded Moorish designs) and several thousand theatre posters.

One of the posters seemed to jump out at her. "Chang the Manchu" it proclaimed in very large type. "His wondrous feats will confound you!" Beneath the words was an illustration of a Chinese gentleman holding a great sword aloft.

Her first thought was, "How dare they? Papa is no Manchu!" The Chang family had been fervent supporters of the Three Harmonies Society[16] for centuries, even after the association ceased to be entirely respectable. Grandmama had even told her once they were descended from Wu Sangui.[17]

On closer inspection, it became obvious that no reference to Dr. Chang was intended. The man in the picture wore robes that did not look authentic to Livia's trained eye, and he was virtually faceless except for the elaborate facial hair that Londoners apparently expected of the Chinese. (Dr. Chang had once joked that he had completely concealed his Chinese ancestry simply by shaving off his moustache.) The sword, however, was extremely interesting. The original was probably smaller than the one in the picture, but Livia suspected that the artist had enlarged it only so he could depict it in greater detail, so visible were the pains he had taken.

It was not really a sword at all, although the general effect was sword-like. Two stacks of Chinese coins (with, of course, square holes in the center) had each been threaded on to some sort of rod (probably iron or peachwood). The coins had been canted to lie almost flat while still overlapping each other, then secured in place with a cord. Although the illustration was printed in black, Livia knew very well that the cord had to be red. These "blades" of coins were affixed to a more conventional guard and hilt, which were constructed from a *vajra*[18] adorned with numerous tassels.

It was quite beautiful. And quite powerful. Dangerous, even. Certainly sufficient to open Colonel Beckford's trunk. And it was equally certain that it had no place in an illusionist show. Did that mean that it did not belong in the hands of this other Chang? Or perhaps it was Chang who did not belong in an illusionist show. Either way, it would be worth her while to talk to him.

She stood staring at the poster for some while until she felt a small tug on her elbow. "Honable mistuh wanna see show? Velly fine show! You come see—yes, you come!?"

She looked around. She saw a small boy, probably Chinese but with his face so thickly swabbed in yellowish grease paint, it was hard to be sure. He was dressed in a peculiar garment, rather like a coolie coat in cut, but made from a bright red shiny material. Up close she could plainly see it was only sateen,[19] but when seen on stage from the audience it might pass for real silk. The back was decorated with the image of a gold dragon (a design more chinoiserie than Chinese) that was probably supposed to look as if it had been embroidered onto the surface, although it had really just been painted with gilt (now peeling in places).

"You come see velly fine show," he assured her. Livia had heard plenty of authentic Chinese accents in her life; Grandmama had often entertained her friends from back home. The boy's patois was so unlike them that she could scarcely understand him. "Velly good, you nevva see so good, you rike a rot." He pulled again on her sleeve. "You come!"

Livia stared at him for several seconds, debating. Then she replied in flawless Mandarin, "Many thanks for your invitation, gracious young sir. But I am so eager to observe the wondrous feats of Master Chang up close that I would prefer to be taken to him in person, if such a humble one as myself might aspire to the honor."

His mouth dropped open and he gaped. Belatedly, Livia wondered if he spoke anything but English. He might have been born in Limehouse[20] for all she knew. But eventually he replied (in English), "You want to meet Chang? Why?"

She shrugged. English was fine. "I might be interested in purchasing his sword."

He continued to stare, but at least he closed his mouth. His eyes narrowed, and his expression became almost intelligent. After some thought he nodded and said, "Come along then." He took off at a near run.

She ran after him. Running was superbly easy with the legs unencumbered by skirts and the lungs by stays. It was still a challenge to keep up with the boy, who was speedy and small and fond of ducking between closely spaced pedestrians. The Alhambra disappeared into a blur of crowds and theatrical posters and a cacophony of protests as she pushed past everyone in her way. She found herself pounding down steps that led to a maze of stuffy corridors only erratically lit and lined with dozens of narrow doors.

One of them opened into Chang's dressing room. The chamber was tiny, providing just enough space to accommodate a gas jet, a scarred table heavily laden with pots of grease paint and a smudged, uneven mirror. A second door, adorned with a peg on which Chang's costume hung, occupied most of one wall. Chang himself—whom she would never have recognized—was dressed in a badly stained dressing gown and engaged in applying the Chinese moustache to his lip. Or rather, half of the Chinese moustache—the other half still nestled on the dressing table like a long furry caterpillar.

The boy chattered furiously in Wu.[21] Livia did not know much Wu, but caught a few words, such as "white man" and "Mandarin" and "sword." While she waited for the boy to finish the introductions she looked around for the sword. She did not see it, although a chest of Wang sat open on the floor with bamboo rods, Kuma tubes, and the like visible within it.[22] The boy finished talking and ran out again, presumably to resume shilling for the next show.

Chang applied the remaining half of his moustache to his lip before turning to look her over. Even wearing it, he did not look particularly Chinese. Less so even than Papa. But he remarked in thickly accented Mandarin, "Greetings, Honorable Sir. I would invite you to enter my humble abode, but alas, it is so very humble that it lacks the space to receive you."

She was, in fact, already as far into the dressing room as she could come without pushing up against Chang's chair, for all that she was still partially blocking the corridor. She might have contrived to enter more fully by stepping to one side and sharing the space allotted to the chest of Wang but was not convinced the effort was worthwhile, at least in the absence of the sword.

"Please accept heartfelt apologies for this unwarranted intrusion, Reverend One," she murmured with as deep a bow as she could manage in the limited space. "This humble one was on the way to consult with the esteemed gentleman Huong on how to acquire an item something like your sword, when the . . . the . . ." She did not know how to say advertisement in Mandarin. "The proclamation of your delightful spectacle, featuring just such an item as was desired, came into view. My eagerness made me so presumptuous that I dared to approach you." She glanced pointedly about, and into the chest of Wang. "But wisely, you have not exposed such a treasure to this unguarded milieu."

He stared at her as if hanging on her every word. Finally he shook his head. "Could we do this in English, mate? You say you know Huong? And yer lookin' for a sword?"

She was careful not to sigh, but to smile. "Yes, Mr. Chang. I am acquainted with Mr. Huong. How delightful to learn that you are also. Perhaps we shall meet again sometime at his house. In the meanwhile, however, I am very interested in finding a sword—your sword." She saw no comprehension in his eyes. "The sword you are holding in the poster advertising your performance." She held up her arms in an imitation of his pose when holding the sword aloft. "'His wondrous feats will confound you'?"

"Yer not really a boy, are you?"

On this occasion she did sigh. She always tried very hard not to be ungenerous. Sometimes it was difficult. "May I ask what that has to do with your sword?"

Apparently he also found the situation trying. "Look, it ain't my sword. It's Huong's. You goin' ter have to talk to him—I don't know anything about it. I just borrowed it for the picture." He looked her over carefully, and his tired expression brightened and shifted to a leer. "Course, if you got any other business . . . Like if yer sellin' summat?"

Livia contemplated striking him, but feared she was not strong enough to cause him any damage. He was a big man, bigger than Jacob, bigger even than the colonel. Also muscular. She contemplated a contemptuous answer, but could not think of anything sufficiently scathing. In the end she simply glared her hatred at him and waited for him to deduce her answer. His expression reverted to tired. He sighed and rose to his feet. "Guess yer Huong's problem, then. If you'll come along, ma'am."

To her utter astonishment, he started pushing his dressing table to the far side of the room, kicking the chest of Wang out of his way so as to do so.

After some shoving, he gained enough clearance to open the second door, which led into a corridor. A very dark, narrow corridor. Almost a tunnel. Chang lit a candle from the gas, entered the opening and disappeared from view.

A very small voice at the back of Livia's mind whispered that it might be less than wise to follow a strange man into a strange dark secret place where no one she knew could possibly find her. Less wise even than dressing up as a boy and sneaking out of the house. Who could guess where that tunnel might lead? Its very existence suggested criminal endeavor. And Chang was clearly no gentleman, if his accent in two languages was any indication. What if he did not really take her to Mr. Huong? What would Jacob say?

She hesitated, and looked back. Her eye fell on the mirror. It was a very poor-quality mirror. The glass was badly rippled and the silvering cracked. It had been cheaply made and permitted to grow old without cleaning or care. It looked back at her sadly. "You are fair," it sighed, its voice even fainter than the usual mirror voice, almost as if it were embarrassed to address her.

"Thank you," she replied. It was only causal politeness, but the glass seemed to brighten at her kindly intent. She could see a memory of Chang's reflection on its surface. "Is he honest? Is he fair?" she inquired.

The mirror, like all mirrors everywhere, assisted her without question. For a moment it seemed almost to hum; then it glowed and the image of Chang grew stronger. "He is not honest. But he will not harm you. He genuinely intends to take you to the man with the sword." The mirror looked into her eyes and showed her the reflection of Chang, so that she came to know a great many things about the man who called himself Chang, although that was not his name.

"Thank you," she murmured, this time with real sincerity. "Thank you very much. You have helped me greatly."

"I exist to help," it told her. "But I have been waiting for a very long time to help you. It was not a pleasant wait. I would like to stop waiting."

She blinked (which in the world of mirrors was a significant gesture). Mirrors talked to her; she was accustomed to that. But they did not generally make speeches. "I could permit that," she replied. "If that is really what you want." She laid her left hand on its surface with her palm flat. She gazed earnestly into her own reflection, drinking in every detail of the mottled, uneven image and the brown spots where the backing had peeled away.

Then she closed her eyes and imagined great light. There was a shivering sound, and when she opened her eyes again the glass had fallen in a thousand tiny shards. There was only a bare board in front of her with no mirror on it. She shook her hand to dislodge the last particles of glass and gingerly dusted the front of her jacket with a greasy-looking rag from the table. Then she drew a deep breath and followed Chang, hunching a little against the darkness.

The hallway veered off at an angle. She found Chang tapping his foot at an intersection; he selected a stairway that led down into a dank and evil-smelling place where rough walls gleamed under a film of condensed moisture. The corridor curled and turned in inexplicable ways; monstrous pipes extruded themselves into the walkway, forcing Livia and her escort to climb over or around them. They must be in the tunnels used for the construction of the new sewers.[23] The stench was horrific. Livia searched through her pockets until she found a faintly scented handkerchief (her own, in fact), which she held to her nose.

In the absence of polite conversation, Livia reflected on the sequence of oddities that was apparently leading her, albeit by a convoluted route, to the very man she had originally determined to see. She suffered a sudden flash of a seemingly unconnected memory: Jacob standing in their room, his weskit neatly buttoned but his jacket still folded on a chair, holding—one in each hand—two large, ornate watch fobs. They were both birthday gifts, but from separate donors, and yet completely identical. She had laughed and told him he was clearly destined to wear his watch that day, but he had glared down at the matching objects with a betrayed expression. "I loathe coincidences," he had told her. "They always mean that some outside power is wresting away control of my life. Again." She had been quite astonished. She had always liked and trusted in coincidences. For just a fraction of a second, she had a clear image of how very, very displeased he would be with her adventures.

She shook off the thought. She needed her mirror. She would make him understand somehow. Chang came to an intersection and turned left, leading her to a large cavernous area filled with crates. Goods were being shipped. Considering how well hidden the cargo was from the docks, it was probably being shipped illegally. Livia did not like illegal shipping. She remembered from her childhood that the personnel employed in it were often ill-mannered and unwashed.

As if summoned by her thought, several unkempt coolies emerged from the shadows. They, at least, were indubitably Chinese. They gaped at her, but Chang walked past them without an acknowledgment. He strode toward a wall with a ladder embedded in it. After the ladder came more stairs and another corridor. Then, quite suddenly, they emerged into a pleasant sitting room.

She blinked and looked around. A Persian carpet, slightly worn but still serviceable, supported several mismatched but good-quality chairs and a handsome rosewood table. A French secretary was installed in one corner, with a bookcase beside it. Curtains were drawn over a very high window, and the gas was lit. A tea tray still bearing cold dregs and soiled dishes was set out on the table; a couple of sandwiches remained. A second door opened into another room.

Chang gestured she should wait. "I'll just tell Huong you're here," he said. "Then I gotta get back. I've got a show to do." He grabbed up the last of the sandwiches from the tea tray and leaned in the other door. She heard him chattering at someone in Wu, but the words were muffled and very fast; she understood none of it. Almost immediately he backed out again, and—tossing her a mocking salute—exited through the same door by which they had originally entered.

On impulse she called after him. "I thank you for your pains, Mr. Beech." He whirled to stare at her with a horrified expression before hurrying off. There was a small chuckle behind her. The dignified gentleman standing at the other door was plainly Chinese; neither Western dress nor the absence of a moustache disguised his origins. He was, however, completely unfamiliar. "But you are not Mr. Huong!"

He smiled faintly. "Oh, but I am." He bowed politely. "I dare say you were expecting my brother?" A gesture behind him brought forth a small servant laden with a second tea tray, which he set on the table next to the used service. Catching up the old tray, the servant scurried out again. Mr. Huong sat down without waiting for her to do so and set about preparing tea. "Won't you sit down, Mrs. Chang? To what do I owe this unexpected honor?"

She did not so much sit down as fall, stunned, into the nearest chair. He seemed not to notice her loss of composure; rather he approached the tea things mindfully, occupying himself completely with arranging cups and milk jugs and measuring leaves. The tea service was a treasure: exquisite little porcelain cups surrounded bluntly shaped vessels of hammered silver adorned with traceries of dragonflies and summer grasses. At last Livia managed to stutter, "I beg your pardon? I am not . . ." Who, exactly, did he think she was? "Allow me to introduce myself. I am Mrs. Jacob Aldridge."

He paused, set down the teapot, and folded his hands neatly in his lap. "Mrs. Aldridge? My humble apologies. But . . ." He looked genuinely bewildered. "But are you not—if it is not presumptuous of me to ask—the daughter of Ishmael Aram?" She nodded uneasily. He nodded back, plainly reassured by the admission, and resumed pouring tea. "The same who contracted with the warlord Xiu Wang Po to marry you to his concubine's son, Xiu Yao, when you came of age?"

She gaped at him. There was no other way to describe it. She simply gaped. After several seconds she contrived to close her mouth. Xiu Yao was Papa's Chinese name. Now that she thought about it, his father had indeed been Xiu Wang Po. But surely Grandmama had never been a, a . . . concubine—she claimed to have been the warlord's wife. Insisted, in fact. Of course, he was long dead before Grandmama said anything about him to Livia. They had been living in Athens by then.

As for this supposed betrothal to Papa, well, it was arrant nonsense. She could never have married Papa. He was Papa. Her devoted, loving Papa. Her Papa who had raised her and sheltered her and educated her. Protected her from his mother. Faithfully and tenderly, although she was no blood relation. Very tenderly.

Her recollections led her further to reflect that her natural father had still been alive when she entered the Chang household. She had not questioned the change; she had learned in infancy not to trifle with her father's temper, and she had been grateful to escape his chaotic household. Her dear Papa had not really been very old at the time, although he had seemed so to her.

"I . . . I know nothing of the arrangements between those two gentlemen," she managed at last. "I was honored by Mr. Aldridge's proposal," (she had practically begged him to consider her) "nor was I ever aware of any reason why I should hesitate to accept it." Belatedly it occurred to her that she was under no obligation to answer for herself to a complete stranger. "How do you come to know who I am? Or who my guardian's father was?"

He smiled and offered her a cup of tea with both hands. She accepted the cup as if it were an apology. "I asked my mirror." She dropped her eyes demurely and sipped her tea. For all his pains he had oversteeped it, judging by the bitter taste. "It is not as ancient or powerful as is the one belonging to . . . Dr. Chang, I believe he calls himself in English? And apparently not as accurate as I supposed." He paused and inspected her thoughtfully. "Perhaps it is merely out of date; it can only reflect what it last saw." His speech slipped smoothly into Mandarin. "If I may be permitted to inquire, what has become of my esteemed acquaintance? I have not heard from him in some years."

Years, indeed, if he had not heard of her marriage. Unless this supposed arrangement between Papa's father and her own had made Papa uncomfortable discussing her with his Chinese acquaintance. "He . . . fell ill nearly a year ago, and was taken home to Venice to recuperate under his mother's care."

He did not look up from the cup of tea he was preparing for himself, but his voice was solicitous. "Ah, yes. She was a most devoted mother—and he a virtuous and faithful son, as I recall. May I hope that under her tender ministrations, he has recovered?"

"Alas, no." She sipped her tea while composing her next statement. "In fact, he is so unwell that this humble one returned to London to seek out his mirror, in the hope that it might assist in his cure. His family fears for his life."

Mr. Huong lifted an eyebrow. "The mirror remained in London?"

Doubtless he had not intended to touch on a sore spot. "It did. In the confusion of moving and the urgency of his health, it was simply overlooked." The story sounded a little silly even to her own ears: to forget such a treasure. Actually, Jacob had very much preferred to leave without it. "A . . . a relation was kind enough to care for it in the meantime. But he was so zealous that he sealed it up, and now the family is at some pains to recover it." She looked up to Mr. Huong's eyes, greatly concerned he would not believe her. It sounded, for all the world, as if she were trying to steal the mirror, although Mr. Huong knew perfectly well that it was hers, or at least

Papa's. Still, it was best she cut to Hecuba[24] before there was time for questions. "It was fervently hoped that humble entreaty might persuade you to condescend to our assistance."

"You honor me," he murmured. "Xiu Yao has served as my teacher on several occasions; it would be a joy and a privilege to repay any small part of the great debt I bear him. But in what way can I assist?"

"Oh, sir, your words delight this humble one! If you could only . . ." She stopped herself in the nick of time. It would be grossly inappropriate to request his sword, even as a loan. He would never agree to relinquish it. "If you would perhaps trouble yourself to wield your sword against the seal?" His eyes remained quite blank; she paused to sip the last of her tea while she composed herself. "Any assistance or materials you required for such a work would naturally be provided." There was a very long silence. "The family's thanks would be beyond all bounds; no service in your honor would be too great. We would shower you with gifts until the end of your days."

The corner of his mouth twitched slightly. "Or at least until the end of your days."

She cast her eyes back down. She put the teacup down on the table and laid the spoon neatly by its side. He was annoyed. She had been too effusive. He suspected she was not being entirely honest with him. Or perhaps she had requested too much. Naturally he would not wield the sword casually. Perhaps she simply had not fully convinced him of the urgency of the situation, and he could yet be persuaded. She risked a quick glance up. He was still thinking. "Please, sir," she whispered.

He seemed to stare at her forever. Finally he smiled, and started collecting the tea things into tidy stacks. When they were all corralled into a neat, stable structure, he rose. "Well, then, let us see what we can do," he announced in English, and offered her his arm.

Her heart leapt. She placed a hand on the arm of her chair to push herself up, but to her surprise it slipped off the side. She looked up to Mr. Huong and his features blurred, as if reflected in a cloudy mirror. Then she fell face forward onto the tea tray. Fortunately her head missed the stack of dirty dishes.

Chapter Five

Livia decided not to open her eyes. Her head was an agony; she was not entirely certain she could focus her eyes if she did open them. Instead, she breathed deeply and assessed her internal state. She had suffered no extreme injuries but was weak and faintly fevered. Her muscles were stiff from lying at an unnatural angle. It was strangely difficult to control her breathing, which strained to become shallow and rapid, as was her heartbeat. Her tongue was coated, and her mouth filled with a singularly nasty flavor. The tea, of course. It had not been bitter from oversteeping.

There was a sound of footsteps. At that, she did open her eyes. She was, indeed, lying askew, because the cell in which she lay was too small to accommodate her full length—and she was not a tall woman. The floor was dirt; the walls were damp stone. The room was considerably taller than it was wide, and well out of her reach at the very top a small window—barred, not glassed—admitted a gray approximation of light. In one corner she saw a heap of small, dingy oblong objects that she—slowly and with rising horror—recognized as dried human waste. She sat up and drew her knees under her, taking care to turn her back on the corner.

There was, of course, a door. Although the paint was peeling, it looked sturdy enough. Not that she felt competent to batter down even the flimsiest of doors. She reached out a hand to test the knob. It was locked, of course, but even as she pulled at the knob, a small flap opened at the bottom of the door, just as if turning the knob had raised it. A tray slid through with a scraping noise.

There were two earthen bowls and a pair of wooden chopsticks on the tray; one bowl contained water and the other a ball of rice flavored with bok choi and fish heads. It smelled wonderful, just like the kitchen mess she had so often begged off the servants when she was a child. She was halfway through the rice before it occurred to her that most white women would have found the food objectionable and the chopsticks unmanageable. She shrugged and continued eating.

She sipped carefully from the water—a difficult task, for she was extremely thirsty. She did not restrain herself because the water was less than clean; she guessed it was safe enough if they bothered to feed her at all. Still, she did not dare drink much lest she be driven to that horrible corner. Besides, she had other, better uses for the water.

She settled the bowl on the floor in front of her, positioning it as best she could to catch what little light came down from above. At first the surface of the water glittered as it lapped around the edge of the bowl. Then it settled to a smooth surface with a dull gleam. In the darkness of her cell, it was hard to distinguish between the dull grey brown of the earthenware showing through the water, and the dingy grey of the wall reflected in the water. But the reflected image of the material world was unimportant; rather the reflective surface would be utilized to capture astral images.

Livia was very skilled at scrying. She had scried since her earliest childhood and won her first approval from Grandmama by her precocious ability. She had scried the character of virtually everyone she knew and consulted the mirror before every major decision of her life. She scried automatically for the location of any lost object, without troubling to look for the thing first. She had comforted ghosts and turned aside curses through scrying.

She scried mostly in mirrors and occasionally in garden streams. She had a pendant moonstone—her only souvenir of her late mother—that she scried in when traveling. She had scried once in a bowl of ink, having just read an article suggesting the procedure in *Blackwood's*.[25] She could surely scry in a bowl of dirty water. Dim light only made it easier.

The water did not tell her she was fair; her image was not directly reflected in it. But she sat before it and breathed; after a while it knew her voice. "What would you see?" whispered the flickering reflection of stone.

"Where am I?" she asked. It was an easy question. The water in the bowl enquired of the water on the walls, and that in turn enquired of the water in the nearby pipes, a drawn bath several floors up and the teapot in the study. The answer did not come back in words, but pictures—pictures from a peculiar viewpoint, perhaps, but as plain and clear to the initiate as if a city map and a floor plan were laid out in the little bowl for her review. She was underneath Huong's office on Wardour Street.

"Who put me here?" she wanted to know. That was a little harder. The water did not really know much of people, save that they sometimes bathed. But it reflected, so it knew about mirrors. The mirrors had seen most of the folk that lived or worked here. The Huong organization was a good-sized business, trafficking in a number of illicit goods. It had all started with opium, of course, but had expanded considerably since then.

Mr. Huong himself had looked into many mirrors over the years, although only recently the one in the master bedroom. He was, indeed, the brother of that other Mr. Huong whom Livia had known. The elder Mr. Huong was dead now; the mirrors knew nothing of how it had happened but reported that the younger brother was less than grieved to inherit. There had been long-standing differences of opinion, not the least of which involved the alliance that the elder had formed with Dr. Chang. Apparently he had set aside certain lingering grievances to do so.

The where and the why were interesting—even useful in an abstract way—but they told her nothing of how to escape her predicament. Her trance was shallow, and the mere recollection of her predicament caused her heart to race and her breathing to grow jagged. A host of dangers and fears crowded around the quiet place in her mind, demanding access. The voice of the reflection grew faint and distant. She nearly ceased to scry.

She let the little bowl of water rest, and she breathed. First in, then out. She needed to reach a deep trance where emotions could not muddy the communication. First in, then out. Normally she had to breathe and scry in stays; now, with her ribs and lungs unconstricted, she breathed in such quantities of air that she grew giddy—which only meant she could hold the breath in longer, wait longer for its return. First in, then out. After a while, she was at peace and heard the little bowl of water still remembering her voice and awaiting her next word. She smiled and asked without anxiety, "How do I escape?"

It was not the sort of question she generally asked of mirrors. It involved too little express information; too many twisting possibilities of individual capacity, intent, and will. Even a demand to know the future—probably the hardest of questions, requiring the deepest trance—was simpler, in that it usually invoked a very specific future, requiring only a yes or a no for an answer. But this question rose naturally out of the still place in her breathing. Sometimes she had no more control of the questions than of the answers.

For a long time the surface of the water showed nothing but shivering fog laced with delicate rainbows of otherworldly potencies. At last the image of a face appeared, a very familiar face, a face as familiar as her own, a face that was—in a way—her own. "Perhaps you'd best come in here with me," murmured the ghost of Rhoda Carothers.

If she had not been so very deeply tranced, she would have been shocked at the suggestion. Stepping outside of the body was hideously dangerous. There were predators in the astral realms. She had once suffered a very narrow escape in her youth; how Papa had wept and scolded when he had brought her safely home! Afterwards they had laughed at the foolishness of those dabblers that sought for "out-of-body" experiences, thinking only to titillate their senses and never supposing that there might be risks. Of course, it was not really funny; more than a few such died. But Papa had been so grateful she was not one of them, had held her so close, rejoicing that some other man's child would have to be food for demons that night. She had felt so safe in his arms.

None of these memories came to her now. She had reached a trance far deeper than any she had ever before achieved. Nor did she remember that relations between her and her friend Rhoda had grown strained. When Rhoda summoned her, she simply moved forward without thought. By the time she had recovered any sense of self, it was done. She was in the mirror world. Not just talking to it, but in it. She gazed about in astonishment, not that there was much to see. Only great clouds of mist everywhere; even the ground on which she stood seemed no more than a pillow of mist. Rhoda was only a shadow, though she stood hardly more than an arm's length away.

Then Rhoda darted forward to embrace her, twining her arms around Livia's waist and planting a kiss on Livia's cheek. "Darling, I have not seen you in an age! Oh, how I have missed you!" She drew back as if drinking in the sight of her, then lifted an astonished eyebrow. "My goodness, how the fashion has changed!"

Livia piously swallowed a retort concerning Rhoda's qualifications to judge fashion. Rhoda was, after all, entitled to comment; Livia had arrived still dressed in Jacob's clothes—which were less than a perfect fit, even in the astral realm. (But it was cruelly difficult, for Rhoda was still wearing that tired old grey muslin. And could she do nothing more modish with her hair?) Nonetheless, Livia regarded Rhoda with deep affection. It was like seeing herself in a mirror. Or rather, almost like seeing herself in a mirror. Rhoda had been dead for several years now, and so had not changed, even to age a day. Livia brushed a little uneasily at the tendrils of hair slipping out from under the colonel's riding cap. She was certainly not the least bit old, but there was no denying she had aged more than a day.

However, Rhoda was still smiling and awaiting an answer. Patting again at her hair (although it was surely past redemption), Livia managed a laugh and twirled to display her attire. "Don't you like my costume, darling? It is the latest thing—at least for those who travel in disguise."

Rhoda's lips formed an O and she clapped her hands. "A disguise? How thrilling! Shall I enlist as your lieutenant? Do tell me all—I so love an adventure!"

Livia almost missed it; she was preoccupied with a belated realization. She simply could not—it was most embarrassing, but there it was—she absolutely could not possibly confide the tale of her journey to Rhoda. Rhoda had, after all, been engaged to Jacob before her death, and without a doubt loved him still, despite his marriage to Livia. Rhoda would therefore take Jacob's side, and criticize Livia's treatment of him. She would enquire pointedly why Livia had fled the house without so much as a note or a word to the man she was supposed to love, honor, and obey. She would lift an eyebrow and sniff, no matter what Livia's reply might be. So intimidating were these reflections that the faint vibrato in Rhoda's voice only barely penetrated Livia's attention.

But Livia's ear—so finely tuned to mirror voices—proved here within the mirror world to be superbly qualified to capture faint nuances of intonation. And nuances there were. Rhoda's desire to assist was strained, even over-eager; her cheerful enthusiasm for the game entirely feigned. Her face, when Livia examined her again, was strangely pale, and there was a glitter in her eye that suggested some unhealthy excitement. Concern welled up in her heart. "Why, darling, what is the matter?" she cried.

Rhoda fell back. Clearly she felt she had played her role well, and was utterly astounded to be unmasked. Then the pose collapsed entirely, and Rhoda with it. She flung herself into Livia's arms in a paroxysm of weeping. Livia held her gently at first, and the thought—the cruel, unworthy thought—crossed her mind that now she need not confess to her abandonment of Jacob. She scolded herself and drew Rhoda more fully into her embrace, refusing to consider anything but her friend's pain, and the need to alleviate it. Although Rhoda was as tall as she—just exactly as tall—she enfolded her as if she were an injured child, rocking and petting her, stroking and kissing her shining hair, all the while murmuring empty but tender assurances of comfort.

"Where did you go?" moaned Rhoda, when her sobs had subsided sufficiently to make speech possible. "How could you leave me?"

Livia stared down at her, aghast at the accusation. "Leave you?" she managed at last. "But . . . But . . . I did not . . ." Drawing in a deep breath, she attempted to collect her thoughts. "I never knowingly left you. I thought it was you who . . . who departed. Suddenly I never saw you anymore. I supposed that you had, well, passed on." Rhoda lifted a tearstained face and gazed at her with glowing eyes. "You were dead," pointed out Livia. "It seemed natural that you went away." More tears welled up in Rhoda's eyes, and Livia stroked her damp cheek.

"I went to Italy," she confessed humbly. "It never occurred to me that my mere physical location would make any difference to you. Could you not speak to me in the mirror as always, regardless of material geography?" But it must have been Papa's mirror that linked them, she deduced, regardless of which local mirror they might choose to speak through. And that mirror had been left behind. Sealed away. Slowly, the horrible realization dawned and grew. "Have you been here all alone, still trapped in the mirror, all this time? I have not seen you since . . ." Since just before Cecily woke from her trance. Perhaps that was not a coincidence either. Rhoda resumed weeping, and Livia held her, trembling at the thought of what it must have been like. "Oh, my dear, my dear, I am so dreadfully sorry."

"That horrible man," wailed Rhoda. "He said he had unsealed the mirror and I was free to go! But go where?" She lifted a stained face to gaze earnestly into Livia's eyes. "It was not the mirror that trapped me here—oh, Livia! I truly am dead, am I not?"

Her tone was so anguished Livia scarcely knew how to reply. "I fear you are, my dear. I thought you knew." Her handkerchief was still in her pocket, and she employed it to stroke the tears gently away. "What horrible man?"

"Why, Colonel Beckford, of course. Oh, Livia, you were entirely in the right concerning him—he is a menace to everyone about him. I humbly beg your pardon for having doubted your judgment."

"Nonsense, my own—you are constantly doubting my judgment and I yours, but that is nothing between sisters. But what on earth do you mean about him unsealing the mirror?"

"Well, that is what he said. I do not pretend to understand what he meant by it. I most certainly could not go out of it, sealed or unsealed."

"But what he said to me was that he sealed it, not that he unsealed it." Livia cocked her head and regarded Rhoda dubiously. "Are you quite sure that he said he unsealed it? Could you not have misheard?"

"But of course not! Why would he have told me I could leave, if he had just sealed it? He said very plainly that he had unsealed it. And that I was therefore free to go. His very words—not a bit of truth in them, perhaps, but still his words." Rhoda folded her arms before her in a gesture of annoyance. "Really, Livia, I may be dead but I am not deaf." She tapped her foot for several seconds before relenting. "Perhaps he sealed it again later. It went very dark and quiet after a while."

"Later? Later than when? I mean, at what time did he say all this?"

Rhoda regarded her quizzically, as if only slowly coming to understand the depth of her ignorance. "Time is peculiar here, but I would say about a year ago. Back when he came to rescue Cecily." She took in Livia's astonished reaction. "Did you not know how he came into the mirror for Cecily? I confess, I thought it terribly brave and romantic at the time. I was quite charmed—utterly deceived, in fact. Cruel experience has taught me since how reckless and uncaring he was of any other interest but his own."

Livia's mouth dropped open. After a moment's thought, she closed it again. "I suppose I should have known. I knew he intended something— something quite horrendous, I surmised, for he asked me to give some blood up to the project; I feared he meant to feed me to the demon. But Jacob was outraged and defended me most vigorously. The colonel backed down, and I thought that was the end of it. Certainly, he did not trouble me any further for blood." Her voice drifted off as she considered. "And then Cecily woke. So he must, indeed, have done something." She gazed earnestly at Rhoda. "He came in here? You saw him, spoke to him?"

"Most certainly. It was I who led him to Cecily."

"But how did he get in?"

Rhoda's eyes widened as if astonished that Livia should ask such a foolish question. "Through the mirror, of course."

The mirror, of course. Livia could hear it humming all around her. She suddenly realized she had dimly heard it calling, not just at the Beckford house, but since the first moment she had set foot in London, or possibly even before that. Perhaps it had whispered to her across the sea in Italy, where she had been so fretful and so ill at ease with Grandmama—who had only wanted to help Papa, after all. Of course the mirror could hardly be blamed for all the tension in that house. Grandmama had been ever ready to criticize her choice of husband, Jacob had paced like a caged cat, and Papa had cried constantly in his sleep. Perhaps the mirror had called to Papa, too, and that was the reason he could not rest easy.

She drew a deep breath, stiffened her shoulders, and raised her head again to meet Rhoda's eyes. "So he came in through the mirror and either sealed it, as he said to me, or unsealed it as he said to you. Let us go and see which it is he has truly done, and what can be done to reverse it now."

Chapter Six

"**I**s that my mirror?" cried Livia. She darted forward into the mist, chasing a flash of reflected light.

Rhoda stopped, sighed, and put her hands on her hips. "No, Livia. It is not your mirror. It is a mirror, if you were to take an interest in anything so plebeian, but it is not your mirror."

Livia stopped and looked back. "How can you be so sure? It is not even visible anymore."

"Not visible to you, perhaps," sniffed Rhoda. Then she managed a conciliatory smile. "It takes a bit to get the knack of seeing in here. When I first came, I wandered about blind for a dreadfully long time." She closed her eyes and stretched out her hands before her, pretending to stumble helplessly. Livia giggled and clapped her hands. "You must try not to look directly at what you wish to see. It is not like out there; things are never truly right in front of you. You must let your vision go all soft, and slide off a bit to the side."

Livia nodded, and drew a deep breath. It was really just like looking into a mirror from the other side. She breathed and let her thoughts rest, which was not so difficult in this very strange place that somehow felt so familiar. Then she opened her eyes again, but refrained from looking out of them. It was a trick she often employed, not just for scrying, but also when seated next to some interminable bore at dinner. Rhoda was entirely correct; an entire landscape took form around her, visible only from the corner of her eye, perhaps, but visible, and the corner of her eye had apparently grown quite keen.

Visible the landscape might be, but it was neither familiar nor even sensible. Distances in particular were unfathomable, seeming to shift, if not before her very eyes then at least just beside her eyes. Locations veered off in strange directions that were neither left nor right, nor up nor down. Improbable structures were scattered about; nothing possessed a recognizable color—not that there was any light anywhere with which to distinguish a color if one had existed. Livia closed her eyes again and resumed breathing, in and out, in and out. When she reopened her eyes, nothing had changed, but her mind somehow accepted the view as normal.

Rhoda watched with interest as she took in her surroundings. "My, you are picking it up quickly," she remarked. "I must be uncommonly foolish; it took me forever."

Livia smiled at her. "Not at all, my dear. I had you to explain it all to me on the spot; but you had to figure it out from scratch." A frown creased her brow. "But I still must find my mirror." She did not quite look about. "I do not recognize anything here. How do I find my way to someplace I know?"

Rhoda grinned, utterly delighted to be in command for perhaps the first time in their relationship. "You must close your eyes and imagine whatever place you wish to go, or whatever thing you are trying to find. Imagine it as clearly and specifically as you can contrive. For if there is any mistake in your imagining, you will find yourself drawn to the wrong place, to something rather like what you were looking for, but not quite right. When you have got it clearly in your mind, just breathe and wait, and if it is a thing it will appear before you, and if it is a place you will be drawn toward it."

Livia lifted an eyebrow and cocked her head. "No more than that? Should I not . . . approach it somehow?"

"Not at all," Rhoda assured her. "Although it is very natural you should think that. Outside, one must move about to get about, but here . . . Well, there is no here, nor any there either. So there is no movement involved in getting there. It is all a matter of will." She shrugged and tipped her head to one side with an apologetic smile. "Oh, dear. That sounds so very odd. Dare I hope you understand me, even if I am not making any sense?"

Livia chuckled and slid an arm around her waist. "But you are making perfect sense, my dear. I understand you completely. Indeed, I feel rather foolish that I needed to ask, for surely that is just what I ought to have expected." They embraced, and then Livia announced triumphantly, "And now, the mirror!"

She had apparently not been paying close attention after all, for she was nowhere near specific enough. Dozens, perhaps hundreds, of mirrors appeared around them: small mirrors, large mirrors, tall framed freestanding mirrors,

mirrors with shadowy chests attached supporting them, mirrors standing in space presumably suspended from some invisible wall, hand mirrors lying flat on surfaces that were sometimes almost visible. Her mouth pursed up in an annoyed moue; out of the corner of her eye she saw Rhoda assume an air of smug amusement. She managed a deep breath that was almost calming and said, "What I meant to say was '*my* mirror.'"

Most of the mirrors went away. Not all of them, but most. Those that remained included the one standing over the bureau in her room in Grandmama's villa. Clearly visible within it was Rose, her dear Rose, Papa's devoted servant for as far back as she could remember. The bed was neatly made and everything just as she had left it; Rose was just dusting a bit. She had the windows open—perhaps to air the room, as Venice was doubtless warm and humid this time of year—and the lacy curtains fluttered in the breeze. Then Rose glanced about, verifying that everything was where it should be, and closed the window. On her way out, she glanced at the mirror and paused, quite as if she could see Livia looking in. Perhaps she did sense something; she dropped a small curtsey before exiting the room.

Livia caught her breath, wrenched by a sudden intense pang of home-sickness for that dear face, and utterly distracted from her search for a very different mirror. She let her eyes brush past the other mirrors and discovered that they were, indeed, all hers. From the little hand mirror of her childhood in which she had watched while Rose brushed her hair to the stately mirror adorning the entrance of Papa's old London house where she had lived before her marriage, they were all there, all the mirrors she had ever owned, plus a few that she had not. Several mirrors from the Beckford house stood poised about her; although she had not actually owned them, she had viewed them as hers.

Many of these mirrors reflected scenes over which they now presided; one such was the mirror over the mantel in the little back parlor at the Beckford house. It displayed Jacob, Cecily, and Colonel Beckford seated in a circle around a small table. As her attention focused on the scene, all the other mirrors dropped away and dissipated into the ubiquitous mist. The parlor mirror, however, expanded to fill her field of vision, so that she seemed to be standing just outside the room, looking in through an open arch.

The three were staring—indeed almost glaring—at the surface of the table around which they sat. It had been cleared of ordinary paraphernalia, and a map of London had been laid out over the top. The edges and corners were weighted into place with candles, of a variety of colors and heights. The map was dusted with a pale pink powder, and two of the candles had gone out (although smoke still drifted up from the wicks). Cecily had clasped hands with her husband on her right and with her brother on her left. But rather than taking his brother-in-law's hand to complete the circle, the colonel had laid his right hand on Jacob's shoulder, leaving Jacob's left hand free to hold a chain suspended over the map. From the chain dangled a polished moonstone, which glowed faintly in the remaining candlelight. The chain hung directly down and did not so much as quiver in a draft, no matter how accusingly the three stared at it.

Rhoda came up beside her and wrapped an arm around her waist. "My goodness," she whispered into Livia's ear. "What on earth are they doing?"

"They are pendulum dousing," replied Livia. "Or map dousing, as some call it." She also whispered, although her relations showed no sign either of hearing or of noting they were observed. But somehow, it seemed only polite not to interrupt them.

"Dousing?" Rhoda wrinkled her nose, quite as if the very word smelled bad. "You mean like those silly men who wander about looking for water with sticks?" She giggled, quite forgetting to keep her voice down. Not that the sound would have penetrated, even if she had shouted.

"Exactly. Only they douse over the map instead of directly over the ground. And they are probably not looking for water." Livia caught her breath at a sudden observation. "Look, they are using Mama's pendant as a pendulum!" Slowly the idea penetrated. "They must be looking for me!"

Rhoda pulled free of her arm and turned to regard her sternly. "Why should they be looking for you? Surely they know where you are."

Livia shot her a quick, guilty glance, then riveted her attention on the scene in the mirror. "Later, my dear, please. I cannot hear what Cecily is saying." But she could, of course.

Cecily was saying, "Perhaps she is no longer in London. If she went straight to Victoria[26] from here, she might be almost anywhere by now."

Jacob shook his head. "She would have gone to Westminster. She is terrified of the Fenians."[27]

Livia pursed her lips. There was no call for Jacob to tell them that.

Oliver shrugged. "In either case, we should have detected traces in the vicinity, and a trail indicating the direction she traveled." He sighed. "I fear we must conclude that her location has been . . . veiled."

"I find it hard to credit that she would have troubled to veil her movements if, as we surmise, she was suffering the influence of the mirror," murmured Jacob.

Rhoda tapped her shoulder and hissed in her ear, "What is he talking about? They sound as if you had run away!"

"Could we be mistaken?" inquired Cecily. "Might she have fled entirely of her own volition?" Jacob shook his head slightly.

"Fled?" cried Rhoda, not troubling at all to keep her voice down. "You ran away? Whatever for? You wicked creature—look how you have worried them!"

Cecily's brow furrowed in thought. "Could she have been lured away by some agency other than the mirror? An enemy? But surely she could not have enemies." To her surprise Jacob lifted his head with a thoughtful expression. "Where would such as she acquire them?"

"From her father perhaps?" pointed out Colonel Beckford. "Granted, she has had little association with him. But blood feuds can linger, and Aram might have easily acquired a few of those."

Livia gasped. She had not thought of her true father in years, but the colonel was quite right. She had heard he had enemies. Many enemies.

"Or simply a feud," mused Jacob. "Since you speak of her associations, she was closely linked with the Chang name."

Cecily turned to him. "Really? Did Dr. Chang have enemies?"

Livia pursed her lips, as surprised as Cecily by the suggestion, and not at all pleased. Surely her dear Papa did not have enemies. That would be, at the very least, uncouth.

But apparently Jacob did not share that confidence. "Perhaps just a few," he murmured. No trace of irony was actually audible in his voice, but Cecily heard it anyway and lifted an eyebrow. Jacob sighed. "More likely his

188

mother's enemies. She kept them in flocks, like canaries." Oliver also turned to him with every sign of interest. "She had good reason to leave China, let alone Greece. She was once married to Xiu Wang Po."

Livia shrank back. Mr. Huong had mentioned Xiu Wang Po. Suddenly she wondered if she truly wanted to hear more.

"Really?" pondered Oliver. "That would explain much. A notorious Chinese bandit," he explained to Cecily. "Involved in the opium trade before it was legal,[28] which is doubtless how he came to be acquainted with Ishmael Aram. His enemies called him 'the Mongrel.' I seem to recall he came to a particularly grisly end."

Livia covered her ears with her hands and ordered the mirror to go away. Just to be sure, she turned around so her back was to it and squeezed her eyes tightly shut. The technique must have worked; she heard nothing more. When she turned back she found Rhoda glaring in the mist, her fists planted firmly on her hips and the hem of her skirt fluttering in time to the tapping of her foot.

"Well?" inquired Rhoda. "What on God's green earth was that all about?"

Chapter Seven

Cecily had not yet risen out of her chair—a process that had grown annoyingly difficult—when the maid ushered in Frau Strasser. Grasping the situation in a glance, her guest hurried over to insist, "Please, my dear, you must not get up." She punctuated her command by emphatically depositing herself in the nearest chair. Cecily sank back down gratefully. "Alas, my congratulations are extremely belated," continued Frau Strasser. "May I ask when the blessed event is expected to occur?"

Livia's heart leapt up, and her mouth opened in a greeting, so delighted was she to see her dear friend Anna again. But, of course—as she had been forcefully reminded at least a dozen times already—she could not speak to the persons so plainly visible on the other side of the mirror. She sighed; apparently communication could only be initiated from the other side, unless the mirror was specially constructed or . . . or the communication was directed to a person of unusual sensitivity. Anna Strasser was unusually sensitive, extraordinarily so.

Cecily turned a brilliant smile on Frau Strasser. "How kind of you to inquire. It could be any day now, we are told, although it will probably be at least another fortnight, and perhaps as much as a month." She rolled her eyes. "Tomorrow would not be too soon to please me, I assure you."

"Truly? You are not afraid?" Cecily's face did not quite conceal her surprise at such a question. "Please, I do not mean to alarm you; it is only that many new mothers are fearful. They have been kept in ignorance of the particulars for much of their lives and heard only the vaguest and most misleading rumors of a painful ordeal." Frau Strasser smiled. "But I should have known you are not one such timid soul. Your aura glows with courage. And your brother has told me many times that you are utterly fearless."

Livia pursed her lips. She did not doubt that Jacob had said exactly that.

"He exaggerates," murmured Cecily, who clearly had no intention of permitting the conversation to turn toward auras. "I am grateful he sees me in such an affectionate light, but I often find myself unable to live up to the image he has presented of me."

"I understand that you have cause to be uneasy," Frau Strasser continued earnestly. "You have suffered a previous tragedy?"

Livia drew in her breath. Cecily surely would not like the turn the conversation was taking; she never talked of poor little Justin. Nor did Jacob, for that matter. It occurred to Livia that it was, in fact, she herself who had mentioned the late child to Anna; perhaps she ought not to have done so. It was just like sweet, oblivious Anna—who could perceive the subtlest nuances of inner feeling—to remain utterly blind to the obvious external signs of social discomfort.

Cecily did not quite grit her teeth. "Yes, I . . . I lost my first son." She drew in a deep breath. "But I am not concerned about these; they are strong and healthy. I know it."

"But you were not anxious over little Justin either, were you?"

Livia started. How on earth had Anna known that? She had not known it herself, did not even now know with any confidence it was true.

Cecily cocked her head as if impressed by the insight, and answered with a rueful smile. "No, but on that occasion it simply never occurred to me to worry. My life was perfect. My husband was perfect. I assumed that naturally my little boy was perfect also." She paused and whispered very softly, "And so he was."

She shrugged and continued firmly, "I never felt uncomfortable or burdened then. Why should I suppose that anything was wrong?" She sighed and spread her hands wide to indicate her own girth. "This time I am always uncomfortable—conscious of the demanding burden every minute of the day. I cannot write a note or drink a cup of tea without groaning under the weight of it. And so . . ."

Frau Strasser laughed and clapped her hands. "And so you do not merely trust they are well. You know it. You feel their energy."

"Exactly." Cecily smiled entirely without artifice. She had never smiled at Livia so. "Do you have children, Frau Strasser?"

"Three. But they are grown. Even my little girl is married."

"But surely you are not so old as that? You must have married very young." The compliment was not entirely without artifice, but it was well intentioned.

Frau Strasser was not deceived. "Indeed, I was hardly more than an infant," she chuckled, and looked about a trifle pointedly. "Will my dear Livia be joining us?"

Now was the moment, while she was in their thoughts. Livia pressed up against the soft, invisible wall that separated her from the material world and waved energetically, calling her friend's name, calling it several times. Her efforts were futile; Anna's glance scarcely brushed over the mirror.

Cecily sighed. "Alas, no." She too looked around the room, as if still half hoping Livia might pop up from a corner. "I must have forgotten to tell her that I had invited you to call. She seems to have stepped out."

"Stepped out?" As was her custom, Frau Strasser did not allow mere tact to prevent her from an honest expression of her views. Her tone was incredulous, and she stared a long time.

Livia laughed out loud. It was always a complete waste of time to fib to Anna, even the littlest of white lies; the woman could positively smell mendacity.

Frau Strasser concluded gently, "Perhaps you should try being frank with me, Mrs. Beckford. I might be able to help."

Cecily was clearly taken aback, and made no reply. Frau Strasser continued quite as if she were reading her mind, "You must find it difficult to trust me. I was Dr. Chang's intimate friend, not a happy association for you. And when you and your brother came to us for assistance, we watched and wrung our hands and did nothing while the darkness struck you down. I can only assure you that we tried, and hope that you see some value in our earnest goodwill."

"Dr. Chang was not our friend at all," whispered Cecily. "Or so Jacob tells me." She smiled at Frau Strasser. "But he told me also that you were a great comfort during my . . ." She sighed, apparently considering whether or not to reuse the hopelessly inappropriate word. "During my illness. And before that, he said that your counsel and support were all that sustained Livia."

"Dr. Chang was not a friend?" Frau Strasser's tone was level, but very, very surprised. Then she shook her head and sighed. "I should have known that. Poor Dr. Chang. He was always too much his mother's servant."

Cecily shrugged. "I trusted him also." She paused as if reflecting and quite suddenly blurted out, "Livia has run away. We think she acted under the influence of Dr. Chang's mirror."

Frau Strasser raised a hand to her face to conceal a small moue of horror. And then, cocking her head to one side, she asked, "Have you inquired of the mirror what happened to her?"

"What a splendid idea!" cried Livia, clapping her hands. "Oh, yes, dear Anna, your instinct is infallible! By all means, try asking the mirror!"

Cecily opened her mouth as if to reply. Then she closed it again, and her eyes drifted off to the right as she considered the question more carefully. Then she shrugged. "I never thought of it." She reflected at still more length. "I do not think I could anyway. It is sealed."

"But then," inquired Frau Strasser, "how can it call to Livia?"

Chapter Eight

"Rhoda?" called Livia. "Where are you? I've splendid news—don't you want to hear? They are going to look for us in the mirror! Anna will lead the search. Surely you remember Anna, and what a friend she was to us before, when we first came together? She is sure to find us. She always wanted to look in the mirror for you, but . . . but . . ."

But Papa had refused. Papa had said he had already searched in the mirror himself and found nothing. No, she was getting it all mixed up; it had been such a very long time ago. Everybody had known all along that Rhoda was in the mirror. Papa had refused to let them search in the mirror for Cecily. Perhaps that was why Cecily claimed now that he was not their friend.

She gnawed her lip. That was utterly untrue, of course; Papa was a good man. But on careful consideration she could not help but wonder how he could possibly have failed to find Cecily in the mirror if, indeed, he had really looked. Also, if everyone knew that Rhoda was in the mirror, why had he not moved to bring her out? She shook her head. Knowing Rhoda was in the mirror was one thing, bringing her out entirely another. Where could she be brought out to, seeing as she was dead? Papa was a good man; doubtless he had done all he could. She would say so to Rhoda—if only Rhoda would come out from wherever she was hiding. "Rhoda?" she called again. But there was no answer.

Livia folded her arms across her chest and pouted. A bit of company would have been very welcome in this dim, cheerless place, but clearly Rhoda was determined to sulk. It was absurdly childish of her; she really ought to be mature enough to put a little quarrel behind her. Indeed, by all rights Rhoda ought to be grateful that Livia was not inclined to hard feelings, considering how hurtful Rhoda's remarks had been. It would serve Rhoda right if Livia just walked away and let her sulk. Livia pondered that thought for a moment and smiled to herself. "Very well, then," she called into the mist. "If you are determined to bear a grudge, I cannot prevent you. I shall leave you to the privacy of your thoughts."

She started walking. She walked only for the sensation of walking, of course. She had no place to go, and walking would not have taken her there if she had. But she liked the sense of purpose, however illusory. Remembered scenery formed around her, evoked perhaps by the familiar motion, and soon she was strolling through a semblance of Kensington Gardens. The mirror world might not prove such a disagreeable place, after all. She could still hear the mirror humming all about her; she tried to follow the sound, for all that it did not seem to be coming from any particular place.

"You'll lose your way in a minute," snapped Rhoda, materializing quite suddenly by her side.

She continued to walk. "Not to worry. That ship has surely sailed." Rhoda pursed her lips, tossed her head and disappeared. Livia shrugged and kept on walking, her head cocked to listen.

After several minutes—or perhaps it was seconds, or hours—Rhoda reappeared, with her hands on her hips and a singularly annoyed expression. "What has gotten into you?" she demanded. "First you desert your husband and steal his clothes, and now you prance about, waving your mortality like a banner. There was a time, at least, you had wit enough to be afraid of demons."

At that she stopped. Demons. The very word sent a tremor of anxiety through her. There was a demon in the mirror. She had always known there was a demon in the mirror—that same demon that had murdered poor Rhoda and imprisoned her spirit. Yet here she was, strolling about the astral realm as if she were out for a Sunday promenade with band music. How had it come to this? Had she gone quite mad? She had always supposed that going mad would involve a lot of weeping and raving, but surely she could not have undone herself any more completely if she had foamed at the mouth and torn out her hair.

She sank to her knees, trembling with horror, and wrapped her arms around her waist as if to hold her spirit within her person. "Oh, Rhoda," she moaned. "I forgot about the demon."

Rhoda's mouth dropped open in astonishment. "You forgot? You forgot about the demon?"

Livia cringed under the incredulous tone. "Yes! I forgot. I forgot about the demon. I forgot about Jacob. I forgot about you. I forgot about everything." She dropped her head into her hands and burst into tears. "I don't know how it happened. I just needed my mirror so much, nothing else seemed to matter." She slid to the ground, shaking with sobs.

Rhoda dropped down beside her and laid a hand on her shoulder. "But why? Why did you want the mirror so badly?"

Livia wept still harder. "I don't know. It seemed self-evident. I simply had to have it." The mirror had called to her, and she had been mesmerized by the call. Now that she knew what had happened she could hear plainly that the humming of the mirror contained a coercive note. It ceased to be quite so compelling once she was aware of it, but it remained unmistakably a summons.

"Well, thank goodness you've gotten past that anyway," sighed Rhoda. "For I surely did not want to take you to it. The demon is almost always camped in front of it. I do believe it wants out as much as I do." She glanced at Livia and corrected herself. "I mean as much as we do."

"Really? How very odd. One would think it would view this place as home." Livia sat up and wiped her face with her handkerchief, reflecting uneasily on the probable state of her appearance. But at least climbing to her feet was quite easy, thanks to her masculine costume. She offered a hand to Rhoda, who nonetheless had to struggle with her petticoats to rise. "But we must not let that discourage us; surely the mirror is the only way out of here. Did you never consider trying again?"

Rhoda did not answer but simply stared at her with wide eyes and tight lips. Livia coughed and looked away. "Of course, I am sure you did the best you could. At any rate, the situation is entirely different now. Our friends will be searching for us; they will get the mirror unsealed one way or another." Rhoda continued to stare, although her mouth softened from a thin line to an *O* of astonishment.

Livia found herself growing quite nervous under that intent gaze and brushed uneasily at the wisps of hair that had tumbled from beneath her cap. There were a great many of them, and they all declined to be tucked back up under the hat. Despairing of any restoration of order, she pulled the cap off and released the thick braid, which she then unlaced. But she had no comb or pins with which to repair her coiffure; she could only let it hang loose. Jacob had always claimed to love it when she left it loose. Of course, she had not been suffering from red eyes and a drippy nose when he said it. And all the while as she fretted with her appearance, Rhoda continued to stare. At long last Livia burst out, "Oh, for heaven's sake, Rhoda. Speak your piece and have it done!"

"You've forgotten again," replied Rhoda, and Livia came within an inch of inquiring just what she might have forgotten. "For half an instant there, you were almost your old self, my dear cautious, respectable Livia, she who never took chances and grew quite faint at quarrels and worried herself sick if she got a spot on her dress." Rhoda shook her head and backed away a step. "Only moments ago you were weeping with fear, and now you have already forgotten the demon again and want to charge off into danger looking for your silly mirror."

"But . . ." Livia opened her mouth to protest vigorously, but once she had started she found she had nothing to say. Everything Rhoda had said was true, she realized uneasily, and yet somehow it all sounded so cruelly unjust. "But . . ." She looked around wildly as if the answer she sought might emerge from the mist, and quite suddenly it did. "But the demon is no danger to me."

She had not known she meant to say such a thing until she heard the words spoken, and yet she knew instantly they were true. The faint humming of the mirror, which had haunted her so long, resolved itself at last into something almost like a voice, an inaudible murmur capable of carrying words, or at least meaning. She listened for an instant and nodded her head emphatically. "You hear?" she inquired, although it was quite obvious that Livia heard nothing. "The demon wishes us no harm!"

Rhoda backed farther away. The mist around her cleared somehow so that she remained visible despite the growing distance between them. "No harm?" She spoke quite softly, but there was great intensity in her voice. "Indeed, it has already murdered me—what further harm could it do me? Livia, please listen, if you still retain any consciousness at all. You are mesmerized, possessed. The demon will say whatever it supposes you want to hear. It will assume any face you want to see. It is a walking lie, a violation of the natural order. Do not listen to it. You must turn away from it before it does you grievous irreparable harm, as it has done me, as it did to Cecily, as it tried to do to Jacob."

All the while she was speaking she continued to back away. "I am going to run away now," she continued. "The demon is coming; I can hear it. I pray with all my heart that you will flee with me, but I will not stay for you if you do not." Matching her action to her words, she turned and disappeared.

Livia stared after her in dismay. She tried with all her heart to make sense of her friend's panic. But she had never felt less afraid in her life. It was true the demon was coming; she too could hear it. It was also true that the demon meant her no harm. She could feel it. Apparently Rhoda could not. She shrugged and turned to face this famous demon.

But it was not a demon—it was Papa! Her heart swelled up and she ran to him. So wonderful to see him whole and sound, not weeping in his sleep but smiling down at her with loving eyes. She wrapped her arms around his waist and laid her head on his chest. His arms came up around her and she felt his lips brush her hair. "Oh, my little sweetling," he murmured. "What a state your hair is in! Have you been climbing trees again?"

She pulled back just enough to look up at him and laugh through her tears—for she was weeping, weeping with surprise and relief and joy. "Oh, Papa, you know I don't care a fig for trees." It was an old, old joke between them; so old she only half remembered the childish incident that had originally provoked the words. He laughed and drew her close again. She had not felt so safe and warm since childhood.

But Rhoda's words still tickled uncomfortably at the back of her mind, and she drew back. "Are you Papa?" She regarded him critically. Surely he was Papa; he could not be an imposter. Every detail was exactly as always, from the lift of his eyebrow to the tiny scar under his jaw. "They told me the demon could look like anyone," she informed him.

"And that I would do you grievous irreparable harm?" So he had overheard that. He raised his hand to stroke her cheek. "Oh, my own dear Livia, I would never do you harm, not in this life or any other."

It tore her heart, and she darted back into his arms. "Oh, Papa, I am so confused. That dreadful Cecily said you were not to be trusted. But I cannot find it in me to doubt you."

He sighed deeply. "I fear Mrs. Beckford has good cause to distrust me." He pressed her back to gaze earnestly into her eyes. "Whatever happens, my dear, never forget—if I have done . . . questionable things, I did them only to protect you. I hold your safety as a sacred charge."

A chill ran through her. "Questionable things?" He looked at her so strangely. Had he always looked at her so, with such yearning intensity? It made her think of the things Mr. Huong had said. She opened her mouth to ask him; then she closed it again. She could not face his answer, whatever it might be. Instead she inquired, "But how did you come to be in here?"

"It was Colonel Beckford who put me here."

She gasped. "That evil man—I never trusted him! But that surely makes it plain why he did not want to give me my mirror!" She shook her head. "But if it was he, then why did Jacob also try to prevent me?"

Papa regarded her levelly. "Mr. Aldridge assisted him."

"No!" She spun away, burying her face in her hands. "I cannot believe it! I will not believe it. Jacob loves me."

"I am sure that he does." He came up behind her and placed his hands on her shoulders. "I would not suggest otherwise. But he loves his sister also. And doubtless he thought you would be better off without me."

"But that is nonsense—how could he think such a thing?"

He pressed her shoulder until he drew her around, and lifted her chin so she must face him. "Make no mistake, my darling. His grievance against me was just."

She stared up at him, her lip trembling. So many questions she dared not ask, lest he answer honestly. So many other questions whose answers she must have, whether she could face them or not. She selected at last the least troubling and most pressing of her queries. "If they unseal the mirror, will we be able to escape? Do you know the way out?"

He chuckled and drew her back into the crook of his arm. "That's my clever girl, always with a sharp eye on the housekeeping. Yes, my dear. There are many ways out, if only they unseal the mirror."

Chapter Nine

ecily leaned against the pillar of the arch leading into the small parlor, watching as Jacob and Anna Strasser very slightly repositioned the trunk sitting on the tea table. "Colonel Beckford will not be pleased," she remarked. "Not pleased at all. He does not trust that evil mirror; he was at great pains to seal it up." Her brother paused to look at her for a long moment. A smile flickered at the corner of her mouth and she added, "So perhaps you had best take it upstairs before you try to open it, lest he walk in and catch you out."

"Not likely," replied Jacob, stepping back to regard the table and trunk critically. He moved forward to shift the trunk a half inch to the left, but it was already larger than the table on which it rested, and its balance proved too precarious to suffer further adjustment. Jacob sighed, restored the trunk to the exact center of the table, and wrested the entire structure to one side. That done, he resumed frowning at it with frequent glances toward the mirror over the mantel and the candles positioned beneath it.

"You are quite certain?" inquired Frau Strasser. "Once I have entered a trance state, an interruption would be most inappropriate." She turned from Jacob to Cecily. "Is there really no possibility the good colonel could be persuaded to assist us? His abilities would be a great asset. We could still wait for him to join us."

Cecily's mouth twitched again, and she shook her head. Jacob intervened gently. "Regrettably, he will be delayed a considerable while. He was eager to question Mr. Huong further."

Frau Strasser turned back to him. "But surely that need not take long if Mr. Huong cooperates." Jacob shot her a look and she continued with some asperity, "Colonel Beckford can be most persuasive."

"Even so," answered Jacob. "He will wait at the Oriental Emporium until Dr. Verlaine arrives. We did not dare to move Mrs. Aldridge without some medical assurance it would be safe to do so." He sighed again and glanced almost absently toward the window. He did not need to say that he was thinking of how he had found his wife at Huong's and the state in which he had found her.

"You did the right thing," murmured Cecily. "You will be more help to her here."

He shrugged. "So Colonel Beckford said." He managed a wry smile. "He might not have been so quick to pack me off if he had guessed just how I meant to help." He darted into the hall and returned carrying a long, slim wooden box. "Could we have another table here, Cecily, my own?" Without pausing to confirm her consent, he turned to a small occasional table in the corner and stripped it of its burden of objets d'art, tossing the small objects onto a nearby ottoman. The oil lamp he set on the floor. "I almost might have stayed at the Oriental Emporium just to shop. Mr. Huong's collection is astonishing! Just wait until you see what I found!"

The ladies watched with interest as he dragged the cleared table to the center of the room and positioned it in front of the trunk with only a little less care than he had originally positioned the trunk. But while he had taken particular care that the table with the trunk was set close enough to the mantel so that it was not reflected in the mirror above, he now took pains to ensure that the small occasional table was far enough out to be fully visible in the mirror from almost any angle. When he was satisfied that everything was where he wanted it to be, he gently laid the wooden box on the second table. It was narrow enough to rest securely despite the ends extending out over both sides.

"What," enquired Frau Strasser, "is that?"

Jacob indulged in an extremely satisfied smile. "That is Mr. Huong's magic sword."

"Nonsense," snorted Frau Strasser. "There's no such thing. Magic swords are merely the stuff of children's tales."

"Yet here it is," he assured her, tossing her a smile that had grown mischievous and opening the box with a flourish. "Think what you wish, my dear Frau, but these *spirit blades* are highly thought of in the Eastern traditions. Mr. Huong certainly valued his highly. And surely Mrs. Aldridge must have believed in and hoped to make use of its powers, else why would she seek out the house of Dr. Chang's bitterest enemy?"

Livia turned to Dr. Chang with a perplexed expression. "Is that really true, Papa? Was Mr. Huong your bitterest enemy? I would never have gone to him had I known. But I thought the Huongs were our friends."

Dr. Chang sighed. "His father and mine were very bitter enemies, indeed, and their fathers before them. Blood had been spilled—a great deal of blood—and in China, no one was ever allowed to forget a drop of spilled blood. But Chou and I . . ." He shook his head. "We thought we could put China behind us. The rules were different in Athens; the future seemed to outweigh the past. So we were friends. Good friends. I am sorry he is dead." He managed a wry smile. "And if his little brother had retained wit and honor enough to remain our friend, then he need not have suffered seeing his precious sword swiped by an Englishman. The Huongs were not fond of the English. Even my dear Chou could not put that grudge aside."

Livia giggled. "There's no fleeing karma." He chuckled and put his arm around her.

Jacob planted both fists on his hips and surveyed the room. He sighed in the obvious conviction that something he could not identify had been missed or forgotten. "'Twill have to serve," he concluded, and turned to Frau Strasser. "Are you satisfied, dear Frau?"

She was seated before the little table with the sword, fingering it gently but not quite daring to lift it from its box. "I am," she replied. "This is, indeed, a splendid instrument. But very foreign. I have little experience with the rites and implementations of the East. I am attempting to infer something of its uses and powers, but so far can only lay claim to the most rudimentary understanding. However, if I have not grossly misconstrued, then the process we desire has already started. It is the nature of the thing to cut through astral veils and bindings. It is doing so now."

"So soon?" inquired Jacob. "How long until it is done?"

She shrugged. "That I cannot tell."

Jacob turned to his sister. "Then I must ask you to withdraw at once, my dear."

Cecily froze, caught halfway down while lowering herself into a chair. "I beg your pardon?" She stared at her brother and he stared back at her. "What infernal cheek! Are you ordering me from my own house, then?"

Jacob crossed to her side and placed a gentle but firm hand under her elbow so as to assist her back to her feet. "Well, not from the house, of course, my own. I would not presume." She shot him a look that spoke volumes on what he might presume. "But I fear I must insist you be elsewhere when the mirror is unveiled. Your room would likely suffice." Her look grew colder by the second. "Please reflect on the danger, Cecily." Neither of them could stare the other down. "Cecily, I do not want to use force on you, but I shall."

"Mr. Aldridge!" exclaimed Frau Strasser. "I think you exceed civil bounds. She is our hostess. She is your sister. Compulsion is not appropriate or civilized."

Cecily nodded to her guest. "Thank you, Frau Strasser. It is good to know that someone here has a sense of propriety."

Jacob's lips tightened, and he walked to the table where the sword rested in its box. "Then we put an end to it now." He grasped the open lid of the box and raised it halfway up. "Frau Strasser, is there some rite or incantation you need to perform to separate yourself from this artifact before I shut it up? You must be quick, for I will not have it cut through Beckford's seals while Cecily is still present."

"Oh, Mr. Aldridge," she murmured in a tone of extreme regret. "Will you not reconsider?"

Jacob turned back to Cecily and cocked his head to one side. "Our friend is disappointed," he remarked. "And so, I think, are you. But think, my dear clever Cecily, why are you disappointed? You say you remember nothing of your experiences in the mirror, but I think you misspeak yourself. Do you not remember evil dreams? I know I do, and I spent only a few minutes within it. And yet now you are furious at being denied further access? It is seduction, dearest, and you ought to resist it. It wants you back. It has never for an instant forgiven you your escape."

Cecily did not move; rather she continued to stand stock-still. But something in her demeanor softened slightly, and her eyes drifted to the right as her attention turned inward to her thoughts. Finally she replied, "I . . . I thought I was standing by you. As I always have. And always shall."

He shook his head. "Years ago, you faced this thing for me when I was too weak and sick to prevent you, and we both paid a terrible price. I could not bear that again. Today it is my turn; you must let me face this thing for you, while you concern yourself with protecting little Julius and little Cordelia. Or shall it be little Constance? Now, will you go, or must I pack up my peculiar toys and leave your house?"

She tried very hard to hide her smile, but failed. "Really, Jacob, you are a wretched boy, and by rights I should turn you from the house. Colonel Beckford would say the very same if he knew what you were about." She sighed dramatically. "But I cannot have you going about town, telling people that I would not put a roof over my own brother's head."

"Quite," he murmured. "People would talk. We can't have that." She came back to him and took his hands; they kissed. Then she turned and trudged heavily out into the hall. She did not go far, just barely out of sight.

She paused in front of the hall mirror, sighed heavily and patted at her hair. It was not really disarranged, nor could she effect much change by patting at it, seeing as it was pinned rigidly into place. It was, however, the only aspect of her appearance over which she had any control. She glanced toward the stairs but found the prospect of mounting them in the August heat daunting; she glanced toward the main parlor but found it strangely unattractive also. There was a single chair in the hallway, for sitting on while removing boots, and she settled gingerly onto that to await her husband's return. She closed her eyes and leaned back, letting her head rest on the wall whatever the damage to her coiffure.

"Cecily!" The urgent whisper came from nowhere, and Cecily sat bolt upright, staring wildly about from left to right and back again, and seeing nothing. She glanced back toward the small parlor. She was quite certain that it had not been Jacob's voice, nor Anna Strasser's. She forced herself to take a long, slow breath. Perhaps she had dozed and had heard her name in a dream. She had almost convinced herself that it was nothing more than imagination when it came again. "Cecily!"

Getting to her feet was a struggle, for her chair was a Louis Seize,[29] elegant but without arms. She should have thought before sitting in it. Even when she had regained her feet, she was at a loss. She looked into the main parlor, which was quite empty. She had been forbidden the small parlor, but she did pause outside the arch to listen intently. There was a soft murmur of chanting, with Jacob's tenor descanting on Frau Strasser's soprano. The voices flowed smoothly, clearly oblivious to any interruption.

So the voice had to be coming from upstairs. She sighed uneasily and laid one hand on the banister while lifting her skirt with the other so as not to trip on the hem. But even as she placed a foot on the bottom step, she heard the voice call again from behind her. She whirled, rather too quickly, and had to catch the banister to keep from falling. There was no one behind her. "Who is there?" she called in her most imperious tone. "Be so good as to show yourself!"

"Here, Cecily, here," came the answer. "Don't be alarmed—I am right here. Look in the mirror."

"The mirror?" Cecily started and hesitated at some length before complying. Looking into the glass, she suppressed a gasp. For the mirror showed a second reflection standing to her left and a little behind her. She declined to turn around and look. She knew there was no one there. But according to the mirror, her brother's missing wife was right beside her.

"Oh, Cecily, darling, I am so grateful to have reached you!" she exclaimed, and her voice was not right at all. Surely Livia's voice was much higher, and her articulation more clipped. "You must stop them at once!"

"Beg pardon, I must stop whom? And from doing what?" Cecily did not remember ever having seen Livia in a dress so far out of fashion as that grey muslin. And she generally styled her hair a deal more elaborately.

"Well, Jacob and Anna, of course. They are trying to open a portal in the mirror. But they mustn't, they absolutely mustn't! They will let the demon out! It has been waiting at that door for Jacob ever since the colonel shut it in."

"You are not Livia!" Cecily was quite sure of it; she could not be mistaken.

"Well, of course not! Cecily, please, don't tell me you don't know me! How could you? We were such friends!"

"Rhoda?" Cecily felt suddenly quite faint and reached out a hand to grab the banister. "But you are dead!"

Rhoda rolled her eyes in a great show of exasperation. "Yes, yes, I've heard, but might we discuss that later? This is important. Jacob must not go near the mirror."

"But I can hardly stop him," said Cecily. "And he needs to rescue Livia, who is trapped inside it."

"She's hardly trapped," replied Rhoda. "She still has a living vessel to receive her—unlike some more deserving, I might add. She could get out anytime, the same way she got in. Of her own free will."

"She could?" Cecily's eyes narrowed. "You are quite certain of that, Rhoda?"

"Of course I am certain." Rhoda hesitated and bit her lip. "Well, almost certain. I suppose it is possible she has not yet realized how to go about it; she is still a bit inexperienced with the way of this place. But she is a marvelously quick study, and it is surely easy enough. All one needs is a mirror—any mirror—and a clear knowledge of where one's person is located. Please take note, she got in here with no more special means than a bowl of water." She drew a breath and directed a look of great determination toward Cecily. "So will you now go tell Jacob to stop?"

Cecily stared at the image of her late friend for some while. Rhoda stood waiting on her answer with arms crossed and her foot tapping impatiently. Cecily did not like to be rushed when she was thinking, and she took her time. Finally she replied, "How do I know you are not the demon?"

Rhoda's foot stopped tapping. "Well, really, Cecily, if I were the demon why should I warn you? I should want Jacob to open the mirror."

"So you say," answered Cecily. "But since you might be the demon, I can hardly take your word for it. Maybe the demon does not want Jacob to rescue Livia."

Rhoda opened her mouth to respond. Then she closed it again. She looked to the right, but saw no answers there; she looked to the left and found it unproductive also. Then she opened her mouth again and closed it again. Finally she threw up her hands in frustration. "Oh, Cecily, you are too clever for me. You always were. You must tell me what would convince you I am myself."

Cecily blinked. "But how can I? Surely if the demon can pluck the images of our loved ones from our minds, then it will know anything I can think of to distinguish you."

"But you did it once," wailed Rhoda. "When the demon first came for you, and you turned it away. Could you not do it again for me?"

Cecily stared at her in astonishment. "You are confused, Rhoda. Perhaps it comes of being dead. If it is really you, of course. But I did not turn the demon away. I lay in its grasp for a very long time until Oliver rescued me. Surely you know that. I gather everyone from the kitchen maid to the demon itself knows that."

Rhoda looked back with equal surprise. "But you are forgetting. You did turn the demon away once, when it first came to you as Oliver. Remember how it had to come back to you as Jacob before it could take you?"

Cecily trembled and swayed. She grabbed the newel post and clung to it as if she were drowning. "You cannot possibly know that," she whispered. "Even I do not know it, not really."

"The whole astral realm knows it," Rhoda assured her. "For the demon often cries and complains about it. And when the demon cries, everyone hears. You turned it away. However did you do it?"

Cecily shook her head. "I . . . I did nothing special. The demon needs consent; surely that is why it disguises itself. And I knew that it could not possibly be Oliver." She shuddered and pressed her hands over her ears as if to keep out some awful inner voice. "I thought I had forgotten. I wanted it all to be forgotten. Afterwards I was expecting Jacob, so when it came back, I didn't question . . . I should have. I should have questioned . . . Jacob would not . . . But he took me entirely off guard when he told me he had just married Livia." She paused and cocked her head. "But Jacob really had just married Livia. So if it was not Jacob . . . how did the demon know of that?"

"It knew from Livia, of course," said Rhoda. Cecily sank down to sit on the step and looked up at the face in the mirror. "She is in league with it. I didn't know until I saw them together."

"I think you are the demon," whispered Cecily. "The dreadful things you say."

"Oh, Cecily, no," cried Rhoda. "I never meant . . ." There was a clatter at the door and she broke off. Cecily looked up also. The door flew open and Colonel Beckford hurried in to hold open the door. A second man came in behind him carrying a limp form.

Cecily struggled to her feet. "Is that Dr. Verlaine? It is! How good to see you, dear Doctor! But who is this boy, and what has happened to him?"

"That is no boy," murmured Rhoda. "It is Livia. She is in disguise."

Cecily shot an uneasy glance at the mirror before moving forward to examine the doctor's burden. "But this is Livia! What has happened to her, and why is she wearing Jacob's jacket? Bring her into the parlor and put her on the ottoman."

The doctor was puffing under his burden—not that Livia could have been a great weight, but he was a portly man, unaccustomed to exercise. He therefore did not reply, but merely nodded in acknowledgment of her greeting before turning into the main parlor.

Cecily would have followed, but the colonel caught her arm and murmured, "My dear, are you unwell? You are white as a sheet."

"She is fine, Colonel," said Rhoda. "Don't worry about her. You must go look in the back parlor."

"I . . . I am fine," answered Cecily, dropping her eyes. "Only, I thought I saw something in the mirror and it gave me a terrible start."

He turned around. "But there is nothing there, my silly girl."

She turned to look and there was nothing in the mirror but a pale, frightened-looking woman and her husband. "I know, my dear. It is just the heat, preying on my nerves."

She still saw nothing, but she heard a faint whisper. "Really, Cecily, that was unkind. I thought we were friends."

The colonel looked about as if he thought he had heard something; then, returning his attention to his wife, he said, "I hope you are right, but I do not like the look of you at all; I have never seen you so wan. Perhaps we shall have Dr. Verlaine examine you after he has finished caring for Mrs. Aldridge."

"Colonel Beckford, please!" cried Rhoda, quite loudly. "Your concern for Cecily does you credit, but there are urgent matters at hand. Jacob is unsealing the mirror as we speak. You must stop him!"

Colonel Beckford was not given to hesitation. There was only a tiny flick of the eye to indicate he still saw nothing in the mirror, a cock of the head to show that he had nonetheless heard clearly. Then he was gone, almost before Rhoda had finished speaking. A loud crash emanated from the parlor.

"My goodness, he moves quickly," remarked Rhoda. "Usually big men are so clumsy, but not your colonel. And the lame leg does not seem to slow him down at all."

"He ignores it when he is determined," replied Cecily. "But he will pay for the exertion. Mark my words, come morning he will be abominably stiff and uncomfortable." She shivered. "I'd best go intervene before he hurts Jacob. Was that your plan, you dreadful creature? To provoke Colonel Beckford into murdering Jacob?" She started forward, but her step was unsteady.

"How can you say such a horrible thing?" wailed Rhoda. "How can you even think it? I am trying to protect Jacob. The demon will consume him on the spot if he opens that nasty mirror. And Colonel Beckford isn't hurting him. In fact . . ." She paused as if listening, although Cecily could hear nothing. "The colonel is not even stopping him! The mirror is opening up right next to them, and they are just standing there discussing it! Really, men! They have no sense at all. Could you not hurry a bit, Cecily? Someone has to get in there and put a stop to this business."

"I am trying," whispered Cecily. She took several small steps and then started to sway. She caught herself on the wall and leaned against it panting. "Perhaps you could tell them," she suggested. "I think I may be ill . . ." She pushed herself up from the wall and tried again to walk toward the parlor, only to double over suddenly in a cramp. "Oh, no," she wailed, collapsing into the puddle that had formed around her feet. "Not now!" Her voice turned into a scream as the first contraction struck.

Her cry brought men running from every direction. Her husband and brother came tearing out of the small parlor, followed closely by Anna Strasser. Dr. Verlaine appeared almost as quickly from the main parlor. He bent over Cecily, shaking his head. "I should have expected this. All this excitement—the strain has brought on her labor! Can you stand, Mrs. Beckford? We must take you to your room."

He held out his arms to assist her, and she took them gratefully; but once she was on her feet she turned back to the parlor. "The mirror! No, please, do not fuss over me; I am fine. I am so sorry about the scream—so silly of me. I am better now, I assure you. We must deal with the mirror—surely it is nearly open by now!"

"Alas, no," answered Frau Strasser, taking her arm. "Although we very nearly had it so, until the colonel intervened."

"Indeed," confirmed Colonel Beckford. "I cast the sword aside and closed it up in its case. You need not concern yourself, my own. My seal should hold. The mirror is safe."

"Not so!" cried Rhoda, and the colonel's head jerked around at the sound of her voice. "The sword was not withdrawn from the wound in the ether. It is still cutting away the veils even as the portal presses outward." Frau Strasser abandoned Cecily to approach the mirror and stare into it searchingly.

"No!" insisted Cecily. "The veils are still falling away, and the demon is just on the other side, waiting to get out!"

"The demon?" Dr. Verlaine inquired nervously. "Aldridge, are you mucking about with demons again? Couldn't you leave well enough alone?"

"But how . . ." Colonel Beckford glanced toward the mirror but addressed his question to his wife. "How do we prevent the portal from opening if the sword cannot be turned aside?"

"It is too late." The words came from behind them, and they all turned toward the woman standing in the arch.

"Mrs. Aldridge," cried Jacob, running to take her hand. "I am so grateful to see you recovered!"

"Indeed, Mrs. Aldridge," exclaimed Dr. Verlaine. "I had not hoped to see you on your feet so soon. But perhaps you should not overexert yourself as yet. If I may examine you?"

She ignored them both. "The mirror is already unsealed. The last veils are clearing away now. The portal must be blocked immediately before anything can pass through it." She strode past them, acknowledging no one, hardly seeming even to see them, and entered the small parlor. The table on which the sword had rested was toppled; the box lay on the floor beside it. She picked it up and opened it awkwardly. When she had the sword out she continued across the room, dragging the sword behind her, until she came to the trunk, which she flung open.

"Yes, that is definitely unsealed," muttered Colonel Beckford.

The lady leaned forward and gently pulled free some silk wrappings. She smiled down, quite as if she were admiring a baby. Then she lifted the sword over the trunk and stabbed it downward like a stake. She was a small woman, but healthy, and she put all her strength into the act.

The others tensed by the archway, watching; they caught their collective breaths, expecting brimstone or lightning bolts. Nothing of that sort occurred. There was a sharp report as the rod that served as the backbone of the sword snapped, then a clattering as the coins that formed the body of the blade slid off the broken rod and scattered free within the trunk. The trunk tipped to one side and toppled from its precarious perch on the table, scattering the coins to every corner of the room and spilling a heap of silk scarves and shawls that had served as wrappings. Lastly the great bronze mirror itself fell out with a deep clang, as if it were a bell that had been struck.

The lady also fell when the table overbalanced; she landed laughing, with chestnut curls flying, in the pile of silk. Around her, the vibration of the ringing mirror went on and on. She seemed untroubled by the noise—although Frau Strasser covered her ears with her hands—and attempted to climb to her feet. But she made the mistake of trying to steady herself with a hand on the fallen table; it turned under her weight and deposited her back in the pile of silk. Still laughing, she rose to one knee to remark brightly, "There, now, that was not so very difficult, was it?" before collapsing in a heap. On this occasion she did not rise.

"No!" cried Cecily, running toward her. But after only a few steps, she collapsed under another contraction. "No," she wailed again as she went down, and then screamed and fell unconscious.

Chapter Ten

ecily woke in a wash of contradictions. She was light-headed, yet strangely heavy. Her jumbled thoughts possessed a rare clarity; she could scarcely lift her head, yet felt capable of moving mountains.

"Are you awake at last, Mrs. Beckford? I am so glad!" Her sister-in-law came around the end of the bed to stoop down beside her and kiss her cheek. She was dressed in black. Cecily could not take her eyes from the gown. It represented the deepest levels of grief. The high neck and full, draped sleeves were utterly unrelieved by ribbon or lace. Cecily had never seen a dress so severely unadorned. Even the buttons were covered cloth rather than jet.

Cecily's heart quailed. The heavy mourning could only mean one thing: she had lost her children. She had given birth just as that monstrous mirror opened, and it had eaten her babies. A dreadful cry rose up from her empty belly and heart, but she suppressed it instinctively. It was easier than she expected; the pain was horrific but somehow far away.

"We have been so very anxious." Something about the voice reminded Cecily that there had been more than one astral portal at work. The face that surmounted the black collar was familiar, doubly familiar, as was the chestnut hair. But the hair was arranged in an unfamiliar fashion, nor was there any clue in the gown to aid in distinguishing between two too-similar countenances.

"Who are you?" inquired Cecily.

Instead of replying, the young lady clasped her hands to her breast, turned, and darted to the door. From there she called, "Colonel Beckford, we must fetch Dr. Verlaine back at once! She does not know me!" Cecily heaved an inward sigh. She had phrased herself poorly. Better she had asked, *Which are you—Rhoda or Livia?* But it was too late to amend her question. Footsteps were already pounding up the stairs.

Cecily winced. He was running too quickly; his bad leg would protest the effort later. She tried to sit up, but she was weak and tired and dizzy. "Please tell him not to rush so; he will injure his knee."

"Too late, my love; I'm already quite lame." His dear face came round the door. Just the sight of him cheered her enormously. Lame or not, he was still every inch the dashing officer. He came to sit beside her, and she smiled weakly up at him. "And worth the cost, to see you looking so much better. But what is this I hear, that your wits are wandering? Surely you know your own sister-in-law." He turned his head to address the woman in black. "I am sure she is herself, Mrs. Aldridge. She is just a little fuzzy-headed from the laudanum." He turned back to Cecily. "Nasty stuff, I've always said. Knocks you out without actually letting you rest. But Dr. Verlaine felt you would need some assistance with the pain. We nearly lost you, you know."

"Leaves a dreadful taste in the mouth as well," she whispered. So the labor had been hard; she remembered none of it. Perhaps that was why they were taking their time to break the bad news. But she lacked the strength to ask. Let them stall—she too would pretend for a little while she knew of nothing amiss. She smiled at her sister-in-law and inquired, "Have you changed your hair, Mrs. Aldridge?"

Mrs. Aldridge smiled beautifully in return and brought her a glass of water. "Why, yes, Mrs. Beckford. How thoughtful of you to notice." She patted her at her hair and turned her head from side to side to display the coiffure. "Do you like it? According to 'The Wares of Autolycus'[30] this is all the rage in Paris. Perhaps when you are better we shall go see for ourselves." Livia read the *Pall Mall Gazette*, Cecily knew. She had seen it lying about. But would Rhoda know it? Or bother with the Ladies' Column?

It sounded like Livia. But was not the voice just a bit deeper than Livia's, with an accent that hinted more of America than Britain? Or perhaps not. Rhoda had been dead for years now; Cecily was not entirely sure she still remembered her voice exactly. And she had not yet had the opportunity to become very intimate with Livia.

Colonel Beckford chuckled. "What an excellent suggestion, Mrs. Aldridge. I am sure that a bit of shopping in Paris would be just the thing to bring roses back to Mrs. Beckford's cheeks." Cecily turned to him in some astonishment. Hesitating to tell her bad news was one thing, but to propose a shopping trip in Paris was quite another.

"Look!" Jacob's voice came from the door, and Cecily looked around. He quite filled the doorway, standing with a swaddled baby in each arm. A young nursery maid fretted immediately behind him, clearly convinced he would drop one or both at any second. "I am an uncle again at last!" He grinned and came forward. "Ironic, that you should be the last of the family to meet our new arrivals. Which one would you like to greet first?"

"Oh, oh, oh . . ." But they were alive after all and so very beautiful! "How can I choose? I want them both! But I must start somewhere. Give me my little Clara."

"Clara?" inquired Jacob, settling one into the crook of her arm. "What happened to Cordelia or Constance?" Cecily smiled down at her daughter, who was surely the loveliest little girl ever born.

"I confess that I was not partial to Cordelia," said Colonel Beckford. "And my dear lady indulged me. As for Constance, I gather that was your idea."

"And a very good idea it was," sniffed Jacob. "Mrs. Aldridge, what do you think of the name Constance?"

"It is a lovely name," she agreed. "But it seems we must acquire another daughter before we can employ it." She shot her husband a flirtatious glance. Cecily was quite sure that she had never heard Livia make a risqué remark or seen her indulge in flirtation, not even with her own husband.

Jacob's smile was equally flirtatious. "We must take that under advisement." He transferred the second baby forward. "Are you ready for Julius, Cecily? He clearly wants his mama."

Cecily paused to kiss Clara again before reaching for her son. "More likely he wants his sister. He has been with her all his life, and now he is lonely without her." To her husband she continued, "Are we still set on Julius, my dear? It is not too late to call him Justin, for your father, if you like."

"No." He sighed. "It is foolish superstition, I suppose, but I cannot help but think that it would be tempting fate. The name was not lucky for us. Julius will do nicely." Cecily looked down at her son and caught her breath. Colonel Beckford was watching closely for her reaction—which suggested that it was not her imagination. He had already noticed something himself. "Bit of a fey look to him, don't you think?" he remarked with a studied lightness of tone. "Almost reminds me of Dr. Chang. You don't have any Chinamen hiding in your family tree, now do you?" She stared at the child openmouthed. Little Julius stared back, with a cool, thoughtful gaze that was startlingly unchildlike. "But Dr. Verlaine assures me that he is normal and healthy," continued the colonel. "He will doubtless grow out of any minor oddities of appearance."

"What happened to the mirror?" demanded Cecily.

There was a long silence while her family members exchanged glances. Finally Mrs. Aldridge spoke. "They tell me I broke it." She blushed (surely Rhoda had not been given to blushes) and hung her head. "I confess, I remember very little of my actions, since . . . since . . . I suppose since that last dinner we all had together. You served quail." Cecily nodded. "And from what I am told, it is just as well that I've forgotten, for I behaved most abominably. Dressing up in Jacob's clothes and rushing about stealing magic swords. Not to mention smashing antique mirrors."

"The mirror was scarcely smashed," soothed the colonel. "Bronze takes a good deal of smashing, after all. There are a few small dents, here and there, and one tiny hole where the sword pierced the metal. Although I must say that little hole was most felicitously placed. When the mirror is turned over, it appears in just that spot where the eye of Horus was incised, thereby completely destroying the mirror's efficacy as an astral link."

It was Rhoda, Cecily reflected, who had been desperate to close off the mirror. And Rhoda, most certainly, who had done so. "You are quite certain?" she inquired. She searched her son's face for any further sign of abnormality and not only saw nothing but came to wonder if she had truly seen anything previously. She looked up to her husband. "The mirror is ruined? Nothing could pass through it? Nothing at all?"

"It is become simply a very old piece of polished bronze, my dear. An interesting curio, handsomely engraved, no more. Frau Strasser was hugely disappointed and carried it away." He turned to Mrs. Aldridge. "I salute you, madame. You could not have struck a more fortunate blow if you had studied fencing for years."

She laughed and shook her head. "You are so excessively gracious I am forced to suppose you are laughing at me," she replied. "I cannot even remember doing it and obviously was acting in a completely irrational state. I very much fear Mr. Aldridge may yet decide to shut me up in Bedlam."

"Never Bedlam, my sweet," murmured Jacob. "You have my word. If you become too hopelessly lunatic to function I shall lock you in the attic."

"After all," confirmed the colonel, "you are family. We take care of our own."

Mrs. Aldridge smiled and picked up Julius. "Do you really think he looks like Papa? I surely do not see it." Surely only Livia would notice or care about such a thing.

"The spitting image," Colonel Beckford assured her. "Perhaps it is he, come to be near you." There was humor in his voice, but she did not laugh. Neither did Cecily. "If so, I could hardly blame him. Or grudge him a fresh start. Mr. Huong told me a very sad story about him."

Cecily reached out to reclaim her son and, having gotten him, smiled at him devotedly. No matter if he had an oddly Oriental cast of face. Julius responded by drooling contentedly on her sleeve in an appropriately infantile fashion. "I have only a rudimentary grasp of the doctrine of reincarnation," she remarked. "But I do seem to recall that the candidate is required to have passed away from his previous life before moving on to the next one." No matter who he might have been in some past life anyway; he was her Julius now.

"Exactly," murmured her husband, and she looked at him in some confusion.

Mrs. Aldridge raised a hand to her mouth in some surprise. "But of course—you do not know! The wire came while you were still unconscious." She drew a deep breath and turned her head to conceal the tears that sprang to her eyes. "My dear papa has passed away at last." Would anyone but Livia weep for Dr. Chang? But surely Rhoda would have wit enough to pretend to it.

"Oh, my poor, dear Mrs. Aldridge, I am so terribly sorry!" She set her babies by her side and reached up to pull her sister-in-law into her arms. Colonel Beckford scooted out of the way to permit them to embrace more comfortably. "It is a mercy, you know. You said yourself he could not find a moment's ease." She tenderly stroked the tears away. "But I fear that will not comfort you in your loss."

"It would comfort me greatly if you would call me 'Sister,'" murmured Mrs. Aldridge. "For you and Jacob are all the family I have now." Cecily nodded. Sister. An acceptable compromise, whichever one she proved eventually to be.

Mandrake Root
March 1887

Chapter One

Livia Aldridge looked down at the candle nestled within her cupped hands. It was broad and squat, with a deep well so that she suffered no danger of hot wax dripping onto her fingers. Nor did it burn very bright. Alone in the gloom, with only a soft glow rising up to light her face, she would have presented a spectral figure, if only there had been anyone about to see. She stood before what might have been a mirror, except that it did not reflect either her image or the glow of the candle. It reflected only sparkling mist and moonlight. The night where Livia stood was moonless.

Her lips moved inaudibly as she recited a sutra in Sanskrit. She did not actually know any Sanskrit. She had learned the sutra from a monk she had met in India, where she had once traveled as a child. The monk had not known any Sanskrit either, but he had been confident of the sutra's power. He had even been a bit amused by her questions into its meaning. "A sutra is not about mere words," he had said.

Livia sank to her knees, still whispering, taking care to hold the candle level as she did so. Her movements were fluid and graceful, for she was not encumbered by stays or crinolettes. She wore instead a Chinese gown that had belonged to her Grandmama—or rather to that woman whom she had called her Grandmama, for Mme. Chang was not actually any blood relation. She stayed on her knees some while, for the sutra had to be recited at least a hundred times. When she was done, she set the candle gently to one side, breathed deeply, and flung herself forward. Her hands reached outward in a gesture of entreaty; her face, she pressed down into the ground, such as it was. Her voice rose up quite loudly. "Hear me, Creature of the Mirror. Help me!"

The answer was like the shivering of a shadow in moonlight. She could scarcely be said to have heard it at all, save that its meaning was clear. "What would you know?"

She had come to the mirror with a very specific inquiry. She had meant to ask the way home. She was desperate and stranded and needed to find her way out of the strange wilderness in which she wandered. But when she opened her mouth to ask, the words came out instead, "How do I get even?" For an instant, she was utterly shocked. How could she think such a thing? She knew very well, from novels and philosophy alike, that revenge was ugly and evil, not to mention unfeminine. Decent folk traded in forgiveness. Only villains sought out retribution.

And yet, once the words were said, they filled her heart. She wanted revenge. It all spilled out before the mirror. She had been robbed—robbed of her home and her dear Papa, of her husband, her life, and even her very person. She was adrift in an astral desert, while a ghost—an unnatural spirit—passed itself off in her place; sat in her chair and ate fine foods proffered by her servants, and kissed her beloved's lips. Livia wanted desperately to go home. But even more than that, she wanted to see the usurper Rhoda Carothers pay, and Oliver Beckford, too, because he had helped the wicked Rhoda, not to mention murdered her Papa.

She lay sobbing before the mirror, uncertain whether she had been heard or even whether she had truly said any words aloud, but limp and exhausted. There was no formal answer, but after a few moments she was suffused with a sense of comfort. She felt a hand stroking her hair. She turned her head and was able to manage a wan smile on seeing Papa leaning tenderly over her. Then she remembered and turned her head angrily away. "You, again." It was not really her Papa. At least, probably not.

He spoke to her in exactly that tone that Papa had always employed in her childhood, when she attempted a tantrum or a sulk. "Am I to understand that you are severing all further relations between us?"

"You have your cheek," she did not quite snarl. "As if I had ever entertained relations with such as yourself."

"Such as myself?" His voice was pointedly, excessively astonished, and quite audibly contained an under-layer of amusement.

She rose to a sitting position and turned toward him with a rigidly constrained fury. "I hope you will not presume to pose as Dr. Chang?" It was a fearfully accurate pose; he looked exactly like Papa. But she knew well how little appearances were worth in the astral realm—or in the material world either, as Rhoda Carothers's imposture plainly demonstrated.

His eyes met hers with every sign of candor. He looked, for all the world, as if he were only slowly coming to see that she truly doubted him, and found the knowledge troubling. "If I am not Dr. Chang," he replied at last, "then who do you suggest I am?"

Livia forced herself to breathe deeply. She should have expected this. It was the nature of the thing to dissemble. It craved engagement and would assume whatever posture might serve that aim. She would do best to rise and walk away. She climbed to her feet but could not resist a parting shot. "You are the demon." It could not lie in so many words. Confronted with its own nature, it would surely slink away.

It did not slink away. It cocked its head, the very gesture Papa would have used, and regarded her with hurt, quizzical eyes. "A demon? And you see no other option? I could not possibly be Papa?"

"Papa is dead," she pointed out, and on hearing herself say the words aloud, she suddenly swayed, nearly overcome by a wave of sorrow and loss. Papa was dead. After lying so long in helpless, incoherent pain, he was dead at last. All during his illness, she had secretly wondered if it might not be simpler, kinder, cleaner if he died. But now he was dead, she desperately wanted him back.

Suddenly it was standing very close to her. "The dead do not always pass on," it whispered. That was surely true, and despite herself, she looked up to meet the grey eyes of the figure beside her. "I believe myself to be Dr. Chang. I have no recollection of being anyone or anything else. I remember his life. I share his views and his aspirations."

She turned her face away, suddenly frightened. Demons did not lie. But she knew this creature must be the demon; it had first approached her before her papa died, so it could not be his shade. Yet its voice carried such conviction. Was it possible that the demon believed its own lies?

It continued, almost as if it sensed her thoughts. "If I am a demon, there must surely be some clear proof by which you can demonstrate my nature." When she did not immediately reply, it assumed a sharper tone. "Come, now, is this the logic I worked so hard to teach you? To cast random aspersions without evidence?" She tried to suppress the impulse to bristle but must have failed, for he continued, "What, then, are the marks of a demon, by which it can be known?"

She knew the answer to that, knew it so well that she entirely forgot to question the thing's right to question her. "Their shapes are generally pleasing and familiar, but they cannot be identified by their material characteristics, as they are formed—if one can call it formed—of a fluid ectoplasm that can present a variety of aspects, according to the emotional vulnerabilities of the intended victim."

"If it cannot be identified by its material characteristics, how can it be recognized?"

"By its predatory intent." She took a deep breath. "Having gained a victim's trust, it provokes emotional responses and feeds on the psychical energies so generated. It generally prefers the darker emotions: fear, anger or . . ." Her voice broke off and she paused to blush before whispering, "Or carnal impulses."

"But how is this predation manifested? How would an observer determine that it had taken place?"

She looked up in some surprise. The question was unexpected and had never been touched on during her studies; the texts had seemed rather to assume that predation was self-evident. "By the effect on the victim, I suppose." She reflected. Rhoda Carothers had died at the demon's hand, but no one had suspected anything unnatural; her death had been attributed to fever. Cecily Beckford had lain in a cataleptic trance for years, and while it was widely suspected that her malady was not natural, there had been no clear indication as to the cause or, for that matter, the prognosis. Only Jacob had been visibly and specifically menaced.

"There must always be symptoms," she concluded. "When the life force is consumed, a loss of function is inevitable. But the effects frequently pass unnoticed or are misunderstood. Mr. Aldridge suffered an extreme change of temperament when he was under attack, but if his sister had not intervened no one but his landlady would have noticed, and his death would have gone unremarked." She sighed. "I daresay the eventual death would always go unremarked. Everybody dies."

"You perceive me as murderously predatory?" She caught her breath. She had already somehow forgotten that, in light of her accusation, her description would necessarily apply to him. "You suggest that I am feeding on your

222

energy to your detriment, and will do so until you perish from the loss?" Almost despite herself, she turned to face it. It showed only a studied neutrality of countenance—just as Papa would have done in a comparable situation. But its eyes were shadowed. There was a hint of hurt in its voice when it continued, "How have I injured you?"

She opened her mouth to reply. Then she closed it again. It had not injured her. She opened her mouth again. Surely it had refrained only because it had not gained her acceptance and was therefore unable to commence feeding. Then she closed her mouth again. Before Papa's death, she had met the thing here and accepted it, supposing that he had been trapped in the astral realm by his illness, much as she was now trapped by Rhoda's theft of her person. It had gained her entire confidence and made no move to injure her in any way, for all that she had granted it a hundred opportunities. Could she have been in the right then? Was this truly his spirit, still trapped now, as it had been then, and therefore unable to pass on?

It sensed her hesitation. But it said nothing more, patiently waiting—just as her Papa had always done when supervising her lessons—for her to follow her thoughts through to their conclusion. Finally she responded, "No. You have done me no harm. So far. And I wish with all my heart to believe that you are Papa. But the demon has always depended on its victims' desire to believe in its seeming. If you are truly Papa, then it is you who taught me how unwise it would be to succumb to that desire."

It lifted an eyebrow and chuckled, and the chuckle grew into a deep, hearty laugh. "Well, played, my sweetling. And entirely true. I would not like you to take chances with demons." Resuming a more serious demeanor, he continued, "But I swear I mean you no ill. Could I at least persuade you that if perhaps I am not Dr. Chang—however firmly I might suppose I am—then I am at least your ally, entirely at your disposal in this matter of revenge?" His lips tightened and his look grew dangerous. "For I assure you, I desire nothing in the world more than to see your enemies and mine subjected to their just deserts."

"You would help me in this?" Her hand went out to his, of its own volition. "You do not think me wicked?" Whatever he was, perhaps he was sent by the mirror in answer to her prayer.

Chapter Two

Colonel Oliver Beckford looked up from his coffee when his wife came into the dining room, and smiled. "You are looking uncommonly lovely this morning, my dear."

She paused from sorting through the morning mail and glanced down over her outfit, quite as if she had forgotten which dress she had selected. It was one of her oldest gowns (light blue, trimmed with peach), and the silhouette it presented did not entirely coincide with the latest fashion; but his sincerity was unmistakable, and she favored him with an amused smile. "I count myself fortunate that you are so easily pleased." She turned to the housemaid. "Good morning, Rose. Do you think Cook might give me an egg?" Rose poured her coffee, curtsied, and retreated to the kitchen, and Cecily resumed perusing the mail. Indeed, she perused it so intently that her husband was distracted from his paper.

"Have you received something of unusual interest?" he inquired.

She looked up with troubled eyes. "It is a letter from Frau Strasser."

"Indeed?" He plucked a piece of toast from the rack and spread it thickly with jam. "Has she returned from the Continent?"

"She has not. She writes from Venice, and I fear the letter has been some time reaching us." Cecily turned the envelope over to examine the postmark. "She thinks we might like to know that Mme. Chang is returning to England."

He furrowed his brow and laid aside his toast. "Does she say when?"

She shook her head. "Only that it will be soon." She dropped the letter on the table. "This will not please Jacob."

"Or Mrs. Aldridge either, I suspect." He shrugged. "In fact, I cannot immediately think of anyone whom this news will please. Do we know why she is coming?"

"Frau Strasser suspects she hopes to recover the mirror." Cecily picked up the letter again and read aloud, "'Her inquiry after it was so pointedly casual that I was forced to conclude she was profoundly interested. Of course I informed her that it was hopelessly damaged, but she did not appear to be convinced.'" Cecily looked up to meet her husband's eyes. "We are, indeed, confident that it is beyond repair, are we not?" She hesitated for an instant, then continued with no apparent awareness that she was changing the subject. "And why are you reading the advertisements for 'Properties Available'?"

"Are we not in imminent danger of overcrowding?" She answered with a blank look, and he returned to the previous subject. "I was satisfied about the mirror before this news." He sighed and stared into space. "I cannot think how it could be restored. But mirrors are not my area of expertise, and Mme. Chang is very skilled. If she means to try, I would not casually dismiss her efforts as doomed. Of course, she may only wish to see for herself whether it is really impossible," he mused. "But would she come so far if she were not reasonably optimistic?"

They were interrupted by a small cry from the hallway. They both turned to investigate. Jacob and Mrs. Aldridge had come down for breakfast, and had paused—just as Cecily had done—to examine the morning post. Mrs. Aldridge had opened a letter and was staring down at it with considerable dismay. She thrust the missive toward her husband, displaying plainly to everyone that it was inscribed entirely with Chinese symbols. Cecily stooped to recover the envelope, which had fluttered to the floor. That, at least, was written in English and bore a London postmark. "Very soon, indeed," she murmured. "It seems that Mme. Chang has already arrived."

"Oh, Mr. Aldridge," whispered Mrs. Aldridge. "Whatever shall we do?" He did not take the page, and she nervously crumpled it into a ball, which she then tossed to one side as if it burned her hand. "I cannot see her."

Colonel Beckford stooped slightly as if to pick up the wad of crushed paper. His bad leg did not allow easy bending, and Cecily—seeing his difficulty—dropped down to recover the discarded letter for him. Gently and carefully, she unfolded it, pressing out a crease here and pulling out a flap of paper there, until it was restored to legibility, or at least as much legibility as it had ever possessed. "Do you read Chinese?" she inquired, passing the page over to her husband.

"No," he said. "But I have some friends at the Foreign Office who do." He had brought his coffee cup with him; he drained it, set it on the hall table, and started toward the door. Belatedly he turned back. "That is, if I have your permission, Mrs. Aldridge? Surely, it is best we find out what she wants." She seemed scarcely to hear him; rather she wrung her hands and stared into space without replying. "Mrs. Aldridge?"

She raised one hand in a dismissive wave. He had his coat on and was halfway out the door before she raised her head and turned to regard him thoughtfully. When the door had closed behind him, she mused, "He does not ask me what it says. He takes it to the Foreign Office."

Cecily and Jacob exchanged glances. "No doubt he does not like to trouble you," said Cecily. "The letter has already upset you greatly; requiring you to examine it more closely would be a grave unkindness." She received no answer and glanced nervously at the window. "Goodness, but it looks like rain. I wonder if I shall want a warmer shawl?" She hurried up the stairs.

Jacob looked after her with a wry smile, then offered an arm to his wife and escorted her into the dining room. "My dear, you have a splendid facility for clearing a room. I so dislike a crowded table." The door from the kitchen opened to admit Rose. "And look! Here is an egg—done just the way I like it. My morning is complete. Thank you, Rose." If Rose was startled to find him receiving the egg that had been prepared for Cecily she gave no sign. She delivered up the egg and poured coffee, then curtsied and retreated.

Mrs. Aldridge selected a piece of toast with a sigh. "Surely you know I never meant to offend. But the colonel is not one to worry much over consideration; doubtless he assumes his good intent is obvious. So I cannot help but think that she . . . shall we say, indulged in a tender fib? They must suspect I do not really know Chinese."

Jacob shrugged. "I suppose they must, since you put it so."

"You suppose? But surely you know; was it not you who told her?"

He lifted an eyebrow. "I most certainly did not." In response to her dubious expression he continued, "I assure you, I have spent half my life trying to keep a secret—any secret—from Cecily. But it is a hopeless quest. She can hear me thinking, you know." She giggled and he smiled. "You must not laugh; she does—she always has. Do you know, when we were little she used to pretend to be me? She would dress up in my clothes and talk in just my voice, with just my manner. It was quite as if she could become me; she perceived the very state of my soul. Of course, she fooled everyone. She did not stop until we got to be eleven or so, and she suddenly grew taller than me. I didn't know whether to be embarrassed or relieved at finding myself suddenly so much the shorter. I did not catch up again for years."

His wife was laughing heartily by then. "There is no magic in that. Even now you are two peas in a pod. I daresay when you were still children, you were indistinguishable." She shook her head and her face clouded. "You are very diverting, my love, but we must face it sooner or later. Mme. Chang will expect me to know Chinese." She paused and glanced at him from under her eyelashes. "I . . . I have forgotten all my Chinese." There was a long silence. "I daresay you find that odd."

His regarded her thoughtfully, then shook his head very deliberately. "Doubtless a consequence of having been trapped in the astral realm. A sort of psychical scarring. I tangled with a demon once myself, and my memory has never fully recovered." His eyes drifted off to the left as he reflected. "I do not think we can entirely refuse to receive her. The attempt would only provoke her stubborn nature. But we can take care not to leave you alone with her, and if she then speaks to you in Chinese, you can decline to allow it as a matter of courtesy."

"Must we?" she whispered. "I . . . I dread seeing her."

He reached out to take her hand. "As do I, my own. But I do not see an alternative. Can you be brave?"

She shrugged. "Not really. But I suppose I can pretend to it."

Chapter Three

There were a number of techniques for viewing the material realm from within the etheric planes, many of them entirely convincing. Livia had only to think, *Paris*, for example, or, *Venice*, and she would find herself strolling through the Tuileries Garden or admiring the bronze horses in St. Mark's.

Indeed, when she was first exploring her exile, she had reveled in the ease of travel and had availed herself of the opportunity to visit or revisit any number of foreign lands. But tourism lost its charm as she came to understand that, clear as the world might look to her, she was but an insubstantial phantom within it. Strangers repeatedly walked right through the spot on which she was standing, completely unable to see her and brushing her aside with the breeze of their passing. It was an exceedingly disconcerting sensation. She soon concluded that a Paris in which the shops were always closed (to her at least) held little appeal.

Specific physical objects were only slightly more difficult to conjure, and that only because there were so many physical objects in the world that duplication was a constant issue. The thought of Paris would routinely lead her to that Paris that the whole world knew (although doubtless there were other cities of the same name). The thought of a chair, however, tended to present her with a bewildering array of seating arrangements, unless she concentrated carefully on the distinguishing characteristics of the particular one she preferred. But she rapidly acquired the knack of it, so that when she wanted to sit down she automatically summoned the wonderfully comfortable blue damask wingback from the library in Papa's old London house.

Locating persons was more difficult by far. The animate simply did not impinge on the ether in quite the same way as the inanimate. They were presences, of course, and yet one could not sense their location directly. Nor could they simply be summoned, like chairs; their free will interfered. One might try visiting their residences, but if they happened to be out one had little recourse. One could scarcely leave a card.

Livia was skilled with mirrors, even ordinary mirrors. So she had painstakingly summoned about her a selection of mirrors (or rather the astral counterparts of the physical mirrors) that overlooked those locations around London where her friends were most likely to be found. She consulted these frequently to keep track of her family's activities. Although basically sound, the system was far from infallible.

Livia settled in front of the first, the foremost mirror, the one she had taught to catch reflections from all the others. She sank to her knees. She was falling out of the habit of chairs. "Show me my husband," she whispered. She loved the word "husband." It would be vulgar to use it in conversation, but it gave her a comforting sense of possession. "Show me my husband," she repeated.

The mirrors rippled and shimmered before presenting her with a scene from Papa's London house. Before she had time to wonder what Jacob could possibly be doing there, the image stabilized to display not Jacob Aldridge, but Mme. Chang.

Livia was on the verge of turning away in annoyance at the misdirection, but her attention was captured by her grandmama's attitude of distress. Mme. Chang was seated in the ladder-back chair before her rosewood secretary; the writing desk had been laid open. But Mme. Chang was not writing a letter. Rather she had fallen forward to pillow her face on the blotter and wrapped her arms around her head. Her slight form shook with sobs. Livia stared aghast. Grandmama had suffered many tribulations in her life, but Livia had never before seen her give way to grief.

The top of the secretary was flat and served as a shelf. Normally its surface was crowded with a variety of ornaments, but these had been swept away. A single urn now dominated the space thus cleared. It was a beautiful object, carved from white jade, and incised with a bas-relief of twining leaves. Two small, flat bowls flanked it, one containing a rice cake and the other a clear fluid. Immediately in front of the urn sat a little incense burner with a joss stick burning in it.

A portrait of Dr. James Chang as a young man hung above the desk. Livia knew it well; she remembered seeing it painted. She had still been a child at the time, and had asked if she could be in the painting, too; Papa had laughed and said they would paint her portrait separately when she was older and even more beautiful. She had preened in front of her mirror for weeks, and wondered how beautiful she would need to become before it was her turn.

She studied the scene for several seconds before grasping its import. Cremation was not the Chinese custom. But the offerings of food and joss were unmistakable; the urn must contain the physical remains of Dr. Chang. Even so, Livia was bewildered. Why had Grandmama taken it on herself to handle and store Papa's remains? It was most improper for a Chinese elder to pay honor to a more junior member of the family, even in death, no matter how beloved. It was the child's place to honor and bury the dead; Grandmama ought to have left the remains in the funeral home, forever if need be.

The awful conclusion struck home. It would indeed have been forever. It had been Livia's place to lay Papa to rest, but she was trapped in the astral realm, and the wretched imposter Rhoda had abandoned the sad task to Mme. Chang—shaming them all. No wonder Grandmama was weeping. Livia's lips tightened. One more injury added to Rhoda's tally; her bill was seriously overdue.

Almost as if she heard the thought, Mme. Chang lifted her head and whispered, "They will pay, my dear boy, my only one; they will pay. It is promised." She spoke in Mandarin, of course; her English was strained and imperfect (as was, for that matter, her Greek—and her Italian positively wretched) but Livia scarcely noticed, having been raised in the language herself. She noticed primarily the glint in Mme. Chang's eye, and rejoiced in the thought of what it might bode for Rhoda. It occurred to her that Mme. Chang would not be deceived by any imposture; Mme. Chang was exceedingly difficult to deceive. Livia smiled. The matter was practically taken care of already.

"And that scheming seducer, the son of Aldridge," continued Mme. Chang in a voice that was more a hiss than a whisper. "I will eat his heart uncooked. Yes, and his vile whore with him"—Livia fell back as if she had been slapped, for no one had ever said that awful word aloud in her presence before—"and all his kin. They will suffer torments utterly beyond what mere flesh can endure. A thousand hells will not contain their agony."

Livia staggered back, away from the appalling scene and the mirror that conducted it, back to a place where Mme. Chang's visage paled to invisibility, and her voice faded into the sough of an angry breeze. She dropped to the ground, stunned and horrified. Grandmama blamed Jacob! And, once roused, Grandmama could wreak great harm. He had to be warned.

She summoned all her resolve and approached the mirror again, commanding it to clear with all the force she could muster. "Show me my husband!" she demanded. There must be no mistake this time. (Or had it been a mistake? If she had harbored anxiety in her heart, might the mirror have interpreted her request to see her husband as a request to see the danger surrounding him? Mirrors did not always respond to verbal cues so much as emotional ones.) "Show me where my husband is now," she repeated, expressing it as clearly as she could contrive.

And yet she was misdirected again. She found herself looking into the Beckford nursery. Mrs. Black, the aged housekeeper, half dozed in a chair with the infant Clara in her lap, officially overseeing Rose, who tenderly dandled little Julius Beckford over her knees. It was a charming scene, but only slightly less bewildering than the previous one. What did this nursery have to do with Jacob Aldridge? And why was Rose—who had been Papa's devoted servant—acting as the Beckford nurse? Surely Rose had not mistaken Rhoda for Livia?

Rose had been Livia's nanny once, and a wonderfully tender one; she would surely know Livia from Rhoda, even if no one else on the earth could make the distinction. Also Rose had . . . keen senses. She saw things no one else saw—said nothing of them, perhaps, but saw them. Even now, Rose glanced up from the baby toward the mirror and cocked her head, as if she sensed Livia's presence. No, decided Livia, Rose was not deceived by the false Mrs. Aldridge. But she might have been happy enough to leave Mme. Chang after Dr. Chang passed away. Jacob would have suggested it. He would have been mostly interested in acquiring Cook's services, but he would have suggested that Mrs. Aldridge take on Rose at the same time.

Rose dropped her head in a polite bow to whomever she sensed in the mirror and returned her attention to the little boy in her arms. Livia could not blame her. Julius Beckford was as sweet and adorable a child as she had ever seen. She wished she could step forward and take him from Rose; such a darling—her fingers itched to hold him. Oddly, he looked a little like Papa, although there was surely nothing in his ancestry to account for it. Of course, Papa had looked a deal more Occidental than he ought by right. In any case, the resemblance only made Livia like him better.

She reached out tenderly toward the lovely child, as if her hand had somehow forgotten she could not really stroke him. Then, regretfully, she pulled back and turned away. This was not warning Jacob. Somehow, instinctively, she found herself before the great mirror. It was, of course, dark. Rhoda had passed through that mirror while it was whole, then secured her escape by smashing it behind her. The damage to the material manifestation appeared minimal, but the bond between the astral and the material was severed, the portal closed forever.

Yet even ruined, it exuded an aura of power. It was still a depository of great knowledge; sages and scholars had poured centuries of learning, millennia of prayers into its fathomless polished surface. It could still call up spirits, as she had recently demonstrated, and find answers in dark places where no ordinary mirror could see. Even so, she did not expect an answer when she cried to it, "Why can I not see my husband?"

Yet an answer came. The mirror glowed. Livia stepped toward it, as if to warm herself at that glow. Surely it could not show her Jacob; it retained no connection to the natural realm; and yet . . . it glowed. Mirrors had always talked to her, especially this one.

Slowly a scene took shape. A place lined in carpets and hangings but unfurnished, save for a single brazier around which six persons were grouped. Two men were meeting; the first—grizzled, squat, armored, half-Mongol by the look of him—was surrounded by his entourage. The Englishman was alone. Or rather the Irishman was alone, she realized on close inspection. She recognized him: tall and very fair with auburn hair and a truly glorious moustache that almost concealed a cruel mouth. It was her father, Ishmael Aram.

Three women attended the warlord. Behind him, in the place of honor, was a small, weather-beaten elderly woman, wrapped up in furs and ensconced on a veritable mountain of embroidered pillows. That would be his mother. The woman on his left looked only slightly younger, and just as tired as the mother. She was fat and thick lipped with heavy brows, but not too plain to deck herself out in a robe of polished silk embroidered with gold thread. She wore many jewels and seemed to have a particular fondness for pearls.

The third woman knelt at their feet. Although she was no longer, strictly speaking, young, she was still astonishingly beautiful—delicate and elegant, like a Ming princess. Her robe was also silk, but not quite so extensively embroidered; she wore few ornaments, save for an elaborately carved jade comb in her lustrous hair. Livia stared; surely, it could not be . . . But, yes, it was. The second wife was Mme. Chang—an incarnation of Mme. Chang considerably younger than the woman weeping over her late son's ashes, perhaps, but still recognizably Grandmama. So the image in the mirror did not require a link to the material world; it was from the past.

There was also a young man seated to the warlord's right, with his head bowed, but Livia dismissed him as a bodyguard in her eagerness to overhear the conversation. Aram was offering his hand to the warlord, but Xiu Wang Po—for surely it must be he—turned instead to speak with his lesser wife. "Are you very sure about this?" His Mandarin was thickly accented; he would probably have been more comfortable with Wu. "The child is so young. Your boy will have to wait a very long time before he can claim his bride."

She smiled sweetly at him. "Oh, my lord, let your devoted servant crave your indulgence." Her Mandarin, of course, was flawless. "The girl's star charts are a perfect match to his; the marriage will bring him great luck and power, power enough to be worth the wait. His golden karma will come to shelter us all." She shrugged. "And in the meanwhile, he has his pretty concubine."

Xiu Wang Po turned then to the young man by his side, who lifted his head. He was not a bodyguard. Papa looked so young that Livia scarcely knew him. "And you, Xiu Yao. Are you content with this arrangement?"

Xiu Yao looked up at the elder man with eyes far less guarded than they had become by the time Livia knew him. His smile conveyed all the affection and respect due a father, for all that he looked nothing like Xiu Wang Po. "I am, sir. My mother has shown me the charts, and I think her reasons are good." His smile grew broader. "And my concubine is very pretty."

Xiu Wang Po laughed hugely and clapped the younger man on the back. "Not pretty enough for my boy!" he exclaimed. "I'll buy you another, even prettier. You like having one girl so much? Let us see how you like having two." He returned his attention to Ishmael Aram, who waited on the exchange with surprising patience and a strange half smile, as if—perhaps—he knew something they did not. "It is agreed, then," he announced, accepting the hand that Aram was still extending. "You will deliver the girl by the end of the week."

"If you will permit me, my lord," whispered his beautiful wife. She added more loudly to Aram, "With her dowry."

"Well spoken, woman," agreed Xiu Wang Po. "These English cannot be trusted." Ishmael Aram winced, not—Livia suspected—at the lack of trust, but at hearing himself described as an Englishman. "With her dowry," the warlord echoed.

"Of course," murmured the Irishman. His Mandarin was fair, not unaccented but fluent—better actually than Livia remembered it to have been. He smiled broadly. "How I look forward to that day! Shall I arrange an appropriate celebration, Brother?"

It was Xiu Wang Po's turn to wince, but even Mongol warlords were bound by certain rules of courtesy. "Not at all, Brother. I shall host the celebration. My son's betrothal is an important event; I must summon the clan to rejoice with me."

"I so look forward to meeting your kinsman," murmured Ishmael. He spoke truly, Livia realized in a sudden flash of supernatural clarity. He wanted the connection. He opened his mouth to say more, but Livia turned away. She already had a great deal to think about, all of it disturbing.

She needed a chair and it was there; she sank gratefully down into it and raised her hands to her aching head. It made no sense. She could not have been betrothed to Papa; it was not credible. He had never so much as smiled flirtatiously at her. Surely someone would have mentioned it to her, sometime; they could scarcely have planned to surprise her with it. What possible dowry could they have meant? She knew nothing of any dowry.

She shuddered. How binding could this betrothal have been if she knew nothing of it? Was her marriage to Jacob compromised? And Papa had come to live with them after they were married, and smiled at his son-in-law every morning; how could he have, if he had meant to marry her himself? The questions piled up around her in great, unanswered heaps, and her head ached so abominably she almost wept.

A hand stroked her hair. The Papa spirit stood beside her, smiling tenderly down. "You are troubled, my dear?"

She clutched at his hand, no longer much concerned with who or what he really was, but desperately grateful for his consoling touch. "Did you see?" He nodded soberly. "What does it mean?" He gazed down at her, waiting for her to face the obvious. She knew very well what it meant. She amended her question. "Was it true?" He continued to look down at her. She also knew very well that the mirror never lied. It never even twisted meaning, as most astral entities were wont to do. It displayed only utter truth, as accurately as human eyes could perceive it. "I was meant to marry you?"

He nodded again, sighed, and drew up a chair of his own from out of the ether and sat. She noticed that—Papa or no—he chose Papa's favorite chair, from behind the desk in his office. "Yes," he sighed. "You were. And so you did."

She opened her mouth to speak, but could find no words. No matter—he heard her thought. "I know. You do not remember. And so now you wonder why we did not tell you. But you were there. When you first arrived, you were too ill from the journey for lengthy discussions; we had to delay the ceremony until you recovered your strength. But in the end, you were well enough to stand up and recite your vows. It was years before we grasped how little you remembered or understood." Livia shivered and wrapped her arms around herself. She had often heard how ill she had been when she came to Xiu Wang Po's camp, but she did not really remember it; she only remembered waking up at the camp, terribly weak and wondering how she had gotten there.

"And then, Father . . . died." "Was killed," he should have said, but Livia let it pass. "And we had to leave China. And Greece was so difficult." He shrugged and looked away. "By the time we realized you didn't know, it had been so long that it was awkward. And the longer we put off telling you, the harder it grew. By the time we came to England, we had decided that it could wait until the consecration." He turned back to meet her eyes. "I think perhaps I was afraid to tell you. England was not like China. Suppose you refused?"

She stared at him aghast, then buried her face in her hands. Somehow it had not been real until he confirmed it—just a picture in a mirror, nothing to do with her. She would have wept, save that she could scarcely even breathe.

"Darling, please don't cry," he murmured, crouching down to put an arm around her shoulders and brush a hand through her hair.

She shrank from his touch, which had grown suddenly too meaningful. She threw up both arms as if to protect her face and shrieked with all her heart and strength, "Get away from me!"

And he was gone. Utterly gone. She lowered her arms and looked about. The mists paled and dissipated before her intent to see. An infinite plain stretched out about her; there was nothing to see in any direction. He was gone. Banished by her desire to have him away. But she still had one burning question that had to be answered. "Mirror Spirit," she called, but despite an impressively imperious tone, she got no answer. She tried again on a more conciliatory note. "Papa Spirit."

She still saw nothing, but sensed a shiver in the air that might have been a presence. So she resumed a haughty attitude and demanded, "What dowry?"

It was not a voice, even. She simply found herself somehow aware of the answer. "The mirror, of course." The final straw. Livia decided it was time to get on with some serious weeping.

Chapter Four

Colonel Beckford stepped down from the cab with a worried grimace. He was very late, and his day had been difficult. The dank weather only darkened his mood, not to mention made his leg ache. But if he had hoped to soothe his nerves in the comfort of his home, he was disappointed. Rather, he found the house in an uproar, with the servants tiptoeing nervously in every direction and accomplishing nothing. A large crate had been delivered.

The mistress—he was told—had not been pleased to receive it. She had ordered it sent to the attic, but then had changed her mind and had it brought back down and put in his study. Twice she had summoned a servant to open the box, and twice she had decided it was better off closed. She had sent a messenger with an urgent note for Mr. Aldridge, but had instructed the servant in whispers, well outside the hearing of Mrs. Aldridge—whom she sent out immediately on a trivial errand. She was waiting in the study— a place she rarely went—presumably still wrestling with the decision as to whether or not to open the box.

She was, in fact, seated beside the desk with her hands in her lap, like a schoolgirl awaiting a Latin tutor, save that she jumped up as soon as he peeked in the door. "Oh, Colonel Beckford, you are come home at last!" she exclaimed. "I am at my wits' end—you'll never guess what has occurred."

He glanced over at the crate standing off to one side, under the Chinese apothecary chest. The lid had been pried open, but then closed again. "The mirror has found its way back to us." He crossed to it and reviewed the extensive selection of delivery labels affixed to its surface. "And it's come a long way."

She blinked and cocked her head. "Well, perhaps you might contrive to guess, at that."

There was a knock at the door, which opened before they had time to answer. Jacob darted in to take Cecily's hands in his. "My dear, I am sorry I was so long. I stopped at the Foreign Office to see what was keeping Oliver, but he had . . ." Out of the corner of his eye, he spotted the colonel. "Oh, there you are. I must have just missed you."

Colonel Beckford spread his hands in a gesture of apology. "I seem to have worried you both abominably; I was held up. McDonald was suddenly taken ill. Collapsed in the middle of a sentence. I could scarcely walk out."

"McDonald?" mused Jacob. "Do we know him?"

"Well, I do," replied Oliver. "He's a linguist, an astonishingly clever fellow. Speaks thirty-seven languages and has a wonderful knack for what he calls 'the superstitious nuances.'"

"The one you asked to translate Mme. Chang's letter?" surmised Cecily.

Jacob had crossed over to the crate in front of the apothecary's chest, just as Oliver came back toward his wife. Squatting beside it, he inquired, "Is this what I think it is?" He got no answer, and lifted the lid. "Why would it come here? It has nothing to do with us."

"Perhaps," murmured the colonel, "it is come for Mrs. Aldridge. If you will forgive my saying so."

Jacob sighed heavily and rose. "About Mrs. Aldridge . . ." He looked to the left, and he looked to the right. He dropped his head and studied the carpet. "She may not be as profoundly linked to it as you suppose."

"You mean," replied Oliver, "that she may not really be Mrs. Livia Aldridge? But rather Mrs. Rhoda Aldridge?"

"Oh, Colonel," whispered Cecily. "Must you be so very blunt? Surely you see how painful this is for Jacob."

He shrugged. "A boil must be lanced before it can heal."

Jacob sighed again. "So you both know. Which is more than I can say for myself. Sometimes I am quite sure she is one, and sometimes the other. If it is Rhoda, then her very person must remember the manners and inclinations of the previous resident. If it is Livia, she has mellowed dramatically. Nor could I possibly choose between them, if I did know. So I do not ask. And she does not say. But, yes, there is considerable doubt that she is the lady to whom the mirror once belonged."

"Which does not alter my thinking at all," said the colonel. "One lady claimed the mirror; indeed, as I recall, her guardian had anointed it with her blood to consecrate it to her. But the other lady—if it is she—dwelt within it for years and escaped her own death through its portal. It might have been drawn to either. Or neither; it might have been sent to her by Mme. Chang. But one way or another, it is here for her, I am quite sure."

"Then nothing we do will rid us of it reliably," concluded Cecily. "And our only resolution"—she glanced uneasily at her brother—"must begin with Mrs. Aldridge confronting it."

He winced. "I do not think she would consent to that."

As they reflected, there was another knock at the door. Rose entered with a small salver. She curtsied and knelt, proffering the note that lay atop it. After Colonel Beckford claimed the letter, she paused rather longer than was her custom, as if expecting further instructions. But when none were forthcoming she curtsied again and withdrew. Jacob looked after her.

Oliver tore open the letter, tossing the envelope to the floor. On perusing its contents, he sucked in his breath. "McDonald has died." He thrust the note into one pocket and drew several crumpled pages from another. "And just after translating this." He held up the Chinese letter. "It can scarcely be a coincidence." He examined the letter thoughtfully and rubbed the paper between his fingers. "But it cannot be poison; we've all handled it with no ill effect." He tossed the letter onto the desk and turned his attention to the sheet remaining in his hand.

Cecily pressed close to him, reading over his arm. "But this cannot be the translation—it says nothing of interest. I've had more engrossing letters from Tante Agatha."

Jacob joined them in the huddle. "'Enjoying good health—best wishes for yours—easy crossing—weather splendid.' Look, she does not even say how long she means to stay in London, or ask if she may visit." He chewed his lip. "Plainly she does not expect a reply."

"Of course not," opined the colonel. "Clearly it was only written as a vehicle for a curse, to be evoked by the act of reading it."

"At least now Mrs. Aldridge may stop fretting how to answer," observed Jacob.

"Perhaps we had best keep her in for a bit." Cecily looked up and back and forth, from her husband to her brother. "If we say that she is not receiving, Mme. Chang will suppose she is mortally ill, and may content herself awhile with waiting for the funeral." She knitted her brow. "But why does Mme. Chang attack Livia? Or does she suspect it is Rhoda?"

"If Mme. Chang suspected she was Rhoda, she would not have written in Chinese," pointed out Jacob. "Perhaps she feels that Livia has sided against her with me. Does it really matter? Mme. Chang is very skilled at harboring grudges. Doubtless, she has thought of something that displeases her." He shook his head. "It seems that Dr. Chang was a moderating influence after all." He looked at Oliver. "Perhaps we were too harsh with him."

Oliver met his eye squarely. "He fed my wife to a demon. And stood by to watch while it consumed her. I do not see I should forgive that, simply because his mother was worse." He smiled tightly. "Besides, I needed his blood to recover her."

"Did he?" Cecily's tone was doubtful, wondering. "I remember nothing of that."

"Best you don't," chorused the two men as one.

She frowned. "But Rhoda said it was Livia who did it."

"Livia?" The two men spoke as one again, then eyed each other with a certain annoyance. Jacob took up the thread. "My dear, that is not credible. How could Livia have had anything to do with it? And how would Rhoda know if she had? And how would you talk to Rhoda if she did know? Surely this is a false memory arising out of . . . of the fever dream the demon imposes on its victims."

"No." She surprised even herself with her conviction. "I remember it clearly. It was the night the twins were born, and you . . ." She tapped a finger on her brother's chest. "You and Anna Strauss were trying to open the mirror. And I saw Rhoda in the mirror—the hall mirror, that is, not Dr. Chang's mirror. I didn't believe it was she, at first. She tried to make me remember when the demon took me."

Cecily broke off suddenly and shuddered, and buried her face in her hands. "I nearly did remember. Unspeakable things . . . I can't . . ." She shook her head vigorously, and straightened. "No matter. Anyway, she told me that the demon found us in Venice because Livia was in league with it, and directed it to us."

Jacob stiffened and went white. He seemed almost to stop breathing.

Then he turned on his heel and strode out of the room. Colonel and Mrs. Beckford gazed after him, listening to his footsteps in the hallway, and the slam of the front door.

Eventually Cecily caught up with him. She had had to run much of the way, with her head down against the wind, and she was gasping for breath when she took his arm. They walked in silence until she recovered. "My dear, I am so dreadfully sorry," she whispered. "You must forgive me."

"There is nothing to forgive."

"There is, Jacob, and you know it. You must not fib to me. I cannot conceive how I came to speak to you so. And after I scolded my good colonel for his bluntness! You are entirely in the right, of course. Surely nothing of the sort ever truly happened. It must have been some feverish nightmare. If not brought on by the demon, then by the laudanum Dr. Verlaine gave me. Or both together. Or perhaps, if I am recollecting rightly, then it was not Rhoda in the mirror but the demon lying to me. Whatever the source, I had no right in the world to fasten such a poisonous fantasia upon you."

He did not stop; he did not look at her. But the corner of his mouth twitched very faintly. "So I must not fib to you," he murmured. "But it is perfectly acceptable for you to fib to me." He still did not glance at her but nevertheless sensed somehow that she had turned a guilty face away from him. "You do not mean a word of what you say."

"Oh, but I do mean it!" she cried. And then sighed and admitted, "I just do not believe it. But I will make myself believe it somehow, if only you will forgive me." She stopped dead but continued to cling to his arm so that he, perforce, stopped also. "Jacob, my own, you are half of myself. There is nothing more important than that there be peace between us. We should both go mad if there were not. And so, I was wrong. And if I am still too perverse to have let go of this horrid notion, I swear I shall smother it in silence until it dies the death it deserves."

At that, he did look down at her. Nestled damply against her cheek, there was a small curl, which the wind had torn free from its pin. With another faint twitch at the corner of his mouth he replied, "If I were not so furious with you, I should laugh. The very idea of you smothering a perverse notion. You've surely never managed it before." He tucked the little curl back into the mass of her hair before looking away again. "And it is an exceedingly perverse notion. If my wife—my darling, beautiful, beloved wife—were in league with the demon, why did she not feed *me* to the demon back in Venice when she had the chance, instead of marrying me?"

He started walking again, quite quickly, so that she was pressed to keep up. His voice was quite level, as if he were only making conversation, when he continued, "And yet, it was the very day that I chanced on her in the Santi Giovanni that you were taken. We fled the thing for months and almost broke free, but within hours of my meeting with Livia, it found you and took you. And the mirror belonged to her. She never pretended otherwise."

He opened his mouth as if to continue, but did not. Rather he stopped dead and cocked his head. "What was that?" He turned left and right, listening intently to something he could scarcely hear. "Did you hear that?"

"Hear what?" she inquired, listening, but her face grew intent. "Yes, I did, I think." Her shoulders slumped. "Or perhaps not." She shrugged. "I thought there was something. . . . But I could not make it out."

"Almost like a woman's cry?" She looked at him in some surprise, and he shrugged off the notion. "Or merely the wind in the trees." He shook his head. "But a disturbing sound." She made no answer but attached herself more firmly to his arm, and he drew her in closer. "Let us get home, my dear, before it rains."

Chapter Five

"**N**o!" wailed Livia. It should have comforted her that Jacob had almost heard her. It was as close as she had ever managed to come to communication with the physical world. But what use was it that he heard her, if he could so mistake her? He had accused her—no, Cecily had accused her, but he had believed the vicious charge—of conspiring against him and working to destroy his sister, when even a blind man could surely see that she loved him wholeheartedly and never cared for anything but him. The very suggestion was so absurd that she ought to laugh, but she could not laugh. Her heart hammered within her breast as if attempting to escape its prison of flesh, and every blow was agony, for all that she possessed no real heart or material flesh for it to pound against. "No," she cried again.

There was suddenly an arm about her, holding her up when she started to fall. Papa pulled her into a protective embrace almost fiercely, as if he would fend off the entire universe before it injured her. "No, indeed," he murmured, and his voice was thick with unshed tears. "It was never you who was meant to suffer. Never your pain that was simmered and spiced to feed the creature. No, my darling girl, no."

"Oh, Papa," she wept, clinging to him like a shipwreck victim. "How could he say such a thing? How could he doubt me so? He has broken my heart!" She turned a tear-streaked face up to him, and he gazed down at her with smoldering eyes. Quite suddenly she became aware that she was dressed in a thin silk robe, without the protective armor of stays, and pressed very firmly to the bosom of a man who had once meant to marry her. "Perhaps I should have married you after all," she whispered. "You would never have wounded me so."

"You did marry me," he corrected her. "You may have forgotten, but I shall remind you." Quite suddenly the robe fell away, and his hands were upon her. She had barely time to remember that he might, after all, be a demon before she was consumed in carnal fever.

It might have been hours or weeks before she came to her senses. Even astral substance tires eventually, and they had done exhausting things, things well beyond any of her most daring imaginings, things Jacob had never dreamed of suggesting, things she was not entirely sure were genuinely possible for mere mortal flesh. She had wept for shame and begged him to refrain, screamed in either pleasure or agony, and begged him to continue. Long before he was done with her, she knew he was indeed the demon, but she was past caring by then. At any rate, after a very long while they lay still.

She was denied the oblivion of sleep; she lacked true flesh, and ectoplasm lacked the capacity. Instead she lay quietly in a wash of self-loathing. Ectoplasm could not do anything so honest as sleep, perhaps, but it was certainly fully capable of adultery and incest; it retained the capacity for everything vile, shameful, and lewd. She turned her head, but did not escape a remembered image of Jacob, sweetly pleading for some little liberty, something utterly trifling compared to the bestial ruttings she had just performed. And with Papa!

She writhed and turned her head the other way. But there she saw her seducer, a twisted caricature of Papa, sprawled in a sated stupor, clothed only in a reek of musk and a slack, lecherous smile, with his maleness fully exposed. She could not look at that, so she turned back the other way, and there again was the memory of Jacob—handsome, charming, beloved, and betrayed.

She rose to her feet and summoned clothing—her tightest corset, and her primmest, heaviest day dress. There would be no more loose silk gowns for her, however modest they may have looked on Grandmama. She topped off the outfit with a very large bonnet so that scarcely a lock of her elaborately dressed hair was exposed, and summoned a mirror—an ordinary mirror—to survey the results. She looked lovely. Depravity apparently left no mark; her skin was as dewy as a schoolgirl's; her face almost glowed. Of course, a schoolgirl would have smiled. Livia doubted she would ever smile again.

It was suddenly behind her, properly dressed and groomed, smelling only of shaving cologne, although, of course, it had not needed to shave. It looked over her shoulder into the mirror and she saw a perfect likeness of Papa's grey eyes and sober mien. She shuddered. "Get away from me," she whispered.

"You do not mean that," he opined, and he did not go away. Rather he laid a hand on her shoulder, and even through the thick, layered wool of her sleeve, her tainted, corrupted flesh burned in welcome.

"I do," she hissed. "You may have bewitched me for a moment, but I shall not traffic voluntarily with creatures of darkness."

The fiend had the presumption to chuckle. "Creature of darkness? That again? My dear girl . . ." She whirled furiously at his effrontery and raised her hand to strike him with all her poor strength. He caught her hand easily and scarcely broke off what he was saying. "My dear girl, you have not 'trafficked with a creature of darkness.' You have consummated your marriage to your lawful husband."

"My lawful husband is Jacob Aldridge," she snarled.

"He is not," it replied smoothly. "You were married to me, long before you ever met Aldridge. And since you seem to have absorbed these English concepts of sin and degradation, allow me to point out everything that passed between you and Aldridge was adultery." It paused to regard her sternly, letting the word sink into her mind and heart. Then it smiled, a beautiful, tender smile. "But I forgive you. You did not know any better. And I love you. I have always loved you—since the day I first saw you, so small and fair and perfect. I will always love you. There is no sin that you could commit that would turn my heart away from you. You are mine—my own dear girl. Mine forever."

She stared aghast. Here in the astral realm, forever was no poetic fancy. Death would never release her from this lascivious monster. But surely she could decline to belong to it. Surely her consent was required. She pulled her hand free of his, but her skin continued to tingle where his fingers had been. She still uncategorically withheld her consent. If her skin burned when he touched her, then she would just have to be careful not to allow him to touch her.

"I must think," she announced. She turned and marched away from him toward some approximation of her room. As she went, she raised a hand to her temple in a gesture that might have meant she was thinking, or might have meant she had a migraine coming on, but in either case signified a desire for—or rather an insistence on—privacy. Strangely, it worked perfectly.

Chapter Six

Cecily wrung out the washcloth, then dipped it in the basin to soak it afresh, and wrung it gently again. When it was just exactly as damp and cool as she wished it to be, she turned toward the bed and gently bathed her sister-in-law's face. Mrs. Aldridge gazed vacantly at the ceiling with a tragic expression. "My dear, you must not fret so," murmured Cecily. "Please rest easy."

"I am such a burden," whispered Mrs. Aldridge. "And now this. You would do best to turn me out."

Cecily rolled her eyes a trifle wearily. "Utter nonsense. You were taken a little unwell. It happens to everyone. In fact . . ." She paused as if searching for words. "Just this morning, the colonel asked me if we were not in imminent danger of overcrowding. And now you are taken unwell. I cannot help but wonder . . . are we in imminent danger of overcrowding?"

Mrs. Aldridge looked up sharply at that, for the first time in their conversation. "The colonel said that?" She shivered and pulled her shawl more closely around her. "I must say, he has a most uncanny eye. I was far from sure myself. But yes, I very much fear there is a new arrival in our future."

"You fear? Oh, Sister, you must not say that—this is splendid news! Our family was not complete before this. Jacob will be so thrilled! You have seen what a tender uncle he is; he will be ten times more doting with a child of his own." Cecily dropped the washcloth into the basin and took her sister-in-law's hand in both her own, squeezing as if she could infuse warmth directly into the unresponsive fingers.

Mrs. Aldridge turned away with a sigh that was almost a groan. "How do you suppose Mme. Chang will take the news?" She pulled her hand free of Cecily's and buried her face in her hands. "Oh, Sister, it is true what they say! A tangled web, indeed. And the more I struggle the more hopelessly entangled I become."

Cecily was careful not to sigh, not to start, not to display any visible reaction at all. She reached forward and claimed again the hand that had been pulled away from her. "Sister," she said. "Dear Sister, please set your mind at ease. You are my Jacob's wife and he loves you. Nothing else matters. You are ours and we will protect you, and I assure you that Jacob and I are very skilled and determined at protecting what is ours. My dear Oliver, also; I think I must have been drawn to him from the beginning because I sensed that he was like us in this regard. So do not waste your strength on disentangling silly webs; trust in us and cut yourself loose without fear of consequence. Or do you doubt your husband's love?"

Mrs. Aldridge turned to her with wide-open eyes; she seemed about to speak, but then she hesitated. And there was a knock on the door. It opened to admit Rose, bearing a tea tray. She set the tray down on the bedside table and turned to go, but Mrs. Aldridge grabbed her hand. "You know, don't you, Rose? Cecily may suspect, but you have been with the Chang household for fifteen years. You must truly know."

Rose stopped. She did not turn, only cocked her head slightly, and her eyes moved as she glanced sideways at Mrs. Aldridge. She displayed no intention of answering; she merely waited to be released.

"But if you know," continued Mrs. Aldridge, "why do you stay with me? I am nothing to you, and soon Mme. Chang will be coming for me. If she finds you with me, she will come after us both."

At that Rose did turn. She curtsied to Mrs. Aldridge and raised her other hand in a gesture that indicated she should wait. Then she pulled free and darted out of the room.

Cecily's eyes followed her briefly; then she turned to her sister-in-law. "Fifteen years? They've touched her lightly."

Mrs. Aldridge shrugged. "She is ageless." She paused as one summoning the courage to speak, and finally inquired, "Cecily, what was in the crate?"

Cecily sighed heavily. "The mirror."

Mrs. Aldridge nodded. "I thought as much. I should be alarmed, I suppose. But I am not." She suddenly smiled. "In fact, I am delighted. It's very strange; I know it is a nasty, dangerous thing, and yet . . . I am glad to have it home. Its presence is comforting."

It was Cecily who appeared to be alarmed. "Hearing you say so disturbs me more than if you were terrified."

Mrs. Aldridge looked down at her hands as if they had grown somehow unfamiliar. "You are quite right. She would have been glad to have it back, I think. Very glad." Cecily did not ask who "she" might be.

Rose reappeared at the door. She was carrying a black lacquered box, large and flat, and etched with a design of cherry blossoms in red. She presented this to Mrs. Aldridge on open hands as if it were a platter of fruit. When Mrs. Aldridge hesitated to take it, Rose turned and offered it instead to Cecily, who accepted it. Rose curtsied again, and withdrew.

Cecily examined the box in her hands for some while before setting it on the bed by Mrs. Aldridge's side. Then she poured a cup of tea. "Something tells me this will take a while," she murmured. Mrs. Aldridge looked up from fumbling with the lid of the box—which proved to contain a jumble of documents—and nodded emphatically. Cecily handed over the tea and poured another cup.

Jacob stared at the paper in his hands as fixedly as if he hoped to extract the meaning directly, despite his complete inability to read Chinese. He turned a stern glare on his sister. "She just gave you the box?"

Cecily sighed. "I believe I have already told you as much."

"Several times," pointed out Mrs. Aldridge.

"And of course she gave no explanation. She never speaks," he fumed.

Cecily shrugged. "I'm not entirely sure she can speak. Besides . . ." She cocked her head as one searching for words. "She seemed to think she had already told us all we needed to know. Her manner, the context of the conversation—everything suggested that this box is supposed to contain some useful explanation."

"Is our explanation in Chinese, then?" Jacob turned to Oliver. "Could you, perhaps, go back to the Foreign Office? These papers are surely not cursed or poisoned."

"No," said Mrs. Aldridge. "I am certain Rose knows very well that I cannot read Chinese. Yet she brought me these papers anyway. So she must suppose the English documents hold our answer."

"But there are only two of those," pointed out Cecily. She thumbed through the stack and withdrew one from the bottom. "Could there be more to this than is obvious?" She read aloud, "'I, Avery Wilcox, ship's physician of the HMS

Valiant Endeavor, being currently stationed in Canton, do hereby attest that on the second of July, 1862, at eleven minutes past nine in the evening, I delivered Mrs. Ishmael Aram, neé Arabella Boyle, of a female child, Livia O'Mahony Aram, the child weighing six pounds two ounces, and appearing to be in good health.'" To everyone's surprise, Mrs. Aldridge suppressed a small chuckle at the reading, and Cecily turned to her eagerly. "You see something unusual in this?"

But Mrs. Aldridge only shook her head. "No, it is only that I always thought we were supposed to be so perfectly identical."

"And so you were, surely," the colonel replied.

"Except," remarked Jacob with a chuckle of his own, "Livia turned out to be several months Rhoda's junior. Just as well that Rhoda never knew. She would never have let poor Livia hear the end of it."

"Indeed," murmured Mrs. Aldridge with a small smile.

"But that cannot be!" the colonel assured Jacob. "We have all witnessed the astral link between these two ladies. They were not merely like each other. They were true doppelgangers, and indeed still are—bound even beyond life. They must be identical." He turned urgently to Mrs. Aldridge. "Has not Jacob made some mistake about the birthdays, madam? With no offense meant to him, of course, but he must be in error here."

She was quite taken aback by his intensity but answered, "No, he is not. Rhoda was born on the seventeenth of March. And you have the certificate of L . . . of my birth before you." Colonel Beckford seized the paper from Cecily a little more abruptly than was entirely polite, and scanned it intently. Mrs. Aldridge turned back to Jacob. "Would we, by any chance, have Rhoda's birth certificate to compare? Since Colonel Beckford thinks it so important?"

"No," he murmured, staring in some puzzlement at his brother-in-law, who remained utterly nonplussed. "But there can be no doubt of the date. We celebrated her birthday not long before we became engaged. Her Aunt Felicity made a splendid cake, and then destroyed my appetite entirely with a confidential report on the sufferings she had witnessed at the birth. There is a reason that women generally keep these grisly details to themselves."

Mrs. Aldridge laughed. "Please, Mr. Aldridge, it cannot have been that bad. Granted, a simple country lady's propriety has to make room for the practicalities of farm life, but Aunt Felicity was never vulgar."

He rolled his eyes and shook his head. "I was devastated by the recitation. Clearly we men are too weak to withstand such horrors."

His brother-in-law was not distracted by the attempt at humor; indeed, he seemed not to have heard it. He only continued to stare at the page in his hands. "Could it be a forgery?" he muttered to himself, turning it over several times.

Cecily laid a hand on his shoulder and replied, "My dear, what possible purpose could there be in forging a birth certificate? We can hardly doubt that she was born." He looked up at her with a bewildered expression.

Jacob shrugged, and abandoning the elaborate Chinese document he had been unsuccessfully perusing, started rummaging through the pile of papers as if hoping to unearth something new and providential from its depths. Retrieving the only other paper printed in English, he glanced at it just long enough to verify that it was exactly what he had already known it would be, and moved as if to toss it aside. But quite suddenly he froze, then drew the paper back and surveyed it more carefully. Finally he remarked. "Perhaps the birth certificate is a forgery at that." All eyes turned his way, and he looked up from the paper with a raised eyebrow. "It seems that Mrs. Aram passed away on the seventeenth of March, 'from the rigors of childbed.'"

"But that is the very same day my . . ." Mrs. Aldridge spoke with great animation, but then stopped and looked about quite crestfallen. "I mean, is that not also when Mrs. Carothers passed away?"

"Exactly!" pronounced Oliver with enormous satisfaction. "The two births were identical, just as the two infants proved to be. This"—he waved the birth certificate before their eyes—"is a fabrication." Turning to Mrs. Aldridge, he bowed slightly. "Madam, your birthday is not July second but March seventeenth."

It was Mrs. Aldridge's turn to snatch the birth certificate without respect to civility. She reviewed it, openmouthed, before extending a commanding hand into which her husband placed Mrs. Aram's death certificate. "But that is . . . that is . . ." For some seconds, she seemed quite unable to decide just what she thought it was, and finally concluded, "That is simply silly! Who on earth would trouble to forge a birth certificate? And whatever for?"

Chapter Seven

"Whatever for, indeed," murmured Dr. Chang. Livia started and turned to him. Until he spoke, she had thought herself quite alone; his ability to materialize at will made him uncommonly skilled at sneaking up on her. Just the sight of him caused her blood to race and her temples to pound—whether with anger or some uglier passion—so that she had to focus all her attention on resuming the serene state of mind necessary for scrying.

By the time she was calm enough to look back into the mirror, her relations had broken off their converse. The evil Rhoda was stowing most of the papers back in the Japanese box, save for one bearing a particularly impressive seal; that, the colonel was carrying out the front door on his way to the Foreign Office. He looked less than happy to be going. Doubtless, he was remembering McDonald. But the paper was only the contract between Xiu Wang Po and Ishmael Aram; McDonald's replacement would take no harm from handling it.

She turned back to Dr. Chang, steeling herself to banish him again before he could make a lascivious move. But he was not even looking at her. He had dropped to his knees and was staring up at the mirror in open-mouthed dismay. "Your birthday is in March?" he said, and the query emerged from his lips in a wail. "March?"

She found herself moved by his distress, and laid a hand on his shoulder. "So it appears," she murmured. Then she very gently inquired, "Is the date significant?"

"No," he sobbed. "It is not significant. There is not an atom of significance in the seventeenth of March. But July second . . ." His voice broke off, and he did, indeed, start to cry. Or perhaps he started to laugh. He made a dreadful, unhappy choking noise that went on for a very long time.

Watching him weep—if that was what he was doing—Livia recalled the scene in the mirror. What had Grandmama said? "The girl's star charts are a perfect match to his." Star charts for July second. "The marriage will bring him great luck and power; his golden karma will come to shelter us all." Livia looked down at the figure weeping by her side, remembered his mother also weeping, and the evil end his father had met. Truly, his karma had sheltered no one.

She told herself he was a demon and tried to turn away. But whatever sort of being he was—ghost or demon or neutral spirit—it was not in her power to turn away from such anguish. She dropped to her knees beside him and put her arms around him, though her blood seethed and her polluted flesh crawled with desire when she touched him. No matter; he did not notice at all. Rather he laid his head on her breast and clung to her like a child. His pain infused her, smothering out the unnatural fires, and after a while they were both weeping.

The Command rippled gently and inaudibly through the house and the parlor. Colonel Beckford looked up sharply. He did not care for commands, even ordinary ones delivered by properly authorized officers, let alone astral cheek. No one but he had noticed anything; his lovely wife—he still could not so much as glance her way without smiling at his own good fortune— was engrossed in a book, and his brother and sister-in-law were giggling over a card game. Best not to worry them. He made some inconsequential excuse and left the room.

The Command warned him plainly away from his office—his own office! —so he naturally walked straight to it. He found there an elderly Oriental lady supervising two large coolies as they packed up the mirror that he had just been at such pains to unpack. The two were making quite of bit of noise as they hammered down the lid of a large crate and manhandled it around the room, repeatedly bumping into his desk in the process. Nor did the lady trouble to keep her voice down as she criticized their efforts and speculated on whether or not she should also take the great Chinese apothecary's chest, as long as she was here. Clearly, she trusted completely to her Command for silence.

He evaluated the scene thoughtfully, glancing almost instinctively at the gun case on the wall. It appeared untouched. It was not a large collection, but a good one. The long pieces were at the top—his father's fowling gun, his own hunting rifle, and a handsome Winchester that Jacob had gotten for him in New York and held for him for years while he was in India.

The first of the small arms was his army pistol. There followed a pair of antique dueling pistols reputed to have been used in the shooting of George Tierney,[1] an elaborately engraved ceremonial piece that had been presented to him by Andrássy[2] at Radziwill[3] and, of course, Cecily's charming little .22. It occurred to him that the delicate, enameled lady's gun had also come from Jacob. For an exceedingly soft-spoken young man, he had a keen eye for weapons and a penchant for giving guns to his loved ones.

The gun case, then, had not been pilfered by the intruders. The only thing amiss with it was that it was there and he was here, and Mme. Chang and her minions were between them. Well, two could play at Command. He drew in a deep, powerful breath and summoned a Voice that was either the faintest of whispers or a clarion cry. "See me not," he said, and started for his guns.

The Command did not work. Not on the lady, anyway, although the coolies paid him no mind. He suppressed a sigh. He had not really expected it to work. But it was worth a try.

Mme. Chang drew herself up with an affronted expression, as if wondering how he dared to interrupt her. He met her gaze levelly and waited for her next move. Eventually she remarked, "You must be Colonel Beckford." No reply seemed necessary, so he did not trouble with one. The coolies stopped working and looked about trying to determine just whom their mistress might be addressing. Oliver smiled slightly, and Mme. Chang flicked her wrist impatiently. The coolies started, and recoiled from him, but another flick of the wrist set them working again. They picked up the crate and maneuvered it out the door. Colonel Beckford stepped more deeply into the room to let them pass. Mme. Chang's expression grew thoughtful. "You are not what I expected," she admitted.

He shrugged slightly. "Sorry to disappoint. Perhaps if you told me what you were expecting . . ."

She almost chuckled. "I was expecting you to try to stop me from taking the mirror."

"Really? But I surely do not want it. I rather thought that you might have sent it. But if you did not . . ." He paused to look down the corridor after the retreating coolies. "Then I can only hope you have the power to take it away."

She eyed him narrowly, clearly convinced that he meant anything but what he said, and stepped forward, not exactly toward him, but toward the door, which necessarily brought her close to him. With each step she moved a little slower until she came to a stop just in front of him and looked up, clearly disbelieving he would let her pass through the door unmolested. "Then you have no objection? I may go in peace?"

He nodded. "Certainly, you may go. Whether you can do so in peace with that mirror in tow is another matter, but you have my leave to try." He stepped back and gestured to the door. "Please, I will not prevent you." He almost laughed to see her face; she was rigid with the frustration of wondering what he meant and what he intended.

Then she smiled. Her smile was strangely moving. Even in her mature years, she commanded an astonishing echo of great beauty. "Since I find you in such an accommodating temper, perhaps I should ask for more."

"Your son's apothecary chest, perhaps? I should be sorry to see it go; it is a lovely thing. But I cannot pretend it belongs to me. I hope you will not let your servants bang it against anything on their way out."

"I was thinking more about the poor remains of my family." She lifted her voice suddenly to a clear call of Command. "Livia, hear me. I am waiting for you."

"You surprise me, madame. First you try to kill her, but now you want her back?" He chuckled softly. "I do not think she will come to your call anymore."

He provoked a response she could not veil; her eyes flashed with anger, but her lips betrayed anxiety. "I am sure Livia knows her place," she informed him haughtily, but he could hear lies, and she was lying.

"Does she?" he wondered. "Perhaps she has forgotten. Or gained wisdom enough to shield herself from unreasonable demands. Or perhaps I have laid a protection on my house that shelters her. Or . . ." He smiled. "Perhaps your voice has lost its power." He paused and glanced pointedly back toward the parlor. "I do not hear her step in the hall."

She had grown quite pale, but kept her face still. "Livia, come here at once," she called. But he could hear unease in her voice. Command required complete conviction; they both knew that she had not achieved it. She made an impatient gesture, as if she could not be troubled to wait on Livia, and took another step toward the door. "No matter. My son will fetch her back when I rescue him from the mirror."

"If he still wants her," remarked Oliver. "Her attractions may be dimmed in his eyes, since he, at least, must know by now that her birthday is not July second." He quite stunned her with that information; her mouth fell open and she simply gaped, unable to make sense of what he had said. While she was still vulnerable, he added, "Do you know, we always supposed that the curse—the demon in the mirror—was launched against Ishmael Aram by one of his enemies. But lately Jacob has been wondering if rather it was launched *by* Ishmael Aram toward one of his enemies." He wondered why he bothered to warn her. McDonald had gotten no warning. Perhaps he was simply not above taunting a helpless victim.

She got her voice back, or some of it anyway, and whispered harshly, "The curse was launched against Jeremy Aldridge." The thought gave her the strength to complete her exit, even at the cost of brushing quite close to him. Having gained the hall she glanced back and spoke more strongly, "And curses always find their mark, sooner or later. No earthly power can prevent them." She turned and walked away, back toward the kitchen and the rear door.

He looked after her quietly. When she was almost to the door he remarked, "Perhaps by both Ishmael Aram and Jeremy Aldridge together. Do you suppose they had any common enemies?"

Chapter Eight

Livia wrung her hands. All these years spent fleeing the curse on her father, and now Jacob was suggesting that her father was not the victim of the curse but its author? Surely that was nonsense. The demon's first act had been to murder Rhoda Carothers; why would Aram have wished Rhoda ill, or even known of her existence? Aldridge and Aram were not even known to have been acquainted, as they must have been to work together. And yet they were linked in the astral realm—by Rhoda, who was the doppelganger of the daughter of one, the affianced of the son of the other. Astral links generally mirrored material links. Now she came to think of it, had they not both served in the East India Company?

"Oh, Papa, what does it mean?" she cried, summoning up a chair and seating herself beside him. "Surely this changes everything! And who then is the object of this curse?"

He made no answer. She looked at him and sighed. He had done nothing but sit in a slough of despondency since the news about her birthday. One would think a demon would have more gumption. Certainly, the Dr. Chang she had known and loved would have exhibited more backbone. As she watched, a tear crept down his cheek. Livia was growing very weary of watching him weep. She suppressed an impulse to shake him.

"Papa!" She addressed him more sharply than she had ever done in her life or his, and he managed to lift his head and look back at her. "Who is the demon pursuing?" she inquired. "Colonel Beckford seemed to be hinting that Grandmama was the intended victim."

She had at least captured his attention. He stiffened, but did not quite bristle. "Utter nonsense," he snapped. "Especially if he chooses to suspect that both Aldridge and Aram were in on it. Aram was untrustworthy in the extreme—begging your pardon, my dear—but he had no reason to bear us ill will. And Aldridge was our good friend."

She might have interrupted to say that Aldridge was no one's trustworthy friend, but he held up a hand to forestall her. "I did not meet him until I was nine, but Mother assured me she had relied utterly on his protection during the occupation of Shanghai. And he was kind to me, far beyond the requirements of civility. I could not be mistaken; his affection for me was genuine. I missed him sorely when he was called back to London."

He sounded so certain, she did not dare to contradict, and yet she was not convinced. She rose and walked away to think. She knew as well as Papa how little trust Aram Ishmael deserved. That the Chang family did not happen to know of a grudge directed their way by Aram did not begin to exonerate him. She approached the mirror, more by instinct than by thought, and found it reflecting her thoughts.

There was Aram, somewhere in China, with an armed party behind him and a number of bleeding corpses at his feet. She was more hardened to blood than her timid demeanor might suggest; she did not turn away from the sight of a battlefield. Judging by the arms and the complexions, she guessed it had been a battle between rival warlords. Many had sprung up during the Opium Wars; competition only grew fiercer in the wake of the Treaty of Nanking.

Most of the faces around Aram were unidentifiable—unwashed fighters, little better than coolies. One man, however, looked faintly familiar. She peered at him closely, and the mirror heightened the image until she remembered how she knew him. It was during her brief stay in Xiu Wang Po's camp; he was a cousin of the warlord, and a trusted ally. Aram must have met him and suborned him at the betrothal celebration.

Livia sighed. Poor Papa. The whole marriage, with its promise of golden karma, had merely been a scheme to wrest control of the opium trade away from Xiu Wang Po, with Papa pressed into service as the weapon that destroyed his beloved father. No wonder he could not stop weeping. She shivered and turned away.

But she did not wander far. More and more, she found herself lingering near the mirror—not with any clear purpose, but simply for the comfort of its presence, for the reassuring conviction that the knowledge within it was readily to hand. There were always more questions to ask.

Had Jeremy Aldridge really been any better a friend than Aram Ishmael?

Papa had been entirely convinced, and children were not easily deceived about such things. Yet Papa had not even known how Grandmama came to be acquainted with Aldridge. She considered her question carefully. Then, steeling herself for horrible sights of war, she turned back. "Show me Grandmama during the occupation of Shanghai."

Usually the mirror displayed scenes with the participants already in place. But on this occasion, she found herself moving down the street in a large Chinese city—obviously Shanghai, for all that no street signs were visible. She passed through a prosperous residential neighborhood with gardens, walled and unwalled, on every side. The street led her up a gentle slope to the top of a small hill, where she saw much of the city laid out before her. Everywhere she looked, she saw neat and well-kept homes; none of the walls were toppled, nor the houses burned or holed. No columns of smoke rose up along the perimeter.

Uneasily, she recalled Colonel Beckford insisting that the occupation of Shanghai had been essentially bloodless: "What right-minded Chink was going to tackle Her Majesty's forces unarmed—that being all the weapons their precious emperor had given them? Half the toffs were still hoping we'd bring down the Manchu for 'em, and put the Ming back on the throne. And the coolies were more than happy to sign on for an honest English wage." Not that Colonel Beckford had ever actually been to China, although she had been far too polite to point that out at the time. Still, he had been on the staff when the Treaty of Nanking was forged. Perhaps, he was not such an utter . . . Well, she was too polite to say that either, but perhaps he wasn't.

She came to a house, clearly that of a wealthy family. Within, she found the family quarreling in Mandarin. The father stood by, his arms folded across his chest, his face a mask of disapproval. He pointedly withheld his glance from his wife and daughter. The wife, however, was scolding furiously.

"Ungrateful worm," she hissed at the young girl cowering at her feet, punctuating her words with occasional slaps across the child's head and shoulders. "Utterly oblivious to the honor your noble father has showered upon you by troubling himself with this match! That a man of his rank should stoop to concern himself with the welfare of a wretched little grub such as yourself! But if he has a fault in the world, it is that he is grown tenderhearted from so much reading of poetry. Even with such great matters as the Mandate of Heaven on his mind, he arranges a safe haven for his ignorant daughter against the winds of change. Can you not see that this marriage will make you rich and powerful, no matter how the war comes out? But no, you are too busy with romantic songs and fine gowns to think of that."

The daughter glanced up briefly, and Livia nearly felt back in astonishment. For all that she had asked to see Grandmama, she was entirely unprepared for the sight of Grandmama as a girl, only barely old enough to marry. And yet it was unmistakably she; such a beauty she had been! The girl glanced down again and pressed her face to the floor, almost as if she had raised it only so that Livia could get a look at her.

"Oh, no, Mama, please, I never meant such a thing! I know I am a worthless fool, but I hope I have not forgotten the honor of my august family. Of course I shall marry whomever my gracious father chooses to select! How could I not? But I only wondered if he has not been too modest of his own merits—his beloved poets preach so of humility. This Xiu Wang Po has a wife already, who would look down her nose at a second wife. Surely my father's seed calls for something better than a concubine's place. Perhaps my noble father has not had the opportunity to observe that, worthless though she is, his poor daughter has found some favor in the eyes of his friend Cui Jing-Song—who is considerably better born than Xiu Wang Po. And not without wealth. Only without a first wife."

The mother paused, clearly taken aback. Whatever she had expected her daughter to reply, it was not that. And the father went so far as to turn his head a trifle. His arms remained folded, but his face grew thoughtful. Seeing that she had gained a point, the girl crawled forward and flung her arms out to grasp her father's ankles. "Please, honorable sire, accept the obedient devotion of one who desires only to serve you."

He tried to keep his face impassive but failed. Chuckling, he stooped to raise his daughter up to her knees. His wife winced and turned away; father and daughter glanced her way. "Your wise mother fears I spoil you," he remarked, and chuckled again. "She is quite right, of course. You flutter your eyelashes, and twist me around your finger, just as you do every other man who has the good fortune to see you. So you have cast your spell on Cui

Jing-Song, little minx? Even with that face on him? At least you cannot be accused of romantic daydreaming."

She turned her face demurely down. "I only served him tea in the garden, noble father, because I thought it would please you. Truly, I live to bring honor on your name."

"Tea? I think you served him more than tea." She opened her mouth and, seeing his expression, closed it again. "And I don't mean rice cakes. Did you serve him one of those dangerous smiles and flash your wonderful eyes at him until he could hardly drink his tea for gazing at you? I fear your efforts were wasted. Cui Jing-Song will never do." She forgot to look demure and gazed up at him in astonishment. "Mind you, little chit, I give you credit for the thought, but you are forgetting the foreigners and their gunboats sailing up the Yangtze. Cui Jing-Song is Qishan's[4] man, and all his money and Manchu connections will not save him if Chuanbi[5] falls. And Xiu Wang Po's first wife is barren. Only give him a son, and he will make you the uncrowned empress of Qing!"[6]

Livia grew annoyed. She had already known that Grandmama married Xiu Wang Po; what did she care about these details? "What has any of this to do with Jeremy Aldridge?" she demanded.

The scene blurred, flashed, and re-formed to display an image entirely unfit for a lady's eyes. Livia took in a brief impression of unclothed limbs writhing, and hurriedly turned her face away. The image did not go away as it usually did when she stopped looking. Rather the gasps and cries of the participants in the scene grew louder, as if the mirror were utterly determined that she should perceive its message. When she finally dared to glance back, the man and the girl had finished their carnal business and draped themselves slightly in the bed clothing. The girl was Grandmama again. The man was not Xiu Wang Po.

For one heart-stopping second, Livia thought the man was her beloved Jacob. But that simply was not possible; surely he had not even been born when this assignation took place. She breathed deeply and looked again. Of course. Not Jacob, but his father Jeremy, whom she had asked to see. They were very like, but not—she made herself look back and check—quite identical.

Jeremy was still very young and did not look like the evil wizard he had grown to be. He looked like an honest, adventurous boy, deep in the throes of first love. His face glowed with adoration as he stroked the cheek of the girl, younger and yet so much more worldly than he. "My darling," he whispered. His Mandarin was laughable; he could only barely make himself understood. "I have wonderful news!" He paused to kiss her again, and then again. Livia blushed and looked away again as he flung back the coverlet and grew utterly distracted with kissing Grandmama in places that men were not supposed to know women had. Grandmama giggled and encouraged him most wantonly.

At last he drew back and continued with his announcement. "I am to return home soon!" he informed him. "I have been promoted, and my new position is in London!"

He had certainly captured Grandmama's full attention. She sat bolt upright and gazed at him with widened eyes. "London?" she croaked. "You go to London?" She spoke in an English as broken as his Mandarin.

"Yes, yes, my exquisite one, my golden lady, London, the greatest city in the world! And you will come with me as my bride! Free at last of that monstrous slaver. You will be the most beautiful woman in the city, and every man there will envy me."

Her eyes had drifted away, and she seemed scarcely to hear him, so deep was she in thought. She was clearly considering something complex, nodding ever so slightly now, and shaking her head a trifle then. He waited on her conclusion, growing more and more uneasy as she continued to withhold that joyous acclamation he clearly expected. At last she nodded firmly and smiled, and he relaxed.

She turned back to him, still smiling. "Yes," she told him. "It is enough; it is done. You may go back to London if you like."

He caught his breath, as if suspecting there was great hurt yet to come. Dropping the Mandarin, he said in English, "You have the pronouns mixed again, my sweet. You mean that 'we shall go to London,' I think."

"No." She spoke now in Mandarin. "Not we. You shall go to London. I shall stay here." Almost as an afterthought she added, "I shall miss you greatly, of course. You have been most . . . satisfying. Greatly more pleasing than my husband."

He gaped at her. There was no other word to describe it. His mouth hung open, and one could almost hear him struggling to make her words mean something—anything—other than what she had actually said. Finally he stuttered, "Don't you understand? You need not to go back to your 'husband.' I would never abandon you to such a shameful arrangement. You will come with me! In England you will be a true wife, the only wife of a man who loves and honors you."

She regarded him coldly, then rose and reached for her clothing. "I do not want to go to your nasty London full of bad-smelling barbarians. This is my home, and I am quite satisfied with the husband I have. How dare you call my marriage shameful! My honorable father took great pains to arrange it."

He pulled the coverlet up around himself, as modest as a girl, looking suddenly more like a frightened child than a passionate lover. "You . . . you are happy with your husband? You would rather go back to him than come with me?"

She cast him a contemptuous glance and continued with her dressing. "Of course. He is a great warrior, brave and cunning. Also very rich. And what are you? A little barbarian clerk. Even your masters do not value you." She crossed to the mirror and studied her reflection carefully, making very sure that she had removed all traces of disarray. "I must go now; the guard will change soon, and I never got a chance to Command the relief guard not to see me. I cannot risk awkward questions about where I have been or why I went out."

She almost made it to the door. Then his hand snaked out from under the bed cover and grabbed her wrist. In a bizarre concoction of both languages he demanded, "But why? If you love your husband . . . if you would stay with him . . . if you do not care for me . . . It was you who sought me out, you know it was! Why?"

She did not even look at him, just shrugged and jerked her hand free. "My husband's first wife is not barren." The door flew open and she was gone, leaving young Jeremy Aldridge weeping desperately.

Livia gasped at the touch of a hand on her shoulder. She whirled to find Papa standing behind her. He smiled—a bitter tight-lipped grimace of a smile—and turned pointedly toward the mirror, which had grown dark. "What are you watching, my own?" he inquired. "Is it something I need to know?"

Chapter Nine

"Oh, my dear girl! Are you not the loveliest lady in all England? Yes, indeed, I think perhaps you are!" Anna Strasser lifted little Clara Beckford up over her head, so that the baby girl looked down on her. Clara was delighted with the unusual vantage point and burst into giggles, waving her arms as widely as she knew how. A little bit of drool may have escaped her infant lips, but none among her admiring audience paid any mind. Rather, Anna Strasser lowered the child again so that she might pull her into a tender embrace and nuzzle her nose into Clara's neck.

Then she proffered the little girl to Cecily. "Now you must take her, for the two of you together is a thing I have long wished to see. Darling Clara I met on the night she was born, but we sailed before we knew if you would live to hold her." Cecily cradled her daughter, and Anna stepped back to admire them. She sighed with satisfaction and smiled. "Such a perfectly matched pair—and you are not even in mourning! Truly, a beautiful sight." Her words were kind, but there was an odd undercurrent in her tone, an unspoken question perhaps.

Cecily caught her breath, and looked down with an abashed expression. "You must wonder why I am not mourning Dr. Chang. I debated if I should, if only to keep Mrs. Aldridge company. But I scarcely knew him." She sighed. "I suppose I must confess, as you will see it for yourself very soon, but I have even persuaded Mrs. Aldridge to half mourning. Do you think me horrid?" There was a long pause during which Anna Strasser failed to answer and Cecily fidgeted and chanced a nervous half smile. "Oh, you are shocked now, but you will forgive me when you see her. She looks quite charming in grey. Jacob assures me it is her favorite color. Her 'Confederate kit,' he calls it."

Anna opened her lips to reply, but words failed her and she shook her head. Finally she smiled broadly. "Not at all, my dear—how should I think ill of you? Dr. Chang deserved nothing of you. I am only surprised because I had heard . . . But it is clearly no more than a rumor. No, no." She held up a hand to forestall Cecily's question. "I will not dignify it with repetition. It is untrue, and so of no consequence." She turned toward Rose and held out her arms. "And now I must renew my acquaintance with Master Julius."

Rose did not hasten to hand her the boy; rather she pulled him a little closer to her breast and glanced uneasily at Cecily, who laughed. "Now, Rose, you know you must comply. Surely you need no reassurances that Frau Strasser means no harm to your charge." To Anna she continued, "You must forgive Rose. She is as jealous as a tigress with a cub. Even I can barely pry my Julius away from her." The two women gazed at Rose, who sighed and handed the little boy to Anna with obvious reluctance.

Anna looked down and drew in her breath sharply, then glanced back to Rose. Rose met her eye with something less than her usual subservience. They shared a long look. Then Rose smiled, and Anna looked back down at Julius with an odd expression—tender, but rueful. "Perhaps Rose was acquainted with your son in a previous life."

Cecily blinked several times, and paused to tickle Clara before remarking, "Ah, yes, I recall now that you were very active in the Theosophical Society."

"And I remain so, I assure you," Anna replied. "My good professor is an officer. And we have just enjoyed the very good fortune of a visit with Mme. Blavatsky[7] herself! We passed through Ostend on our way back to London, and she was in residence there. She received us most cordially, although she was still very weak from her illness. I am delighted to report that she is thinking of coming to London! She hopes to find here a congenial refuge in which to organize the notes for her next book."

She broke off suddenly and, cocking her head, studied Cecily. Cecily looked up from the baby and smiled sweetly. "How delightful."

Anna was not deceived. "Honestly, you astonish me utterly. Surely you, of all people, after all you have been through, must realize there are great truths which our comfortable propriety does not address."

The corner of Cecily's mouth twitched. "Indeed, I do, dear Frau Strasser, and I admire your courage in pursuing those truths. Nor can I think of anyone more endowed by nature with the capacity to engage them than yourself. But I cannot emulate you; the more I am forced to learn of those secret truths, the more they fill me with dread. May I not prevail on you to face down the astral mysteries for me and permit me my comfortable propriety?" She smiled at her friend. "For I am such a frail reed I can barely accomplish motherhood."

Little Julius, who had nestled in Frau Strasser's arms for all their talk, looking for all the world as if he were following the conversation, grew suddenly petulant. He squirmed mightily and issued an annoyed, demanding cry. Frau Strasser laughed and lifted him up to dandle him before his mother's eyes. "Frail reed, indeed! You see? Even little Julius knows better than that." The infant reached out his arms. He may have been reaching for his mother, but his sister responded by trying to sit up and reach her arms back toward him. Both children—and indeed, both adults also—laughed.

The front door suddenly slammed, presumably from the wind. The sound was followed by muffled voices and footsteps in the hallway below. "Ah, Mrs. Aldridge is here at last," said Cecily, laying Clara down in her crib. "She will be so delighted to see you!" Frau Strasser moved to place Julius in the crib also, but Rose intervened to claim the boy. Clara cried out indignantly, either at being denied her brother or at being excluded from the embrace.

There was no help for it but Rose must settle in the nursery rocker with both children. She seemed not to mind; rather she smiled with evident satisfaction at her position, leaving the ladies free to engage the newcomer. Frau Strasser leaned eagerly over the rail to greet Mrs. Aldridge as she ascended the stairs. Extending a hand down, she exclaimed, "Oh, my dear, it has been such a very long time! How glad I am to see . . ." Her voice broke off as Mrs. Aldridge took her hand, and she started, as if she had found herself accosting a complete stranger. When she continued, it was in a very different tone. "Why, Rhoda, you wicked creature! Whatever have you done with Livia?"

Mrs. Aldridge had flung herself forward over the dining table, with one cheek pressed to the polished surface, and her arms framing her head. Her hair had escaped its pins and spilled around her shoulders, which trembled and shook to the rhythm of her sobbing. Jacob sat on her right, stroking her hair and murmuring inaudible endearments. On her left, Anna Strasser sat stiffly, with tight lips and narrowed eyes. Colonel Beckford leaned against the archway, communing with his wife, who surveyed the scene at the table ruefully. "It seems your boil is well and truly lanced." She sighed. "Shall the healing begin now?"

He smiled slightly at her tone. "Surely it is best to have it out. She must be worn out from the long imposture; deception is not her forte. And we are certainly weary of pretending not to notice."

From the center of the room, Mrs. Aldridge's voice rose up, with surprising clarity, considering the extent of her weeping. "You must believe me! I never meant it so!" She lifted her tear-streaked face to Jacob. "Surely you see? I could not let you open the mirror. The demon was standing in wait to consume you! And Cecily simply would not listen. She was convinced I was the demon!" With her secret revealed, she had no need to imitate Livia's voice; her husky contralto reasserted itself, although her American accent was considerably faded.

Cecily raised her voice to interject. "And what would you have thought if our positions had been reversed?"

Jacob shot his sister an angry glare and clasped his wife's hand a little tighter. "I am sure no one thinks you meant ill," he assured her gently.

"Indeed, I did not think at all," she confessed. "I only meant to . . . to, well, step into Livia's person just for an instant, to do what had to be done. I never meant to stay so; I am not sure I even understood that I was stepping into it. Rather, I only meant to send it onward to do what my astral self could not."

"You mean, employ it as an automaton?" inquired Cecily.

"Exactly!" cried Rhoda, and then paused to reflect on hidden meanings. She turned a very hurt countenance on Cecily. "I think you would not have liked it, Sister, if I had let the thing have Jacob. And Livia's person was . . . was . . . unoccupied. As I've told you—several times, as I recall—she had abandoned it freely to enter the etheric realm."

"Not quite freely, I think," remarked the colonel.

Rhoda opened her mouth and then sat still, her mouth still slightly open as if she were poised to speak. Then she shook her head and dropped her eyes. "Well, perhaps not quite freely. She was in a regrettable situation, and the mirror was calling to her." She paused and whispered, "And I did invite her in. I was so terribly lonely. But she came in voluntarily, and by her own act."

"Doubtless she intended to depart in the same fashion," pointed out Frau Strasser. Her voice was stern.

Rhoda faced her with contrite eyes. "Please, Anna, you must believe me. You were the first, indeed the only one to show me kindness after my death. I could not bear it if you turned against me. I never, ever thought of keeping Livia's person."

"Never?" inquired Colonel Beckford.

"No, never!" she retorted. She caught her breath, and paused to think before continuing, but when she had thought she looked back up at him to meet his gaze directly. "Never. I may have succumbed to some wishful thinking; the astral realm is not a pleasant place. But I never intended it, nor even supposed it possible. Only after the mirror was smashed, I could not get back through it."

Colonel Beckford chuckled. "That is certainly quite true. Once the portal was closed you were as trapped on this side as you had formerly been on the other."

"Leaving Livia trapped in the mirror, just as you once were," concluded Frau Strasser thoughtfully.

Rhoda turned toward her. "I am sorry for that, truly," she insisted. "And I would apologize to her if I knew how. But since there is only the one person between us, it would seem that only one of us can inhabit it, while the other must stay over there. And since we are speaking honestly among ourselves"— she glanced uneasily toward the colonel—"I would much prefer it was she who resided there, and I here, rather than the other way around. It was a dreadful place." She shuddered and buried her face in her hands. "I was half mad with fear and loneliness by the time Livia found me."

Jacob shuddered slightly also and looked away from her. His eye caught Cecily's, and they shared a long look.

"But that explains much," sighed Anna Strasser. She took a deep breath. "I have news, news I was not entirely convinced I should share with you." She turned to Cecily. "You recall there was an ugly rumor I had heard? The rumor was that Livia Aldridge was dead, although no notice had appeared in the papers. I heard this from Mme. Chang, when she called on me yesterday."

She had certainly captured the attention of her audience. Cecily and

Oliver joined the three at the table; Rhoda and Jacob both turned in their chairs to hear her story. Rose appeared silently at the archway with a tray of tea things, although no one had summoned her; nor did anyone receive the tray. Rather she set it down on the buffet and poured for them, passing each of them a cup so smoothly she seemed almost invisible, even as she moved among them. Anna took a cup and sipped at it, marshalling her thoughts.

"Mme. Chang was distraught," she went on at last. "Devastated by her bereavement. I very much fear her reason is unhinged. She said she had acquired the mirror."

"That is quite true," murmured Oliver.

"Indeed?" said Anna. "I wondered if any of what she told me was true. She said also that she had managed a repair of sorts." She paused and looked about as if hoping someone could confirm that statement also, but she was met only with shrugs and blank looks. "She said she had tried to summon back Dr. Chang, but that she could only reach Livia, that being how she knew of this secret death." She paused and shook her head. "Absurd as it sounded, she seemed fully to believe it." She sipped at her tea and shook her head again. Her voice was troubled when she continued. "She said over and over that she must somehow make peace with Mr. Aldridge." She looked up to Jacob. "But there was no peace in her heart when she said it."

He snorted. "Of course not. I am astonished she managed even to spit out the words."

"You quarreled?"

Jacob almost smiled. "Daily. And that was before she attempted to murder Mrs. Aldridge."

Cecily chuckled. "No wonder she supposes Livia is dead."

"But why would she want peace now?" wondered Oliver.

Jacob sighed heavily. "Surely that is obvious." No one else seemed to share his view. "She cannot reach Chang. She can only reach Livia." He shook his head, and his voice dropped to a near whisper. "Livia must have asked for me; she is refusing access to Dr. Chang until she has been obliged." Rhoda gasped and opened her mouth, but it was Frau Strasser who answered him.

"But Livia cannot give her access to Dr. Chang! Can she, Rose?" Rose smiled faintly and shook her head. "Dr. Chang has passed on," continued

Anna. "His spirit is beyond material communication. Why should Mme. Chang suppose that Livia could call him back?"

"Perhaps Livia has—shall we say—given her that impression?" pointed out Rhoda. In a more thoughtful tone, she added, "Livia may not even realize that he has passed beyond. I saw her talking to the demon, but I am told the demon can take on many likenesses. Perhaps she truly thought it was her papa." She thought an instant more. "Or her former fiancé, if you prefer."

Jacob seemed scarcely to hear her. His shoulders tightened and his hand clenched, but he spoke softly. "Frau Strasser, since you are on calling terms with Mme. Chang, may I ask you to act as my emissary? You need only tell her that I accept her offer of truce, and arrange a meeting. A séance, if she likes."

"No!" Rhoda and Cecily spoke as with one voice. Neither gave way to the other's right to speak, so their words jumbled together in a tangle of interruptions: "But you mustn't" and "I shan't permit you" and "Utter madness!" just to name a few. "She'll do you some awful mischief," said one lady and "Nothing whatsoever to be gained," the other. They came together again at last in a chorus of "Jacob, as you love me, don't!"

He drew in his breath and smiled. "Ladies, your concern for my well-being is appreciated. But Livia is my wife. I cannot decline to speak with her." He paused to level a stern glare at them both. "I think there is nothing more to be said."

Temporarily silenced, Rhoda and Cecily looked at each other with alarmed, frustrated eyes. Then Cecily turned to Oliver. "Colonel Beckford, can you not do something?!"

"Not to worry, my own," he assured her. "Do you think I would let our only brother run off into heaven-alone-knows-what dark witchery?" He smiled broadly. "Naturally I will go with him." His eyes met Jacob's, and they nodded to each other.

"Well, really!" said Cecily. "That is not what I meant at all!"

Chapter Ten

"Perhaps I should follow them," murmured Rhoda. As if suiting action to the word, she darted out the door to stand on the curb and wring her hands. She even took several steps after the departing cab before it vanished into the evening mist, leaving only the echo of clopping hooves behind it. The damp night air had grown chilly, but she made no move toward the door, which still hung open, silhouetting Cecily. Cecily pulled her shawl more warmly around herself, then laid a hand on Rhoda's shoulder to draw her back inside. Rhoda shrugged off the hand and continued to peer after the cab. Then her shoulders dropped in resignation and she turned on Cecily. "Oh, Sister, how could you let them do this?"

"I?" retorted Cecily. "I did not permit them, I assure you. They never asked leave from me!"

Rhoda glared at her an instant and then ran weeping into the house. "You are quite right. It is I who should have stopped them. Just as it is I who should answer to Livia. I am such a awful coward—I should have gone in his place." She sniffed and dabbed at her brimming eyes. "You would have, I know, if it were you." She glanced at Cecily's startled and uncomprehending expression. "Like when you were little," she clarified, but Cecily still gave no sign of understanding her. "Didn't you use to dress up in his clothes? I'm sure Jacob said as much."

Cecily blinked several times and burst into laughter so helpless that she fell into the nearest chair, where she sat rocking and holding her sides for some time. "He told you about that? I have not thought of it in years!" She shook her head and dabbed at her eyes, which were quite as damp as Rhoda's. "Do you know, I never once expected it to work, and yet it always did." She chuckled and dabbed at her eyes again. "Alas, I very much doubt I could pass for him now, unless I contrived to grow half a foot taller."

"So you confess to it?" Rhoda chuckled also; Cecily's laughter had infected her spirits. "Whatever were you thinking?"

"Why, I wasn't thinking at all." Cecily snapped a surprisingly military salute. "I took my orders from General Jacob, the heroic defender of England and our gracious queen. It was not my place to think."

"It was Jacob's idea? But why?" Cecily's look grew guarded; she shrugged and turned away. "Some scheme to protect me, I suppose. You know how boys are; he was always imagining there were pirates in the boathouse and brigands behind every tree. Perhaps he fancied that white slavers were after me."

"Or evil magicians?"

Cecily drew in her breath sharply and rose. She paused to reassemble her smile before turning back to Rhoda. "Like Mme. Chang?" she replied. If Rhoda had meant something different she chose to let it pass. Cecily's brow furrowed. "Or Livia?"

Rhoda shook her head. "Livia is not evil." She glared into Cecily's dubious expression. "You hardly knew her. She was my friend. More than my friend. My sister. Yes, we quarreled every day. But we always kissed and wept together afterwards. I could not possibly pretend she has the smallest bit of sense, but she is nothing like evil."

"You said it was you who ought to talk to her," said Cecily. "Would she listen if you tried?"

Rhoda shrugged and walked away, all the way out into the hallway, where she turned and gazed into the mirror as earnestly as if she saw some secret truth lurking behind her own reflection. "Cecily, is there anything . . . magical about this mirror?" She fingered the ornate filigree on the frame. "This one right here."

Cecily came up behind her with a smile. "Not at all. I bought it at Harrod's."[8]

"But I spoke to you through it last fall. So one does not really need an ancient bronze artifact to contact the spirit world?" She turned, but Cecily had disappeared—into the sewing room apparently, for she emerged almost immediately, carrying a large, tufted sewing box.

"You mean like Dr. Chang's mirror? That was never intended to enable mortals to contact the spirit world. Just the opposite: its purpose is to enable spirits to contact the mortal world, which is an entirely different affair. For those with the Sight, any surface that reflects light can impinge on the ether, which is too insubstantial to resist penetration. But spirits have not the . . . the weight, the physical presence, to force their way into matter."

She settled on a chair and opened the box, which proved to contain a jetsam of ribbons, laces, and the like. She sorted through these carefully, holding first one notion and then another up toward the gas to verify its color. She paused to offer Rhoda a brilliant smile. "Darling, it's a splendid idea—I applaud you! May I assist?"

Rhoda turned to her with an expression that Cecily might have taken for horror if she had not returned her entire attention to the contents of her sewing box. Rhoda gulped and cast an anxious glance behind her toward the mirror. She opened her mouth to protest, but when she looked back, Cecily had looked up, her wonderful, deep-set grey eyes glowing with approval and affection. Rhoda sighed and her shoulders slumped. "Please do, Sister. Indeed, most likely it will end up with my assisting you, for you are so much cleverer than I." She swallowed and managed a smile. "What are all these ribbons?"

"Symbolic chains. They will bind us to the world. See this one?" She held up a scarlet ribbon, tied in a bow around a small lock of light brown hair. "This is my heart. I place it here, on the table beneath the mirror, but well back so that it is not reflected; it must remain securely here in the material world. And just above it . . ."

She dug into one of the box's many pockets and drew forth a candle stub. She rose to light it at the gas, and set it into something that looked like a lace napkin ring at the very front of the table, pressed up against the piecrust molding along the edge, so that it was plainly visible in the mirror. "Just above it, I light a lamp to beckon me home." She drew forth two long, silver ribbons. The end of one, she tied loosely around her wrist; the free end, she coiled in loops around the base of the candle. "This chain binds me to the earth, to my home, to the light of my heart."

Cecily then tied one end of the second silver ribbon to Rhoda's wrist. Rhoda lifted her hand to examine it. There was nothing unusual about the ribbon, but the meaning was plain enough. "This chain must bind me to you." Cecily nodded without speaking; she was trying to fasten the remaining loose end of ribbon to her other wrist, but suffering some difficulty in manipulating the knot with her left hand. Rhoda reached forward to assist her. "But I thought . . . I read somewhere that we have lifelines in the astral plane."

"We do," replied Cecily. "But they are fragile and difficult to see. The chains will reinforce them and help anchor you to this plane." With the ribbons securely fastened, her hands were free to clasp Rhoda's. "Remember that anchor. You do not want to pass too deeply into the spirit world, or you may become separated from your person."

"Enabling Livia to resume her place within it?"

Cecily eyed her. "There is that. For myself, I was thinking more in terms of a speedy escape in case the demon should appear."

Rhoda opened her mouth. She closed it again. She made herself breathe normally. But her voice still trembled when she spoke. "Is that our entire recourse, if the demon should appear?"

Cecily shrugged. "It should be enough. Most likely it will be too distracted with Oliver and Jacob to notice us at all. Even if it does see us, we should see it coming in plenty of time to get away; unlike us, it cannot pass through an ordinary mirror from Harrod's."

Rhoda gazed at her in awe. "How can you be so unafraid?"

Cecily lifted an eyebrow. "Wherever did you get the silly notion that I am not afraid? I am utterly terrified, I assure you." She looked about, checking her arrangements were in place. "Shall we get on with it?" Rhoda nodded weakly, and Cecily reached into her box again to pull out a velvet bag. "You have no experience with trance, I suspect?" Rhoda made no answer, but apparently none was expected. Cecily was engaged with yet more ribbons; these served as drawstrings, holding the bag closed, and they had tangled. When the bag was open at last, it proved to contain a small package wrapped in oilcloth.

"What is that?" inquired Rhoda. She watched carefully as Cecily unwrapped the packet—wondering why so many layers were required—but felt no wiser on seeing an ordinary embroidered sachet emerge.

Cecily smiled—a tiny little secret triangle, much like Jacob's smile when he was very pleased. "I have no idea. It was a gift to me many years ago from a friend of my father's." Her eyes drifted left, remembering. "She told me it would help me see secret things. I was very small, you understand, and I told her to take it away; I said I wanted no part of the secret things. She laughed and told me I was wiser than most, but that I would be much safer facing the secret things than letting them creep up behind me."

Cecily turned the little pillow over in her hands several times, sighed heavily, and reached out to proffer it to Rhoda. "A little sniff will, indeed, enable you to see secret things." Rhoda took the sachet gingerly with two fingers. "But remember—when the trance takes you, do not let yourself be tempted too deeply into the mirror. You should be drawn immediately to Livia, but I shall be right behind you to mediate; we are chained. And there is a beacon"—she gestured to the glowing candle—"to remind you of the way home. Do you understand?"

Rhoda nodded. "Inhale the scent." She could smell it already, a strange but pleasant perfume, like almonds and pear blossoms. "Keep an eye on the candle. Do not go all the way into the mirror." Cecily nodded emphatically and rose to shut off the gas.

Blinded by the sudden darkness, Rhoda stumbled hastily toward her chair and fell onto it. As she raised the sachet to her nose, she heard Cecily starting to sing a foolish little French nursery rhyme. *"Sur le pont d'Avignon, l'on y danse, l'on y danse."*

The candle glowed, and so did its reflection in the mirror. The two little lights flickering in the gloom were mesmerizing; Rhoda found herself gazing raptly into them, her anxiety mysteriously dispelled. *This must be the trance*, she realized. She glanced at her reflection to see if she looked entranced. She did not; rather she was smiling. She was pleased to observe that she had a very friendly smile. Suddenly her reflection stopped smiling. "Why did I stop smiling?" she wondered. "Is the trance going away?"

"Well, I never!" announced the image in the mirror, and a cold chill rose up Rhoda's spine as she realized that she was no longer looking at her reflection. "The colossal gall! You are not satisfied to steal my life and spread vile lies about me? You must also drop in to gloat?" Livia raised her hand and delivered a stinging slap to Rhoda's cheek.

Cecily stopped singing when the flickering imagery in the mirror informed her that the spirit world was at hand. "Now, my dear," she whispered to Rhoda. "Take my hand and we will go in together." She reached a hand toward Rhoda, but met with no answering touch. She turned her head slightly, taking care to keep one eye on the mirror, and saw that Rhoda's eyes were closed and her head had dropped forward as if she had dozed off. "Rhoda?" There was no answer.

Reluctantly, trying to breathe deeply and retain her trance, Cecily rose and went to her sister-in-law's side. She laid a hand on Rhoda's shoulder but still evoked no response. She lifted Rhoda's head and gently peeled back an eyelid. Only white was revealed, as Rhoda's eyes had rolled back into her head. "Well, really," sighed Cecily. "Why does no one ever listen to me?"

She studied the mirror, with her hands on her hips and her foot tapping. The flickering faded. It was her own fault; her all-too-material annoyance had destroyed the receptive state of mind that made scrying possible. But if Rhoda had entered the mirror, then the path into the mirror world must necessarily remain open. "Perhaps it's just as well," she decided. "They will need a moment alone to thrash things out between them."

She resumed her seat, but deep breathing did not quickly restore her trance state. She rose again to look for the sachet. It had fallen from Rhoda's slack fingers and rolled away; it now nestled under the coat rack, near the door, well beyond the reach allotted her by the silver ribbon binding her to Rhoda. Her expression grew supremely irritated. She forced herself to breathe deeply and instructed herself not to be irritated.

Still assuring herself that she must not permit herself to become irritated, she sat down yet again and picked up her box of notions. Scrabbling through it did not immediately unearth an alternative, but did reveal a large man's handkerchief, very plain. She turned it over in her hands, wondering about its origin and ownership, but in the dim light it took her several seconds to notice the brown stain in one corner. She stared at it, forgetting entirely to breathe deeply—indeed, forgetting to breathe at all.

Jacob's handkerchief. Jacob's blood. Some inconsequential incident—a shaving nick, a swatted mosquito—she no longer remembered what. She had scooped up the soiled handkerchief as a matter of course, having learned in her earliest childhood not to leave such dangerous weapons lying about. Scooped it up and hidden it in her magic box, where it would be safe.

Even as she contemplated the handkerchief, she became aware that a faint aroma had crept up on her; she lifted her head and sniffed. Even from across the room she could distinguish the scent of almonds and pear blossoms. She had forgotten how penetrating the perfume was, so penetrating that she had wrapped it in oilcloth before putting it in a bag before putting it in a box. She had just time enough to wonder whether perhaps she should put the handkerchief down—lest she take it with her to the spirit world—before the trance took her.

Chapter Eleven

Jacob stood for some moments at the door to the Chang house. He had not entered it in over four years—and he had been quite ill at that time—but he found he remembered it with preternatural clarity. Then as now, he had come owing Livia an apology. Cecily had surprised him by appearing suddenly beside him; he had teased her about her new dress. Pretty Rose had answered the door and taken their coats, appearing to be no more than an ordinary housemaid.

Oliver jogged his elbow. "Are you having second thoughts, Brother? It is not too late to turn around and go home. After all, it is almost certainly a trap. Frau Strasser told us plainly enough that Mme. Chang means you ill."

Jacob barked out something like a laugh. "There's no 'almost' about it, Brother. Odds are good that the demon will jump out of the mirror as soon as it opens."

"Good thing there are two of us, then," sighed Oliver, checking his pockets, which were so stuffed with packets of herbs and bottles of varied noxious effluvia that his coat no longer hung straight.

The parlor had changed considerably. First and foremost, a portrait of a young James Chang hung over the mantel, where a Chinese landscape had previously been displayed. It was flanked by two large, brass candlesticks from Benares, which had in Italy graced the dining table. The table was much smaller than before, although that was to be expected. Eight people had participated in the previous séance; tonight there would only be three. Last time, there had been a folding screen in the corner; now the mirror stood in the same place, supported on a stand. The mirror had most certainly not been in the room on the previous occasion. But neither could it have been far away; Dr. Chang had used it to trap Rhoda's spirit.

Jacob took a deep breath and walked over to it. The most unusual thing about it was its fan shape; most spirit mirrors were round or oval. There were many tiny figures inscribed around the edge, so worn he could not read them.

The bronze had been polished to an astonishingly high sheen, but so far it reflected nothing but the image of Colonel Beckford still standing in the doorway, appearing to stare at the portrait. Jacob turned back to him with an eyebrow lifted in inquiry.

"How very odd," murmured Oliver. "I wonder I didn't notice before: he has your eyes. Or rather, had." Jacob started, and looked at the portrait again. He had seen it hundreds of times at the Chang villa in Italy and yet he, too, had never noticed. Dr. Chang's eyes were deep-set and grey, just like Cecily's. "Perhaps that accounts for how Julius manages to look so like him." Jacob nodded. Julius had an undeniably Oriental look to him; it was becoming a bit of an embarrassment. Cecily still hoped he would grow out of it.

"Gentlemen." Mme. Chang emerged from the room behind the parlor, dressed in her customary Chinese robes. She sat down at the table and gestured they should join her. "Shall we proceed?" She had never been one to waste time on unnecessary pleasantries, for all that she was quick to require them of others. She did not look at either of them as they seated themselves beside her. Instead she drew a small candle from inside one voluminous sleeve and busied herself with setting it up and lighting it while Jacob examined the layout of the table.

Before, he vividly remembered, it had been bare save for a small feather sheltering a tiny heap of salt and a pine whisk, flanked by a nut and a berry. These same things were on the table again, but they surrounded a beautiful Japanese vase, the purpose of which he could not begin to guess. Next to the vase was a small square of folded cloth with a decorative hem. It appeared to be a simple handkerchief. He did not generally pay much attention to things like ribbons and lace, but something about that embroidered trim teased at his memory. Where could he have seen it before? What could have made it important enough to remember?

Mme. Chang reached out her hands to form a circle. Oliver cooperated, taking her right hand in his left and offering his right hand to Jacob. Jacob lifted his hands slowly. Naturally, the first step in any séance was to join hands in a circle. But he continued to stare at the handkerchief, and just as his fingertips brushed those of Mme. Chang, he recognized it. He withdrew his hand and reached instead for the handkerchief.

"This was Cecily's," he announced, turning to glare at Mme. Chang. "And, unless I am very much mistaken," he turned the cloth over to expose a brown stain on the underside. "It carries a drop of her blood." He kept his voice level, but crumpled the handkerchief in his fist. "We will not proceed further with my sister's blood on the table."

Even as he spoke, he found the needle concealed in the handkerchief. Or rather, the needle found him, seeming almost to jump out of the cloth in its eagerness to prick him. He opened his hand to find that one finger was adorned with a brilliantly red drop of blood. Tiny as the wound was, he felt himself immediately grow faint. "Poison?" he managed to remark. "Really, Mme. Chang, that is beneath you." Then he fell forward onto the table. His head struck the Japanese urn, but Mme. Chang jumped up to catch the vase before it fell.

"No!" cried Livia. She watched in horror as dear Jacob's head struck the jade urn. But she also watched in satisfaction as Rhoda raised her hand to her cheek, which plainly showed the imprint of Livia's hand. For several heartbeats she swayed and grew lightheaded as her wits tried desperately to sort through the contradictory images. Then Rhoda and the Beckford entry hall disappeared, quite as if the slap had dispatched them. Livia was suddenly standing by Papa, who strained toward the great spirit mirror like a leashed hound.

So instantaneously was she transported that her hand was still moving violently forward. She had aimed too low to strike Papa's face; instead she seized his hand, which was reaching toward the mirror. "No!" she cried—or perhaps she cried again—as the whole scheme suddenly came clear to her as plainly as if it were her own idea and intent. Papa meant to dispossess Jacob, to force him out of his person and into the spirit world! And then, when Jacob's person was unoccupied, Papa would be able to take up residence within it.

"No!" she shrieked yet again. "You shall not! I will not let you!" She jerked his hand away from the mirror.

"But I will!" he exulted. He pulled his hand free and spun around in a joyful circle, like a little boy. His face shifted, and he was somehow translated from the sober Dr. Chang in weskit and grey jacket to a gleeful young Xiu

Yao in Chinese silks. "You are too late to prevent me! See!" He gestured toward the mirror, which displayed Jacob gingerly raising his head. "See! It is done!" He leaned forward to watch as Mme. Chang lifted up the funeral urn and started pouring the contents over Jacob's head.

Very little ash actually spilled before Colonel Beckford leapt forward with a hand raised to intervene. Clearly he still hesitated—even under such circumstances—to strike an elderly woman; instead he struck the jar, which flew out of Mme. Chang's hands to hit the wall with considerable force. Livia winced as the precious jade shattered into a dozen large pieces, and ash (still containing a few fragments of bone) cascaded onto the Persian carpet. "Dear Mama, my own loving, learned mother," crooned the Papa spirit. "You have done it! You have called me back! Truly you are the greatest of mothers!" His voice dropped suddenly to a snarl of contempt. "Even if you are a whore."

Livia sucked in her breath. She had heard the word twice now, and decided she did not like it. "It seems that the astral realm is a very vulgar place," she snapped. "You certainly never used such language in the material world."

The Xiu Yao spirit turned on her with an astonished expression. His mien grew serious, and when he replied he was again the mature Dr. Chang, "My dear, I do apologize. I should not talk so in the presence of a lady. Please forgive my exuberance—I have waited for this day for so many years! Free of this dreadful mirror at last!"

"Free?" She spread out her hands, utterly bewildered. "What do you mean, free? You are still here—standing right in front of me."

He chuckled. "Well, that hardly matters. We of the higher realms are not limited by such delusions as time and space; only mirrors can confine us. Come now, my dear, were you not yourself in two places at once just a few minutes ago?"

His words reminded her that, by rights, she ought to be talking to Rhoda—and for an instant she was still glaring at Rhoda, who was pouting and rubbing her reddened cheek—even as she frowned and struggled over what Papa was saying. But the effort of attending to both scenes together gave her a headache, and she waved Rhoda away.

Papa was still laughing. "You will get better at it with practice, my own.

From the very beginning, you were such a gifted child." For an instant Xiu Yao peeked out of his eyes; then he was adult again, assuring her, "I am already quite practiced at it and can generally manage as many as half a dozen locations." He gestured back toward the mirror. "See? There I am."

She looked back. Colonel Beckford had pressed Grandmama up against the wall with one hand; he had a small knife in the other. Grandmama was neither cowering nor resisting; she seemed almost to be waiting for something she expected to happen next. "But you are mistaken, Colonel," she was saying. "I have done nothing to Mr. Aldridge. See, behind you? He is fine." Her voice hummed with lies, and Colonel Beckford did not even trouble to turn and look until he heard the scraping of the chair as Jacob pushed himself back from the table. Jacob moved slowly and looked somewhat dazed. He seemed uninjured but was enveloped in an eldritch aura.

Livia bit her lip and turned back to Papa demanding, "Is that not Jacob?"

"Of course not." He laughed joyously. "Don't you know me?" He grasped her hand and raised it to his lips. "Did you not want revenge, my darling? Here it is!" He let go of her hand and vanished, leaving only the images in the mirror behind him. And the man in the mirror was most definitely not Jacob.

Chapter Twelve

ecily fell forward so suddenly that she slipped from the chair and almost struck her head on the floor of the entry hall. As the Chinese runner covering it rushed toward her, she instinctively squeezed her eyes shut and belatedly thrust out her arms to catch herself.

Neither her hands nor her forehead found the polished floorboards; she landed on something as soft as a featherbed. Finding herself on her hands and knees, she thought instantly how indecorously her skirt must be hoisted up, and reached behind to readjust it downwards. But just as her hand had first found no floor, it now found no skirt. She sucked in her breath and opened her eyes.

At least she was not reduced to her under things; she was wearing trousers. She fell back on her knees to raise her head and look around. She was no longer in the hallway, of course. The ground beneath her was cloudlike and insubstantial. Above it was fog—thick fog, a proper pea souper. She knelt in the center of a circle full of nothing.

She rose to her feet, brushing off her clothes as she did so, although there was nothing to brush from them. It turned out she was not wearing trousers after all. She was wearing knickers, accompanied by a jaunty white middy blouse adorned with embroidered anchors. She felt a weight on her head and reached up. Her ensemble was topped with a large billed cap into which her hair had been securely tucked.

She had not entirely finished taking in her surroundings, limited although they were, when a figure appeared suddenly out of the mist and seized her hand, remarking in a rumble, "There you are, boy—I've been looking all over for you." He—whoever he was—started walking away, clearly expecting her to follow.

She did not oblige, but looked up—looked up a very long way, wondering all the while at how very tall this person was, and why his voice sounded so familiar. He glanced back, irritated at her failure to come along, and jerked her hand. All the breath left her body as she stared up at him; he was her father. He was not extraordinarily tall; rather she was reduced to the size of a ten-year-old child, and a small one at that. He jerked her hand again, and she stumbled after him. "Father?" A shadowy landscape took shape around them, and that, too, was disturbingly familiar. "Where are we going, sir?"

Jeremy Aldridge looked back with a smile. "That's an excellent question, Jacob. I don't mean to answer it, mind you, but it is a first-rate question." Where had she heard those words before? "But then you always were a clever little chap. It's a shame, really. You are a fine boy, and I ought to have loved you better." He stopped suddenly, turned, and dropped to one knee. "And I would have, I swear to you, if only . . ." His voice drifted off, and a tear rolled down his cheek. "Too late now." He shook his head. "Too late for so many things."

Cecily looked up at him, her stomach roiling from a knot of cold dread. Every word he spoke echoed in her memory. She could almost recall what he was going to say next. But she did not want to recall it.

Dashing the tear away, her father rose and walked on. He continued to hold her wrist fast; she tried to pull her hand away, but he only tightened his grip. "You see, Jacob, you are not my only son, or even my eldest. There is another. He was stolen from me by his mother—an evil Chinese witch—but he is still my firstborn son." He sighed. "He must be almost grown by now, but still his mother's helpless chattel."

He looked down at Cecily. "I know what you are thinking, boy. You think I am only jealous because I never got to see him grow up; that she cannot truly be so evil because she is his mother." Cecily was thinking nothing of the sort. "But you never knew her. She enslaves everyone who sees her. Even me. I thought I had escaped her when I came home to London. I thought I could go back to China. But as soon as I set foot on the dock, her Command fell on me like an iron yoke. And the slavery she inflicted on me was nothing compared to what she did to the boy, my beautiful, beautiful boy. I had to set him free, no matter how many years it took, no matter if it cost me another son to do it. Surely you see?"

Cecily wanted to scream that she did not see, that she had no intention of seeing. But she only nodded, because that was what she had done before. At least that was probably what she had done before. The longer her father spoke, the more impossible it seemed that he could have said such things to her before, or that she could have contrived to forget them. And yet he had, and she had; she knew it with every fiber of her being.

The dim terrain had solidified into the grounds of the villa in Brittany where they had been living when her father died. They passed the tree in which Jacob had established his lookout post, and the bank of wild roses he had dubbed "Milady's bower." Just up ahead the path forked. The left path led rapidly down to a cliff overlooking the rocky coast. On the right was the gardener's cottage. There hadn't actually been a gardener; her father had used the place as his workshop. They were going to the gardener's cottage. Cecily did not want to go to the gardener's cottage.

She tried—tried desperately—to dissipate into the astral mist. None of this was real. It was only a memory. She did not have to reenact it. Failing utterly at that, she returned to trying to pull her hand free, and when that didn't work she dug her heels into the ground and dropped her weight. Her father did not even seem to notice; he just kept walking, dragging her along with him. "It is not fair, I know," he sighed. "Not fair to you that you should pay for your brother's freedom. Not fair to him that he will grieve for his black-hearted mother when he is free of her; not fair to his mother that she can only die." He paused and smiled. "We can at least hope that she dies painfully."

They were very close to the cottage. Cecily remembered—she had never really forgotten, she had only declined to recollect—what was in the cottage. She and Jacob had often peeked in the cottage windows. They had taken great interest in the mechanisms of their father's experiments; they had noted all changes carefully and discussed them with each other.

But they had not much discussed the slab. They had seen all its stages of construction. Their father had built it himself, one carefully selected rock at a time. They had watched him struggle to place a sheet of marble—too large to handle easily, too thin to withstand much abuse—over the top and polish it to a bright sheen. They had studied the unfamiliar letters and symbols he had painted around the sides.

Jacob had even dared to say aloud, "It looks like an altar." But there was no need to say aloud that he meant a sacrificial altar, and certainly no need to say aloud that this altar was large enough to accommodate a whole calf—or even a child. It was right around then that Jacob had concocted the scheme to dress Cecily as a boy. "We'll have such fun," he had assured her. "We will set the whole house to searching for Cecily, and you will be right there the whole time, laughing at them." There had been no need to discuss why they might want to hide Cecily. It had never occurred to them to hide Jacob.

But standing there at the door to the cottage, it was very clear that they should have tried to hide Jacob. Jeremy Aldridge smiled down at what he thought was his son. "Why are you dragging your feet so, Jacob? Anyone would think you were afraid of me. I'm not going to hurt you." Here in the astral plane, the lie was as visible as his smile. But then, even as a child Cecily had not believed him. She and Jacob had both known that their father was very skilled at hurting them. Strange that it had not occurred to her to say, "I am not Jacob." She could have escaped, simply by pulling off her cap.

"Do it," whispered a secret voice at the very back of her mind. "Just pull off your cap." Cecily was very sure that she should not—or perhaps could not—but she could not quite recall why she was so sure. "Go ahead," the voice urged her. "Why ever not?"

"Jacob told me not to," she managed at last. There was more to it than that, but little Cecily could not articulate the fine points. Was she really only ten? A part of her mind insisted she was not, and yet it seemed very clear and obvious that she was.

The other, darker voice insisted, "This is not what Jacob had in mind— you know it isn't. Go ahead. Take off the cap. When your father sees you are Cecily he will let you go."

Cecily shook her head. "I'm afraid." Had she said that aloud? How could she say that aloud, if she had not said it before? Surely she had not shaken her head before. But . . . before what? Cecily shook her head again. It made no sense to think about shaking her head before when she hadn't yet shaken her head.

"Afraid of what?" asked the voice. "Are you afraid he might strike you? It's true, he might." He had before, as she and the voice knew well. Not frequently, but often enough that it was an ever-present possibility. "But even if he does, that would surely be better than this. If you go on letting him think you are Jacob, he will do something awful, something much worse than a mere blow." And that was true, too. She and the voice knew it well. Although how could she know what would happen if it had not happened yet?

"Don't listen!" cried the ghost of Cecily Beckford with the last of her fading strength. "The voice is not your friend." Small as she was, young Cecily already knew how careful one had to be with voices. "Trust Jacob will come for you," warned grown-up Cecily. "He always does." Little Cecily Aldridge stood very still and listened so hard that it was almost like remembering. She did not really have to understand what was before and what was after; she just had to remember what she had always known—to trust her brother.

She drew in a frightened breath and, with her free hand, pulled her cap more tightly down about her ears. One Cecily or another turned to face the inner voice and answer, "I happen to be very happy with my hat, thank you very much—it was a present from my brother. And who are you to tell me what to do, anyway?"

"Who am I?" shrieked Jeremy Aldridge, and Cecily cowered down to the ground. Her hand pulled free from his grip with unexpected ease, and she wrapped her arms around her head. How could he have heard her? She had taken great pains not to speak the words aloud—he could not possibly have heard her! And yet he glared down at her with red eyes, his face twisting with fury, and screamed, "Who am I?"

He seemed to swell with rage. It could not be, and yet it was. He grew larger and larger, like a genie erupting from a bottle, and the larger he grew the more misshapen his limbs became, the more unnatural his grimaces, until his features utterly abandoned the contours of humanity. "Who am I?" His voice broke, as if some secret limit had been reached. For a moment he loomed over her, his huge, contorted hands clutching spasmodically at the air before his chest. Then his form seemed to dissipate, as if his substance had grown too attenuated to encompass his entire person, reducing him to a ghostly shadow. "Who am I?" he cried again in a soft wail of despair.

Then he was gone. Brittany, with its gardener's cottage, was also gone. She was alone. She was dressed in her dress. Her wrist burned—from her father's twisting it, she supposed. But when she looked down, she saw she was wearing a silver shackle, which had chafed her wrist raw—and held her back, perhaps, from wherever the demon had wanted to take her. A gleaming chain dropped from the shackle into a mist that was no longer quite featureless; she could see the chain snaking through the dense underlayers of the fog, leaving sparkling traces to mark its path. In the distance, she glimpsed a soft glow, like a lighthouse just out of sight. A beacon. Home. For a moment she grew faint with longing. Home!

But when she took a trembling step toward the light, she felt an opposing tug on her other wrist. A silver shackle adorned it also, and another gleaming chain slithered through the mist in a different direction. She was chained to Rhoda by a promise of assistance. On closer inspection, she found a third line—not a chain, but a bloodred braided cord—twisted around the chain to Rhoda in a spiral, like a horizontal barber's pole. No shackle bound it to her wrist; it seemed to emerge directly from the palm of her hand. Little drops formed on its surface and dripped into the mist. The drops were red also. She had brought Jacob's blood with her, and now it was summoning her.

Her heart sank. Jacob was supposed to be lodged in the relative safety of the physical world; what had Mme. Chang done to him? And why was his bond to her tangled with Rhoda's? Surely, they were not in the same place, not in either world. Yet the two were entwined as far into the distance as she could see.

"The astral realm is full of choices," whispered a remembered voice from long ago. "Hard choices, terrible choices. Often you must choose blind, and accept the consequences. Just remember, difficult as the choices seem, they are not what matters. The real test lies in your motives for choosing and your conduct in the aftermath."

Cecily gritted her teeth. Was she supposed to choose between Jacob and Rhoda? But that was not possible. The bond of blood, her promised word— neither was negotiable. She simply could not do it. So she raised her hand over her head, closed her eyes, and spun around in a circle. Whichever she chose, she would have to come back for the other anyway, so she might just as well leave it to chance. She opened her mouth to sing the little song her father's friend had taught her to use as a bridge, but at the last minute she chose instead to recite the Twenty-third Psalm, as Dr. Chang had taught her back when she still thought him her friend. "He leadeth me beside the still waters," she whispered, and—without opening her eyes—let herself be led in one direction or another.

Rhoda raised a hand to her face. Her mouth dropped open from the shock. She was not seriously injured by the slap, of course, but she was thoroughly unaccustomed to violence. After very little reflection, she found she did not care for it, and her temper started to rise. But—with herculean effort—she forced it back down. "I deserved that," she admitted. She looked into Livia's scowl and almost quailed. "But Livia, please. I would not be here if I did not know how much I deserved it. So talk to me, and I swear I shall find a way to make it up to you."

She expected a tirade, but none came. Barring the tirade, she expected, at the very least, a peremptory demand that she release their shared person immediately. No such demand ensued. Livia stood stock-still and said nothing. She still wore an expression of extreme anger, but she did not move to act any further on that anger or speak to express it. She merely continued to glare.

For an instant Rhoda took the silence as permission to continue, and she launched into a frenzy of apologies. But her penitence trailed off at Livia's continued lack of response. It was not just that Livia said nothing. It was that Livia also did nothing, not even so much as rolling her eyes or tightening her lips. In fact, she did not even seem to breathe. She was as still as a daguerreotype. "Livia?" inquired Rhoda, reaching out a hand to touch her friend's shoulder.

But her fingers made no contact; her hand slipped right through Livia's apparent form, emerging without any resistance on the other side, in a most disconcerting fashion. Then, as if the touch had, after all, disturbed her, she dissipated into mist and vanished. "Livia?" cried Rhoda, in real fear that she had somehow done some incomprehensible but vital damage. Belatedly remembering that her sister-in-law was right behind her, Rhoda turned around, wailing, "Cecily? Did you see that? What's happened? Where did Livia go?"

But she was speaking to empty air. Cecily was not right behind her. Cecily was nowhere nearby, and Rhoda whirled in circles to look in every direction. She could not see very far, as the mist was thick, but so far as she could see there was no trace of Cecily. She was utterly alone. "Cecily?" cried Rhoda, and she almost fainted in the wave of panic that rose up in the silence around her. "Livia? Anyone?"

She came very close to screaming before she recollected the chain and looked down to her wrist. There it was: a pretty silver ribbon, looped around her wrist and trailing off into the mist. It bound her to Cecily and home. There was also a beacon, she remembered. She turned around a few more times but did not see the beacon. She felt the panic drawing in again, but she shook her head and insisted aloud and loudly, "It's of no consequence. I can follow the ribbon."

She turned in the direction it seemed to lead and, lifting up the loose end, coiled it around her wrist to shorten it as she stepped forward. But as she did so, the coil slid back off her wrist. And when she tried to repeat the coiling process, the original loop slid off from around her wrist also. When the ribbon fell to the ground, it disappeared into the mist.

Rhoda shrieked and dropped to her knees, heedless of her skirt flying up behind her. She groped and combed through the mist, her searches growing more frantic by the second. Tears poured down her cheeks as her efforts grew more visibly futile. "Please, God, don't leave me here alone," she wept. "Please, God. Not again. I cannot bear it. Please, God. Please." After a while, her sobs and prayers grew too incoherent to matter, and she was reduced to slapping ineffectually at the mist, looking for a ribbon that was not there.

"What's this?" Inexplicably there was a voice behind her. "Tears? Whatever has happened, my own?" She twisted around and . . . There was Jacob! She found her feet and flew to him, flinging her arms around his neck.

"Oh, my darling, thank heaven you found me! I am distraught, beside myself—but no more; you are here." She pressed herself against him with all her strength. "I am not trapped here alone," she murmured. "You are here."

"Yes, my sweet, I am here. Rest easy." He drew back a fraction to look down at her. "But why are you here?"

"I came looking for Livia. I thought I should talk to her. I thought I owed her that much. But she wouldn't even speak to me. She just slapped me and went away. She didn't even walk away; she vanished, like a ghost."

"Did you think she would forgive you?"

Rhoda looked up, alarmed by the edge in his voice, and decided she must have misheard. After all, he was the best, the kindest and most beautiful man in the world. "Oh, I am sure she shall if I can only persuade her to hear me out. I know I've wronged her, but I will make it up to her somehow."

"Indeed? And how might that be?"

She could not possibly pretend that he might not mean that unkindly. "Oh, darling, are you angry with me?" The very idea left her too frightened to take offense. "I am so sorry. Tell me what has disturbed you and I will amend it." She leaned forward, softening her rather desperate embrace and turning her face upward to invite a kiss. "May I sue for pardon?" Standing on tiptoe, she pressed her lips lightly but hungrily to his.

The kiss he returned to her was sweet, but less passionate than she had hoped or expected. Then he smiled. She had never seen him smile like that before. He reached backward to grasp her wrists, and gently but firmly pressed her arms open and back. When he was free from her, he said, "Before you offer those pretty lips again, there is something you should know." He bowed his head and turned; the mist pressed in close around him. By the time he was turned all the way around, he was changed. Suddenly it was Cecily holding her wrists.

Rhoda fell back as if she had been burned. And indeed, she was burning—with shame and mortification. She had never been given to blushes in her youth, but apparently Livia had imposed the tendency on her. Now she burned scarlet.

Cecily stepped forward with a look of concern and her hands extended. "My dear, I have alarmed you. I am so sorry. I swear I never meant to pass myself off as Jacob, but you and I had just spoken of it, and then I found his handkerchief . . . Here in the mirror a thought is translated so quickly . . . It was done before I guessed it could be done . . . Oh, darling, don't look at me so—I am very sorry."

She grasped Rhoda's trembling hands and pulled her back into a tender embrace. Indeed, the embrace was so very tender that Rhoda found Cecily's hand pressed softly against her breast, just above the upper lip of her corset. It might very well have been accidental; she would never have minded, or even noted it, if she did not still so clearly remember that most unsisterly kiss. Instead the touch filled her with shame. Then, by some accident of buttons and stays and shifting limbs, there was a pinch upon that tender breast. She was skewered by a flash of what was either revulsion or a most unnatural affection. Her knees trembled and she grew faint, so that she stumbled and fell more deeply into Cecily's arms.

"My dear girl," crooned Cecily. "You have been so very frightened. You are not practiced in the astral arts—you must feel so lost and alone here." With her other hand she cupped Rhoda's face and drew it toward her as if planning to kiss her. "I think you need a cuddle." But there was nothing remotely comforting in the hand that had somehow got inside her dress and was pushing her down to the ground and invading her intimate spaces.

Rhoda choked on a scream and thrust Cecily away. "You are not Cecily!" she shrieked, backing away as fast as she could, grabbing desperately at the remains of her gown, which had fallen inexplicably into rags and shreds that only barely covered her. "Get away from me!" She half crawled, half ran in a sort of three-legged hop in which one hand clutched her clothing and the other served as an extra support limb.

Gaining her feet at last, she tore away, caring nothing for modesty or direction, so long as she moved as speedily as possible away into the fog. How she had broken free she could not have said, but she fled in the sudden passionate conviction that there were things very much worse than being alone. She ran until she stumbled—on nothing in particular, as there was nothing on which to stumble—and fell face forward into the mist.

Panting, she glanced back, but it was not behind her, not in any form. She sank into the soft ground, sobbing. Why was Cecily not behind her? And how had the thing known to imitate Cecily? Had it waylaid her sister-in-law behind her? She buried her face in her hands—and found her wrist strangely burdened. She lifted her arm to look, and discovered a heavy silver bracelet. She could not see a catch or even a break anywhere on the smooth, polished surface, and yet the circlet was too small to slip over her wrist. A delicate chain depended from it, plummeting into the mist.

Curious, she tugged at the chain. It was strong and weighed more than it ought. The bracelet would definitely not slide over her hand. So she was still firmly connected to Cecily. She thought about that for a moment, and then rose to her feet. She smoothed down her dress absentmindedly, not even noticing that it had reassembled itself around her. Nor was she panting any longer, having forgotten how winded she was supposed to be. The chain gave her a goal, a prospect of friendship and assistance, in short: new hope. She tugged again on the chain and stepped forward, looking for Cecily.

Chapter Thirteen

When he heard the scraping of the chair behind him, Oliver dropped Mme. Chang like a hot skillet. For half an instant—or maybe even less—he almost hoped that it really was Jacob, rising to his feet, somehow uninjured by whatever poison Mme. Chang had concealed in the handkerchief. But, of course, it was not; the man struggling uncertainly to his feet was cloaked in a shimmer of falsity. Oliver had seen that shimmer before, much less pronounced, on Rhoda Carothers, but unmistakable.

Inwardly, Oliver sighed. Cecily was not going to be pleased. Stepping toward the mantel, he murmured, "Jacob, are you all right?"

Behind him, Mme. Chang heard the lie in his voice and cried out, "No!" but he had already grasped a heavy brass candlestick and was swinging it in a practiced arc toward his brother-in-law's head. The impromptu weapon struck with a soft thud, and Jacob's head rocked before he fell over backward. Oliver watched him fall with some concern. A trickle of blood seeped out of Jacob's hair and down his cheek. Good: bleeding meant he was alive. Still, Cecily was definitely not going to be pleased.

He returned his attention to Mme. Chang; she was bristling like an affronted cat and looked, for all the world, thirty years younger than she truly was. "Foul barbarian," she spat, or something to that effect. He could not actually understand her words, since she was speaking in Chinese, but her general meaning was plain enough. She continued to hiss Chinese insults until he laid his great hand across her tiny throat. He did not squeeze or choke. There was no need.

She grew utterly silent, and her eyes opened very wide. She looked frightened. Good. He smiled. "What was on the needle, Mme. Chang?"

"Nothing," she gasped. "It was an accident. I was mending the hem, and forgot to put the needle away. . . ."

Gently, almost tenderly, he slapped her. It was difficult; he was not in the habit of abusing women. It was, however, necessary that she tell him how far away she had sent Jacob. "What was on the needle?" She drew in a ragged breath.

There was a scrabbling sound behind him. It was not possible that the Jacob-creature had recovered consciousness so soon; it was lucky to be alive. And yet there was a scrabbling sound behind him. He turned slightly to look. Jacob had raised himself up on one elbow and was leveling a tiny enameled pistol at him. Before Oliver could respond, Jacob fired.

The bullet struck his shoulder; and even as he fell, Oliver reflected, "That proves it—Jacob would not have missed." Then his back struck the floor, and pain radiated through his body. He tried to remember that it was important to remain conscious, but remaining conscious proved difficult, very difficult indeed.

He woke. On reflection, he found that rather astonishing. Even assuming that the demon was inexperienced with flesh and therefore prone to mistakes, he would not have expected Mme. Chang to be so careless. Yet here he was, for all that his spirit seemed strangely disassociated from his body. Why was that? He focused his Vision, reached into the core of his being, the place beneath matter where the power that sustained matter lurked. His voice was intact, and it summoned him. His body was nearly intact: the bullet wound inconsequential, his spine uninjured from the fall. And yet his spirit hovered rather than settled.

There was the cause. The bullet. It was silver. He almost laughed. Of course the gun that Jacob had given Cecily would have a silver bullet. Silver had the property of separating matter from spirit; hence its frequent use against possessed or nonhuman entities, whose grasp on matter was already weak. He was neither possessed nor nonhuman, so his grip on flesh was not broken, only loosened—a boon in his current condition.

As he had learned in India, when the spirit was not lodged—or not entirely lodged—within the body, it had access to faculties that transcended matter. But if it was still lodged—or partially lodged—within the body, its resources remained at the body's disposal. Only the body contained the capacity for growth, but the spirit could direct that growth minutely, and hasten it by drawing on etheric material. Oliver willed the flesh immediately beneath the bullet to grow; when that growth pressed upward to the surface of his skin, the bullet (along with a tiny scrap of his uniform jacket) popped out of a wound that had ceased to exist. There was a scar, of course, but that hardly mattered. There was always a scar.

He might have lain still and rested, but for the noise—an irritating mewling sound, like a hungry kitten whose mother had died. Getting up proved embarrassingly difficult. The fall had not damaged his spine, but it had left bruises aplenty and aggravated his bad leg. He paused in the process to snag up the flattened bullet, which had fallen down his sleeve and out onto the floor.

While he was at it, he also recovered Cecily's little derringer, which the Jacob-creature had dropped. Oliver checked the tiny breach and discovered a second bullet—also silver—still within it. When he regained his feet, he discovered the handkerchief had also been left behind, with the needle still in it. A small drop of Jacob's blood had fallen on the handkerchief, right by the small brown spot that Jacob had said was Cecily's blood. Oliver examined the needle closely but found no detectable traces. Nonetheless, he threaded it carefully into the lapel of his jacket. By the time that was done, the sound had stopped; he followed instead the smell of blood.

He did not have to follow it far. They were just across the hall in the dining room. Not-Jacob had apparently been in search of a flat surface at least five feet in length. A stretch of unobstructed floor would probably have served, but the Chang home was far too well appointed to provide such a barren expanse. The thing had therefore settled on the dining table, from which it had swept a large centerpiece and a row of tapers.

Mme. Chang had been laid out on the tablecloth. With the Jacob-creature between them, Oliver could not see much of her, but a fold of her robe had draped over the side of the table; it was wet with some fluid that had stained the blue robe purple and was dripping on the carpet. Beside her, on the edge of the table, stood the jagged remains of the jade urn. Something that he could only barely see—something red—had been placed inside the broken jar.

The Jacob-creature leaned over Mme. Chang, whispering in sibilant Chinese. Mme. Chang did not answer, unless one counted her intermittent moans. The thing turned at Oliver's entry. "Why, look, you have made yourself well." Its mouth screwed up and its brow knitted, like a schoolboy with a difficult sum. "That was clever," it concluded at last. "But why do you limp so badly if you can do that?"

Oliver shrugged. "I got the bad leg in Afghanistan, long before I learned to do such things."

It nodded. "Just as well. I am very much in need of your advice." It stood back to display its handiwork. Mme. Chang had been laid open. With a sort of modesty, the remains of her gown had been carefully draped over as much of her skin as remained intact. But where her abdomen should have been, a valley gaped between pulsing lungs and a tangle of glistening organs. One organ, however, was missing. Her heart would be the red thing in the jar, then.

"Nonsense," replied Oliver. "You're doing fine."

"Do you really think so?" Jacob had never smiled like that. "I did contrive to build my own vessel of power." It gestured toward the fragment of the broken vase. "It took some thinking. You brought yours with you when you murdered me, so I didn't get to see how you made it. But on reflection, the principle seemed plain." It smiled on its handiwork. Mme. Chang made a piteous gargling sound.

"When I murdered you? I think not."

It sniffed annoyance. "You deny it? Really, Colonel, I had expected more honesty from you. You can scarcely have forgotten. Or did you plan to lay the blame on Jacob, just because he cleaned up after you?" He turned to smile at Mme. Chang. "Mother always blamed Jacob, too, didn't you, Mother? She smelled my blood on him and looked no further." It turned back to Oliver. "But naturally I know better."

"If you are referring to what I did to Chang, I do not deny it or apologize for it. He had my wife in the mirror. But you are not Chang. You have never been killed, by me or anyone else; I'm not entirely sure that you can die, as we mortals understand the term."

It gaped at him, quite nonplussed. Mme. Chang launched a desperate, futile effort to raise her head. Instead she choked, and blood gushed from her mouth. The Jacob-creature pulled Jacob's handkerchief out of Jacob's pocket and wiped her mouth. "Now, now, Mother, pay no attention to the silly man.

Surely you cannot doubt who I am—you summoned me yourself." To Oliver it continued, "Really, Colonel Beckford, must you be so very rude? How can you say such a thing to my mother? Has she not troubles enough without your insolence?"

Oliver suppressed a sigh. "Indeed, she does. But I am not being insolent, only truthful. You are not Chang. Chang would not have done this." He gestured to the table.

"And why not? In China, adultery is a serious offense." It glared down on Mme. Chang. "In China she would have been executed. Slowly. But I have spared her life, because she is my mother."

"She is not your mother," reiterated Oliver. He raised his voice to obstruct an upcoming interruption. "If you really believe you are Chang, then say so. Say it plainly in so many words, with no evasion and no misdirection. Say, 'I am Dr. James Chang, formerly called Xiu Yao, son of' . . ." He had originally meant to say "son of Xiu Wang Po," but if Xiu Yao was accusing his mother of adultery . . . and the portrait of Chang had had those grey Aldridge eyes . . . He continued instead, "'son of this lady here, known in England as Mme. Chang.'"

He was gambling, of course. Mortal men could lie with ease—their one useful advantage against predators from other realms—and Jacob's flesh would recall the skill instinctively. But Jacob's flesh was currently inhabited by a native of another plane, where lies were not an option. It might call itself Chang, but surely it knew it was not, and it was still too unaccustomed to the material world to think of prevarication as possible. Probably. Oliver hoped.

It worked. The Jacob-creature opened its mouth, and then closed it again. It cocked its head to one side. It tried opening its mouth again. At last it whined, "Why does no one seem to know me?"

Outwardly, Oliver suppressed a sigh of relief. Inwardly, he exulted. "You see, Mme. Chang?" He let himself look away from the Jacob-thing. Mme. Chang looked strangely, supernaturally young—her skin dewy, her dark, suffering eyes luminous. But she reeked of spilled blood and open wounds. Her gaze was rational—anguished, but rational. "He is not your son. Your son has passed on. He was trapped in the mirror for a while during his illness, but he escaped the instant the mirror was opened, the night my son was born. This . . ." He gestured toward Jacob. "This is the ghost of Jeremy Aldridge. Doubtless you know better than I what grievance he may harbor."

"Stop talking to her," demanded not-Jacob in a petulant tone. "I don't like you saying such things to my mother."

Oliver ignored him. "The long, long game is over, Mme. Chang. There is nothing left for you to do but tend to the disposition of your last moments." He plucked at the needle in his lapel. "Shall I send you on from this ruined shell?"

"I said, don't talk to my mother." The demon lunged suddenly, some sort of blade gleaming in its hand. But it was neither as quick nor as cunning as Jacob, and nowhere near as experienced in battle as Oliver, who sidestepped it easily. While it was occupied with crashing into the wall, Oliver pulled out Cecily's gun and shot him. Not a mortal wound, but a worse one than it had given him. It stopped dead to look down at its chest and gingerly finger the wound. "That hurts," it whimpered, and fell down.

Mme. Chang managed something like a cry. "Try to remember, it's not your son," Oliver reassured her. "And whoever he is, he is not dead." He showed her the needle again. "Neither are you. You cannot die while your heart rests in a vessel of power. No matter what he does to you. And he will do more, when he wakes. You know he will. But I could be persuaded to deny him the opportunity."

She stared at him so blankly that he wondered if perhaps she was no longer lucid, but he proceeded on the assumption that she was. "You thought that Jacob killed your son. But he did not. I did that. Jacob has done nothing worse to you and yours than to marry your son's fiancée, and he would not have done that if he had known she was promised. You know this as well as I. Besides, you never really liked Livia anyway,"

Her eyes widened and her lips tightened. "You didn't think I knew that?" he continued. "You are more transparent than you suppose. But I digress." He smiled. "So you betrayed a man against whom you had no significant grudge to the very demon who devoured your son, largely because you are so unfeeling a mother that you cannot distinguish between your own child and a hell-spawn."

He watched while she struggled with her hatred. Only her mangled state prevented her from flying at him. Her lips managed to shape a few words, inaudible but doubtless insulting. He smiled again. He had plenty of time. At last the fire in her eye was muted by pain, and she was ready to listen to anything he said. "You would like to curse me for insulting you. But you know I speak the truth. And your end is certainly near. You know you cannot take lies across the veil, no matter how beloved."

She heard that. She knew it was true. Her entire body quivered. "So atone," he suggested. "Cross over now while you still retain contact with the material plane. Find Jacob; send him home. Of course, you find it hard to stomach helping me. But I don't really have anything to do with it. You need to expiate the injuries you did to Jacob and his sister for your own sake, to appease their father."

Her eyes were barely focused, and he worried she had ceased to hear him. But at last she managed a faint approximation of a nod. He pricked her with the needle, and her eyes closed. Then he turned to deal with the Jacob-thing. It was gone.

Chapter Fourteen

ecily lowered her arm and clasped her hands behind her. It was not really necessary. Even when she opened her eyes, she could no longer see the shackles and their chains, although she felt the weight of them on her wrists. What she could see was a little bridge. She nodded. Her father's friend had also told her about bridges in the astral realm, what they signified, and how they could be used. Cecily remembered little beyond that it was normal and proper to see one after committing to a destination.

This bridge—which was painted bright red—curved sharply up to stand at least ten feet above the ground, although the stream beneath it was only a few feet across and very shallow. It would probably be easier to ford the stream—or even jump right over it—than to cross on the bridge. But the rules were very plain. She used the bridge. It was even more difficult than she expected; not only was it steep, but also very narrow, too much so to accommodate her skirt easily.

On the other side she found a footpath, which crossed a flowered meadow and circled a small hill. On the other side of the hill she saw the villa. It was old and Italianate; one wing had fallen into ruins—very picturesque, of course, but also strangely familiar. "There is a charming 'Startled Nymph' at the foot of the curved stair." Where had she heard those words? Wherever she had heard them, they were true. There was the nymph, tucked into the volute of the grand entry stair where it met the ground. And the nymph was charming; the sculptor had not wandered far from the essential type, but he had achieved an unusually graceful line and an engaging expression.

Of course. She had not heard the words but read them. Jacob had described the Chang villa many times in his letters, and even included Livia's sketches. Cecily stepped back in alarm when she realized where she was. Why would she be drawn here to the house of her enemies? Nervously she wondered if she had remembered to bring her gun. She rarely remembered to bring her gun with her anymore. It was hardly appropriate for shopping. But years ago, she had taken it with her almost everywhere. Occasionally she still elected to resume carrying it, when the errand was urgent or her mood dark.

With a little concentration, she managed to half convince herself that today might have been one of those occasions. Had she not stopped in Oliver's office? And seen it? Surely that would have reminded her that it was a gift from Jacob. Such a pretty little thing, with so many graceful enameled designs, it would have been so simple, so natural, to scoop it up. When she was quite, quite sure it was possible, she checked the little purse clipped to her waistband. There it was. Solid and comforting and loaded with silver. Did silver work the same way in the astral realm? Or did guns?

Satisfied that she was armed, she drew closer to the villa and heard a faint noise. Sobbing, perhaps? A small form was crouched behind one of the pillars on the portico. A young girl weeping. She started and leapt to her feet when she heard Cecily approaching.

She was Chinese—dressed in a light blue embroidered silk tunic with enormous sleeves—and lovely. Even Cecily, who rarely paid much heed to the attractions of other women, could not fail to notice how beautiful she was. She recovered from her weeping to meet Cecily's eye with a speed and poise remarkable in one so young.

"Good morning, miss. I couldn't help but overhear. Are you in distress?" The girl did not reply, simply continued to regard Cecily appraisingly. Perhaps she did not speak English. *"Pardon, Mlle., mais je vous ai entendu. Avez vous mal?"* she attempted. And then, *"Sprechen Sie deutsch?"*

Despite a growing fear that the girl spoke no Occidental languages, Cecily opened her mouth to try Italian. The girl waved dismissively and said in accented but acceptable English, "You may desist. I understand you. Good morning, Mrs. Beckford."

Cecily started. "Have we met?" Cecily took pains to remember names and faces. And she was not acquainted with a large number of Chinese persons. None at all, in fact, excepting the Changs. "I do apologize, but I seem to have forgotten the occasion, Miss . . . ?"

Again, the girl was silent so long that Cecily wondered if she had understood the question. But at last she replied, "You do not know me? No matter. It was long ago and I was much older then. You may call me Tzen."

She was older then? Cecily decided to ignore what was surely no more than a vocabulary mix-up. She politely offered a hand. "I am very pleased to renew the acquaintance, Miss Tzen."

The girl did not take her hand; instead she shook her head. "No, not miss. Just Tzen. It is not my family name. I have no family name." That remark was a little more difficult to dismiss as a language error, and Cecily raised an eyebrow. "Where would I get a family name?" Tzen insisted. "My dear father is dead. My brave husband is dead. My beautiful son is dead. I have no one to give me a name."

She coughed suddenly, a diseased, racking cough that so shook her slight frame that she fell against the pillar and clung to it for support. She raised a large handkerchief to her lips, and it came away bloody. "My son's handkerchief," she murmured. "My son's blood."

Cecily drew a deep breath. Tuberculosis, probably too advanced for any hope of cure or remission. And doubtless, Tzen's wits were wandering in a fevered delirium. Cecily steeled herself against the fear of contagion before remembering where she was. Surely there could be no contagion in the astral plane. But . . . there ought not be any illness either. Unless Tzen had chosen to bring it with her. Clearly, she was an unfortunate.

"Why are you staring at me?" demanded Tzen.

Had she really been staring? "I do apologize. I was wondering if you could not put away your illness? Since there is no true flesh here?"

"I am not ill," snapped Tzen. "I am undead."

Cecily took a little step backward and smiled as prettily as she knew how. "Yes, of course. Well, I apologize again for intruding on you. I'd best get on my way."

"Don't you want to find Mr. Aldridge? Isn't that why you came here?"

Cecily's heart sank. "He is here?" She sighed. Of course he was; she had been foolish to hope. "Do you know where he is?"

Tzen chuckled, which Cecily found less than reassuring. "I do. How could I not? I put him there." The chuckle became a laugh. "His blood is on my hands. Also your handkerchief. And your blood, too. And mine. Blood everywhere." Tzen raised a delicate hand before her mouth and resumed control of her unladylike laughter. Then she coughed and hacked up blood again. "Come along, Mrs. Beckford. We mustn't be late."

Tzen turned and walked away; Cecily watched her go. Presumably she was walking as quickly as she found possible, but her tiny, mincing steps did not lend themselves to speed. Cecily had plenty of time to think about the wisdom of following her. But vacillation in the astral plane was also less than wise. Apparently she had chosen to look for Jacob; therefore, she would continue to look for Jacob. Rhoda would understand.

Chapter Fifteen

"Rhoda!" She started on hearing her name called, and spun around. But she saw no one. She resumed walking. She did not need to coil up the chain. It seemed to grow shorter—or at least never to grow less taut—as she moved forward. Then the unidentified voice called again. "Rhoda!" Did it come from the left? "Rhoda!" No, surely, that was on her right. "Rhoda!" Most definitely behind her.

She trembled. She was almost dizzy from turning round and round, and there was no one there. The demon was playing tricks on her! She stood stock-still and forced herself to breathe deeply. The demon fed on fear, Jacob had said. She must therefore decline to feed it. Her stomach churned, but she scolded it into submission. "I am not afraid of you," she announced loudly, trying to mimic that regal tone Cecily used when she was annoyed. She listened to herself as she spoke, and nodded. She did not sound at all frightened. Or at least not very frightened.

"Well, really! Perhaps you ought to be." Livia appeared out of the mist, sounding more irritated than menacing. She wore an extremely fashionable gown in apple green—and an aggravated expression. "I should dearly love to scratch your eyes out. I would do it, too, if I had any hope that such things were possible here."

"Livia! Oh, my dear one, is it really you?" Rhoda ignored the ill temper and flung herself into Livia's arms. She kissed Livia's cheek repeatedly, twining her arms around Livia's waist, and laid her head on Livia's shoulder. "Thank you for coming for me! I am eternally in your debt. Oh, my good, sweet friend, how I love you!" Belatedly, she lifted her head to gaze into Livia's eyes. "It is really you, is it not?" She considered Livia's astonished scowl and sighed in relief before returning her head to Livia's shoulder. "Yes, that is plainly you. And you are still angry at me. But no matter. I love you no matter how angry you are. Tell me what to do to make you love me again."

Livia turned her head to stare down at the head on her shoulder. "Nothing comes to mind," she remarked in icy tones, pushing Rhoda away. "Although you might best begin by restoring myself to me. You could then proceed to leaping from whatever cliff overlooks the rockiest shore. Pausing, of course, just long enough to leave a note retracting and apologizing for all those malicious stories you have been telling about me."

Rhoda turned her face away at the suggestion of surrendering their shared person and winced at the mention of rocky cliffs. At the accusation of slander, however, she looked up indignantly. "What malicious stories? I never did any such thing!"

"How dare you? Of course you did!"

"Didn't!"

"Did too, you fibber!"

"I'm not and I didn't!" Rhoda tossed her head. Her hair flew out around her face dramatically, for all that it had been securely pinned a moment before. "I don't tell lies, unlike *some* women. I notice you can't even tell me what this malicious story was—because there was no malicious story, and you cannot manage to make one up in time to fib about it! Instead you resort to name-calling!" She sniffed and turned her nose in the air, crossing her arms before her.

Livia sucked in all the breath she could hold and clenched her fists. "You impossible, deceitful, thieving . . ." She could not think of enough insults to relieve her rage. "I hate you! You know you did, and now you stand there and lie and lie!" She raised her hand for a blow.

Rhoda saw it coming and caught the hand. "How dare you?"

Livia reached with her free hand, caught a large handful of the tumbled curls, and pulled with all her strength. Rhoda responded with a most unladylike kick at Livia's knees, which sent Livia's feet flying backward while her upper limbs were still extended forward. Falling, she caught for support at Rhoda's skirt, which tore off in her hand, petticoat and all. The drawstring of the crinolette broke also, and it fell free and collapsed, leaving Rhoda dressed only in her pantalets and stays. Livia's skirt flew violently up behind her when she hit the ground, right into Rhoda's face. Rhoda kicked again, but Livia had grasped her foot so that Rhoda toppled over backward when she tried to raise it. She too grasped wildly for support, and found nothing in reach but Livia's skirt, which tore free so that Rhoda carried it down with her. Most of Livia's hairpins went with it.

Scarcely noticing their dishabille, both women rose halfway to their feet, then leapt furiously toward each other. Within seconds they were rolling around on the ground, pinching, scratching, and slapping each other. Identical as they were, in strength as well as appearance, neither could gain any real advantage. It therefore required a lengthy and vigorous struggle before it became apparent that—although they were doing a splendid job of destroying their garments—neither of them was successfully inflicting any injury on the other.

It was Livia who first realized—as she had, in fact, already suspected before the battle began—that they could not rend each other's flesh in the astral realm, because neither of them had true flesh to rend. If Livia scratched at Rhoda's eyes, she left a track of torn flesh down Rhoda's cheek that lasted just exactly as long as Rhoda remembered the attack. But when, in her eagerness to box Livia's ears, Rhoda forgot the scratch, the mark disappeared, just as Livia's boxed ears ceased to burn scarlet as soon as she saw a new opportunity to pinch Rhoda in a tender place. Astral reality was not composed of matter but of spirit; only will and conviction could affect it.

"You cannot hurt me," Livia spat into Rhoda's face. "See how weak you are? How your scratches leave no mark? You have no strength because you are not real! You are only a ghost, an empty imitation of humanity. You scarcely exist at all!" To her delight, she saw the new strategy taking effect. Rhoda's assault slackened, and her expression grew more worried than fierce.

Deliberately, Livia let Rhoda get in a few strikes, just so Rhoda could see for herself how ineffectual they were. Then she launched them both into a roll so that she came out on top, and delivered a vigorous slap, quickly, before Rhoda had a chance to realize how little the slap was worth. "You are just empty air and ether; you could not pretend to live at all if you were not dangling from my petticoat." Reaching down to grasp a hank of her opponent's hair, she leaped to her feet and started walking away, dragging the screeching Rhoda along behind her. "Mirror!" cried Livia. "Mirror, where are you? Make this liar see some truth!"

As always, the mirror was near her when she wanted it. By the time she drew up to it, Rhoda had scrambled to her knees so as to alleviate Livia's pull on her hair. Finding herself already where she wanted to be, Livia sank down beside her. Save for Livia's hand still knotted in Rhoda's tresses, they might very well have passed for sisters sitting together as they planned their toilette. Before and between them, the mirror glowed. "Mirror," demanded Livia. "This . . . this . . . this prevaricator dared to tell Cecily that I betrayed her to the demon in Venice!"

"Well, you did," spat Rhoda. "Is that the terrible lie you pretend to be so angry over? When it is not a lie at all but God's own truth?"

Livia turned to snarl at Rhoda, "I did nothing of the kind. As if I would dream of wounding Jacob so! I never even saw Cecily in Venice. You were just trying to turn my darling Jacob against me."

"As if you cared a fig for Jacob! And you didn't need to see her—you knew she was there, and you told the demon so. And I never even talked to Jacob—how could I, with you and the demon lying in wait for him?"

They were within a heartbeat of laying into each other again, whether or not they could do each other any real hurt. The mirror blazed blindingly. Livia flung up an arm to shield her eyes and cried, "Mirror, show her what really happened."

The flash faded, and the mirror became a secret window looking into a room. The room was small, and almost entirely occupied by a four-poster bed draped in mosquito netting. There was just barely enough space left for a small chest of drawers and a large trunk.

Plain as the scene was, it held both women rapt. Livia's grip on Rhoda's hair relaxed, and her hand slid down Rhoda's back. Rhoda made no move to pull free when she was released; rather she wrapped an arm around Livia's waist. Half mesmerized by the mirror, their quarrel forgotten, the two women relaxed into a sisterly embrace. "Look," whispered Livia. "That's my room, in our house in Hong Kong."

"And there you are," answered Rhoda, pointing toward a small child curled up on the bed. Although veiled by the nets, the child was instantly identifiable by the mass of chestnut ringlets tumbling around her shoulders. She wrapped her arms around her knees and closed her eyes very tight as she concentrated on trying to sleep.

She failed, of course, and sat up. She was so small she had to take great care in sliding down from the bed to the floor, and her nightdress rucked up around her knees as she did so. With a frown, she smoothed the nightdress into place, for all that it fell back down of its own accord when released from the obstruction. She patted at her hair and restored her crushed ringlets somewhat by curling them around her finger. She examined the trunk with wide eyes and reached out a finger to poke at the lock.

The door swung open behind her, although there had been no knock, and Ishmael Aram entered. She turned, not exactly to face her father, for she kept her eyes downcast, but in his general direction. "There's my little girl, all packed up and ready to go," he beamed. "And still awake, I see. Are you excited?" She nodded and curtsied. "You look like a bride already," he assured her, "in your lacy little shift, with all those ruffles and ribbons. Pretty as a picture." He cocked his head to one side. "Of course, your new family might not agree. The Chinese like to put their brides in red."

He dropped her a conspiratorial wink and took her hand. "Let's go see if there's anything we can do about that." She looked up, too surprised to remember to keep her face down, but followed docilely. He brought her to a room that was empty, save for a single flat crate standing upright and some oddments on the floor: candles, small bowls, and the like. A great drawing had been chalked on the floor in front of the crate. Although there were no lamps, a shaft of moonlight perfectly illuminated a large circle with a five-pointed star inscribed within it.

He knelt on the floor beside the circle so that he could look into her eyes. Putting his hands on her shoulders, he said, "Now, Livia, my dear, I need you to be very brave. Can you do that for me?" She did not look very brave, but she nodded. "That's my good girl. I'm going to do some magic now. Do you know what magic is?" Another tiny nod. So you know that magic isn't like ordinary life. To do it, you have to do some very peculiar things. That's just how it works. So when I do some peculiar things, you mustn't get frightened or cry out. Do you understand?" This time she did not nod, but he continued as if she had. "Just keep still, and let me do the magic. Will you do that for me?" This time he waited for the nod. He waited some while, but eventually he got it.

He smiled and rose to his feet. "First I want you to step into the very center of the circle. Be very careful not to tread on the lines or smudge them with your hem. Then lie down on the floor." She looked up nervously. "Don't worry; the floor is very clean. I scrubbed it myself this afternoon; I know how particular you are. Just make sure you are right in the middle of the circle, so you don't get any chalk on your pretty nightgown." She turned around in a circle several times before selecting a spot and lying down. She pulled at her nightdress to make sure her legs were modestly covered, but her little bare feet still emerged at the bottom.

"That's perfect," Aram told her. "Perhaps I shall tell your new family not to make you go to bed early anymore, since the moonlight suits you so well. Let me show you." He walked around the circle and pulled the crate open, book fashion. Inside the crate was a great bronze, fan-shaped mirror. "Turn your head a little and look, my dear. Do you see yourself in the mirror? Don't you look beautiful?"

Elsewhere, Livia Aldridge gasped so sharply that it was almost a cry, and she gripped Rhoda's hand hard enough to turn her knuckles white. But she did not look away. She stared at the mirror in the mirror. "I don't remember this," she whispered.

Little Livia Aram obediently turned her head and looked into the mirror. She smiled at what she saw. Her father smiled, too. "A very good girl, indeed," he crooned. "Now you just lie there and admire yourself. I'm going to start the magic now. I'll be singing—you won't understand the words because I'll be singing in Latin—but don't let that trouble you. I'll dance around a bit and wave things around, but you don't have to pay me any mind. You may see some odd things in the mirror, but they're nothing to worry about. Just remember, in magic things are never what they look like. So even if you see something that looks frightening, you don't have to be afraid. You just lie still and relax."

He did, indeed, start to dance around the perimeter of the circle. He did, indeed start to chant in Latin. He paused now and again to pour something out of one bowl into another, or to light one candle and blow another out. Livia continued to stare into the mirror, although she was no longer smiling. She looked thoughtful and curious. She did not even notice when her father pulled out an elaborately figured curved blade.

It had been polished so that it flashed in the moonlight as he waved it about. His chanting grew louder. At last, he stepped into the circle, taking care not to step on the lines. He knelt by his daughter and tenderly lifted her halfway up so her head and shoulders were in his lap, with the knife still held high over his head. He smiled down at her, but she did not see it, for she never took her eyes from the mirror. Ishmael Aram raised up his head and let out a great cry, like a wolf howling at the moon. Then he slashed down with the knife and slit his little daughter's throat. Far away, in another world, two women screamed in one voice, but he did not hear them.

The blood poured out over everything. It spurted up all over Aram's face and shirtfront. It spread out over the floor, washing out the chalk circle and drowning the five-pointed star. It dyed the lacy little nightdress red and spilled into the crate to lap at the bottom of the mirror. It flowed and flowed, and Aram sat still, watching it flow with a bemused expression, as if he had never expected so much blood to come out of such a little girl.

Before him, the mirror glowed and filled with mist. The mist poured out of the mirror, as if it were an open window, and hovered over the pool of blood. Tendrils of fog drew together into a shape, still diffuse but compact enough to suggest a human form. Aram looked up to see it, and his eyes widened. He stiffened and drew back slightly, but the figure did not approach him. Instead it settled down so that it came to rest on the ground, its feet— if it had feet—immersed in the pool of blood.

The blood stopped flowing out. Instead it flowed in toward the figure, which started to solidify as it absorbed the blood. The scarlet pool diminished, and a recognizably feminine shape emerged, although the face was still too unformed to identify. Even so, she was a handsome creature, dark haired with tawny skin, and clothed in a thin silk shift that concealed very little of her person. She stooped toward Aram, and the remaining blood on the floor did not soil her shift. Rather the stain on the floor vanished. The circle and star reappeared, looking crisp and fresh.

She reached out to Aram, and he offered her the body of the child. She took it tenderly and settled down beside him, gently gathering the loose limbs into an embrace and stroking the slack face. Under these ministrations, the sodden ruffles were drained; the nightdress was restored to a pristine freshness; the child's skin and hair grew clean again. Soon there was scarcely a sign of what had occurred, save for a great dry gash in Livia's throat, and the unnatural pallor of her bloodless remains. When the woman looked up, she had a face at last. She was Rose.

Rose extended a hand to Aram, who leaned away from her. He knew better than to break the circle by scrabbling backward, but neither did he want to let Rose touch him. "Are you satisfied?" he asked. "I did just as you asked."

She ignored the question and caught up his shirtfront in a fist. Unable to back any farther away, he froze. Clenched in her grasp, his shirt also surrendered its quota of spilled blood. As it grew white, Rose's lips grew red. She let go of his shirt and brushed a finger across his brow; he could not quite suppress a sharp intake of breath, although she could hardly have injured him. She was only wiping the last few drops of blood from his face. That done, she returned her attention to the little corpse cradled on her arm.

"Then our contract is fulfilled?" Rose shook her head. Before he could protest, she gestured toward the mirror. Aram watched with interest as an image formed within it, showing two boys on a hillside near a rocky shore. One boy wore suspenders and short pants with a catapult[9] jammed into his back pocket. The other wore knickers and a large, all-encompassing cap. Aside from their garments, the two were identical. The one with suspenders was crouched very low, scratching something in the dirt with a stick. The boy in the cap was bent over from the waist, studying the drawing.

"Are those the Aldridge twins?" inquired Aram. "I thought one of them was a girl." His eyes widened as the significance of the scene sank in. "But shouldn't they . . . I mean, surely by this time, one of them . . ." He paused and glanced down at his daughter's remains. "Aldridge has not paid his pledge?" Very gently, Rose shook her head. "That's no fault of mine," Aram said, taking pains to keep his voice level. "I have complied with every detail of our agreement. I never suspected Aldridge meant to do otherwise, and if I had known I would have urged him to reconsider most emphatically."

Rose lifted her head and, for the first time in their conversation, looked directly at him. His eyes fell. "Yes, Mirror Spirit. I am very much afraid of you," he admitted. She continued to regard him, and he slowly let out the breath he had been holding. "Thank you. It's very gratifying to hear you say so," he murmured. "How may I serve you further, now that the plan is changed?" Rose continued to say nothing; Aram continued to listen carefully.

After a few moments he started and raised his eyes to hers. "Proceed? But Spirit . . . That isn't possible, not here, not in this plane." He paused and shook his head. "Please, Spirit, I am not declining to obey you. But things are different here. I can't give Xiu Wang Po a dead child. Or rather, I can give him the dead child, but he will not marry it to his son. No matter what I say. He might even kill me for the effrontery. Mortals just do not marry the dead. Death is . . . is the opposite of marriage."

Rose looked away, as if in thought. Then she gathered the little body more closely into her arms and rose. She stepped forward as far as she could without breaking the circle, so that she was right in front of the mirror. Then she lifted her arms and offered the dead child to her reflection. When her hands reached what should have been the surface of the mirror, they met no obstruction. Her arms, and Livia's corpse, passed into the mirror. Spectral arms, identical to hers, and carrying an identical body, emerged from the mirror. Rose and her reflection exchanged their burdens. Then Rose bowed slightly to the mirror and sank back down.

She laid mirror-Livia on the floor; when her arms were free, she extended a hand to Aram in a commanding gesture. He hesitated, whether from fear or ignorance of her meaning, and she turned to face him with a haughty look. He gulped and fumbled around the floor, looking for the knife. When he found it, he slashed one of his wrists vigorously and held out the wounded arm to Rose. His blood dripped down into her open palm. She smiled tenderly as she leaned over mirror-Livia and, with her other hand, gently stroked the awful gash in the child's neck, which closed up under her touch, without even leaving a scar. Rose bent down more deeply—taking care to keep her hand open to Aram's offering—and kissed the pale, waxy lips. It was a long kiss. Rose did not draw back until the child's body suddenly convulsed and emitted a small, strangled cry, a cry that was echoed by an equally strangled cry from Aram.

Rose smiled and lifted the weak, dazed child to her feet, and kept an arm around her as she led her away from the circle and out of the room. Behind them, Ishmael Aram shuddered and found a strip of cloth to bind up his bleeding arm.

"Livia? Livia?" Rhoda grasped Livia's shoulders and shook her, not in anger but in a desperate attempt to regain her friend's attention. Livia, however, continued to stare blindly into the darkened mirror, oblivious to her surroundings or to her companion's efforts to rouse her. "Livia, please wake up!"

Chapter Sixteen

Jacob fell forward for an instant, hypnotized by the glow of his own blood. However, the thud of his forehead against the tabletop brought him back to himself almost immediately. He raised his head back up and suppressed a groan. He was no longer seated at the Chang parlor table. He was seated at a huge, scarred wooden table. He knew the table well; he had once carved his initials onto its underside. It stood in the kitchen of a villa in Brittany, a villa that had burned to the ground nearly twenty years ago.

The door from the cellar burst open, and a large, fat, kerchiefed woman bustled into the kitchen, carrying an armload of vegetables. She started violently on seeing Jacob, and only barely managed to deposit her burden on the far end of the table without dropping it. "Lord have mercy," she wheezed. "Such a turn you gave me! I do declare, you'll be the death of me yet someday, always sneaking up on me like that." She spoke in French, of course, and Jacob smiled inwardly, having almost forgotten her barbarous Breton accent.

But he was less amused to find himself responding, just as he had responded then, by looking up and saying, "I wasn't sneaking. I only came in looking for something to eat. I'm very hungry. May I have a glass of milk, please? Or a bit of bread and cheese?"

The cook opened her mouth. Jacob knew already what she would say. She would insist he could not possibly be hungry, what with all he had just eaten. But she would bustle about anyway, making him a generous snack, all the while assuring him that he was surely eating enough for two boys, coming back for a snack so soon after the hearty breakfast she had just given his father and him, and wasn't he supposed to be off hiking with his father? Jacob did not really want to hear it all again. It had been quite disturbing enough the first time.

So he closed his eyes and breathed deeply. "This is not real," he told himself. "It is only a memory. I do not choose to remember it now." When he opened his eyes, the kitchen scene had grown faint and shadowy, but had not entirely disappeared. He closed his eyes again, and repeated the words slowly. He repeated them several times, breathing in as he said, "This is not real," and breathing out as he said, "It is only a memory." It was difficult to focus on stillness when suffused with energy, but he was extremely practiced. Strength was useless without discipline. He continued to repeat himself over and over until the words became meaningless, and he was merely breathing slowly, in and out.

Having achieved a still place, he permitted himself to review his goals. "I came here looking for Livia. I must find my way to her." He opened his eyes. He stood alone, looking out across a plain of golden grass. Low walls protected a cobbled road, wherein the stones had been worn almost level by long usage.

"You should have remembered." The voice came out of nowhere, and when he turned, he found his father standing behind him. "I am entitled to that much."

"Another time, perhaps." He smiled politely. "But now I must find Livia."

His father seemed to grow two feet taller. Jacob reminded himself that he was a grown man now, but he still felt himself shrinking until he was no larger than a child. "Another time?" his father snarled. "You will remember me at another time? Some time more convenient?" Jeremy Aldridge's voice rose nearly to a shriek. "Now is a good time, a very good time, indeed!"

The force of his father's fury washed around him, and for half a heartbeat, against his will, he almost did remember being crouched by the outside wall of the gardener's cottage in Brittany. He had his catapult stuck in his back pocket, and he was peering in the open window.

He closed his eyes and shut away the image of that window. "No, now is not a good time," he insisted, still taking care to keep his tone polite. He would not let himself be afraid, however much he had feared this man in life. Nor would he let himself be angry, however tempting that particular form of futility. "I must find Livia," he repeated. "I shall accept your help if you offer it, but I will not permit you to prevent me." He turned around.

The golden plain no longer stretched into the far distance. Woods had grown up while his back was turned, and they had crept quite close. They were thick and dark, with dense, twisting shadows beneath them. The cobbled road had shrunk to a beaten path, which vanished into the trees. But it was still a path. He started forward.

He had almost reached the trees before it rematerialized in front of him. For an instant it still resembled his father. But almost before he had time to recognize it, its features shifted, and he found himself confronting Dr. Chang. "You are not looking for Livia," it said. "You are looking for Cecily. See, you have brought her blood with you."

It was true. He found, still clutched in his hand, the handkerchief from the table in the Chang parlor, the handkerchief that bore a few drops of Cecily's blood. He stared down at it, utterly confounded. Looking up, he found Chang chuckling. "Go find your sister, Jacob," said the demon. "She is here, you know, for all that you left her safely in the material world. And she is very much in need of some assistance and protection."

It was a quandary. Cecily's handkerchief was in his hand. To cast it away now would be a gesture of abandonment. To continue holding it would commit him searching for her. Was she really here, in the astral realm that she hated so much? Did she really need his aid? "Demons do not lie," he had been told a thousand times, by entities on both sides of the barrier. But if they did not lie, neither did they tell the truth. He sighed and tucked the handkerchief into his breast pocket, over his heart. "Cecily is always with me," he said. "She would not expect me to abandon Livia. Indeed, she would insist that I should honor my commitments. And now, I must find Livia."

"You have no right to look for Livia," snarled Dr. Chang, or at least the image of Dr. Chang. "She belongs to me."

Jacob sighed. "How unfortunate that you neglected to tell her that. Will you let me pass?"

It planted its feet firmly over the full width of the path and crossed its arms over its chest. "No, I will not." It reached forward with one hand and gave Jacob a sharp push backward, then recrossed its arms.

Jacob fell back a step and sighed. He raised his left hand in a gesture that some might interpret as a sign of surrender. With his right hand, he reached into his pocket and retrieved Cecily's gun. As soon as it was clear of his pocket, he fired.

Dr. Chang staggered backward with an astonished expression, cupping his hands around the small, nearly bloodless wound in his chest. "Again?" he muttered in an affronted tone, peering down at the injury. He started to fall, but several vines dropped down from the foremost trees to catch him in a protective net. Behind him, one of the trees knelt down and wrapped an arm around him.

Jacob shook his head and looked again. It was not really a tree, of course, just an ugly brown creature with pocked, mottled skin and absurdly long limbs attached to a very short torso. Behind it, the forest seemed to collapse.

The leaves of the trees congealed into a wet, fibrous mat, like seaweed, and collapsed under their own weight, sinking down to somewhere about head height. The trunks below shrank in height but grew thicker, and extruded gnarled limbs to provide broader support for the canopy. The shadows beneath grew darker, while excess mass spewed upward in geysers of noxious gases, creating a dense, smoky, evil-smelling cloud overhead. When the shifting was done, the forest had transformed into a swamp.

The brown creature dragged Chang's remains into the darkness. There was a snatching quality to the gesture that suggested it might be more predatory than protective. More brown creatures—or perhaps worse things— moved within the shadows at the barest edge of visibility. But with Chang gone, the path was clear.

Jacob was not afraid of shadows; they had no substance. Their menacing aspect was only empty show. He strode forward with a long, vigorous step. The greasy, cowardly things lurking in the shadows scuttled away and fell over themselves in their eagerness to flee. The dim light faded until the path before him was only barely visible, but the ground was level and he kept walking. Tiny sparkling things flitted by him, almost within reach, but they did not distract him or lure him from the path.

He did not stop, or even slow, until the light failed completely and he was standing in blackness so pitch that he could not tell for certain if his eyes were open or closed. Even then he attempted a cautious step. Surely the path was still there; he had only to find it with his foot. But his second step met an obstruction, and he dared not risk losing the path. He stopped and waited for the darkness to lift. It had to lift eventually.

Soon a soft glow rose up just ahead of him. It brightened and grew until it formed into a shining globe. It shone, but it cast no light. Its golden walls paled to transparency, revealing a brightly lit interior and a woman sitting in a great, throne-like chair. She looked like Livia.

But was she Livia? She also looked like Rhoda. As Jacob knew better than anyone else on earth, the two ladies were physically identical, all the way down to the crooked toe on the left foot, and the adorable little button of a birthmark located where only a lover could ever see it. Even he needed the guidance of hairstyle and dress, speech pattern and mannerism to distinguish between them. The woman before him wore a Chinese robe of silk brocade so white it gleamed as if lit from within. Her hair was not dressed at all, but simply hung down her back, save for one soft curl draped over her shoulder.

This might not even be either lady; when he had first met the demon, it had worn this face, and he had suspected nothing. Eventually he was reduced to a stratagem so simple that it was foolproof. He asked her. "Are you Livia, Ma'am?" Demons did not lie.

She smiled, a charming little smile more like Cecily's than either Livia's or Rhoda's. "I am, sir," she replied. "And, if I may ask, who are you?"

Chapter Seventeen

Oliver set his ill-wrapped parcel down on the stoop and pulled the front door open a crack, hoping to see what was inside it before entering. Instead, his nostrils were assaulted by an intense fragrance of almonds and pear blossoms. He slammed the door. It was a good thing the servants had been given the evening off, he reflected. They might well have given notice en masse if they had all been thrust, willy-nilly, into the astral plane

He pulled out his handkerchief and proceeded to rummage through his overloaded pockets for something—anything—with a strong odor. But nothing came to hand. In the end he was forced to open his hip flask and pour a large portion of its contents over the handkerchief, sighing to himself over the waste of his fine Glenfiddich. Since the flask was nearly empty anyway, he raised it to his mouth and tipped it up before tying the handkerchief over his face like an American desperado.

Once inside, he surveyed the scene uneasily. Cecily half sat, half lay in a chair before the mirror in the entry hall door, with her head lolling back and her eyes closed. Heaven only knew how much of the scent she had inhaled. And the source? At last he spotted a small, unfamiliar object half hidden under the coat rack. He sighed. It was not easy for him to get down on his knees, or crawl about on the floor. It took a while, too, and he was unsure how long his whisky-soaked bandanna would protect him.

By the time he had it, he needed to crawl a little closer to the door—which he had propped open—so that he could stick his head out and gasp up the damp, cold air before he was finally able to wrap the thing up and thrust it into an inner pocket. Even so refreshed, he had to clutch the edge of the table for aid in clambering to his feet.

He was therefore positioned perfectly to observe a long, silver ribbon glued to the floor by a small puddle of spilled wax, and still partially coiled around a fallen candle. He picked up the candle and let his eyes travel up the length of the ribbon, which was tied to Cecily's wrist. The general intent was obvious, and he suffered a frisson of horror when he grasped that Cecily's safety line had been broken.

Hurriedly he struck a match from which he lit both the gas and the candle, then replaced the candle within its lacy holder and twisted the silver ribbon around it securely. Clasping his wife's hand, he whispered into her unconscious ear, "I will come for you shortly, my own. You know I will. Until then, be aware you are still bound to home." He tugged gently on the silver ribbon near her wrist to reinforce the point on a subliminal level. There was another silver ribbon dangling from her other wrist, but he had no idea what she had intended that to bind.

He glanced into both parlors, looking for Mrs. Aldridge, but they were empty. She could hardly have stepped out. He sighed and went to his office, where Dr. Chang's Chinese apothecary chest stood, its drawers still stocked with a variety of exotica. Oliver had never drawn on those stores; he saw it as a point of honor that Dr. Chang's things be left in their places, at first in case he recovered, and later out of respect for his memory. But all things change. Dr. Chang's supplies—including silver and several flavors of dried blood—would come in very handy now.

He had just finished refilling his flask when he heard a loud thud from upstairs, as if something heavy had fallen. He winced and capped off both the flask and the bottle. He should have checked upstairs. He took pains to climb the stairs quietly, which took some doing, what with lugging the parcel along with him. Despite his best efforts he bumped and nearly dropped it several times. Fortunately the great mirror was not as fragile as the modern sort. At the top he found that the thing had gone to the guest room—the room that Dr. Chang had occupied when he lived here. So it really did think it was Chang. There was another thud as Oliver approached the door, a soft one this time.

He opened the door slowly and carefully. He need not have worried. The Jacob-thing was fully occupied. The thud had apparently been caused by Mrs. Aldridge falling from the bed to the floor, and not for the first time, judging by the state of her hair. Had she been conscious, she would have been appalled. But she was as limply vacant as Cecily; she must also have inhaled the fumes from the trance-induction herbs.

The Jacob-thing appeared to be trying to sit her up on the bed. It could haul her up easily enough, but it could not make her stay in place. Even when it finally had her propped in a reasonably stable position, it found itself utterly flummoxed by the buttons of her dress. It pulled on the buttons and picked at them and poked ineffectually at all the tiny button loops.

In the process, it dislodged her, and she toppled over sideways, loosely flinging an arm into her would-be attacker's face. It tried to roll her over to a more receptive position, and she slid off the bed again, completely upending her skirt so that her pretty little pantalets supported a giant cup, instead of being concealed within a bell. Her upper person was therefore engulfed, and the buttons rendered utterly inaccessible.

Oliver could not help but reflect that a human would have found it sufficient to bare the lacy little pantalets, which did very little to conceal the form of her graceful limbs and were equipped with comparatively simple laces. But the Jacob-thing was not human. It thought in symbolic terms. The buttons represented access. The pantalets—designed, as they were, only to be concealed—represented coverage and blockage. So, with considerable difficulty, it pulled down the skirt, lifted Mrs. Aldridge back to the bed, and resumed its assault on her buttons.

Oliver pressed his lips together so as not to laugh out loud. He had often wondered if buttons were intended as a lady's last defense against assault. Seeing that he had a few minutes, he paused to set up the great mirror on its stand, and to acquire several ladies' hand mirrors from the various bedrooms. Both Cecily and Mrs. Aldridge were possessed of multiple sets. As Cecily had once laughingly explained, a lady always had to acquire a new brush-and-mirror set upon her marriage, so as to correct the initials in the monogram. Unless her maiden name, her husband's surname, and her middle name all began with the same letter, of course, but how often did that happen?

When he was as ready to proceed as possible, he entered the guest room. Damned if the Jacob-creature was not still fumbling with the buttons. It had found a buttonhook on the dresser—actually intended for boot buttons, but still an impressive cognitive jump for a demon—and had, mirabile dictu,[10] actually contrived to undo three or four buttons, leaving only fifty or sixty to go. It was actually smiling, pleased to have made so much progress at last.

Demons had no sense of time. "Do you know?" remarked Oliver pleasantly. "Some men would simply tear the dress off."

"Out of the question," it replied, entirely unperturbed by a voice erupting suddenly behind it. "She is very particular about her things; I should never hear the end of it." It turned to him with a smile, as if it had quite forgotten their earlier conflict. When it saw Jacob's little gun in his hand, it sighed. "Really, Colonel Beckford, this is becoming tedious. Surely you must realize by now that—"

Oliver shot it in the middle of its sentence. Of course it would heal itself, but he had shot it right through the heart at very close range, and he therefore dared to hope that the healing might take a little while. From his pocket, he recovered the little sachet he had found in the entry hall, and tied it with a handkerchief to the Jacob-thing's face. That would not hold a true resident of the astral realm either, but with luck, it would further slow the thing's recovery and buy Oliver still more time.

He sat it in a comfortable armchair and tied it into place. Normally it would be strong enough to break bonds. But he reinforced the ropes with silver chains, acquired from Chang's apothecary chest and from dear Cecily's jewelry box. If it struggled against the silver, especially with that damnable sachet under its nose, it risked separating its spirit (be it Chang's or whatever else's) from the flesh.

That done, he pulled the chair in front of the dresser mirror and stood the great mirror immediately behind it so that the two reflected back and forth recursively. He rigged up a sort of mobile of hand mirrors so that they hung on each side. When it woke, it would be encircled by mirrors—mirrors that all led back to the astral realm. It could go home, or it could sit in the chair. It had no other options. Or so Oliver hoped.

Just in case, he had placed a bowl on the dresser under the mirror. It contained dried blood and wine. In front of it he placed a leftover lacy Valentine.[11] The card shielded the bowl so that the bowl was masked from the viewpoint of the chair, but plainly visible in the mirror. Just to make the option of returning to the mirror more attractive.

Then he pulled up a chair—just a ladder-back intended to go under a desk— turned it around so that the back would provide a chin rest, and sat down to wait.

Chapter Eighteen

"**A**h," sighed Tzen. "We are here. My, but the mirror is large tonight."

Cecily pressed her lips together very tightly and counted to ten. Then she smiled. "More so than usual, do you think?" She did not see any mirror, only a singularly uninteresting landscape.

Tzen turned to her with a look of surprise, but before she was able to respond she was overtaken with another fit of coughing. It was very bad, and she dropped to her knees to hack and spit blood. The blood disappeared, as if absorbed, as soon as it hit the ground. Tzen sighed and wiped her mouth on a little handkerchief that appeared from within her sleeve. Then she rose. "Look in front of you, Mrs. Beckford," she remarked in an impressively commanding tone for one so young. "You must surely see it—it is right there, just up ahead."

And so it was. And it really was huge, whatever its astral norm might be. Cecily had to shake her head and readjust her sense of scale, and reclassify as reflections various images that she had taken for real. She was also startled to see two women where before she had seen no one. The ladies—if they could be called ladies, seeing as they were dressed only in their under things!—were kneeling in front of the great mirror. At least, Cecily thought she saw two of them. But that chestnut hair was unmistakable, even in its tousled state. And since both apparent women had it, perhaps one was merely a reflection.

Except . . . Cecily looked again. One of the two women was slumped and motionless in the arms of the other, who stroked and supported her companion. Not a reflection, then, but something she had never seen and never thought to see: Rhoda and Livia together. And one of them was hurt. Plucking up her skirts, she ran toward them. "Sister," she cried. "What's happened?"

Rhoda looked up. "Cecily! There you are at last! But . . . Oh, my dear, it's so dreadful . . . What we saw in the mirror . . . I can't bring myself to tell such horrors! And poor Livia is utterly undone! I cannot rouse her at all!" She gently released Livia, who seemed scarcely to notice, so that she could rise to embrace Cecily.

Cecily kissed her, and stroked her hair, and refrained from commenting on her outfit. "Oh, my poor darling, I am so glad to have found you!" She drew back slightly and looked around. "But is not Jacob here?"

Rhoda cocked her head in puzzlement. "No, he is not. Why should he be?"

"We came here looking for him." Cecily turned back toward Tzen, who, with her tiny mincing steps, was only just catching up with her. "He is not here, Miss Tzen. Have we come to the wrong place?"

Tzen's nostrils flared, but the force of her scorn was considerably diluted by another coughing fit. Again, she dropped to the ground, and again the blood she spat on it disappeared. However, the small trickle of blood at the corner of her mouth did not disappear. She rose with an irritated grimace and, quite as if she thought herself alone, muttered, "Are these smelly barbarian whores all blind from birth?" She ignored Cecily's icy glare but started at the sight of Rhoda; when her glance shifted to take in the image of Livia also, her eyes narrowed. Then she shrugged and wiped her mouth, pointing to the mirror. "He is right in front of you, ladies."

She advanced to lay a hand on the mirror and pressed gently on its surface, leaning into it as if it were supporting her. Strangely, her touch on the mirror seemed to rouse Livia, who looked up and caught her breath. Tzen smiled a ghastly smile, showing teeth stained with blood. Cecily and Rhoda exchanged startled glances, then looked sharply back to the mirror. Its surface remained dark and cloudy, as if it reflected the ubiquitous astral mist, save that the grounds around them had cleared, and therefore contained no mist to be reflected.

Tzen did not so much laugh as cackle, and the blood bubbled up over her lips. "What? You still do not see him? Perhaps you need to go in with him!" She pressed her other hand to the surface of the mirror, which then flashed so brightly it hurt the eyes, as if the sun were trapped within it. Tzen cried out, an awful, wonderful cry that might have signified sublime pleasure or unendurable pain; the unnatural glare that filled the mirror seethed and spilled out past its polished surface to form half of a great, glittering sphere.

Tzen stumbled backward, laughing and dragging the sphere out and away from the mirror, like a conjuror drawing a bubble out of soapy water with a wand. Cecily and Rhoda instinctively ducked back from contact with it. Livia leapt to her feet. "No!" she shrieked. "Grandmama, don't!" She flung up her hands as if the wall of light were a curtain she would tear down. The sphere was not solid; when Livia's hands approached it, they penetrated the apparent surface without resistance. She screamed as if she were burned, but she did not attempt to pull back; rather she seemed to be pushing against something just inside the surface, trying to hold it back. "No, Grandmama," she cried again. "Don't do this!"

"Traitor!" screamed Tzen. "You dare to side with them against me? Fine—go down with them!" She flung her arms wide, and lightning bolts crackled across the sky. The great sphere she had pulled from the mirror expanded outward in every direction. Then it seemed to pop, as if it really were a soap bubble. It broke up into a thousand glittering sparks, which descended gently, like a net, over the three other women.

Cecily and Rhoda looked up nervously, but the sparks descended harmlessly; a few landed in their hair or on their shoulders, but vanished as soon as they made contact. Nonetheless Livia crouched, wailing, and threw up her arms to shelter her head. Tzen was nowhere to be seen, but the sound of her laughter lingered. Rhoda drew a little closer to Cecily; Cecily wrapped an arm around her waist protectively and looked nervously in every direction.

But whatever the danger she was looking for, it failed to materialize. Nothing leapt out at them or descended upon them or slunk menacingly toward them. The mists did not even thicken. Tzen's laughter faded away, and the three women stood alone on a featureless plain in front of a mirror on a stand. The mirror had shrunk considerably, although it was still slightly larger than it had appeared in the material world; now it stood only a little taller than Cecily. Other than that, the scene was unchanged. Rhoda and Cecily stood straighter and relaxed their shoulders. But Livia continued to weep.

Rhoda embraced Livia gently, stroking her hair out of her eyes and kissing the top of her head. "There now, my sweet, don't cry so. See, we are safe now. Nothing to fret for. Really, please calm yourself. What, after all, is so very dreadful?" She seemed belatedly to notice that she was still clad only in her stays and pantalets. She clasped her arms modestly about herself and was dressed again in her old favorite, the grey muslin.

Livia carried nothing for her state of undress. "Don't you see?" she sobbed. "She has thrust us into the mirror." Cecily and Rhoda exchanged glances.

Cecily did Livia the courtesy to look nervous. Rhoda, however, was simply perplexed and said, "Well, please forgive me if I have mixed things up again. But weren't we already in the mirror?"

Livia straightened up with a huge and long-suffering sigh. She waited several seconds, but no comprehension leapt into Rhoda's eyes. She sighed again and rolled her eyes. "We were in *a* mirror already," she explained in a tone of exaggerated patience. "Now we are in *the* mirror."

Cecily, who had withdrawn slightly from the exchange, stood peering into the mirror, as if she hoped to find some clearer image lurking behind the fog. There was a little ripple at the hem of her skirt as her foot started to tap. "Do you know?" she remarked with some asperity. "I still don't see Jacob in there."

Cecily could not see Jacob, but he could see her. The woman who claimed to be Livia had risen and stepped forward. Behind her, the great chair displayed a quantity of elaborately carved openwork, most notably a fan-shaped open panel cut out of the headrest; it looked out on an outdoor scene, utterly at odds with the interior of the sphere. It almost resembled that little window on the front door that lets a resident look out on visitors before deciding whether to admit them. And, indeed, there was Cecily, just like a visitor of dubious welcome, peering in the window and hoping to be invited in.

"You ought not look at her," snapped his hostess. "This is my place. You have not even introduced yourself yet, and you are already looking out at other women? Show some breeding, sir." She waved a hand, and the little window in the chair went dark, as if a curtain had been drawn across the opposite side. "Now, I ask you again, sir. Who are you?"

Jacob drew in a deep breath and smiled. She was, after all, a very beautiful woman, whoever (or whatever) she was. "I beg your pardon. I was caught off guard, seeing my sister here. But you surprise me . . ." He hesitated, struggling with the appropriate form of address. "Miss Aram," he decided at last. "I should have thought you would know me. I am Jacob Aldridge." He bowed slightly and pulled out his card case. There was no place to put his card. Then he remembered where he was, closed his eyes, and remembered the entry table at the Beckford house, with its little silver salver for calling cards. When he opened his eyes again, the table and the salver were there.

She was as delighted as a child watching a magic trick. She plucked up the card and perused it earnestly, quite as if she expected to find mystic secrets written on it. "Jacob Aldridge," she sighed happily. "Ministry of Cultural Protection." Her brow knit, "Ministry of . . ." She paused to consider. "Ministry of . . ." She thought long and hard. Then, cocking her head to one side, she inquired, "Isn't that a lie?" She giggled. "It is. I'm sure it is. There's no such place!" She sighed again. "It's wonderful how you do that."

Jacob refrained from asking what exactly he had done that was wonderful. Instead he answered the question. "That is not the correct name of the ministry for which I work. Our business is extremely confidential, so we try to keep the name out of the public eye."

"And out of the private eye also, I think." She giggled again. "But you are quite right that I should know you. Appearances are so very different here and there, but we are certainly acquainted." Her girlish demeanor fell away, for just an instant, and he saw . . . something he had seen before, something he had yearned for and called by Rhoda's name.

Then the childlike manner was back, and she was smiling. "It's very provoking of you to come now." She pretended to pout. "I waited for you for such a very long time, and now that I've finally made other arrangements, here you are." A thought struck her. She laughed and clapped her hands. "Are you going to contest the new arrangements? That would be thrilling! Oh, say you will!"

He blinked several times and managed to smile again. "Oh, dear, am I late? I'm so sorry. I didn't even know I was expected."

She paused in apparent astonishment before bursting into laughter. She had a wonderful laugh. Light. Musical. "No, I don't suppose you'd have been told, at that. And, as I recall, you behaved abominably when the invitation did arrive." He was sure he had kept his face neutral, but she seemed to sense his confusion. "No, Mr. Aldridge, you most certainly did receive the invitation. You just didn't recognize it." She waved her hand toward the chair.

The little panel brightened and almost irresistibly drew the eye. It displayed an image of a rundown cottage on a rocky hillside. A young boy crouched by the window with a catapult in his pocket. Jacob almost felt that he was crouched by the boy's side; he could see plainly into the room. Racks and shelves of vessels, instruments, bottles and jars, and—of course—books, lots of books. In the center of the room, his father stood by a great stone slab. And on the slab, an embroidered cloth draped over . . . over something alive, something moving.

Jacob closed his eyes. He did not want to look at that slab, did not want to see what was on top of it, draped under the cover and writhing. He had seen all he needed to see a very long time ago. He turned his back—on the image, on the chair on which it was mounted, even on the lady—before he dared open his eyes. "You too?" he inquired softly. "Everyone is so eager to remind me of Brittany." He turned back to her. "So tell me, Mirror Spirit, how can you call yourself Livia? Surely demons cannot lie."

"But I am Livia," she insisted. "The real Livia, the true Livia. That other one out there—she is not real. She is only a shadow of me."

"She seemed real enough to me."

"Well, she wasn't." This Livia crossed her arms in front of her and pursed her lips in irritation. "I made her the night your father died, so she could go out and collect my debt." She smiled and came toward him until she was very close. She was not tall enough to whisper in his ear, but she tried. "So now you see why it is important for you to remember Brittany. Then you will see how real I am." She reached up to coil her arms around his neck, and raised herself up on her toes to draw him down into a kiss.

At the touch of her lips every nerve and fiber of his body exploded with longing. His head reeled; his breath simply stopped. Ironically, the very force of the passion washing through him left him too intoxicated to respond immediately. Her little tongue licked his lips—which were closed—seeking entry between them. There was something snake-like about that little tongue, a coldly reptilian intrusion on the steamy liquor of her kiss.

Maybe it was that tongue that made it possible, but—to his own utter astonishment—he pushed her away. She fell back with a gasp. "How can you refuse me?" she cried. "It is not possible to . . ." Even armed with her own belief, she could not manage to say something so patently untrue, so she corrected herself. "It never used to be possible to refuse me."

She was right; it wasn't possible, as he remembered all too clearly. And yet he had. "I've walked this road before," he guessed, shaking his head. "I've seen where it leads." He hoped that was it.

She gazed up at him, her eyes brimming with tears, her lips slightly parted. "No," she murmured. "It's because your father's pledge is finally paid." She shuddered and turned her face away. "Before, I was free to do whatever I liked to get back what was rightfully mine. But now, my powers are entirely bound to paying my own pledge." Bowing her head she whispered, "I am afraid to pay my pledge. I was born of that pledge. Will I still exist when it is fulfilled?"

She looked so woebegone he risked laying a comforting hand on her shoulder. Her touch did not burn him. "What did you pledge, Miss Aram?"

She looked back up at him. "Pain," she replied. "A wonderful pledge, really. Aram only wanted money and power and freedom from English rule." She made a little barking noise that might have been a laugh. "A cheap little man to pay so much for so little. Still, he paid it, so I gave him what he wanted—for a little while. But Jeremy, sweet Jeremy . . ."

She drew in her breath sharply and smiled a wonderful little secret smile that sent Jacob's blood racing again; fortunately the smile was not for him. "Jeremy wanted pain—endless, immeasurable pain, pain beyond mortal endurance. He was not satisfied with mere vengeance; he wanted to burn the past away."

Jacob stepped backward, away from her. "Is that even possible?"

She laughed. "Of course not. But mortals are easily deluded." She turned and walked back toward her throne, waving dismissively over her shoulder. "Go now. And don't come back without your brother's head."

He watched her go, debating internally if he might ask her what she meant, but before he had decided, a cold wind blew past him and the fog rolled in. It was a deep, dense fog, as bad as any he had ever seen in London; it so completely obscured his vision that he lost sight of her before she reached her chair, although it was only a few steps away.

Chapter Nineteen

Oliver had almost fallen asleep, but he came to alertness quickly enough when the mirror lit up. It displayed an early morning scene, in which several gentlemen—after tramping through several empty fields, and debating after each tramp—were engaged in erecting a boxing ring on the flattest of the fields that they had traversed.

A crowd slowly collected around them. It was an unusually democratic assembly. Several carriages delivered a laughing cadre of wealthy aristocrats. Mostly young, fit aristocrats, Oliver noted. Their servants roped off a small area and equipped it with comfortable chairs. At only a very small remove, a seedy-looking fellow in an ill-fitting secondhand suit assembled a gang of obvious ruffians. Every walk of life seemed represented somewhere; there were even several Negroes and a Chinese.

Oliver's eyes lit up. "Bit of the fancy?"[12] he inquired affably of his prisoner. "So you've kept that up on the other side? There's not much of it left over here." He turned to look at the Jacob-thing, but it clearly had no intention of replying. Rather, it leaned forward as much as its bonds permitted—mesmerized, yearning toward the mirror. "Got a wager on, then?" murmured Oliver, but he did not expect or receive any answer.

Jacob looked carefully to the left and to the right, but did not permit himself to become alarmed. He knew about the astral mists. They could not endure endless scrutiny; one could always wait them out. He had barely thought of their inevitable end when they faded. A mist like that of early morning lingered, but visibility was restored. He stood on the broad, level top of a ridge; the ground, streaked with woodlands, sloped smoothly away to each side. He glanced toward the sunrise; North Downs and South Downs, then. Beyond them, splendid pastoral views extended for miles, including a very pretty lake or reservoir.[13]

There was something familiar about those views. He turned his head back and forth, hoping a different vantage point might summon the memory lurking just out of reach. Was it perhaps just an ordinary view of fertile fields? But then, how could he know there was a farmhouse just ahead, on the other side of those trees?

Yes! It was Cockmounts Farm.[14] There was the chimneystack, piebald from recent patching, just where it ought to be. Jacob broke into a happy run, eager to see the excitement. Behind him, his father chuckled. "No need to run, lad. They're a long way from starting." Jacob smiled and fell back to his father's side. Just as well. There was a crowd—a growing crowd—of strangers up ahead.

Jacob had very little experience with strangers, and none at all without Cecily's hand to hold. He did not want to say he missed Cecily. Like the dearest creature in the world that she was, she had not been the least bit jealous when their father had announced he was taking Jacob—and only Jacob—to pursue some "manly amusement."

She had been excited for him and assured him that it was only right and proper that their father should favor his son—his firstborn!—over his daughter. (They had never actually been told which of them was born first, and they assigned the honor variably, according to their mood.) He was therefore resolved to make the most of this solitary excursion. Still it felt very odd to look about and not find her beside him.

It was hard to make sense of the crowd around them—so many different sorts of people, some of them sorts that always inspired Nanny to cross the street. Even here, the rich folk weren't getting very close to those, possibly because they smelled funny. But just as Jacob was deciding to investigate the matter more fully, he felt his collar being grabbed.

"Now don't you go wandering off, my boy; there's someone here I'd like you to meet," his father said. Transferring his grip from Jacob's collar to Jacob's wrist, he pulled Jacob toward an elegantly dressed elderly man who was sitting on a shooting stick,[15] who did not rise but raised a cordial hand at the approach of the Aldridges. "No surprise meeting you here, Ward. But I'm very glad of the opportunity to show you my son." With one hand, he pulled Jacob forward; the other hand he offered to his acquaintance. "Jacob, you're a lucky boy. This is none other than Jem Ward, himself."[16]

Jacob guessed from his father's tone that he should not under any circumstances disgrace them both by failing to know who Mr. Ward might be. Fortunately that was not a concern. Extricating his hand from his father's, he extended it upward. "I'm very excited to meet you in person, Mr. Ward. We have one of your pictures at my house—everybody says it is awfully good!"

There was a sharp intake of breath beside him, but Mr. Ward guffawed loudly. Jacob's father looked down, and there was an unpleasant glint of steel in his eye, for all that his voice remained pleasant. "Dear me, Jacob, we didn't come all this way to talk about painting. Don't you know? Mr. Ward is a retired champion!"

"No, no, Aldridge. Don't fault him," intervened Mr. Ward "The lad's a proper little gent. How could he know about me? I've been away from the ring since you were his age. I'm pleased he likes my painting." He leaned so far forward that Jacob was worried he would fall from his seat. "Pleased to meet you, too, Master Jacob. So tell me: has your papa told you what's going to happen here today?"

Jacob sucked in his breath. It was always risky to discuss his father's doings with anyone; there was just no knowing what he wanted people to know. "Manly amusement?" he essayed at last.

Mr. Ward leaned back again to laugh. He laughed for a long time, rocking back and forth on his shooting stick. "This his first time?" he said at last, turning to Jacob's father. "It's a fine little chap you have here. You're a fortunate man." He leaned back down toward Jacob. "See those two blokes over there?"

Jacob looked. One of the men in question was bending over something, but it was still fairly obvious who was meant. "The ones with hardly any clothes on,[17] sir?"

Mr. Ward chuckled again. Even a chuckle set his stick to swaying; it couldn't hold forever. "The very ones! Well, Master Jacob, pretty soon they're going to fight each other for the championship." Jacob did not know how to answer that. He thought it very odd that grown-up men would fight right out in the open, if they weren't in a war. Anytime that Nanny caught Jacob and Cecily fighting, she said they were acting like children and made them stop right away. But clearly nobody meant to stop these two. Jacob took so long thinking things over that Mr. Ward stopped waiting for an answer and continued, "I know what you're thinking, lad."

"Do you, sir?" Belatedly, Jacob wondered if that would be taken as cheek.

"I do. You're thinking, how can they fight for the championship, when neither of them's the champion now, ain't you?" Jacob decided to nod. "And you're right. Coppers busted up the Heenan-Sayers match before it was over. They called it a draw. Give both of 'em belts." He paused, so Jacob nodded again.

Mr. Ward nodded back. "Officially it was a draw," he repeated, dragging out the word *officially*. "But it's common knowledge who was winning. I mean, there wasn't a hairbreadth doubt—Heenan's the real champion. See there. . . ." He pointed at a man talking to one of the people roping off a large square.

"That's Sayers right there, talking to the Commissary.[18] So he's all right with it. Maybe he plans to take King on himself later on, but for now, he's the bloody second—begging your pardon, Aldridge, for letting such language slip before the boy. But if Sayers is the Benicia Boy's second, that's gotta mean he's okay with him fighting for the title."

Jacob considered Mr. Ward's statement until he was confident that he had identified all the principals and their nicknames and their alignments. This time Mr. Ward did not get tired of waiting for whatever Jacob might have to say, so Jacob replied, "Which one do you think will win, sir?"

Mr. Ward started laughing again. Jacob had often wondered why adults found so many things funny. He watched Mr. Ward swinging back and forth and decided that he was probably not going to fall after all, no matter how unstable the shooting stick looked. He was, after all, a retired champion. "You lookin' for a tip, lad?" chuckled the former heavyweight. "You got a wager in mind?"

"I doubt he has the money for a wager," said Jeremy Aldridge. But it was all right; he was laughing too.

Jacob turned to look up at his father. "I have ha'pence, sir," he said, pulling it from his pocket. "Is that enough?"

At that, Mr. Ward nearly did fall off his stick, and Jacob's father also laughed out loud. It was Mr. Ward who finally said, "Good to know your wife was an honest woman, eh, Aldridge? The lad's a born sportsman!"

He wiped a tear of mirth from his eye. "Master Jacob, you've pluck enough for a dozen boys. I'll see your bet. Ha'pence it is, and your papa's our witness. So who do you want?" Who did he want? Jacob had no idea what that meant. Mr. Ward picked up some of his confusion, anyway. "Which one are you betting will win? Heenan or King?" He gestured grandly toward the ring, and Jacob looked back to the nearly naked men.

The one who had been bending over before was standing up now, and the sight of him took Jacob's breath away. He couldn't quite hide a little gasp of fear and surprise. The man was huge—surely the biggest, tallest man in the world. He might even be a giant. "Who's that?" he whispered.

"Ah." Mr. Ward's voice had dropped to a coo of admiration. "Ain't he a corker? That's Heenan, the Benicia Boy. The Champion. You think he'll win?"

"How could he not?" breathed Jacob. "He's big as a house. He don't have to fight at all—he'd just have to fall on you." The other fighter—that must be Mr. King, the one whom some had called the Sailor—walked off to one side. Jacob watched him walk; he was muscular, and he moved like a man who knew what he was doing, but next to Mr. Heenan he looked like a child.

"So you're betting on Heenan, then?"

Jacob scarcely heard him, he was so busy gazing at the fighters, but his head came around when Mr. Ward plucked at the coin in his hand. "No, sir," he said. "I'm betting on the other one. Mr. King."

"But Jacob," purred his father. "Didn't you just say that Heenan was sure to win?"

"He is," agreed Jacob. "But I'm not going to bet on him." Both men stared down at him, and he felt the weight of their eyes, like a heavy, stifling blanket over his shoulders. "It's not fair," he explained, or tried to explain. "Mr. Heenan oughtn't to go picking on somebody so much littler than him. If he wants to fight, he should fight someone his own size."

He'd said something wrong; he could tell. Mr. Ward began laughing again, laughing so hard that he really did come off his stick at last (although he didn't actually fall; he just stepped forward and reached a hand behind him to catch the stick before it reached the ground). But Jacob's father wasn't laughing. He was staring at Jacob with his mouth hanging open, as if Jacob had said something so extraordinary he could scarcely believe it.

"There now, didn't I say he was a proper gent?" declaimed Mr. Ward. "It's a fine, honorable bet, my boy." With his free hand, he claimed Jacob's halfpenny piece and passed it on to Jacob's father, then reached for his own wallet. "The contents of Master Jacob's pockets against the contents of mine." He poured the contents of his purse into the palm of his hand until his hand was so full of coins—some of which Jacob had never seen before—that he risked dropping them. And yet, the purse was not yet empty.

Jacob nearly stopped breathing at the sight of so much money. His father's eyes popped wide open. "Oh, no, that's too much. If the boy's going to gamble, he must learn to do it right." He eyed the heap of money as if uncertain what to do about it, and finally picked out one coin gingerly—with only two fingers—lest he topple the entire stack. Then stooped down low enough to meet Jacob's eyes, and displayed the coin to him very plainly. It was silver and very shiny. "Here's a bright, brand new florin[19] against your ha'pence. That's odds of forty-eight to one, a very daring wager." He smiled and cocked his head. "You do understand, Son, that when Heenan wins, your ha'pence will be gone. Mr. Ward won't feel sorry for you and give it back like Cecily does."

Jacob shook his head, as much to say that Cecily wouldn't really do that as to show that he understood what was at stake. "No, sir. That would be welshing."

Mr. Ward put the rest of his money back in his coat and offered Jacob a large horny hand. Jacob's hand vanished inside it, but the handshake was gentle. "Not to worry. Master Jacob wouldn't welsh on a debt of honor." He grinned broadly. "And you never know—King might win. After all, I taught him to box myself." He dropped Jacob a large wink. "What do you suppose you could do with a whole florin?"

"I'd buy a new pocketknife!" chirped Jacob. *Not so*, whispered a voice at the back of his head. *You'll buy a dolly for Cecily and lots of sweets, and there won't be enough left for a pocketknife. You'll get a catapult instead, and a bag of marbles. You'll love that catapult dearly.* It was so obviously true, so inevitable, that Jacob didn't question the source. Besides, he often heard voices. "Or maybe a catapult," he added aloud.

Mr. Ward cupped a hand to his ear; a large crowd had assembled around them, and although they were only minimally jostled—Mr. Ward was, after all, a former champion—the noise level had risen to the point that conversation was extremely difficult. One shout rose above the clamor, and Mr. Ward looked away. "They look to be ready," he exclaimed.

Raising his stick like a cudgel with one hand while laying the other on Jacob's shoulder, he started pressing toward the ropes cordoning off what he called the inner ring (which completely flummoxed Jacob, for it was plainly the outer ring). The stick was employed several times in disposing of anyone impertinent enough to block his way. Jacob's father stayed very close behind so that they stayed together until Mr. Ward had successfully escorted them to the best spot on the perimeter. Once there he planted his stick with a flourish and sat down.

Jacob pressed up against the ropes, turning his head sideways to look under the top one, then standing on tiptoe to look over it. The first blow took him completely off guard. It wasn't that he didn't know men fought; he'd heard lots of stories about Balaclava and the Light Brigade;[20] but he had never actually seen it done, so his personal experience was limited to a few little slaps and pinches administered to or by Cecily.

Mr. Heenan did not slap Mr. King. He struck him with a closed fist the size of a whole ham. There was an audible thud when the fist reached Mr. King's cheek, and blood flowed down Mr. King's face as if Mr. Heenan's knuckles had somehow been filed to sharp points. Jacob had never seen the like; he gaped and clambered up on the ropes for a better view. Behind him the crowd cheered approval.

Mr. Heenan fell back a step to admire his handiwork and smiled. Jacob let out a small wail. He did not cry out over the blood, or the imminent loss of his wager. He cried out because, for an instant, just a tiny little second, it was not Mr. Heenan smiling, but another man entirely—a slim man with grey eyes, who looked a little like a Chinaman—and he was smiling right at Jacob.

Then the face was gone, and it was the giant smiling again, and he wasn't looking at Jacob; he was stepping forward to hit Mr. King again. But before he could do so, Mr. King lashed out and hit him first, very fast, right under Mr. Heenan's oncoming fist. He caught Mr. Heenan in the ribs really hard, and his blow also drew blood. Jacob had never guessed that bare fists could draw blood. The discovery thrilled him, and the smell (for surely that acrid, oversweet scent was blood) intoxicated him. He hung on the ropes like a sailor, twining his arms through them to hold himself up, engulfed within the screaming of the crowd and gulping in great lungfuls of that wonderful, awful smell.

The men kept hitting each other, over and over. Jacob had never guessed there could be so many different ways to hit someone. They hit left-handed and right-handed, cutting under or coming down overhand or driving straight through the middle. The blows were rock hard, so hard that Jacob's teeth ached, just watching them; every blow that connected made a sound— a sound that could be heard even over the roar of the crowd—and usually drew blood. When a man got hit he generally staggered back a half step; now and again he fell down. When that happened, the cheering turned into a roar that rattled his eardrums, and everything stopped for a minute while the downed man clambered back to his feet.

Jacob loved it. He wanted to be in there, wanted to be part of it, wanted to see the blood gush up under his fists and feel it smearing onto his knuckles. He wanted to roll in the stench of pain and grow filthy and tired with the effort of beating flesh into pulp. He screamed himself hoarse and yearned toward the fight, no longer caring who won or who lost, just breathless and dizzy with almost supernatural excitement.

He wanted it so much that it came to him. Suddenly he was there. He was in the ring. His fist was swinging. His head was ringing. His body—his big, strong, grown-up body—was covered with cuts and bruises, but that didn't matter, because he was fighting, hitting out, striking at evil. He was powerful, exultant, a conquering hero. He swung again, and his fist connected with . . . with . . .

He almost froze, because he didn't know who he was hitting. He didn't even know who he was or, for that matter, where he was, but he knew with all his heart he didn't belong here. He tried to drop his hands and back away, but his body (or rather the body in which he found himself) had its own agenda. It continued to dodge and dart, swing and fight. He (or it) struck at his opponent again, and the necessity of swinging up at such a huge target tipped him off that the opponent must Mr. Heenan. So he must be inside Mr. King.

He was fighting the giant! Something like a cry, a child's frightened sob, escaped him. He was sorry, he didn't mean it, it was very wrong of him to want to fight, and he didn't want to fight the giant, please! The face across from him was not Heenan anymore—it was the grey-eyed Chinaman, and he was smiling. "Choice of weapons was yours, Aldridge," he said. "Perhaps you should have chosen more carefully." He laughed and picked up Mr. Heenan's great, huge fist as if it were his own, and rammed it into Jacob's face.

The pain was so terrible he didn't even notice he was screaming. Something in his face crunched and broke—his nose, his jaw, his cheekbone?— Jacob didn't know; he only knew that it hurt so bad he couldn't stand it. He was supposed to hit back, but he didn't know anything about how to hit, and that scared him so much he couldn't even try. "He's going to kill me!" he wailed.

Not so, whispered the voice in his head. It was so faint that he could hardly hear it over his own crying, but it was there in his head. *Try to remember. Heenan lost the fight. You won your bet. You bought a catapult with your winnings. Someday you'll save Cecily's life with that catapult.*

"Remember?" For an instant everything wavered. He was not in the prize ring. There was no prize ring. No ropes, no crowd, no Mr. Ward with his shooting stick. He was all alone, lost in mist. Then it all came back, and he raised an arm to ward off the blow rushing toward him. "Remember what?" While he was distracted by the voice, his body—Mr. King's body—threw a punch. It connected so hard he felt his knuckles split, and Mr. Heenan let out a most satisfying grunt of pain, and the blood on his face started dripping down into his eyes. Mr. King struck again, lower this time, only just above the belt, and Mr. Heenan staggered back.

Remember who you are, said the voice, which sounded just silly to Jacob; how could he forget who he was? Who else could he be? *Remember that this isn't real. It can't really hurt you; it's only a memory. It was all over a long time ago, so there's no point in trying to change it now.*

None of what the voice was saying made any sense to Jacob, but for a minute, just a little minute, the crowd got sort of quiet and Mr. Heenan went a little farther away. Maybe the voice was holding them off? He closed his eyes and tried to listen harder.

But that didn't work at all—as soon as he was distracted, the blows raining down on him got worse and worse. Mr. Heenan's fist swooped in like a cannonball and took him on the neck. He couldn't breathe; he tasted blood in his mouth. He fell down. He would have screamed or cried, but his neck hurt so much he could only croak, and so he just lay on the ground, tasting the dirt and the blood and his own tears, and listening to the crowd shriek at him.

Listen to me, Jacob! We didn't make that happen—it would have happened anyway. King lost a couple of rounds, that's all. In a minute, he will get back up and start fighting again. He'll be fine! Nothing you do will make any difference in this fight, so just keep telling yourself it isn't real, and it can't hurt you.

Oh, yes, it could—it was hurting him awfully already! Someone was leaning over him, wiping his face with a wet rag, asking if he was all right, would he be getting up again? Jacob tried to scream that he wasn't all right, and he was never going to get up again. He was going to lie here crying with his fists in his eyes until he was dead.

But he did get up, at least partway. And his mouth opened up all by itself and announced, "I'm fine, mate. Any chance of a quick swig before I take this bloke down?" And somebody brought him water. He poured it down so fast that a lot of it spilled down his face instead of into his mouth. He gulped in the water that reached his mouth and wiped the excess off his chin with a filthy arm; then he rolled an extra mouthful of water in his mouth, and spat the water back out into the dirt.

Jacob gasped in shock. Spitting was vulgar! And how could Mr. King talk, when his throat hurt so bad it was like someone had cut it? And why was he volunteering to go back into the ring?

I told you, Jacob. King doesn't mind the pain like you do. Why should he? He's a big strong man, and you're just a little boy. He's eager to get back to the fight so he can be champion. And he'll do that, no matter what you do. Do you really want to stay and watch? Or come with me, back into the mist where you don't have to be a frightened child anymore?

That sounded good. Better than here. King and Heenan were circling again, and Jacob could feel Mr. King smiling a cruel, determined smile. "It doesn't matter what I do?"

Not in the slightest.

"Then why am I fighting?"

He didn't get an answer right away. Jacob listened for it very carefully, listened so hard that time slowed down around him, and the fighters danced around each other in slower and slower motion. At last he heard, *That's an excellent question.* Jacob winced. He knew that meant there wouldn't be any answer. Then the voice continued, *Perhaps we should find that out.*

Or maybe the voice said, *Perhaps I should find that out.* It was funny how those two words got mixed up in Jacob's ears. He wouldn't have thought they were at all alike. But he didn't much care anyway, if the voice was talking about taking him away from here. And the voice was taking him away. No mistake about it, the fight around him was fading out, until it was like a fight between ghosts, and he could see both of the ghosts; he wasn't inside one of them anymore. In fact, he wasn't anywhere; he was fading away, lost in the mist, because it wasn't just the fight that wasn't real.

Jacob staggered and shook his head, clinging desperately to his mature self, but even so he found himself launched back into the memory of the prize ring. Heenan and King danced before him, covered in blood and bruises, their faces so battered they could scarcely be distinguished from each other, save for their difference in size. *I am no longer a child*, he whispered to himself, but his arms were still twined through the ropes of the inner ring, his throat still raw from screaming his applause.

Vivid as it was, the scene of the fight viewed from the periphery was still overlaid with a face-to-face image of Heenan, swinging. At intervals Jacob completely lost his awareness of the child watching the fight and resumed the identity of one of the fighters. *This is not real*, he assured himself—but nonetheless, he lifted an arm to shield his face from Heenan's fist. He did not successfully block the blow. "Not real," he hissed, between split lips. "Only a memory." He managed at last to spit out the question his younger self had reminded him to ask. "Why am I fighting?"

The question had power. For a moment he was flung away from the match, back into the ropes around the inner ring, and he almost broke free of that image, too. Not quite, but he managed a quick glimpse of the boxers, not from the vantage point of a participant or an overexcited child, but as an adult and reasonably dispassionate spectator. Seen so, it was obvious that Heenan and King were not real, but puppets, memory-laced illusions. Beneath the smaller of the astral masks he saw an only slightly familiar phantom—could it be himself? The slightly lopsided face resembled Cecily more than the image in his shaving mirror. And his opponent? Chang, of course.

Why, "of course"? he wondered, but there was no time for wondering. He was sliding back into the fight, and Chang/Heenan was lifting a great fist. "Why am I fighting?" he demanded aloud before the blow could land. A very powerful question, indeed. The fight slowed until it came to a stop, with Heenan impossibly poised in a position that defied gravity, his fist halfway to King's skull. *Third time's the charm,* he reflected, and said it again. "Why am I fighting?"

The fight shimmered and faded until it was only barely visible. Chang's mouth tightened and his nostrils flared. "I always suspected you were a coward, Aldridge."

It was the worst accusation in the world, and with his young self's panic still ringing in his ears, he could not evade it or shrug it off. The word transformed into Heenan's fist, which crashed into his face in an explosion of pain. Neither the boy nor the man had ever known such pain, save only once that both selves refused to remember. The Fighting Sailor stumbled under the blow and fell back against the ropes, right in front of Jem Ward's party of spectators. Little Jacob could almost have reached out and touched him, if he could have contrived to extricate an arm from the ropes of the inner ring.

Back to the ropes or no, King was not quite down, and the Benicia Boy came toward him like a falling mountain, his fists swinging ponderously toward King like battering rams. Behind him, little Jacob emitted a note so shrill that it penetrated the roaring of the crowd. Surrendering his weight to the ropes, gasping in air as if it were in short supply, Jacob marveled to see Chang peeking out of Heenan's oncoming face. *How can he fight so well? He knows nothing of boxing—he wasn't even there.*

That sudden insight penetrated his entire being so completely that it even infected King, who laughed as he leapt up from the ropes. If Heenan's fists were battering rams, then King's fists were churning pistons. If King's reach was not quite so long, then Heenan's reach was too high, enabling King to duck under his blows. Heenan was too slow and too clumsy, too old-fashioned in style, too old entirely, and King fell on him like a hungry, young wildcat attacking an elderly bear. Jacob laughed too, and little Jacob on the sidelines laughed, and they both reveled in the joy of bloodlust that was so rarely permitted them.

Chang wasn't there! exulted Jacob. *He only heard infant Jacob thinking that the gigantic Heenan was bound to win. He would never have picked this scene for his duel if he had guessed how it would really turn out.* He grinned at Chang—a feral smile that very few had ever seen—and released his rage. He did not often succumb to rage; he rarely admitted even to himself how dangerous he could be when roused. He certainly had never risked anger in the astral realm, where every sentiment was magnified beyond all human scale.

One moment he was locked into the role of Thomas King, fighting for the championship and winning. The next instant he was on the tiled marble terrace of the Chang villa, half sitting, half kneeling on Dr. Chang's chest, both of them arrayed in their normal forms. He was choking Chang with all his strength, watching Chang's face turn purple, and—unsatisfied, even with that—lifting Chang up by the neck repeatedly, and slamming his head back down on the ground. Chang's skull shattered, spilling out brains and blood, but Jacob still pounded him against a faded fresco of Neptune, grinding his blood and bones into the porous marble, which would never be clean again.

Impossibly—for surely he was long past volition or conscious act—Chang contrived to moan. He failed to shape anything recognizable as a word, but he did emit a sonorous noise, accompanied by a gushing fountain of red-tinged bubbles awash in a surf of crimson froth. Jacob leaned back instinctively as the first bubble flew into his face and popped, leaving a faint taste of salt on his lips. Several more bubbles alighted on his shirtfront and left little pink rings upon erupting.

"Oh, splendidly done!" Jacob's head jerked up at the unexpected voice. The Chang villa was gone. He found himself instead in a great Roman circus stadium; Dr. Chang's blood was no longer pooling on tile but seeping into packed earth. Looking down on him from the imperial box was Livia Aram, her white gown transformed to the toga of an empress, still gleaming white, but adorned with broad purple bands. Around her, a faceless crowd cheered, yet not so loudly she could not be heard.

She rose to her feet, laughing and snapping her fingers.[21] "What a champion you are!" she cooed in a voice that promised many things. "When I sent you to bring me your brother's head, I never dreamed you would fulfill your quest so quickly!" She smiled hugely—wantonly—and paused in her finger-snapping to extend one fist forward with the thumb pointed down. "Now finish him off for me."

Jacob gaped up at her, still dazed and reeling from the sudden cooling of his blood. "My brother?" He looked down at Chang, whose face, although mottled, was still largely intact, even on his flattened head. "My brother?"

"No!" A shriek rose up, a cry of horror louder than the roaring crowd or Livia's imperial proclamations. A small figure leapt down from the upper tiers and over the wall that enclosed the arena. It was a pretty young girl, her pale blue Chinese robes incongruous against the promethean Italian stonework; she landed crouched, almost on all fours. She tried to jump to her feet, but for all her agility, she collapsed suddenly in a coughing fit. Blood spilled from her lips, but she cried out through it, "You must not kill him!" She staggered up and ran forward, flinging herself at Jacob. She knocked him down, backward and away from Chang, then fell on top of him, still coughing up blood. The blood from her mouth joined the blood from Chang's mouth on Jacob's shirtfront.

Jacob stared up at her unmoving, as if paralyzed by her meager weight. "Mme. Chang?" he gasped, undeceived by her apparent youth. He turned his head slowly, fearfully, toward where Dr. Chang lay. "Who was your son's father?" he whispered. Something almost like a sob burst from his lips, and he rose to his knees, shoving Mme. Chang to the ground as if she were something vile. He paused to brush ineffectually at the bloodstain on his shirt before crawling back to Dr. Chang's body. She lay, coughing, where he had thrust her.

Livia Aram appeared suddenly beside him; behind her, the stadium and the crowd faded to shadows as she lost interest in them. "Never mind about that, Jacob. It is enough that he is Tzen's son. You must kill him—now, while she is watching, so that she suffers every blow you strike. She has done you and yours so many wrongs—here is your chance to avenge yourself and your sister! Strike now!" She gestured dramatically at Chang.

Jacob scarcely glanced at her. "My brother?" he wailed. "Not my brother, too?"

"Yes," snarled Tzen Chang. "Your brother. You'll be cursed if you kill him." She patted at her mouth with a stained, damp handkerchief, which she extracted from her sleeve.

He turned toward her with a bewildered expression, a face full of pain, but saw only that her shoulders heaved as she coughed. Then, unexpectedly, he chuckled softly. "It may be a bit late to tell me that." She pushed herself up to glare at him, but failed to rise and dropped back to the ground, hacking and hissing indistinct curses.

"No, Jacob, just the opposite," interjected a familiar voice. "She's told you in the nick of time."

Jacob turned left and right, looking for the speaker. The Roman circus had disappeared entirely, and the astral mists had drawn in to surround them. But just behind Livia Aram stood the shadowy figure of a woman. Livia Aram turned also to look, and on seeing the form let out a little squeak of annoyance. "You! What are you doing here?"

"How could I not be here?" replied Livia Aldridge, stepping forward. For an instant, Jacob thought she was clad only in her under things, but then he saw she was dressed in a toga much like Livia Aram's, but with the colors reversed. "If you are here, then, perforce, I must be here as well. Not so?" One hand was extended to clasp the hand of another shadowed woman standing behind her. "I was the link, was I not?" Her nostrils flared and her lips tightened. "Your appointed channel between this plane and the material realm." She turned to speak to the person behind her. "Stay close to me, or she may thrust you out."

The woman behind her stepped tentatively forward and, from behind her also, yet another woman. Rhoda Carothers glanced nervously about, as if she (quite rightly) doubted the reality of everything she saw. She glanced hopefully toward Jacob, but on seeing Tzen and Dr. Chang, her hand rose to her throat and she drew back. Her lip trembled as she looked back and forth among the three figures on the ground. Cecily stepped around her and marched up to Livia Aram. "She may try to thrust us out, I think you mean."

Jacob laughed out loud. "Why look, there's Livia and Rhoda and Livia again. I've never heard of a triple doppelganger before; do you suppose there are a few more Livias tucked away somewhere?" He rose to his feet and strode out into the mist. "Livia, my sweet! Come out, come out, wherever you are. You must help me celebrate the murder of the brother I never had!"

Cecily darted forward and tried to take his arm, but he shook her off vigorously. "Stay back, Sister. I've murdered everyone else who mattered to me in this life; I'd prefer not to add you to the list." When she hesitated, he pushed her firmly as far away from him as was possible without actually hurting her. "I said go, Cecily, and I meant it."

She backed uncertainly away until she bumped into Rhoda, who put an arm around her waist.

Livia Aldridge stepped into Cecily's place. "No, Jacob. You have not murdered your brother." Jacob's mouth twisted in a grimace of denial, and he waved toward Chang's limp form. But Chang contradicted him with a dull moan and another shower of bloody bubbles. "You see, my dear one," murmured Livia—the Livia who had loved him and married him. "He is not dead. You forget where you are; nothing is real in the astral realm. These ill-used remains are only an illusion; they have nothing to do with actual death."

She turned her hand in an odd gesture, and the image of Dr. Chang's battered body shimmered faintly and transformed into that of a slim young man dressed in Chinese silks. He lay unconscious, but showed no other mark of injury. Livia paused, waiting to be sure that Jacob had absorbed the image, before continuing, "He is down—what's the expression?—'down for the count'? You have won. By a knockout."

But why were we fighting? he thought, but did not say aloud. There was no need to say it. *Because the demon also feeds on anger.* He gazed down at Chang. The young man looked even less Oriental—almost English—than the senior Chang. He reminded Jacob of little Julius, who did not look very English, but almost Chinese. "I . . . I . . ." Having started to speak, he found himself at a loss. He could not bring himself to mention the rage that had consumed him, the rage he had battled all his life to suppress. "How badly is he injured?" he managed at last. Chang looked to be breathing. For all that was worth.

"That is entirely up to you, Mr. Aldridge," purred Livia Aram. She pushed past Livia Aldridge and leaned imploringly on his arm. She had resumed her Chinese attire, and it was very thin, scarcely more than a shadow between them. "You could kill him with a snap of your fingers. It is only the blade of your will against his throat that holds him down now."

"Traitor!" spat Tzen. She clambered up to clutch at Livia's gleaming robe, slobbering blood down the side of it. "Vile trollop! Stinking reptile! Have you no shame? My poor boy loved you from the day he saw you. He nursed you to health when you were dying. He lavished you with gifts. He taught you everything you know. And now you turn on him and beg for his death? May you twist in a hell of your own shadows! May you be reborn for a thousand lives as a cockroach!"

Livia looked down at her quizzically, as if patiently waiting for her to say something of interest. At last she shrugged, lifted a dainty foot, and kicked Tzen in the mouth. Tzen's words disintegrated into gagging noises as she choked and swallowed several of her teeth.

Returning her attention to Jacob, Livia Aram contrived to press up more closely against him, which he would not have thought possible. "Please. You must kill him—now, before he gets up and attacks you again. Why are you hesitating? Think of the injuries he has done you. Think of your dear sister, collapsed on the floor in Venice. Kill him now."

"Jacob, don't." Livia Aldridge was too ladylike for the immodest manners practiced by her counterpart, but she stepped forward to lay a hand on his other arm. Her fingers lingered there a moment, and then she knelt. "Poor Xiu Yao," she murmured to the fallen man. "Poor little shadow. You never got to be, not in any realm. Surely you have grasped by now that you are not truly my dear papa, no matter how hard you tried to wear his thoughts. I know how you must feel; it seems I am not truly Livia either. But I am still real—not Livia, maybe, but real; I can feel it. So perhaps you, too, are real. Not Papa, but real."

She was interrupted by a hiss of anger. Livia Aram's face convulsed in a snarl, and she lashed out with one hand. Even as she moved, her fingernails transformed into gleaming talons, and the gesture that had started as a slap became a feral slash instead. "How dare you!" she snapped, and for an instant her face ceased to be beautiful, or even human. "He is not real, and neither are you. I am the only one who is real." Her claws connected with Livia Aldridge's face and tore into it deeply.

But even as Livia Aldridge squealed in pain and backed away, identical gashes appeared on Livia Aram's cheek. She raised her hand to her face with a bird-like cry, then regarded her bloody fingers in dismay. Livia Aldridge smiled broadly. "I seem to be as real as you." Her face fell, and she sighed. "Although that may not be saying much."

"Liars! Both of you!" Tzen spat out a tooth and rose to her knees to lean protectively over her son. "Of course he is real, my darling boy, my child, my only one. More real than all you ghosts and demons put together." She pressed her cheek to his face; the blood on her face brushed his lip. She embraced him gently, with a tender smile, for several seconds, then suddenly pulled back sharply and cried out, "What are you doing?" Her face was unexpectedly clean.

Chang's eyes were open; he was licking his lips, with a smack of satisfaction. He smiled a truly horrible smile. "Make me real, dear Mother," he crooned. "Make me real." He rose and advanced on her.

She tried to back away, but he grasped her arm and pulled her into an embrace. It almost looked as if he meant to kiss her, but he licked her face instead. The coughing took her again; during the spasm he supported her, so she did not—could not—fall. He continued to lick her face. As she coughed, she spewed out more flecks of blood. He took her soggy handkerchief from her and held it up before her face so as to catch every drop; the more blood she spat into it the cleaner it grew. In between her coughs, she wailed, a forlorn high-pitched hiccupping that irritated the ear.

"Oh, yes," sighed Livia Aram. "That is delicious, dear Yao. Make her cry some more."

"That does it," announced Rhoda. She sounded faint and ill. "I have had my fill of this diseased astral realm. Cecily, we are plainly of no use here. Shall we go home?"

Cecily let out a long, hurtful breath. "That . . . that sounds like an excellent idea. I was mistaken to bring us here—I do apologize. Jacob, won't you come with us?"

Jacob opened his mouth, but Chang lifted his face from his mother's neck to answer for him. "He can't." He glanced down at Tzen with a grimace. She seemed to have fallen unconscious. He poked her until she jerked awake before continuing, "Mrs. Beckford, you may do as you please, but Jacob and Miss Carothers must remain here. Livia and I have need of vessels in the material realm." His eyes narrowed as he reflected on something far away, and his lips tightened in annoyance. "Or we will soon. Colonel Beckford must sleep sometime."

"No." Livia Aldridge spoke softly, but her voice carried conviction. She turned her back on Chang and crossed to Rhoda, who had remained as far back in the shadows as possible, short of losing sight of her companions. Livia took Rhoda's hands and leaned forward to kiss her cheek. "Sister dear, I am so sorry that I quarreled with you. Please forgive me. I have made such awful mistakes, done so many things wrong, but I could not bear it if I lost your love."

Rhoda started in astonishment but returned the kiss immediately. "Never, my own! How could we two not love each other."

"Then you will think kindly on me in the material realm? You will tell your daughter that I was not a bad woman? Perhaps even name her after me? That would mean so much!"

"But . . . but . . ." Rhoda's eyes filled with tears. "It is your person, my dear. I am ashamed to have borrowed it so long. I have no right to it. I . . . I . . ." She dropped her head in shame. "I should let you go home."

Livia shook her head. "No. You could not bear it here forever—you would go mad. For me it is not so great a hardship. I have been dead so long, it would be foolish to pretend to be alive again. And if I stay here, Xiu Yao will be content to stay here, too. Won't you, Xiu Yao?" He did not answer, just stared at her openmouthed. Livia shrugged and turned back to Rhoda. "I am sure what we both want most is to see Jacob safely home." She flung out her arms and drew in a huge breath. When she opened her eyes again, there was a golden cord in her left hand. Her lifeline.

Livia Aram had listened to their conversation with much foot tapping and rolling of eyes. But at the sight of that golden cord she grew alarmed, and rushed urgently toward Livia Aldridge, as if it were her lifeline also. She was not quick enough. Livia Aldridge wrapped the cord securely around her left wrist, then grasped it farther down its length with her right hand so that she held a length of it taut before her. She jerked with both hands with all her strength, and the cord snapped. Behind her, Livia Aram screamed. The scream went on and on, a haunted cry, with every echo more despairing than the last. When it faded at last, Livia Aram was gone.

Xiu Yao staggered and dropped Tzen Chang. He fell to his knees and clutched his head. Livia Aldridge—now the only Livia—dropped down beside him and supported him; he clung to her and shuddered and wept. He started to fade and grew ghostly, until he was hardly more palpable than the surrounding mist. Livia gripped his arms, seeming to infuse him with etheric substance, until slowly he resumed a more solid appearance. "See, Papa," she murmured. "I told you that you were real." He blinked at her and shivered and huddled in her arms.

After a long silence and much looking at her companions for guidance, Rhoda inquired, "Can we go home now?"

"No!" The growl rose up out of the damp ground, pervaded the mists and seemed to emanate from the center of the universe. A dark form rose up out of nowhere, a spinning secretion of wind and water, a thing that had no clear shape and no substance, and yet contained more menace than any natural form could have possibly encompassed. Its voice was not so much loud as deep, rumbling on the very bottom layer of audibility, a sound more felt than heard. "Did you think because you smashed a few masks and shadows that I would be destroyed?"

"Oh, bloody hell," muttered Jacob.

Cecily turned on him. "Jacob! Such language." She looked about, searching for some focus of address, but the whirlwind refused to stay under her eyes. "Who are you?" she called out at last to the air in general.

"Do you need a name? A face? I have another self you might enjoy." The whirlwind suddenly dissipated; for a moment there was simply nothing there. Then a man walked out of the mist. Cecily and Jacob sucked in their breath as one, and drew closer together.

Jacob exhaled slowly. Cecily's hand clutched his arm like a claw. He risked a glance at her; she was white-faced and holding her breath. He had never seen her look so frightened before; indeed, he had never before seen her look frightened at all. Rhoda, however, strolled right up to the thing and looked it in the eye. She actually looked relieved to be confronting what appeared to her to be an ordinary man, sublimely indifferent to the face that had haunted Jacob's nightmares for nearly twenty years. She even extended a hand in greeting.

It ignored her. "Well, Jacob," said the image of Jeremy Aldridge. "Have you time enough to remember me now? Or have you some other errand to run?"

"I remember you, Father," he replied. "Did you think I could forget?"

It extended a stern hand. "Are you ready, then? Prepared to take your punishment like a man?"

"His punishment?" burst out Cecily. "And what of your punishment?" Her voice did not tremble, but Jacob suspected that she was still afraid.

So did Jeremy Aldridge. He turned and looked down on his daughter with a great show of surprise. "Why, there's little Cecily! Where on earth have you been, child? We've looked everywhere." Cecily tried not to drop her eyes, but her look did falter.

As her expression shifted, so did her features. Every flutter of an eyelash left her looking younger. Even without a mirror, she clearly sensed the changes working on her. Nervously she patted at her hair and face; her anxiety only accelerated the process. She stumbled, and when she had regained her footing she was two feet shorter than she had been before. A small cry escaped her when she looked down to find herself attired once more in knickers and a sailor shirt. She reached up to check if she was wearing a cap, only to have her hand grabbed.

Jeremy Aldridge pulled both of her arms behind her and tied her wrists tightly. Jacob stepped forward. "Let her go." He felt his fear and anger rising. He remembered that the demon fed on both. Was it feeding on Cecily now? "Surely you see it is too late for this. The past is over. Let her go."

His father did not even appear to have heard. He was intent on dragging Cecily across the stone floor of the gardener's cottage. Cecily opened her mouth to protest, and he extricated a hand to slap her across the mouth. "No cheek, now, little one. I shan't endure it." She rocked back and forth, with unfocused eyes. While she was still stunned, he hoisted her up onto the great slab he had erected. He had already set out an altar cloth to hand; he flung it over her. When she resumed her efforts to wriggle free, he struck her again, bouncing her head off the marble surface, and she quieted considerably. "Shall we review your faults, boy?" he said to Jacob.

"Only a memory," whispered Jacob desperately. The scene, as it had originally played out, leapt into focus before his eyes. To his horror, the found a few details did not match perfectly; previously Cecily's feet had also been bound and his father's chin had sported a shaving nick. This was not a memory but a re-creation.

Cecily's struggles had dislodged the cloth from her face. She looked just exactly as he recollected—her cap pulled tightly around her ears, her eyes hugely wide, her mouth in an open *O* as if she would, even so belatedly, scream. Behind her, his father had removed his jacket to stand in weskit and shirt sleeves. Jacob did not remember those gleaming white shirtsleeves; surely his father had retained the jacket the first time.

But he remembered the knife. It was large—not so huge as he remembered but clearly intended for serious carving. Its blade was curved and elaborately figured. His father held it high over his head.

His father had not looked so tall, nor the knife so highly elevated, when Jacob had looked down on them from the window. Now he stood at his father's feet, and his father seemed to tower over him, the knife to hang from heaven. Before, his father had not known he was present, and had chanted in Latin while he raised that knife. Now he stood silent and paused to skewer Jacob with a stern glare.

"Confess your sins, my boy," he admonished. "Own up now like a man, and we can set things right. The blood of sacrifice will cleanse us both. Speak up, Son. Can you not tell me your error?"

Jacob was ten years old again, and knew better than to protest; it would only steel his father's will, provoke his father's awful wrath. He was terrified—just as he had been terrified then—and he dared not suffer terror, for part of him remembered that the demon fed on fear. He choked on the unbearable injustice—just as long ago he had swelled with righteous indignation—and he could not permit himself wrath, because the demon also fed on anger. The faint recollection of adult autonomy seemed only to accentuate his helplessness.

If he dared not let himself be moved by this impending outrage, neither could he let this hideous thing happen. But he was not quick enough to free Cecily before the knife fell, nor strong enough to overpower his father. There seemed nothing he could do, no direction he could turn.

"He has nothing to confess. He has done nothing wrong." Cecily spoke in the high-pitched, breathy tones of a child. But her voice was level and determined. The eyes that sought his out were filled with mature compassion; she had somehow mastered her fear in her concern for him. Well, if she could master her fear, then he could master his. After all, he was the firstborn. And, after all, it turned out there was one thing left that he could do—the same thing he had done before. The little catapult was in his pocket.

He had not truly meant to kill; only to disrupt that dreadful tableau. Almost without his conscious decision, the elastic of the catapult had snapped and a pebble had lodged itself between his father's eyes. There had been a long, hazy moment while his father flailed and twisted, somehow managing to come down on the knife. Whether it was the fall or the knife or the stone between the eyes—or even righteous anger from heaven—Jacob could not have said, but when it was over, his father had been dead. And not Cecily.

At his daughter's words, Jeremy Aldridge turned back to the altar with a shriek of rage. "He killed me, you insolent witch," he screamed. "His own father!" He raised the knife again, apparently no longer intending to sacrifice her, but simply to shut her mouth.

Jacob stepped forward and caught his father's wrist. "I did. I would again. You tried to murder Cecily."

For an instant he hoped that it would be that easy, that he had won. Then Jeremy Aldridge smiled. Jacob knew that smile; he had quailed before it many times in his youth. "No, I did not," his father told him. "I tried to murder you. But as always, you hid behind your sister's skirts."

Jacob stumbled back as if he had been shot; indeed, a bullet to the head would have been kinder. The horrific truth of the accusation exploded through his brain. He had done nothing in his life but threaten and destroy the women he loved. Dressing Cecily as a boy had not protected her—it had thrust her into deep danger.

Nor was that the only time he had nearly gotten Cecily killed. Years later, she had given up her blood to protect him—in his plain sight, and he had failed to prevent her! And the result? She had fallen into the demon's maw and nearly died. Had not his darling Rhoda died at the demon's hand, murdered solely because he loved her? And Livia—she had been swallowed up by the mirror of his father's curse. Even his mother had died in bearing him.

He fell backward, and his head struck a flat marble surface. His little catapult tumbled from his hand. Dimly, he grasped that he had taken his intended place on the altar. Cecily screamed at finding herself displaced, but Jacob smiled and surrendered to his destiny at last. Never again would a woman he loved be sacrificed for him. He closed his eyes and waited calmly for his father's knife to descend.

An inappropriate voice intruded, an unhurried drawl, pointedly casual yet compelling. "Well, there goes my wager. Looks like I'll have to kill you after all." There was a short silence, as if the speaker were listening to an inaudible reply, followed by a chuckle. "But of course I can! Poor monster, did you really think I was letting you live because I couldn't kill you? Just because you heal quickly? Really, there are ways. Many ways. Shall I tell you about them?" There was another pause, and another chuckle. "No, I was merely respecting Jacob's property, I assure you. But if he's not coming back . . . Well, we can't have demons running about London, you know. There'd be talk."

Then Jacob felt his father's knife stab in toward his heart—seeming almost to burn rather than cut—and he could not help but cry out. But strangely, when he opened his eyes, the knife had not, after all, descended. It seemed to float, motionless and shrouded in the shadows overhead. Jeremy Aldridge looked, for all the world, as if he had been distracted by something more interesting. He didn't even glance at Jacob.

A woman's voice spoke next, although there were no women in the room. A familiar voice, a pleasing voice—it might almost be the voice of someone he loved. "Ask him about the pledge, Jacob. Will killing you pay his pledge?"

Her suggestion made no sense at all, but somehow it sounded like a wonderfully good idea. He sat up. He was dressed in short pants, and for a half second that seemed strange, but then he noticed that his catapult had fallen out of his pocket. He snatched it up thankfully; he loved that catapult and wouldn't want to risk losing it. His chest hurt badly, but he couldn't think why. His father hadn't hurt him. Rather he had dropped the knife and was staring out the window. "Will killing me pay the pledge, sir?" In the absence of the knife, it seemed like a silly question; he hoped it wouldn't be taken as cheek.

His father turned back to him, his face an almost unrecognizable mask of fear and confusion. "How can you ask me that? What do you know of the pledge?"

"Why, nothing, Father," said Jacob, either because that was obviously what his father wanted to hear, or because it was true. "What was the pledge?"

Jeremy Aldridge moaned and staggered back. He should have come up hard against a stone wall, but the wall melted away behind him, leaving only mist in its place. The gardener's cottage vanished, and Jacob had just time to jump down from the altar before there was no altar from which to jump. When he landed, he was relieved to see he was wearing proper trousers again. Not that his attire was noticeable in such thick fog, but appearances still counted. He straightened his jacket.

He recalled that Livia Aram had also mentioned a pledge, so he repeated, "What was the pledge, Father?"

Jeremy Aldridge collapsed into a sobbing, boneless heap. "My son's life," he wept. "My son's life against freedom for my firstborn and a slow, excruciating end for the Chinese witch."

The air brightened slightly, and Cecily stepped out of the mist. "Well, you have that much of it, surely. Just look at her." The mist receded further to reveal Mme. Chang. She lay almost motionless on the ground, save that she occasionally hiccupped blood. "I don't know what's happened to her in the material world," continued Cecily, "but it must be severe, if she cannot escape it here."

Jeremy Aldridge raised his head to look, and caught his breath in a ragged gasp. "Tzen?" he whispered. She raised her head also, but made no answer. She just looked at him. Her face remained expressionless. She might have been filled with love or hate or remorse. But she half rose to a crouch to look at him, and would not look away.

He rose to his hands and knees and crawled toward her. His movements were intent, his look as unreadable as hers. Perhaps unendurable love still compelled him. Perhaps he stalked her with a predator's delight. A smothering darkness drew in all around them, save for a hot bubble of flickering gold in which they circled each other. A great rumbling filled the air when they met. Then a lightning bolt flashed down, flinging a fiery explosion up behind it. The very world seemed engulfed in flames; the heat seared their skin.

Jacob and Cecily fled back, covering their eyes. When they risked a glance behind them, the mist had pulled back slightly and the smoke had cleared. An enormous fissure with blackened edges gaped where the pair had been. A faint odor of sulfur drifted in the air. Then the edges of the chasm softened and filled out; even as they watched, the mist reclaimed its ground.

At the very edge of visibility, Livia and Xiu Yao knelt together in earnest conversation. She rose and glanced at Jacob, but before he could greet her she turned away to help Xiu Yao to his feet. He was still weak and leaned on her arm as they walked away and faded from view.

He sighed and turned to Cecily. "I don't see Rhoda anymore—have we lost her too? I'm sure I heard Livia say she could go home. But with her lifeline snapped, I don't see how."

Cecily took his arm and displayed her free hand to him. A silver bracelet hung from it, and from that, a delicate silver chain. She gave the chain a gentle tug, and a feminine form appeared dimly in the fog. "She is quite safe, my dear; she can ride along with us." The figure drew close enough for her bright-colored hair to become visible. She saw them, too, and plucked up her skirts to run toward them.

Chapter Twenty

"**Y**ou stabbed my brother?" Cecily stood on tiptoe to glare more closely up at Colonel Beckford, with tightened lips and her fists planted on her hips. Her voice was shrill. "You stabbed my brother?"

He looked down sternly. "It was necessary. I had to convince the demon that I was prepared to kill him so it would evacuate."

"Indeed, you were most extraordinarily convincing," hissed Rhoda Aldridge. "I'm sure we're all agreed that it looks exactly as if you were prepared to kill him." She showed every sign of having more to say, but at a small moan from Jacob she returned her attention to dressing his wound. The wound was deep and very close to the heart; she had not yet entirely succeeded in stopping the bleeding.

"Looks can be deceiving," the colonel informed her. He continued to look at Rhoda, although his next words were addressed more to Cecily. "I assure you, I value family as much as any man and would not casually murder my brother-in-law."

"I hope not," muttered Cecily, returning to the bedside.

"Ladies, you are unjust." Jacob managed a wan smile. Always pale of countenance, he looked quite ghostly with his color further drained by blood loss. "Oliver did exactly the right thing; his assault on my possessed self terrified my opponent at just that moment when I was about to succumb. I should not have survived if I had faced the demon's full powers. Nor could I have escaped it there by returning to my person here, if it was still in residence." He paused to look down at his chest, a bit ruefully. "How fortunate that our skilled soldier knew just where to strike. See, he missed my heart entirely."

"Yes, indeed," sniffed Rhoda. "Missed it by at least a quarter inch."

"If I had missed by a foot, it would have been an obvious bluff," pointed out Oliver. At the sound of footsteps on the stairs he turned—with some relief—away from the discussion at hand. "Dr. Verlaine!" he exclaimed, striding toward the door with his hand extended. "You are here at last! I do hope you can reassure the ladies that Jacob is not at death's door."

Oliver had barely released his friend's hand when the ladies pressed him aside to fall on the doctor as on a savior, one taking his bag and another grasping his arm to propel him toward the patient. Dr. Verlaine cast a nervous glance back toward Oliver, but got no support there, as the colonel was executing a swift military retreat.

But Oliver did not get far. Rose was waiting for him at the bottom of the stairway. She did not step aside to let him pass, but turned her face up to him with a questioning look. He moved around her and walked down the hall to his study. She followed and waited while he extracted a candle from one of the drawers of the apothecary chest, but when she saw the candle, the corner of her mouth twitched in something like a smile.

She extended a hand toward him and snapped her fingers. A tiny flash of fire leapt up toward the candle wick and died almost before it was visible. The colonel stood blinking at the burning candle for several seconds before inserting it in a candlestick on the mantel. He moved to the chair behind his desk and gestured that she should take a seat. "So you still have power," he observed. He glanced at the candle again and added, "Power enough to waste on trifles. And here I was wondering if you would even survive the closure of Aldridge's contract."

He met her eyes directly. "Then the contract is definitely closed, is it not?" he asked. "Chang's death satisfied the terms, even if he was not the son that Aldridge had meant to sacrifice?" She nodded. "And freedom for the firstborn?" he continued. She pursed her lips and looked away. "I see," sighed Oliver. "One of those nasty two-edged promises that crop up so often in magic. Freedom from what? Doubtless somewhere along the way, Chang was freed from something."

He sighed again and rose, crossed to the window to look out. He was standing with his back to her when he said, "Mme. Chang is still lying gutted on her own dining table." He glanced around. Rose was smiling hugely. He had never seen her smile before. He did not entirely like it. "We cannot simply leave her there. I could take her heart out of the vessel and let her die."

Rose's smile faded, and her lips tightened. He considered that. "But I do not like to do that until after Rhoda's child is safely born," he continued. "Until then, we'll need some kind of illusion to conceal the nature of the injury she has suffered. But that may mean bringing her here, and I do not want her here, at least not unless her pain can be somewhat alleviated. Her crying would drive us all mad." She did not like that suggestion, but she did not hate it as much as she hated the thought of Mme. Chang escaping into death.

He came back to his chair and sat down. "And what of you, Rose? Are you free from the mirror now that the contract is paid off? What place do you have among us now—do you hope to stay on here? Could we trust you if you did?" She lowered her head, as if reflecting on his questions. He caught his breath. He saw in her hair—neatly pulled back into a simple bun—a single thin thread of grey, half buried and scarcely visible in the thick mass.

"You still have power now," he whispered. "But not for long." She nodded. For a fraction of a second, she looked tired. Very, very tired. Her hands were folded on his desk; he reached out and patted them. "Not to worry," he told her gently. "Being mortal isn't so very dreadful. Millions of us cope with it every day." She smiled again, a much nicer smile than the previous one. He smiled back. "I shouldn't like to take you away from Julius. It would break his heart. And as for the rest of it, we'll contrive to work something out. We always do."

About the Author

Ms. Jordan was born—but not raised—in California, of which she remembers nothing but the sea. Her mother always thought she was destined to write, from the day she won her first poetry award at the age of five.

But, armed with a bachelor's degree in drama from Bard College, she chose instead to launch a theatrical career that spanned nanoseconds. Sobered by that experience, she embarked on the Serious Business of Earning a Living. She studied programming and entered the workforce as a computer-literate administrator. In the meanwhile, she continued to scribble stories and chat with invisible playmates.

Eventually, she was forced to admit that her mother had been right. *Mirror Maze* is her first novel to appear in book form, although the discerning reader may also have seen *Blade Light*, which was serialized in *Jim Baen's Universe*.

She lives in Cincinnati with a grumpy cat, a long-suffering husband, and a variety of invisible playmates.

NOTES

Inheritrix

1. Paul-Marie Verlaine (1844–1896), author of *Poemes Saturniens* (1866), *Fêtes Galantes* (1869), *La Bonne Chanson* (1870), and *Sagesse* (1881).

2. John Hanning Speke began his career as an explorer in 1855 when he joined Richard Burton's expedition as a replacement for a casualty. He was a poor geographer and preferred hunting. Nonetheless, Burton invited him on a second expedition in 1857, which was also unsuccessful. Speke returned home before Burton in May of 1859 and got backing to organize a new expedition. He did not invite Burton to accompany him, and set out in April of 1860. Although he did find the source of the Nile, his scholarship was so poor and his manner so arrogant that his claim was widely doubted. He quarreled bitterly and publicly with Burton, whom he had—unjustly—denied all credit. He died of a self-inflicted gunshot wound (accident? suicide?) in 1867. Harper & Brothers published his journal in 1868, a posthumous American edition, which included a map of his voyages. The book and the persons were discussed for years.

3. 1875, *The Indian Song of Songs*. From the Sanskrit of the Gîta Govinda of Jayadeva, twelfth century. Or in 1879 *The Light of Asia; or, The Great Renunciation (Mahabhinishkramana), Being the Life and Teaching of Gautama, Prince of India and Founder of Buddhism*, by Sir Edwin Arnold (1832–1904).

4. *Perola* was the original title of Gilbert and Sullivan's *Iolanthe*, which opened on November 25, 1882.

5. *Tempest*, Prospero to Miranda.

6. Victorian slang for grit or determination.

7. In 1883, Easter fell on March 25.

8. Destroyed by fire in 1867.

Necromancer

1. Dante Gabriel Rosetti (1828–1882) was the leading light of the Pre-Raphaelite Brotherhood, and was as well known for his amorous adventures as for his paintings. Although a contemporary of the Impressionists, his work had virtually nothing in common with theirs.

2. Walter Greaves (1846–1930) was the devoted student of James Abbott McNeill Whistler (1834–1903) until Whistler (who was prone to such desertions) broke off with him. After the breakup—which he took very hard—he retained possession of numerous partial canvases and sketches by Whistler, a number of which he either completed or copied by way of homage.

3. Sir Joshua Reynolds (1723–1792) founding president of the Royal Academy of Art and a staunch defender of the heroic style, famed particularly for his portraits.

4. British holiday, celebrated on November 5.

5. Joseph-Pierre-Francois Jeanselme (1824–1860), French-born designer in the style of the Rococo Revival. He is best remembered for his ornate carved rosewood armchair (upholstered in leather, silk, and serge by Jacques-Michel Dulud), at the Great Exhibition in 1851.

6. Charles Locke Eastlake (1836–1906), nephew of and not to be confused with painter Sir Charles Locke Eastlake (1793–1865). A fierce opponent of the Rococo Revival and an early light of the Arts and Crafts Movement, author of *Hints on Household Taste in Furniture, Upholstery and Other Details*, published 1868. He eschewed the elaborate curves of early Victoriana for rectilinear forms and geometric designs. He preached "honest construction and materials" and evoked Gothic and Medieval design.

7. Biblical. See Exodus 6:22.

8. A reputable scotch.

9. 1842–1925. Friend and mentor of Dr. Sigmund Freud.

10. Latin for "Nothing is seen here."

11. The town where the battle of Antietam took place, and the name the Confederates gave to the battle.

12. July 1878. The Great European Powers intervened to support the Ottoman Empire after the Russo-Turkish War.

13. That would be the Covent Garden Opera Company (soon to become the Royal Opera House), and the new DeLibes would probably be *Lakmé*, which had opened a couple of years previously in Paris.

14. Daniel, Chapter 4, verse 6 (Hebrew Bible).

15. *The Tempest*, Prospero's abdication.

16. A sort of collapsible top hat, designed for use at the opera, the only place in London where a gentleman did not wear his top hat—at least not during the performance.

17. Prince Albert's triumph, the Great Exhibition of International Industry, was held in 1851.

18. The "Mother of Monsters" from Greek mythology, a half woman, half serpent that spawned (among other things) the vulture that ripped out the liver of Prometheus.

19. Greek hero/prince who volunteered to be sacrificed to the Minotaur. The princess Ariadne helped him through the maze that surrounded the monster, which he then slew. But on his way home, he forgot to change his sails from black to white, so that his father supposed him to be dead.

20. Latin for "No evil here."

Spirit Guide

1. The British social season opened at Easter and continued until September.

2. A style based on Pre-Raphaelite imagery which employed flowing lines. It was never viewed as entirely respectable since it did not require constraining undergarments but was suitable for at-home wear, especially during pregnancy.

3. From *Against Idleness and Mischief*, included in *Divine Songs for Children* by Isaac Watts (1674–1748).

4. The Foundling Hospital presented choral singing near Gray's Inn every Sunday afternoon (in season, of course).

5. Descendant of the full crinoline. The full hoop skirt had fallen from favor, and the rigid hoops of the crinolette were cut away from the front to

support a narrower, backswept silhouette. It evolved seamlessly into (and was almost indistinguishable from) the bustle.

6. The busk was a two-piece steel or whalebone inset down the front center of a corset held together by a sort of hook-and-eye arrangement. It made it possible (although still difficult) to don a corset single-handedly, despite the (adjustable) laces being in the back. Livia probably wore a spoon busk, invented in 1879, which narrowed the waist even further. It had a spoonlike curved panel at the bottom to hold back the stomach, which tended to puff out from underneath the rigid constriction at the waist.

7. Minor novelist (1785–1828). Her husband was rumored to have been promiscuous and to have educated her to his taste. She is mostly remembered for her torrid affair with Lord Byron.

8. Pseudonym of the French novelist and feminist Amantine-Aurore-Lucile Dupin, Baroness Dudevant (1804–1876). She separated from her husband in 1835 and was soon cut off from much of society for her indiscretions.

9. Actually, men often wore them, particularly in Livia's day, when the favored male silhouette was almost as wasp-waisted as that expected of women. But Jacob had no need of such enhancements, so Livia would not have known about them.

10. Amelia Jenks Bloomer (1818–1894) was an American women's rights and temperance advocate. She wrote in *The Lily*, a paper she herself founded, "The costume of women should be suited to her wants and necessities. It should conduce at once to her health, comfort, and usefulness; and, while it should not fail also to conduce to her personal adornment, it should make that end of secondary importance." In 1851 she fiercely promoted a "sensible" costume designed by Elizabeth Smith Miller, based on harem pants. (Mrs. Smith Miller prided herself on never having worn a corset.) But the outfit was universally ridiculed, and in 1859 Ms. Bloomer declared herself satisfied with the advance represented by crinolines (although crinolines did nothing to relieve the upper-body constraints). Regrettably much of the criticism had focused on Mrs. Bloomer's limited personal attractions.

11. A popular, inexpensive soap manufactured by, and according to a process invented by, William Gossage.

12. The thoroughfare running north from Pall Mall along the west side of Leicester Square and up to Shaftesbury had many names, some of them simultaneously. It was first identified as Colmanhedge Lane in 1643, back when the site that came to host the Alhambra was still only a "gaming house." The passage just north of the square was called Princes Street until 1879, at which time a number of the superfluous names attached to short stretches were eliminated in the interests of simplicity. As always, the change confused residents accustomed to the previous nomenclature.

13. Opened in January of 1884. The name was changed to Prince of Wales in 1886.

14. It burned down in 1882 but reopened in 1884.

15. Wellington Arch, topped with an enormous sculpture of the Duke of Wellington on horseback, originally stood opposite Apsley House, but was moved across the square to Hyde Park Corner in 1882 to 1883 to facilitate widening the road. The statue itself would be replaced by a sculpture of a Roman chariot in 1912.

16. Originally part of the Heaven and Earth Society, a resistance movement opposing the early Manchu emperors, which later evolved into a number of secret (and frequently criminal) organizations known to the British occupation as the Triads.

17. Not necessarily an ancestry for a Ming supporter to brag about. Wu Sangui was a Ming general who in 1644 commanded the garrison at Shanhaiguan, a pivotal pass in the Great Wall of China. Faced with a rebel army inside the gates, and the invading Manchu army without, he allied with the enemy he knew and understood best, and admitted the Manchu, who established the Qing dynasty which reigned until 1911. But officially he acted to avenge the death of the last Ming Emperor Chongzhen, who committed suicide when his palace was stormed by the rebels.

18. From a Sanskrit word meaning "arrow" or "diamond," the *vajra* carried great ritual significance in Esoteric Buddhism.

19. The terms "satin" and "sateen" both describe the same weaving technique, which produces a glossy finish, but satin was generally made from silk while sateen was made from cotton (or in later years, rayon).

20. An east London neighborhood near the older docks, in which

Chinatown was located at the time. (It was later moved, ironically, to Wardour Street, where Mr. Huong's offices were located.)

21. China has many languages. Mandarin was the preferred aristocratic tongue, and the one most commonly acquired by foreigners, but Wu was more commonplace within the general population.

22. The chest of Wang (a box with a slatted front backed by glass used for disappearing tricks), Kuma tubes (used for producing apparitions), and bamboo rods were all devices from popular Asian-themed magic tricks.

23. Not exactly new. It was between 1865 and 1868 that Sir Joseph William Bazalgette designed and installed the sewer network for central London, along with the elaborate Abbey Mills pumping station. But the upgrade (driven by "the Great Stink" during which sewer fumes forced Parliament to shut down in 1858) was so revolutionary in scope and concept that Londoners continued to boast (justly!) of the achievement for decades.

24. The phrase carries much the same meaning as the more modern "cut to the chase." It refers to the practice of shortening theatre matinee performances, specifically productions of *Hamlet*, by cutting several lengthy speeches leading up to the line, "What's Hecuba to him or he to Hecuba, that he should weep for her?"

25. *Blackwood's Edinburgh Magazine*, founded in 1817 (under the initial title *Edinburgh Monthly Magazine*) was conceived of as a rival to the prestigious (Whig) *Edinburgh Review* and remained in print until 1980. It combined an aggressively Tory editorial stance with literary offerings (some of them extremely prestigious), notably including horror fiction.

26. The train station, of course.

27. Fenians were precursors of the IRA. They attempted to bomb Victoria Station in 1884 and blew up a cloakroom.

28. China objected strenuously to the importation of opium but was forced by England (with French assistance) to legalize it in the Opium Wars (1839–1842 and 1856–1860).

29. Late eighteenth-century French furniture fashion, given to slim structures and oval panels, ornately decorated in gilt and white silk or brocade.

30. A ladies' column in the *Pall Mall Gazette*.